HOLLYWOOD CHASE

THE DISCREET DUET: BOOK II

NICOLE FRENCH

raglan

This is a work of fiction. Names, characters, organizations, places, events, and incidents are either products of the author's imagination or rendered fictitiously. Any resemblance to real people or events is purely coincidental.

www.nicolefrenchromance.com

For every woman with a song that's never been sung.
Be loud. Be fierce. Be heard.

PROLOGUE

Will

The flame flies high, translucent in the bright sun. I let it run until the metal burns my fingertips, and finally drop the lighter in my lap so I can suck the sore spots away. I wait a few minutes until it cools enough to touch, then start the whole process again.

I swear to God, I could rip these walls down. Throw the furniture through these fucking fish-bowl windows. Maybe take a match to the angora carpet and watch the whole golden palace burn. I've been sitting in this fancy rattrap for two weeks, ever since Benny practically airlifted me out of Newman Lake right as the entire neighborhood was overrun by photographers looking for their next big payday. I know how it works with the paps. Celebrity photography is a bidding war. Twenty-five dollars for the shot everyone else has…but a shot of me? After four years where everyone thought I was dead? That could earn one of those bastards tens of thousands, maybe more.

So, yeah, after Maggie slammed the door in my face, I had no choice but to cut and run. It was either that or bring the whole fucking circus down on her. And I won't do that. Ever.

"Yo, F. Do you think you could limit the pyromania to the rooftop? I'd like to avoid burning down my apartment."

I extinguish the flame, set the lighter back in the box of incense on the coffee table, then turn around to face Benny, my agent and best friend, who's looking at me like I need a straitjacket. Well...he does know me better than almost anyone else.

"Sorry," I grumble, leaning forward onto my knees. "I'm in a mood."

"Yeah, yeah. What else is new?"

I snort, but don't answer. Benny doesn't need it. He's a schmuck, but the best kind of schmuck—jaded and opportunistic, but fiercely loyal to a select few. Benny grew up in one of the shittiest parts of New York, then proceeded to make himself into one of the most in-demand agents in the business. He's a shark in negotiations and a charmer everywhere else— ask most women in Manhattan, and half in LA too.

We owe each other everything. I began his career by making him my agent when he was starting out, and he helped me put mine behind me. Four years ago, when I left the business for good, Benny was the only one who knew what really happened and where I'd gone. We planned it together—the crash, the escape, all of it. He managed my accounts, sent out the press releases, and funneled every inquiry in the right direction so that although no one officially declared me dead, it looked that way to the point people believed it anyway. Sure, I paid him decent coin to do it, but people don't keep secrets like that without loyalty.

And I'll never, ever forget it.

Benny drops a stack of thick manila envelopes on the glass coffee table in front of me. They land with a loud thud.

I look up. "What are these?"

"What do you think?"

I pick one up. "Scripts, huh? Fucking vultures don't waste time, do they?"

Benny shrugs while he flips through his phone. "You're the hot news. I know you say you want to stay out, man, but there's some top-shelf material in there. Everyone's drooling. Van Sant. Soderberg. Shit, I think even Ava sent something over."

He straightens his cuffs, checking his suit, pocket square, cuff links and hair in one of the many mirrors lining the walls of the living room.

Benny says they make the apartment look twice its size, not that it needs it. My friend has done very well for himself since I've been gone.

"Plus," he added with a smirk, "the ladies love looking at themselves while I—"

I grab the lighter and flip it open, not wanting to hear the rest of that sentence.

"Yo!" he exclaims, snatching it out of my hand. "I said cool the flames, man!"

I shrug. "Sorry."

"There's more, you know." Benny goes back to smoothing his hair. "You can take your pick of Late Night, and the *Today Show*'s been blowing up my phone. *SNL* wants you to host, and every single ladies' talk show is begging to have you on. Who's it gonna be, *papi*? Who gets the first interview?"

I sink into the couch and stare at the stack of scripts. They might as well be shackles, the way their existence weighs on me. Part of me wants to flip through them, see what kind of things are coming my way. I waited most of my career for this kind of demand, after spending so many years as a child actor, then working to break my way into more legitimate roles. Getting requests from some of the most important directors in the world, the ones who define artistic merit rather than abide by it—it's every actor's dream come true. I don't care how famous you are; it feels good to be wanted by the greats.

But then there's the other side of it. Shooting a movie takes three or four weeks, maybe a few months if it's a long shoot. And you have to promote. Interviews. Premieres. Photo shoots. Pap strolls. You're expected—no, *required*—to put every aspect of your life on display for a public that's more unforgiving than anyone dreams. And when you do that, there are no boundaries. There's no privacy. Everything—your trash, your home, your family, your friends—is fair game.

Life becomes a fishbowl. And you're trapped. And sometimes people get hurt.

I look around the mirrors and the picture windows around us. On the forty-eighth floor of Benny's Midtown high-rise, we're suspended well above the purview of the cameras. But I can't help flinching every time I see a news helicopter circling the New York skyline. Even up here, I feel like I'm on display. The only thing I want to do is run for cover.

Into the woods. Into my house. Camp under the safe canopy of pine trees, well off the road, where no one can find me. If I close my eyes long enough, I can smell the lake: the clean, fresh waters, the sharp scent of pine sap. I can hear the gurgle of water playing around the edge of that flat rock where my Lily—I can't think of Maggie Sharp as anything else —gave herself up to me, right there, in front of God and nature and everyone else.

I could be on a plane tomorrow, even if I had to take a full security detail with me. I could build the world's biggest fence around the entire property to keep out the fucking jackals and their telephoto lenses.

But I'm not going back without her. Not the woman who's responsible for every fucking beat of my heart. Without her, I'm dead. It's as simple as that.

"No interviews," I say, knowing that Benny and I are about to have the same argument we've been having since I holed up in his place. He wants me to embrace the chaos. I'm convinced it'll go away if I wait long enough.

Benny flops down on the couch, for once giving no thought to whether it's going to crease his custom Armani suit. "Will, come on. You can't expect them to take that as an answer."

"They'll let it go," I reply stubbornly. "As soon as we find out where she is, we'll be gone too."

"F, you know they'll follow. The media is like fuckin' cats, my friend. Act like they don't exist, they'll be rubbing their ass and getting cat hair all over your tailored pants. Throw 'em a mouse, they'll leave you alone."

"And who's the mouse? Maggie?"

Benny looks at me like I'm crazy, and honest to God, maybe I am. He didn't suggest it, but the thought of giving her up that way makes me feel violent. *Mine.* I said it to her, but the word might as well be written across my forehead, not hers.

He has no idea how deep this runs. Hell, *she* has no idea how deep. She doesn't know the way her voice vibrates in the fucking marrow of my bones. I belong to that girl, body and soul.

Because I never had the chance to tell her. Instead of laying myself bare, the way she did for me, every time she let me inside her in a million tiny ways, I kept it all hidden, thinking it would be better to protect her from the disaster of my life. And now that loss is eating me up inside. I'm a ruined man without her. So much more than I ever was before.

I've done some stupid things. I've hurt plenty of people. But this was the worst. This will always be the worst.

"That bad, huh?"

Benny hasn't lost his touch, that's for sure. It's been four years since we've seen each other, but he can still read my face like a book, even if it is covered with two weeks of beard. Part of me wants to keep shaving it off. The jig is up, as they say, and when I took it off for Maggie, I was glad not to have half my face covered in hair. That shit itches. It really does.

I shrug. "I miss her."

There's no point in hiding it. She's all I think about. Every day I call her mom's house, only to be told again and again that she hasn't returned. Lily is still here, somewhere in this shithole called New York City, maybe a matter of blocks from where I'm sitting right now. And I can't fucking find her.

"Yo, yo! Good news, man."

I look up. "If you tell me again that Ellen wants me to dance on her show, I swear to God, Benny, I will punch you in the face and ruin those pretty veneers of yours."

Benny snorts. He's never been scared of my threats, and he's not about to start. And why would he? He's seen a lot worse than a pissed-off actor from Connecticut.

"Motherfucker, you been gone for too long. These are all natural. Did they not have good dental care in the sticks either?"

"Just tell me your news, asshole."

Benny grins, then turns his phone to me.

"211 Christopher Street," I read off the screen. "What's that?"

"The place I know you're dying to be."

It takes me another half second to register what the fuck he's talking about. When I do, I can't move fast enough.

"Whoa, whoa, whoa, there, my friend. Where do you think you're going?" Benny lays a hand on my chest when I spring up from the couch, readying to run to the elevator.

I jerk to a stop, feeling like a balloon that's been popped. Shit. I forgot. One thought of being with her again, and every piece of common sense gets knocked out of my brain. What do I think I'm going to do? Take a fucking stroll down the middle of Fifth Avenue? Get mobbed within fifteen minutes; have my clothes literally torn off my back within twenty? I'm sure Maggie would love having a psychotic group of teenage girls and photographers arriving at her front door along with the asshole who broke her heart.

"Man, stop the pity party. It'll take five minutes to make sure Garrett and everyone are in place, all right? A little shell game, remember?"

I press my lips together. I tell myself it won't be this bad forever. I don't even look the same as I did four years ago, when I was strung out half the time and about forty pounds lighter. Even the biggest names in the world can lose their draw if they work hard enough at it. There are other actors who have managed to avoid the spotlight. Damon. Fraser. Brosnan. It can be done.

"Yeah, man, but they ain't you."

It takes me a second to realize I said all of that out loud. I frown. "What are you talking about? Pierce Brosnan played James Bond. For a while, it didn't get bigger than him."

"He didn't have the fan base you have," Benny points out. "And that was before social media. If the world thought they had lost Brosnan, even right after *Golden Eye*, they would have been sad, sure. There would have been some tears. But your fans have loved you since you was, what, six? You have a more devout following than DiCaprio in his prime. They've been mourning you for four years. They ain't leaving you anytime soon, my friend."

I rub my face, pressing hard enough that my fingers catch on the skin, pulling a little. It hurts. I don't care.

I drop my hands and stare across the room at the face I haven't looked at—really looked at—in years. "Classically chiseled," they'd say. Whatever the fuck that means. Do I look like a statue?

I tap my chin, briefly wondering what it would be like to take it all off. This stupid fucking face. It wouldn't take much. A bad nose job.

Shave my chin, or maybe some filler. I scowl. I hate that I even know this shit, know that half the people in this industry—men *and* women—have the top five plastic surgeons in the world on speed dial. People have no idea how fake the faces they see on the screen really are. But I could do it. I could disappear again…this time for real.

"Stop it," Benny interrupts as he fixes his tie. He always was a bit vain, but I swear he's gotten worse in the last four years.

I drop my hands and look up. "Stop what?"

"I know what you were thinking," he says. "You looked like you were measuring your face. And ain't no way in *hell* I'm gonna let you go under the knife just to avoid some damn photographers. No way."

I fall back, annoyed that he can read me so easily. I'm not used to it anymore. "Yeah, well. A little shift here and there might be worth losing these assholes."

"And your girl, too?" Benny looks at me knowingly as he fixes his watch. "It wasn't some Freddy Krueger-looking face she fell in love with, F. It was that one, just like everyone else. Would she still love you if it wasn't there?" He finally finishes brushing himself down, and at that moment, his phone buzzes. "Especially if you could see her right now?"

In a second, I'm on my feet, all thoughts of reconstructive surgery vanished. "Everything's ready?"

Benny smiles, showing off his pearly whites. All real, my ass. "Ready and willing. Let's go get your girl."

Fame, like a wayward girl, will still be coy
To those who woo her with too slavish knees,
But makes surrender to some thoughtless boy,
And dotes the more upon a heart at ease.

— John Keats, "On Fame"

CHAPTER ONE

"Maggie Mae, when are you coming home?"

It was the fourth time my mother had asked me that today alone. I'd heard the phrase countless times over the past two weeks, since I'd packed my things and driven out of Newman Lake at breakneck speed.

Again.

It still felt surreal. Like I was doomed to live my life on the run.

One minute I was jogging down the road next to the love of my life. Will Baker. Broody. Stubborn. An absolute heart of gold. He was someone who, within the space of four weeks, had torn through every wall I had with one look from his intense green eyes. With him, I'd finally come to accept that maybe the last eight years, from the time I'd left Newman Lake for a music career in New York to the moment I came back with my tail between my legs, hadn't only been a big failure.

To be fair, I had come close. Had a few big shows, even toured with one of the greats. But everything I worked hard for came crashing down the second I became involved with Theo del Conte. It was a relationship that, among other things, had landed him in jail for rape and sent me packing home. Poor, ruined, off to lick my wounds while I tried to recover any of the self-worth he'd completely destroyed over the years we'd been together.

Will made me feel like maybe that past didn't matter, or at least that it wasn't the only thing that defined me. We found each other, and that made sense in a way that nothing else ever had. So, yeah, maybe my life wasn't exactly where I thought it would be at twenty-six. But I was someplace better…or at least on my way there.

Then we turned a corner, and everything changed.

Will sprinting through the forest.

A mob of cameras coming for him, and then for me too.

The breaking news that Fitz Baker, the actor who had disappeared during a boat wreck off the coast of Maine four years before, had resurfaced in my backyard. And proceeded to make me fall hopelessly in love with him without once telling me who he actually was.

Will Baker. Fitz Baker. I didn't know which one was real. And so I'd left Newman Lake again, fled back to New York, a place I *never* thought would be a refuge, but the only other place in the world I had people to help me. Out of the frying pan and into the fire. There didn't seem to be any in-between for me. Not anymore.

"I don't know, Mama," I mumbled. "We don't know what's going to happen with Theo since he showed up at the lake. I should probably stay a little while longer until I know the dates of the hearing and everything."

That was a lie. I wasn't even sure I'd seen Theo at the bottom of the hill that day, although since getting out of jail, he had been texting me again. My lawyer had filed some kind of charge alleging that he had broken the terms of his parole by contacting me…but I certainly didn't need to be there to tell that to the judge.

"Oh…well, okay then," Mama said. "But you are coming back, right? Everyone's been asking about you. Barb, Linda, Lucas…"

I nodded, even though she couldn't see me. I could imagine the faces of the neighbors and friends. People who were salivating over the gossip, though there were a few who genuinely cared about me too.

"Sure," I said softly. I wished I meant it.

There was a long pause on the other end of the line. Ice clinked in the background. Good lord, it was only noon, and she'd already started. I didn't know why I was surprised.

After we said goodbye, I set my phone on the coffee table and sighed. I hated that I'd left my mother, who was struggling with a disease that only seemed to get worse the older she got. It didn't matter how many times people told me I couldn't cure her alcoholism. I'd never stop feeling guilty that I hadn't intervened more.

Right now, I couldn't bring myself to go back to that either. Everywhere was painful. Here. There. *Because he's gone*, a little voice said.

And what did that matter now? When I didn't even know who *he* really was?

Without thinking too much about it, I reached over to the end of the couch where I'd been sleeping for the last ten days, took my favorite guitar out of its case, and started picking a melody that was in my head. The action felt good. Familiar. The strings bit a little at my uncalloused skin. It had been too long since I'd played consistently. But I went with it, singing softly to myself.

> *The things we used to say, like I*
> *Won't stop, no one loves you like I do…*
> *Did they all justify*
> *The heartache and these tears I cried for you…*
> *Can't tell so I might as well just*
> *Feel the way I do…*
> *Gonna make my way back to lonesome without you.*

"What the hell is that?"

I looked up to find Calliope, my best friend and former manager, standing in the doorway of her bedroom with a look of shock. She fluffed the mass of tight black curls bouncing in all directions around her head, then popped her hip and gave me a very businesslike stare, as if she wasn't currently dressed like Cardi B in rainbow-striped pants and a crop top that showed off her enviable abs. Then again, I supposed, her outfit could count as business professional considering she managed crazy-looking musicians for a living.

Cal gestured toward the guitar, and the chunky gold bangles on her wrist jangled. "Is that new?"

I shrugged as I stowed the instrument. "Something I had in my head."

Cal quirked her brow. "It's good. Really good. We should get that down. Did you bring your recording equipment with you?"

I shook my head. "Of course not. I packed and was out of there in fifteen minutes. Besides, it's rough still. I only have the chorus, maybe one verse."

Callie pressed her lips together, like she was trying to decide if I was lying or not. "Well, it's good," she repeated, then came to sit next to me. "I didn't know you were writing again, babe."

"I'm not."

It was another lie, and by the look on my friend's face, she knew it, too. I didn't have to tell her that the second I'd driven across the Washington border, it was like a faucet had been turned on after more than a year of running dry. More than once on the four-day trek back to New York, I'd stopped on the side of the road, perched awkwardly on the hood of my Passat or dangled from the back seat, and picked melodies into my cell phone while passersby honked.

It was funny. In the past, heartbreak had never been a good catalyst for songwriting. Maybe later—months or even years later—but I hadn't written anything in over a year. Not since the last song I wrote after Theo's verdict was handed down. But right now I had a notebook full of new lyrics in my purse that I'd been writing in almost daily. I couldn't stop.

"Mmm-hmm," Calliope replied as she swiped through her phone. "When do I get to hear the rest, though? You put that on a demo, and I bet I could get another showcase together. People are asking about you again since your face was in the papers. We might as well get something out of this circus, don't you think?"

I pulled my knees to my chest and laid my head on top of them. "We talked about this, Cal. New York doesn't want me. Not like that."

Calliope rolled her eyes. "Is that why you lied to your mom, then? Because you think New York doesn't want you?"

I slumped back on the couch and sighed. "I just don't want to go back right away. It's fine."

"Baby girl, it's never been fine." Callie patted my knee. "I was willing to deal with this whole Queen of Denial crap you've got going on because you're my girl and all. But, babe, it's been almost two weeks. Your mama said several days ago that the press disappeared after Will"—she broke off when she caught my glare—"sorry, Dickhead was seen at Teterboro. It's not that I don't want you in my spot, but, babe, you've got to make some decisions. Tell him off. Take him back. Pick up that guitar. Start playing. Get a job. Go home. I don't know, kid, but you have to do *something*."

I stared despondently at the worn copy of US Weekly sitting on the coffee table. The edges were wrinkled from being handled too much. I'd actually bought three copies, but after flipping through the other two to the point of tearing the thin pages, this was all that was left. Okay, so one I actually tore up on purpose. Maybe you would too if you saw pictures of the man you loved plastered with a different name. Pictures from before, when he had his arm around a beautiful actress they said was once his fiancée. Pictures from now, from a night when you were still in love—pictures that your "friend" sold to buy herself a new Porsche and a trip to Maui.

Okay, that's a lie. Lindsay, that bitchy little she-devil from Newman Lake, wasn't ever my friend.

"I'm going to throw that thing out."

Callie reached over to take the magazine, but I sprang to life, swiping it out of her reach.

"Hey!" I hugged it to my chest.

Calliope's entire body dripped irritation. "Girl. This is pa-the-tic. Stop staring at that rag like he's going to jump out of it and carry you off into the damn sunset. When are you going to admit that you're staying in the city because you're waiting for him to come find you?"

I scowled. "That is *not* what I'm doing."

"The hell it's not. You've been moping around my apartment for ten damn days, playing this passive-aggressive game of hard-to-get. You wouldn't let me reach out to his agent—and I would *love* to have an excuse to call Benny Amaya, by the way, in case you care at all about your own friend's career—but you show absolutely no interest in doing anything else productive. Maggie, seriously, it is time to get the hell off your ass!"

I didn't respond. Calliope waited silently, now that she was done spouting. This was the girl who pulled me out of my shell in college, who sat in the back of my first New York open mic, who, once she graduated and became my manager for real, painstakingly arranged every show, every gig, every opportunity I've ever had. She believed in me for a long time, and for that reason, her disappointment stung worse than most.

Slowly, I set the magazine back on the table. Calliope immediately snatched it away.

I missed him. Of course I missed him. You don't go from opening up your entire soul to someone to acting like they don't exist without a little heartache. Will had carved a space for himself inside me, and now it was empty. The void hurt. It hurt bad.

"I still don't get it," Callie said, looking at the cover as she sat down beside me. "How could you have not known who he was? Even way back when the guy snuck into your dressing room. You talked to him for, what, an hour?"

She still couldn't believe *that* story, in which the world's most famous actor somehow kept himself hidden behind a screen without revealing himself. Even more, she was shocked I didn't recognize his face immediately after spending months falling in love with it.

I sighed. "I don't know, Cal. I just didn't."

I'd been asking myself versions of the same question for the last two weeks. It was the same question everyone asked me. Mama, Lucas, the Forsters, and any number of random people who had recently "found" my number and thought that now was the perfect time to rekindle our acquaintance.

How could I have not known?

It was a combination of things, I guessed. I hadn't exactly been living under a rock, but when "Fitz Baker" was at the height of his fame, I had been interested in music and not much else. I was a poor artist coming out of school, waitressing and playing guitar and singing while I shared a two-bedroom apartment with sometimes four other people. Every penny I had went into living in this city and into my equipment. For several years, I didn't even have a cell phone beyond a prepaid flip phone—that's how poor I was. My life was music and survival…and not much else.

It was the polar opposite of the kind of life Will had once had. His fame was the kind that had probably made him so ubiquitous, he would have been easy for me to ignore. I never looked at the magazines in the checkout counter. I never went to the movies. But it had taken exactly ten minutes of scrolling through Google to make me sick with how…*everywhere* he had been.

Emmy and Golden Globe winner.

Oscar nominee.

Sexiest man alive.

Fiancé.

The last one hurt the most.

The tabloids and various gossip sites said it was understandable how other people missed it when they saw him now. To start with, Will had obviously gone to great lengths to conceal his face, with the long, unruly hair and the beard that reached his chest. He trimmed both back in the weeks that followed—mostly by my request. I couldn't help feeling a little guilty—my desire to see him, really *see* him, may have been his undoing.

But it wasn't only that. When you looked at the before and after pictures that were featured in almost every article and post about his sudden reappearance—usually his "Sexiest Man Alive" cover next to the candid snapshot of the two of us taken just days before the news broke—you saw obvious differences that had to do with maturity. He wasn't quite twenty-five when he had crashed his boat off the coast of Maine and disappeared, presumed dead. Back then, his body was much thinner, lankier even, and his face still had traces of adolescence skating over the razor-sharp cheeks and nose. Four years of swimming, lifting, and the basic labor it takes to maintain a rustic property like his house on the lake had turned Will into a lean, but fully developed column of muscle. He wasn't recognized because until you *really* looked hard enough, you wouldn't have been able to tell who exactly he was.

So most people would never have guessed. Not until he trimmed almost his entire beard and bared his face to the world. For me.

And therein lay the rub. Because I wasn't just "anyone" who hadn't recognized him. I was the one who had "penetrated his secret world," according to the tabloids.

Deep down, I must have known he wasn't normal. He never totally fit into a place like Newman Lake. His tastes, though well hidden, belied a much richer life than you would get in Spokane. And of course, now all of his quirks made sense. The fear of crowds. The screenplays and home movie theater. The stubborn insistence to remain off the grid, without even a cell phone or internet connection.

But before I could say any of this to Calliope, her buzzer blasted through the apartment. She gave me a knowing look, then walked over to pick up the handset.

"Hey, Joe." She listened for a second, nodding to herself. "Sure, let them up." Then she hung up.

I frowned. "Who's coming up?"

"Some clients. You might want to meet them, actually. Both of them are a pretty big deal."

I grimaced at my clothes—a black cotton skirt and a torn-up CBGB t-shirt that hung off one shoulder. I looked like an extra from *Flashdance* or another one of those old eighties movies my mom used to love.

"You'readorable," Calliope said as she fluffed her hair in the mirror. "I, on the other hand, look like Diana Ross. This humidity is killing my hair. I should cut it all off." She clicked her tongue at herself, then headed to the bathroom to primp a bit more.

"Hey!" I called after her. "They're on their way up now!"

"So let them in!" Callie retorted before shutting the door behind her. "You're not getting out of this."

As if right on cue, there was a loud knock at the door.

"Maggie! Maggie, I know you're in there. Open up the damn door."

I froze. I wasn't sure why. Maybe it was because I'd barely seen anyone in two weeks. But as soon as I heard that familiar deep voice, I felt the real reason for my paralysis. My body knew he was here before my mind. Just like always.

I didn't move, looking frantically around for Calliope, who had apparently decided to take up permanent residence in the bathroom.

"Lily!"

His voice—*that name*—cut through my stasis. I scrambled off the couch and to the door, where I struggled to open the deadbolt and unfasten the chain. When I did swing it open, I still wasn't prepared for what I saw, filling the doorway with his broad shoulders, long, lean frame, crossed arms, and fiery glare.

Will. Fitz. Love of my life. Devil of my dreams.

He was here, and I could not have been angrier to see him.

CHAPTER TWO

"**W**hat. The hell. Are you doing here?"

I didn't wait for an answer, instead attempting to slam the door in his face like the last time I'd seen him. Will's broad palm anticipated the move with a harsh slap on the wood.

"I don't think so."

He shoved his way in, followed by a shorter man with close-cut hair and a navy skinny suit that was accented with a pink-striped tie and matching polka-dotted pocket square. The two of them made a bit of an odd couple. With the exception of his beard, which had been trimmed to mostly stubble, Will looked his same scruffy self in a plain pair of jeans, an old Nirvana t-shirt with more than one hole, and his hair piled on top of his head in a messy knot. His beard had grown out some in the last two weeks, but not to the point where it obscured his face. After all, his cover was blown. There would have been no point.

He looked delectable. Every cell in my body wanted to jump him. But I hated him all the more for it.

"Well, look who the cat dragged in." Callie strode out of the bathroom with a broad grin directed at Mr. Suit, who immediately grinned back. He crossed to her and delivered kisses to both of Callie's cheeks.

"How you doin', Calliope?" He looked her up and down. "Damn, girl. You look better every time I see you."

"Cut the shit, Benny. I already told you, she's *not* going to do that interview."

I frowned at Calliope. "I thought you said you hadn't spoken to him."

Callie shrugged. "No, I inferred that I'd love another chance to chat him up. This guy's a riot."

"A riot, huh? How did I get such a rave?" Benny asked while I shrank against the wall.

"Interview?" Will glanced at his friend. "What the fuck, Benny? I *also* told you I'm not doing anything with the goddamn press. Neither of us are."

Benny, whom I guessed was Benny Amaya, the notorious agent and name on the one piece of mail I'd ever seen Will receive, just laughed. It *was* kind of funny. Two years ago, I would have given about anything to stand in the same room as this guy. He was one of those people who held the keys to almost every door in the entertainment industry, whose good word could make a career within a five-minute conversation.

Back then, I would have been falling all over myself to meet him. Now I couldn't care less.

"You don't know what I want," I snapped at Will. "You don't get to speak for me. Especially when I don't know who you even are."

"Maggie—" he started.

I ignored the frustrated, helpless look on his face. "Don't bother."

"Hey, hey, hey." Benny inserted himself between us. "Let's cool it a little, huh? First things first." He extended a hand to me. "Benjamin Amaya. I represent Wi—I mean, Fitz, in well, all sorts of matters."

"Benny, she doesn't know who the fuck Fitz Baker is." Will's deep voice cut sharply through the niceties.

I shook Benny's hand limply. He ignored Will and looked me over with mild recognition. "You look familiar, sweetheart. Where do I know you from?"

"Probably the papers right now," I mumbled as I sat back down on the couch. Will followed. I glared at him and got back up, crossing the room to cower next to Calliope. Will had brought a second. Well, I had mine too.

"No, that's not it…" Benny snapped his fingers. "That's it! You were Theo del Conte's girl, weren't you?"

As soon as the name was out, the room, already somewhat icy, became a tundra. Will's face turned black, and Callie shook her head. I swallowed. It was one more indicator that no matter what, I'd always be defined by someone else's shadow. Ellie Sharp's daughter. Theo del Conte's girl. There was a part of me that was starting to wonder if I'd ever be known for just being me.

This time, Benny didn't seem impervious to the room as he shifted uncomfortably on his wingtips. "Right. Damn. Yeah. I, uh, heard about all of that. You really pissed off an entire empire with that one, didn't you, honey?"

He cocked his head—I didn't have to ask what he was talking about. Everyone in this city knew about my high-profile court battle with the del Conte family, in which I'd pressed charges of rape against Theo, and after a year-long battle, won a small piece of justice when he was sentences to six months behind bars (though he served only a few).

"Which means you'll want to keep it to yourself that she's here," Callie broke in. "For her own safety."

"Why *are* you here, Lil?"

I turned to Will, whose penetrating green gaze—that same, unwavering stare that had appeared, night after night, as soon as I drifted to sleep—wouldn't let me go. "Don't call me that."

"It's your name."

"Like Will?"

"Like *mine*."

My mouth dropped. "Are you here to claim me? Because I am *not* your fucking possession, Baker!"

"Whoa, whoa, whoa," Benny cut in. "Maggie, Will and I came over to make sure you were all right. That's all. No one is claiming anyone right now, isn't that right, F?"

Will grunted. "Li—Maggie. I just want to talk." His voice was curt, but the look in his eyes choked back the next retort I had. "I've been searching for you *everywhere*."

We stared at each other for what felt like several minutes, and the tension in the room flowered. Will's eyes, deep, dark green pools, drowned me with their complexity, all the emotions that his taciturn self could never say.

"Please, Lil," he said, and his voice cracked slightly on the last word. "I'm dying over here."

"Oh, Maggie." Calliope sighed under her breath. Benny shook his head ruefully.

I couldn't speak at all. Finally, after I concentrated on taking at least three full breaths to keep myself from running to him, I tore my gaze away and grabbed my purse off the counter behind me.

"I'm going to go for a walk," I announced. "I need to not be here right now."

All three other people in the room objected at once.

"Maggie, maybe you should wait—"

"Yeah, I wouldn't do that, honey—"

"Lil, no—"

I whirled around at the door. "Listen, all of you. I've been cooped up in this apartment for two weeks, waiting until my face wasn't splattered across every tabloid in the country as the pathetic chick *Fitz* Baker took for a ride. I can't take it anymore. Goodbye."

"Maggie!"

The door shut on Will's cry, and before anyone else could answer, I had already dashed down the hall and four floors down the service stairwell to the entrance of Calliope's walk-up. I strode out onto Christopher Street walking so fast I was practically jogging.

The movement felt good. After training intensely for a triathlon for over a month, I hadn't done anything except yoga in Calliope's small living room. My heart rate was up, pounding away in my chest, and the movement helped clear that excess energy.

I was so intent on escaping that it took me a solid few blocks to realize people were clearing out of my way. The normally bustling Christopher Street emptied as pedestrians crossed the street or ducked down back alleys. A half a block later, I stopped and turned around. The sidewalk was now totally empty with the exception of three massive bodyguards, all of them forming a broad, triangular formation around the person who was doggedly following me: Will.

I rolled my eyes. "What part of 'goodbye' don't you understand, Baker?"

He didn't speak until he'd reached me. "You didn't really think I was going to let you walk out, did you? I've been trying to find you for two goddamn weeks, Lil."

I shrugged. His betrayal was humming through me at this point. I was in no mood to be generous. "I've been around."

"Have you?" He spoke through his teeth, like he was trying not to bite my head off. "Your mother said you left as soon as I did. 'New York' was all she would tell me. I'm not even sure she actually knows more than that, but it was the only clue I had. Why else do you think I'd be in this fucking fishbowl if not to find you?"

"Nobody forced you to leave Newman."

"What was I supposed to do after you slammed the door in my face? Go home to the hundreds of photographers waiting for me? Give myself up to the hunt?"

I shrugged again, but I couldn't connect with his eyes.

Will sighed. "Why didn't you tell your mother where you went?"

I pressed my lips together. "You know as well as I do that Mama can't keep a secret to save her life."

"Lucas doesn't know either. Linda. Barb. None of them have any clue."

"No one does."

"Why?"

And there was the question. I'd screamed out of Newman Lake and left a trail of my heart's blood from one coast to the other. All calls and texts from Lucas and Mama had gone unanswered other than to let them know I needed to take care of some things in the city and that I was safe. My official reason for returning to New York was to report that Theo, my ex-boyfriend, had violated his restraining order. But the cops quickly informed me that the man had a rock-solid alibi and that unless I filed for a no-contact clause in the order, Theo wasn't prohibited from phone calls or texts. My lawyer had done just that, but it would be another week before a hearing.

But I didn't strictly have to be here for the hearing, of course. Callie was right. I needed to find a job. Get off her couch. Figure out what the hell I was doing in New York City if not playing music.

"Maybe I didn't want to be found," was all I said.

Will glowered. "I guess I wanted to find you more."

"I think you're overestimating how much I want to see you."

"You're *under*estimating how much more stubborn I am than you."

"Well, that's the truth," I started, right as a young woman's voice broke through our little detente with an unusual amount of joy.

"Oh my God. Oh. My. *God.* You're—you're Fitz Baker, aren't you?"

We both turned around to find a girl about my age, maybe a little younger, staring at Will with shocked eyes and a dropped jaw. She clutched her purse like she was going to rip it apart.

"Oh my *God!*" she kept saying again and again. "I'm *such* a big fan! I cried when I thought you were dead. I'm not even kidding!"

"Fuck off," Will snarled as he set a hand between my shoulder blades and started guiding me around the girl, whose face immediately fell.

I shook his hand off and dug my heels into the concrete, not even caring that the girl was already pulling out her phone.

"Miss, please." One of the bodyguards was already stepping forward to block the girl. "Mr. Baker is not taking photos at this time."

"It's fine," I said. "Don't be an asshole, *Mr.* Baker," I snapped at Will. "One of your adoring fans wants to say hello." I turned back to the girl, who was still ogling both of us openly as she fumbled with her screen. "I'm sorry for him."

She shook her head, her eyes a bundle of stars. I could understand, for the first time, why they called it "starstruck." She really did look like she had been blinded.

"I *am* an asshole, Lily," he growled, low enough that only I could hear it. "I told you that a long time ago."

"People can change," I hissed.

"Can they?"

"I don't know, *Fitz.* Can they?"

We glared at each other all over again like we didn't have an audience, both of us trying and failing miserably to mask the anger and frustration vibrating out of our bodies. Will's eyes flickered to my lips, and I hated myself for imagining, momentarily, shoving him down a side street and kissing him until I had scratched up his shoulders and given him a fat lip.

"Dang. Talk about sexual tension."

At the sound of the girl's voice, Will ripped himself away and plastered the biggest, fakest smile I had ever seen. And yet, I recognized it. It was the same smile on every single one of the pictures I'd browsed over the last two weeks. Beautiful, blinding. Miserable.

It physically hurt to see it.

"Did you want a picture?" he asked through his teeth.

The girl, flabbergasted all over again, practically fell over herself as she stumbled forward with her phone. "Omigodomigodomigod*YES!*" she squealed, shoving her face as close to his as possible while they posed for a selfie, glee practically oozing out of her pores.

I stood politely off to the side with crossed arms, rolling my eyes at one of the bodyguards. The stoic face did not move.

"Thank you!" the girl said again and again as she put her phone away and begged an autograph from Will. Or *Fitz*, apparently, since that's what he scribbled on the wrinkled receipt she procured from her purse.

"No problem," he said as he handed it back. "Have a good one."

He watched as one of the bodyguards ushered the girl down the sidewalk, listening to her blather about what a great guy *Fitz* was. It was only when she'd crossed the street, and we stood on the block, alone except for his security, that Will turned back to me. The smile disappeared; now he had a face like thunder.

"I hope you're happy. In about ten minutes, this entire block is going to be jammed with a hundred more like her. I guarantee you that photo is already on Twatter or Instashit or whatever bullshit time suck people use to invade other people's privacy. It'll be all over the tabloids within the hour."

He looked around, like he expected another hoard of photographers to jump out of the fire escapes or the bushes at a nearby park. I couldn't see them yet, but it was almost like you could feel the energy growing in the air. The trio of security was clearly nervous, their heads now on constant swivels.

I looked at Will. "This is how it's going to be now, isn't it? We'll never be able to do something like take a walk by ourselves again, will we?"

Will softened a little at the word "we." He opened his mouth, but said nothing, just grabbed the back of his neck and frowned.

I sighed, feeling defeated. "Fine. Let's..."

I almost suggested we go back to Calliope's, but she and Benny would be there. I could see on Will's face that he meant what he said—there was no way I was going to get away from him without at least a conversation. And I wasn't really interested in doing that with any kind of audience.

"Do you know somewhere we can go?"

Will looked up, surprised. "Really?"

I huffed. "Yeah. You said we have to talk. So, let's talk. In private, if that's possible anymore."

He blinked, like he wasn't sure I'd actually agreed to what he wanted. Then, abruptly, he turned to one of the bodyguards, the one who seemed like he was in charge. "Garrett, call the car. We need to get out of here."

CHAPTER THREE

Twenty minutes later, I found myself in an elevator of a building somewhere in Midtown Manhattan. It was one of the high-rises that peered over the city from beside the West Side Highway. The elevator soared up the side of the building, and through the glass wall I watched as the dank streets of Manhattan fell away, leaving me alone with the sky. And Will.

The elevator stopped on the top floor and opened into a spacious penthouse apartment that was almost entirely chrome and white. I was almost scared to walk inside, worried that my Converse might track dirt onto the immaculate floors.

Will, however, stomped in like he didn't look like Pig Pen. It took him until he was on the other side of the massive living room to realize I hadn't immediately followed. He turned around.

"Is—is this yours?" I stammered from my spot in the foyer.

It was so unlike the Will I knew. His house on Newman Lake was nice, sure, but it wasn't terribly big or anything, and everything in it, from the furniture to the clothes to the floors, while of good quality, was definitely used regularly. This place, on the other hand, between its gleaming parquet floors, the all-white furniture, walls, cabinets, and counters, and the bright metal fixtures that had nary a fingerprint, looked like a showroom, not someone's actual apartment.

"Oh," Will said, clearly reading my face. "No. It's Benny's place, not mine." He wrinkled his long, straight nose. "He's barely here. Otherwise, I don't know how he could live in such a damn refrigerator."

I don't know why, but I did find it soothing that Will didn't like the cold, sleek interior. The apartment was all angles and shiny surfaces. I was afraid even touching the couch would leave a mark.

"Come on," Will said, jerking his head to the right. "The stairs are this way."

I followed him past a row of closed doors until we reached a spiral staircase at the end, which we climbed up to the top of the world.

Well, not really. But this was one of the tallest buildings in this part of Manhattan, and from its roof we had a panoramic view of the entire city, the Hudson River below us, across the water to New Jersey, and beyond.

Benny had filled the roof with furniture, a wet bar, even a pool in one corner—all of it meant to host an army of people. But right now, it was only Will and me, sharing no walls in a city where everyone shared at least one. We were out of sight—without even a building close enough to house telephoto lenses from across the street. We were truly alone.

Will strode to the edge of the deck and braced himself against the iron guardrail, making his shoulders and back flex ostentatiously through his t-shirt. He stood at the edge of the building for a long time, surveying the city like a king while the wind whipped strands of hair loose from its messy knot.

But I was too upset to ogle. I was angry, and so was he. And more than that, he looked…tortured. His eyes closed tightly, and a few small lines appeared across his forehead. It was everything I could do not to reach out and smooth them away.

Instead, I sank down into one of the couches assembled around an unlit fire pit. Will stayed at the railing for another minute or two, then stood back up. When he located me, he crossed to the couch and stood in front of me, giving me a good look at his long legs.

"Can I sit next to you, or will you run again?"

There was no trace of resentment in the question. He was asking, honestly. My resolve melted a bit.

"Sit," I mumbled, scooting over a little, though there was really no need. This couch was almost as big as my bed.

We sat there together in silence. Will had never been the type to volunteer much conversation—he kept things bottled up until they had to come out. Big things. Things like his real name. His real identity.

But for once, I didn't want to say anything either. I crossed my arms over my chest and concentrated on breathing. Not the fact that I felt so incredibly lost. Or the fact that I had no idea what was going to happen to me tomorrow, or the next day. I focused on breathing. Inhale. Exhale. And again.

"You didn't let me say sorry."

When I turned, Will was watching me with an expression that was halfway between curious and apologetic.

"I just want to know why," I said quietly.

"Why what?"

"Why you didn't tell me." The pain of his betrayal zigzagged through my chest, making it hard to breathe again. "I told you everything about me. *Everything*. All my worst secrets. All the things about me that I'm ashamed of, that I wouldn't want anyone else to know. About my mom. About Theo—"

My voice broke over the name, and I twisted back to stare at the city skyline. My heart felt like it was breaking, and I couldn't fix it because it wasn't currently in my possession. Instead, it belonged to a stranger, to a man I'd truly believed wanted a future with me. Wanted an "us."

But how could that be, when one half of the equation had never been real from the start?

"Why did you come back to New York?" Will interrupted my spinning thoughts.

I turned. "What?"

"You said you were done with New York for good, Maggie. Why did you come back here?"

I frowned. "Well, to start, I didn't want my mom and neighbors to get completely overrun by photographers."

Will nodded, like he knew exactly what I meant. "Sure. But why *here*?"

I looked away. Somewhere in this city was Theo, fresh out of jail and newly served papers for the hearing. Just the thought of him caused a blade of fear to run straight through me. I could feel his hands on my knees, wrenching them apart as he forced himself between them. I shuddered, curling into myself. He would know I was here. And really, the fact that I hadn't heard from him yet was possibly more frightening than if I had.

"There was another text," I admitted. "It was after you—I—after the race. I came back here to report that he was violating his parole, but that was a no-go. My lawyer says I have to wait until the hearing to request a no-contact addition to the restraining order."

Will started. "What do you mean, violated his parole? Did he do something else besides that?"

"Besides showing up at my race?" I wilted. "Apparently he provided an airtight alibi. He was there, though. I *saw* him. I know I did. But nothing major will come of it."

Will stared at his hands in his lap for a long time. "So when it's done...can we go home?"

I blinked. "What?"

"Home, Lil." He stood up, like he was ready to jump on a plane this instant.

"Home?" The words sounded strange, almost alien in my mouth. "You want to go home? What does that even mean now?"

Will collapsed back down to the couch. "I mean to the lake. Or wherever we can work things out. Away from here and all this craziness."

"And what makes you think I want to work things out at all?"

Will gulped. "Don't say that."

"No, I'm serious." I stood up and paced the deck. "What home? You mean the place where I'm nothing but drunk Ellie Sharp's daughter, good for a pick-up and that's it? Or do you mean your home? The one where you convinced me you were in love with me and forgot to mention, oh, I don't know, your *real fucking identity*!"

I was shrieking by the end, and a spray of pigeons flew off one railing as my voice hit fever pitch.

"What was I supposed to do, Lil?"

Will's voice was even, but shook slightly with a quiet passion—the kind I knew belied much stronger currents running beneath the outward stolid facade. He stretched out his shoulders, then sat back like he was settling in for a long story. Instinctively, I sank back into the cushions of the opposite couch. I was tired, so tired.

"I started working when I was four. *Four years old.* That's when my mother booked my first commercial, and it took less than a month for me to become the official spokeschild for some shitty sugared cereal." Will sighed and pushed a hand through his hair. "I was working eight-hour days before I even had the chance to start kindergarten. I booked a TV series, *Bailey's Life*, when most kids are playing Little League."

I pulled a pillow into my lap and held it to my chest. "I remember that show," I said. "I was little, but I remember thinking the main character was cute."

Will's mouth quirked slightly, but he didn't reply. He was opening up. I didn't dare say more for fear he would stop.

"My mom was my manager, working with a bunch of agents and publicists I hated. I had a tutor on set and rotating chaperones or nannies or whatever the fuck you want to call them. And when I wasn't on set, I was at photo shoots. Movies. Ad spots. Whatever." He sighed. "I had no siblings, no friends. The closest thing to another kid I knew growing up was my costar, Emily Parker, who played the teenager on the show. But she was actually sixteen when the show started. I was seven. We weren't exactly playmates."

I laid my head on the pillow as I listened. I knew all about the show by this point, of course, as well as his explosive film work after it ended. It was one thing to read about it on the internet—scan his extensive filmography, read the list of dates and names and wonder how he could have ever done that in twenty-five short years. But it was another thing completely to hear about the isolation. The strange effect a life like that would have had on a small child who would have probably enjoyed playing Legos as much as anything else.

"I worked on that show for five years," he continued. "It was filmed in the city, so my family didn't have to move out of Connecticut, and we continued to stay there when I started getting film work after that, with trips to LA or wherever else filming occurred, of course. But I don't remember a time when we didn't have bodyguards. When we didn't live in a gated house or community of some sort, with the exception of my dad's old house in Stamford. I don't even remember being able to play at a public park. With other kids. Ever."

He continued through the memories, recounting the years when he started to break out, first as a teenage heartthrob on Disney-style comedies that catered to the preteen masses, and later, as he approached adulthood, the more serious films that started to get him legitimate accolades.

I already knew from my internet searches that this was around the time his fame really blew up, with all of the trappings that went with it. Starlet girlfriends. Embarrassing scandals. And accolade after accolade. Intent on torturing myself, I'd even watched several of his movies, enough to know that he was incredibly talented. If he had already been in a place where having bodyguards was a daily necessity, I couldn't imagine the chaos that went with being crowned Sexiest Man Alive at twenty-two.

Twice he had been mobbed in Central Park and literally had his clothes ripped off his body. His family's homes were broken into at least four times. He'd pressed charges against three different stalkers—one of them was still serving time for attempted murder after breaking into his apartment and stabbing him.

"Jesus," I breathed after he told me that. "That's...terrifying."

Will brushed his hand over a spot on his side, where I knew a thin scar sliced across his skin, so faint I had barely noticed it.

"That's putting it lightly." His hands gripped his pants so hard his knuckles turned white. "I bought a gun after that. But you know what? Having it under my pillow at night made me sleep worse, not better. Something about knowing there was a weapon in such close proximity that could kill somebody. I realized later it was because I thought way too much about using it on myself."

I pressed a hand to my chest. "You wanted to kill yourself?"

Will pressed his lips together and gave a tight nod. "I—sometimes. Yeah. My life was a trap, Maggie. I had no one. Nothing. I bought this massive property in Vermont to get away from the city, but honestly, up there I was even more alone, even more scared. Because there were always ways people could find me. I couldn't run away from this."

He waved a hand in front of his face, toward the obvious changes in his appearance. The hair, the beard, but also his general maturity. He wasn't the lanky, youthful sex symbol from the magazine covers, having gained at least another twenty or thirty pounds of muscle living on the lake. It made his face rounder, his neck, shoulders, and chest bigger. In the pictures from before, Will had looked like a man who could break your heart with one smile. Now he looked like he could break your bones too.

He exhaled heavily, and his shoulders drooped, like they were carrying some heavy, invisible weight.

"What about…" Did I want to ask this question? *Yes*, I realized. I had to. "What about your fiancée?"

Will looked up in surprise. "You know about Amelia?"

My skin prickled. "Yes, I know about her. I have access to Google."

My chest hurt at the memory of the photos of the two of them—an indecently good-looking couple on countless red carpets looking like American royalty. There was one picture in particular, the one where they had attended the Academy Awards the year before he disappeared. Will was nominated for a Best Actor award; she was clearly along for the ride. But the girl hadn't been interested in letting Will have the spotlight. She'd basically dressed as a live version of the Oscar statue in a glittering gold bodycon gown that matched her hair and her tanned, sun-kissed skin. In his tuxedo, Will looked like 007, and she was his picture-perfect Bond girl. I hated that picture. She was everything that I, with my unruly dark hair and imperfect curves, was not.

There was a funny look on Will's face, like the idea of me looking him up on the internet physically hurt.

"Don't believe everything you read," he said finally.

"Were you not engaged?"

"No, we were," he said bitterly. "I got down on one knee and every-thing, gave her a rock the size of Kansas. Is that what you want to hear, Lil? Right under the Hollywood sign, so that when we sold the pictures, we'd be guaranteed a nice chunk of change and Amy would get her pick of designers at the Oscars, not to mention the scripts to follow. I kissed her right in front of all the fans that just happened to be on the trail that day, and everybody clapped, like a goddamn movie."

His words stabbed. I had seen that picture too. I had printed it out in

Calliope's apartment and stared at his mouth on hers, his hands around her impossibly tiny waist and her stupid foot popped off the ground, for a solid hour. And then I had torn it up into about fifty pieces and threw them all out the window.

Will worried the hem of his shirt between his hands, looking like he wanted to tear it up himself. "We were set up," he said. "My mother. Benny. Amy's agent. They put the whole thing together after she requested a date with me. They knew I'd never make a move on anyone. I never had the guts to do anything like that."

That, at least, was believable. I knew Will enough to know how hard it was for him to trust anyone.

"I never knew..." He paused for a moment while he stared out at the skyline. "Whether it was real. She made me believe it for a while, and I wanted it to be. Enough that when I asked her to marry me, I thought it was my idea. But really, she chose the ring, Maggie. She imagined our life. The first time I asked, it was over dinner in my apartment in New York. Amy had me do it again in the Hills for the photo-op."

"But you loved her." I couldn't help it. There was one element in his story that couldn't be faked for the press or anything else.

Will looked at me ruefully. "I thought I did," he said softly. "Until I met you."

Oh. I couldn't pretend his words didn't have an effect. Instead, I looked away as I swiped an errant tear sliding down my cheek. Yeah. Well. I loved him too. That was why this hurt so much.

Will sighed and continued his story.

"And then we had a split, a nice fucking messy one where pictures of me talking to a production assistant were used to make me look like a cheater. Right at the time when Amy was promoting a movie and launching her own awards campaign. That was when I realized it was all for show. And then I really started to spiral."

I'd heard some of this from him before discovering who he really was. Will had disclosed once that he'd struggled with a drug problem, one loosely related to his former "job" working in the industry. For Benny. I snorted. There was something significantly wrong with that configuration.

Again, Google had filled in the blanks. Inevitably, after the articles detailing his split with Amelia, came the clichéd pictures of a playboy in the throes of a crisis. Stumbling out of nightclubs with his arms around two, sometimes even three women, cigarettes dangling from his perfect lips, skin covered with the sheen of intoxication. He was arrested once for cocaine possession, another time for public drunkenness. Both charges were eventually dropped, and it wasn't until the night at Irving Plaza, the concert for which I had been the opener for a much larger act —that strange night where our paths had nearly crossed the first time— that his life had really fallen apart.

"I didn't lie about that night," Will said as he came to when, high and frustrated and losing control of his own life, he'd heard me sing.

"No," I said bitterly. "But you weren't exactly one hundred percent honest either, were you?"

He sighed. "No, I wasn't."

Stricken by stage fright, I had only been coaxed on stage by a stranger who had taken his own refuge in my dressing room—and remained hidden behind a screen the entire time. We had spend an hour talking, even holding hands, but at no point did he reveal himself to me, promising instead to find me after the show.

Will had once admitted he was the man behind the screen. But never the actor who had caused the club to break into chaos after I played.

According to Will, my voice had been a beacon. The insanity of his life had faded away, and he had wanted only to find me and meet me again, this time face to face. But the crowds—his fame—all got in his way, and Will absolutely lost it. Havoc erupted in a crowded club, one man was trampled, and several others landed in the hospital, including Will's father when he suffered a heart attack following the news that his son had been arrested...again. Soon after, wracked with guilt and anger, Will crashed his boat on the coast of Maine and abandoned his life of prestige for a four-year journey of isolation. Which, in the end, led him to me.

When he told me that, only a few weeks ago, I'd said I loved him. Now I wondered if it was too good to be true.

"I had to leave," he said. "I had to get out. And okay, so maybe disappearing wasn't the best idea in the world, but I didn't do anything illegal. There aren't any rules against disappearing and giving a friend power of attorney over your money. No laws banning me from crashing my own boat and having it cleaned up. And nothing says I have to stay in touch with my parents."

"You really trust Benny that much?" I wondered about that. I didn't really know the guy, but he seemed like kind of a schmuck with his pocket squares and glassy apartment.

"With my life," Will said. "Literally." He scrubbed his hands over his face. "Listen. The last four years at Newman Lake…that was the first time in almost my entire life I didn't have a gate and a guard, Maggie. That I didn't have to live inside a cage."

"You still lived in a cage," I replied. "You just made it yourself."

"I had no security. No one watching me. I was lonely, yeah, but I made a place where I belong. With you. Please, Maggie. I just want to go home. I want to go back to where we both belong."

But there was the key issue. Right there.

"I don't know where I belong," I said, no longer able to fight the rest of the tears. "I go home, but it's right back to the same old shit I grew up with. I come back, and all the crap I left is waiting here too. I'm pathetic, this sad little puppy who doesn't know where she's supposed to go, and now I have a broken heart on top of all of it. Back to where we both belong? I don't know *where* I belong, Will!"

"That's because you belong with me!"

His entire body was flexed. Under his thin t-shirt, hints of formidably lean muscle bulged through the cotton; veins popped at his neck. His hair had long fallen from its topknot like streamers, cast in magnificent disarray by the wind. Slowly, the fire that threatened receded, but he didn't move, and his temper still bubbled. That was the thing about Will. His moods would rise and fall until finally, they exploded.

"You—you lied to me," I croaked, viciously swiping across my cheeks. "You lied about who you were. Who you *are*. What am I supposed to do with that? How can you expect that we'll fall right back into what we had?"

I stood up then, unable to remain in one place. The short walk through the Village hadn't been enough. I paced around the deck, finally stopping at the railing that looked out across the Hudson River. For a split second, I could imagine what made people jump. This trapped, hopeless feeling was intolerable.

"Maggie."

A tentative hand landed on my shoulder and gently turned me around. I continued to wipe at my eyes. Every emotion I had was percolating up and out.

"Look at me."

I refused, staring up at the sky.

"Lily, please. *Please*, baby. Look at me."

Finally, I did, and saw the entire universe of pain I felt mirrored in Will's deep green eyes. He was hurting, just like me. His last two weeks had been miserable, just like mine.

"I don't even know you," I whispered.

And that's when, finally, the tears turned to a flood. I hadn't cried in weeks, but today I couldn't stop. I'd been sitting around Calliope's house like a statue, devoid of emotion, devoid of anything. But five minutes with Will, and the waterworks were on, a fucked-up fountain of pain.

"Will—" I started. "I mean, Fitz. I mean—shit, what am I even supposed to call you?!"

"I'm *Will*, Maggie." His voice cracked, and I watched, horrified, as he sank to his knees in front of me and buried his face in my thigh. "I'm *your* Will, baby. And you're mine. *My* Lily pad. Without you…" He turned his face to the side, his eyes closed tightly, his cheeks wet. "Without you, I have no name. Without you, I'm no one at all."

My breath caught as I watched his brow wrinkle with the stress of the words. I had to fight not to stroke his hair away from his face. He inhaled, and with each breath, he seemed to take more and more of my essence, mingling it with his in that way that had always felt so unexplainably *right*.

Which was why slowly, surely, I slid down the railing until I knelt next to him. Will cupped my face, his thumbs stroking softly over my cheeks. A subtle gesture that had only ever made me feel one thing: precious. His light touch made me weep even harder, letting out all of the fury and anger and frustration and sadness.

It was then and only then that I allowed him to pull me into his lap.

He engulfed me in his strong arms and cradled me against his warm, broad chest, rocking me lightly side to side and crooning ever so softly.

"You know me," he whispered fiercely in my ear. "You know me, Maggie Mae Sharp. My Lily pad. Better than anyone else on this fucking planet. I know it doesn't seem like it right now, but, baby, I'm still me. Still the same asshole. Still the same Will. It's just me."

He said it over and over again: *It's just Will. It's just me.* And eventually, the words began to stick, seeping into my body and soul like the tears soaking into my cheeks. The pain might not fade immediately, but I couldn't deny the truth. I needed Will, like he seemed to need me. Whatever happened next, we still had that.

"I'm still mad at you," I whispered as he pressed kisses on top of my head.

One hand wrapped securely around my waist while the other slid up my neck to cup the back of my head and cradle me into his shoulder.

"So be mad," he said. "Be angry. Be upset. But be mad with me, Lil. Just be with me."

CHAPTER FOUR

W e didn't talk or do anything else for several hours really but sit and hold each other, as if both of us needed to recharge some precious stores that had been depleted over the last two weeks. Life was so tenuous for us both. Will had a whole host of demons he was going to have to confront after years in hiding, and I had my own share of skeletons that were bound to come out if I was going to have a relationship with a public figure. Because that's what he was, of course—as public as it got, despite what he wanted. And, I realized, he was scared to death about it.

At some point, after drifting off together on Benny's couch, under the discreet shade of the canopy, we sat up in a daze, smiling shyly at one another. What next? Where would we go? What would we do? What were the next steps in healing?

How would I learn who this person was sitting next to me?

Will pushed back his hair. As he re-tied it, his gaze flickered over my body. I looked down to find my shirt pulled down a little too far in sleep, revealing a generous amount of cleavage while my skirt had bunched up around my thighs. I didn't look indecent or anything, but there was certainly some stuff on display.

I made quick work of fixing and adjusting, but when I finished, Will's expression had turned significantly darker. He sucked on his lip, closed his eyes for a second, then dragged his eyes up my body.

"I missed you, Lil," he said softly.

He leaned in, and like a magnet, I leaned forward too. Our lips brushed, once, twice before he snaked a hand around the back of my neck and pulled me in for a kiss that I'd been craving for the last two weeks. It started out slowly, like he was trying to protect us, as fragile as we were. But quickly, his resolve melted, his mouth opened, mine right along with it.

"Oh!" I moaned as his teeth closed around my bottom lip. He sucked, then slipped his tongue around mine.

"Fucking hell," he muttered as he pulled me onto his lap. In a second, my shirt was pulled up and he was yanking down the lace cups of my bra.

"Will..." I whimpered, my breath hot and ragged.

His mouth closed around one nipple while his fingers pinched the other. His left hand slipped under my skirt, took a thick handful of flesh, and kneaded roughly while he hardened between my thighs. I rocked against him, starving for more.

"What do you need, baby?" His deep voice rumbled over the delicate skin of my neck. He licked under my jaw before taking my earlobe between his teeth and worrying it lightly. "Can I make you come, Lil? I want to watch you fall apart in my arms again."

"And—and then what?" His mouth made it hard to think, especially when the hand on my ass slipped farther down, breaching the elastic edge of my panties and making contact with my slick center.

"I just want to come home, Lil," Will said as his finger slipped inside. "Any way I can."

He captured my mouth again with his, twisting our tongues together in that intoxicating dance that erased all conscious thoughts. All I could feel was pleasure. Belonging. The complete and utter *rightness* of our bodies acting as one. I ground into him, luxuriating in the long, solid length rubbing against my clit. A second finger joined the first as he sucked on my tongue.

"Oh, God." I threaded my fingers through his hair. More. I wanted more. "I'm close," I whimpered.

"Do it," Will urged. "Let go, baby. Let me feel it."

His finger began to thrust more insistently, matching the rocking of my hips as I sought more friction against him. His other hand wrapped around my nape, holding me still so he could plunder my mouth more thoroughly. Higher and higher I rose, riding on the grunts, the growls, the heated breaths we shared between indecent kisses.

But right as I was about to fall apart completely, a tinny, bouncing ringtone rang through the air. I froze, then scrambled to the other side of the couch, feeling like I'd been caught doing something very, very wrong. I struggled to catch my breath, tugging my clothes back into place while Will jumped up.

"Shit!" He dug into the pockets of his jeans.

I gawked, fixing my bra as Will pulled out a sleek iPhone. "*What* is that?!"

Will ignored my astonishment as he awkwardly punched in the passcode. No fingerprint identification for this guy, apparently.

"I had to," he said as he lifted it to his ear. "It was either that or have a gorilla babysitter follow me literally everywhere I went. Ben, *what* the fuck do you want? I'm kind of busy."

I watched curiously as Will talked. He sank back onto the couch and set one foot on the glass table. It was a strange juxtaposition. He was dressed in secondhand rags, but he seemed totally at ease with all of this luxury.

"Okay," he said. "Yeah, we'll be right down."

He ended the call and shoved the phone back in his pocket with a sigh.

"Well, well, well. Will Baker is plugged in. If I felt like I didn't know you before, now you're *really* a complete stranger." I was joking, but it wasn't totally wrong.

Will sent me another withering look, which only made me chuckle. In response, he launched himself across the couch, caging me against the white cushions.

"I'll show you a stranger, smart-ass," he said as he leaned in to continue the kiss from before.

His lips were warm, firm. Familiar. I hadn't realized it until now, but a part of me wondered if this would be different too. Would "Fitz Baker" make love differently than Will?

Their kisses, at least, were the same. As Will teased my mouth open, our tongues were quick to restart that desperate dance our bodies already knew so well, I forgot both of his names. I practically forgot my own.

"Damn," he said as he pulled away, though the movement actually made the obvious evidence of his arousal press harder into my thigh. I rotated my hips into it, enjoying the way his breath hitched.

"You kill me, you know that, Lily pad?" he said, pressing his forehead to mine.

I closed my eyes as his minty, fresh breath washed over me. "You don't need to stop." I wanted more. So much more. I wanted to know it was really him.

Will sighed. "Unfortunately, I do. The cavalry is on their way up."

I opened my eyes. "Benny and Callie?"

Will nodded, then rolled off me. "The devil waits for no man."

I got up, fixing my hair, and followed him back to the stairwell. "I think the saying is that 'time waits for no man,' you goon."

Will sent me a crooked smile over his shoulder. "Eh. It still fits."

"What does it say that you're referring to your best friend as the devil?"

Will held the door open, allowing me to walk down the stairs in front of him. "Well, there's the other saying, right? 'Better the devil you know than the devil you don't'? Benny's one of the devils I know."

"One?"

Will wasn't smiling anymore. "One of many," he confirmed. All humor had left in his voice.

We found Benny and Calliope waiting impatiently in the living room. Calliope was texting madly while Benny chattered at breakneck speed into his Bluetooth. They both stopped when they saw us approaching. Calliope smiled when she caught my hand in Will's.

"I'm going to have to call you back," Benny said before switching off his Bluetooth. "Is champagne in order, or is this a temporary reunion?"

Will squeezed my hand, giving me a shy smile as he raised my knuckles to his lips. "She's stuck with me now. But no champagne needed. Yet."

My eyes widened, and Will winked.

Benny raised an eyebrow. "Wow. You *did* change out there in no man's land."

I smiled back at Will, though I didn't know exactly why. I still felt unsure about so much—like I had to get to know this man all over again —but I wanted to believe he meant what he said. My heart told me he did.

"Babe?" Calliope called from the corner. "Look, don't kill me. But I told a few reps that you've been working on some new stuff. They're interested as soon as you can get a demo together."

I sank onto the big white couch that faced Calliope, followed by Will, who seemed unwilling to be more than a foot away from me. "Cal..."

"Don't hate me yet," she said, still tapping into her phone. "It's only a demo, and you need the money, kid. Those legs bills ain't cheap. Plus, you're Fitz Baker's girl—everyone is interested in you now. We should capitalize on that."

Beside me, Will tensed. "Hey," he said low enough that only I could hear him. "Do you need some help? Because whatever it is, I can cover it."

It was tempting, but I wasn't going to do it. We were already in a situation that was complicated enough without letting Will pay my legal fees. I had absolutely no interest in incurring that kind of debt.

"It's fine," I said. "I'll be fine." I turned to Callie.

The thought of performing—even recording—struck a chord of fear through me, but it was either that or waiting tables. Will was facing his fears by being here. It was time for me to face mine too.

"If you can find me some cheap studio space, I'll do it," I said. "I can probably get my old waitressing job back to pay the fees. But it will be me alone. I don't have the time or money to get a band together."

Calliope grinned. "Perfect. I'll make some calls. A couple of guys at Sony owe me some favors. Make sure you play that new one from this morning."

Will blinked at me. "What new one?"

I shook my head. "Just some messing around."

Calliope shot me a sideways look, but I ignored her. I wasn't ready to talk about the songs I'd written on the drive to New York. They were personal, my way of dealing with emotions I still hadn't straightened out in my mind. Our talk on the roof had helped, but things weren't healed. Nowhere near it.

"So, hold up. What's the plan, now?" Benny asked. "You're not going back to Washington?"

"We're going to need a place to stay." Will tugged me into his side, wrapping a solid arm around my shoulder so he could play with my hair.

I cozied into him easily, almost like the last two weeks hadn't happened. Almost.

Benny brightened. "For how long?"

"Only until Maggie gets her hearing." Will squeezed my shoulders, although Benny's disappointment was obvious. "She has to deal with some harassment from her asshole ex." Will turned to me. "Who's your lawyer?"

"Her name is Jamie Douglass. She was recommended to me when the YWCA couldn't take me on again." Jamie was nice, young, and relatively cheap. She was pretty inexperienced with all of this, but she was also all I could afford, and was willing to take a payment plan.

Will's distaste was palpable. "Huh."

He flickered a glance at Benny, who nodded in response to some unspoken communication between the two of them. Calliope and I both blinked at each other, unsure of what had just happened.

"Listen, I gotta go, babe," Callie said, standing up. "Sadly, I do have other clients." She leaned down to kiss my cheek. "You have the key, right?"

I nodded. "I'll, um, keep you updated on where I'll be later."

"Someone will come get her stuff whenever you can be there to let them in," Will added. "We'll bring it here until we lock down a place."

I turned to him, ready to argue that I could pick up my own things, but he silenced me with a curt shake of his head.

"I can't go there right now," he said quietly. "And where you go, Lil, I go too."

I nodded, understanding he was referring to our little spat on the street and the potential crowds that might be there now. He wasn't over-reacting. #FitzSpotting had become a regular sport on Twitter.

He touched his forehead to mine again, almost like he was trying to telecommunicate the things he couldn't quite say. I understood. There was a lot to say. A lot to know. And not enough time to figure it all out. We had to take one step at a time.

"I'll call you later," Calliope said as she walked to the elevator.

I waved.

"Benny, can you round up a broker for us?" Will asked. "Someone quiet. I'd like to be in a decent place tonight, if possible. We need better security than a hotel can offer." He turned to me. "Do you have time to look at apartments with me?"

I nodded. "I should probably practice tonight, though, if I'm going to be recording."

Will nodded again, though he tensed right along with me at the mention of recording. He had no idea what kinds of butterflies were already flying around my stomach.

"Already done." Benny tapped out a message on his phone—the thing really did seem to be a part of his anatomy. "And…she's here."

As if on cue, the elevator door rang out a new arrival, and beside me Will's entire body seemed to freeze.

"Who's here?" I asked him. "The broker? That was fast."

Will pressed his lips into a tight line, and draped his other arm over his face, like he was blocking out the rays of a particularly strong sun. "No, another devil I know. My mother."

CHAPTER FIVE

"Where is he?"

A pair of heels clicked over the shiny wood floors, announcing the arrival of Tricia Owens-Baker. Her sharp voice came again, echoing the same question again and again with rising levels of hysteria.

"Where is he? Where is my son, Benny?"

She swept into the room, a flurry of designer clothes and flashy yet tasteful jewelry. Even if I hadn't already been told who she was, I still would have known this was Will's mother. I had seen pictures of her, of course. Tricia Owens-Baker was a beautiful woman who looked somewhere in her mid to late fifties, with a head of thick blonde hair that had the same wavy texture as her son's. Hers, of course, was perfectly groomed, falling around her shoulders in manicured tresses that bounced slightly as she walked. And while I knew that Will's physique —his lanky height and swimmer's shoulders—came from his late father, the man who stood next to this woman in most of her photos, his face was one hundred percent inherited from his mother. Same knife-straight bones, same full mouth, same penetrating green eyes.

Only hers contained none of the warmth I usually saw in Will's.

She was dressed down in that way that only rich people can do while still looking like their wealth, in a crisp, sleeveless button-down blouse that didn't have a trace of a wrinkle, dark denim jeans that looked like they had never been worn, and black pumps without so much as a scuff. Her nails were French-manicured, and her jewelry included a diamond pendant, a collection of gold bangles around one wrist, and a very expensive-looking watch that gleamed in the afternoon sun.

Still at the elevator, Calliope glanced between the woman and the rest of us with an alarmed look and mouthed at me, "Should I stay?"

Though I wished she could, I shook my head. Will didn't know Calliope, and he wouldn't want an audience for this reunion. So, with regret, I watched the elevator doors close over my friend, then turned back to the new arrival in the apartment, keeping my hand wrapped securely around Will's as we both stood up.

"Benny." The woman traded air kisses with Benny, then smoothed the nonexistent wrinkles out of her shirt and turned to Will and me. "Oh," she said. Her voice dropped a full octave. "Oh, here he is."

Will swallowed and stepped forward. "Hi...Mom."

They stood about five feet apart, eying each other warily. I was reminded of watching cats meet—generally solitary creatures that never seem to expect to run into the other, but when they do, fur, whiskers, ears, tails, *everything* is on high alert. I half expected one of them to meow.

I took a step forward, unable to do more with Will keeping his tight grip on me. "Hi, I'm Maggie, Will's friend," I said, extended my other hand.

"Girlfriend," Will quickly corrected me. "Right?" He looked down at me hopefully, and I couldn't help but smile.

"Right," I murmured, then turned back to his mother. "Girlfriend. Sorry."

His mother completely ignored me, and after a few seconds standing like an idiot with my hand hanging in the air, I stepped back beside Will and waited.

His mother took a step forward, then another. She examined Will like he was an exhibit at a museum, scanning his body, his clothes, his face, his hair for the tiniest details. Her hand floated out like she was about to stroke his face and pull him in for a hug. But instead, she reached it back and slapped him across the cheek. Hard.

"What the *hell*?" I cried out, while Will touched a hand to his cheek and glared at his mother.

"Trish, Jesus Christ," Benny put in. "*Really*?"

"Well, I see some things haven't changed," Will remarked as he rubbed his face.

"How could you do that to me?" she shrieked. "Four years. *Four years* we thought you were dead! Thought our boy had drowned. We had a memorial. What you put your father and me through, I can't even *begin* to talk about it!"

She pulled her hand back again, and instinctively, I stepped in front of Will, raising my own hands to stop her.

"Don't even think about it," I warned.

"Tricia, back off." Benny's voice was more serious than I'd heard it yet.

"Mom." Will's voice cut through all of the noise, and immediately everyone shut up and turned to him.

"You killed him," Tricia said. "You broke his heart and killed him, and I had to handle *everything* myself!"

"It's not like you were much of a help to him," Will snapped back. "How long has it been since you two lived together? Fourteen, fifteen years now?"

"That is *none* of your business. And don't even think about pretending you cared enough about him to be in his life, Fitz*william*! My husband is gone now, and it is all your fault!"

Will wilted. I already knew from his previous disclosures that he did feel responsible for his father's death. His mother's accusations told me exactly where that came from.

"That's ridiculous," I snapped. "How can he be responsible for something he wasn't even there to do?"

Tricia turned to me, like it had just occurred to her I was present. "And who are *you*?" she asked, as if I hadn't already introduced myself.

I straightened to my full height of five feet, five inches. I was still at least five inches shorter than this woman, who loomed over me in her heels, but I wasn't cowering to her.

"I'm *Maggie*," I gritted out. "Like I said two minutes ago."

She looked me over with the evaluative gaze she had also given Will. "What are you? Hispanic? Filipino?" She looked over my shoulder to Will. "What are you doing, getting involved with trash like this?"

My mouth dropped. "Are you serious, lady? I am *right here*."

"Tricia, you can get the hell out if you're gonna start with that kind of racist bullshit," Benny broke in, the first time I had seen him look or sound anything but unruffled. It was apparent that there was no love lost between him and Will's mother. I couldn't help but wonder if there was more to it than Will's disappearance and Benny's apparent aid with it. Of course, considering that Benny wasn't white either, I had to wonder if he'd gotten his share of this garbage from her too.

Tricia glared at him for a long time, then turned back to Will.

"Whatever," she snapped. "What do you think she's doing here right now? Providing moral support? She probably knew who you were from the start."

"Maggie had no idea, Mom," Will said bitterly. "And when she found out, *she* left me, if you have to know. I'm only in New York because I was looking for her. Not you. Not Benny. Not anyone else. Her." He looked down at me, and the fierceness of his gaze practically knocked me over. "I'd find you anywhere, Lily pad."

I couldn't breathe. Every cell in my body wanted to celebrate his words—wanted to welcome him back and show him that I felt the same way. And I wanted all these people to leave immediately so I could do it right.

"Will, you can't *possibly* be this naive." Tricia pulled our attention back to her. "I don't even recognize you right now. I didn't raise you to throw away your career. I didn't raise you to be stupid. And I certainly didn't raise you to align yourself with every desperate little thing that gloms onto you."

"You didn't *raise* me at all," Will growled. "Or did you forget? Five different nannies. Four separate tutors. Every single director I ever had. Too many production assistants to count."

Tricia's wide green eyes, with their strange lack of anything resembling age, widened. "You ungrateful brat. You always were, too. Who do you think was the one carting you around to auditions while your father wasted his life away on that stupid boat? Who do you think paid for headshots? Networked and schmoozed and did whatever it took to make you a star. It should be *my name* on the Walk of Fame, not yours. You would have nothing if it weren't for me. *Nothing.*" She started to pace, and we all watched her, as if we were entranced by the rhythm of her heels on the parquet. "You'd be some smelly fisherman, just like your father, with high blood pressure and a bad heart, talking about nothing but flounder and lobster while battling the bottle. They're a dime a dozen, Will. You'd be common. That's it."

A slight accent emerged the longer she spoke, belying a working-class history underneath Tricia Owens-Baker's picture-perfect exterior. And in that moment, I knew her secret. Tricia Owens-Baker was a woman who, deep down, hated herself. Hated the town she came from. Hated her lack of manners, education, or refinement—the little things that marked a person who grew up with money from someone who grew up without. The hair, skin, nails, teeth, clothes, jewelry—all of it was a mask, things used to hide a woman who, deep down, was as common as her late husband. As common as me, or anyone else.

But there was something else that struck me in her little speech: the casual use of Will's name. I hadn't heard Benny call him Fitz either—then again, he hadn't really called him anything at all, except maybe "F," which sounded more like it was to get under his skin. Will was telling the truth—he *was* Will, at least to anyone that mattered.

"Common," Will said quietly, "would be better than fucking miserable. But I never got the chance to choose? Did I...*Mom*?"

Tricia opened her perfectly painted mouth, then closed it tight before whirling around to Benny.

"And you," she hissed. "You knew about this the entire time, didn't you? I should sue you for fraud, you ungrateful little shit! My son and *my* assistance made your career. You'd have absolutely nothing if it weren't for me, and then you had to steal away my most important asset."

"Come now, Trish, let's all take a breath," Benny said smoothly, holding his arms out like he wanted to give her a hug. "I did what my client asked, from the time he was eighteen and allowed to make those decisions for himself. You can't really blame me for that, can you? It's not my fault he didn't want his mother to manage his career any longer."

He smirked, like he was really enjoying this. Tricia looked like she wanted to tear his head off.

"That's all I was anyway, wasn't I, Mom?"

It was amazing, really, the way with just a few words, all the attention in the room went right back to Will. I was willing to bet that more than anything else, that was what had made him a star. No amount of headshots or auditions could give someone that kind of presence. They called it the "it" factor. Star power. You either had it or you didn't.

"An 'asset,'" Will repeated acidly. "I wasn't a person. I stopped being your son the second you signed my life away to that fucking television show. You want to know why I disappeared? It was that. Right fucking there."

Tricia's mouth dropped. "*What*?"

Will sighed. "What do you want, Mom?"

Tricia examined him again, took a deep breath, and smoothed her hair.

"To start," she said. "I wanted to see you. See if you were real. That you were—that you were actually alive."

Will swallowed again, and when he spoke, his voice was thick. "Well…here I am. What else?"

She looked him over once more. "You look like you've been living in a dumpster for four years. Honestly, Will, didn't they have clothes where you were hiding? What have you been doing out there all this time?"

Will frowned. "Is that all?"

Tricia sighed, then took a deep breath. "No. No, it's not." She took a step forward, and when she reached out again, Will flinched, leaning away from her fingers.

"I'm sorry I slapped you," she said. "I shouldn't have done that."

Still nothing. Slowly, like she was reaching toward a wild animal, she tried again, and placed a hand lightly on his cheek—the same hand that had hit him earlier, now fitting its fingers to the red print splotched over his skin. Will closed his eyes, as if the touch caused him more pain than anything else. Her fingers lingered for a moment, and then he pulled away, taking a half step behind me.

Tricia started, like the tenderness caused her legitimate shock. Almost as if she was less in control of her actions than when she had physically hit her son.

"Dinner," she said abruptly. "I want dinner. I deserve that at least, Will. *At least.*"

I wanted to tell her no. That there was no way in hell Will was going to spend an hour sitting across from a woman who had assaulted him at the first opportunity. I didn't need more than fifteen minutes with Tricia Owens-Baker to imagine what had driven Will to fake his own death. The woman was positively awful.

But right as Will opened his mouth to respond, Benny's phone rang.

"Yeah," he answered. "Hey. Yeah, we'll be there soon. Okay, sure. Yeah, bye."

He stowed his phone back in his pocket and turned to Will. "Broker's waiting. They are going to show the apartment to someone else if we don't get over there now."

"Apartment?" Tricia's green eyes were wide, innocently blinking, like a lost puppy's. "You're staying in New York? Can I come?"

Gone was the furious, intense woman whose first reaction to seeing her son again had been to slap him across the face. It was clear that Will had also inherited his mercurial nature from her—her emotions changed on a dime. One minute she was ready to slap him again, the next she wanted to be close. Was she moody or sociopathic? I wasn't sure I wanted to know.

Will studied her for a long time, and she waited patiently, as if she knew it was only a matter of time before he broke down. I didn't like the feeling. Not one bit.

"No," he said finally, as if the one word cost him most of his energy. "No, I think we'll do this one on our own, Mom."

Fury bloomed again on Tricia's face—you could practically see her temperature rising. For a second, I thought she was going to slap her son all over again. My fist flexed involuntarily. I wanted her to get the hell away from us.

But then she took a deep breath, reached back to fluff her hair, and exhaled.

"Dinner, then," she snapped, already flouncing toward the elevators.

"Eight o'clock. Le Corbeau. I'll tell them to have the back entrance open for you, like always. Don't be late, and *don't* go disappearing again."

The elevator opened as soon as she pressed the button, and the three of us watched as she sauntered into the car. After the doors shut, Will shuddered, then slid down onto the couch and bent over, dropping his head into his hands.

"Will," Benny said, checking his phone again. "I'm sorry, but we need to go, man."

"I need a minute," Will said, his voice shaking slightly.

I sat beside him and slipped a hand over his shoulders, a feeble gesture of comfort. He turned and wrapped his arms around my waist, pulling me onto his lap with no regard for the fact that we had an audience.

"Don't leave me again, Lil," he whispered as he buried his face into my neck. "I can't do this without you."

We rocked silently together, ignoring Benny's pacing, ignoring the way the rest of the world already seemed to be closing in on us.

"I love you." His voice was muffled by my skin, but the words were clear enough. I hadn't realized how badly I'd needed to hear them again until they were out there. Maybe they were said in desperation, but I was feeling pretty desperate myself these days.

He loved me. Fitz. Will. Whoever he was, whoever he had to be, that simple fact hadn't changed.

"I'm here," I said as I stroked his hair. "I'm here."

Slowly, Will's shoulders relaxed, though he didn't move his face for several more minutes. It was only when his heartbeat, pounding next to mine, reached a somewhat normal cadence that he finally released me from his stone grip and blew a long breath out between his teeth.

"Okay," he said with closed eyes. "Okay, let's go."

CHAPTER SIX

"No."

Benny mashed his lips around and pressed a hand atop his close-cut hair. "Is he always like this?" he asked me. "No, don't answer that. I already know." He turned back to Will. "You've gotten way harder to please living in solitary confinement, my friend. Tell me what the fuck is wrong now."

Will rapped a knuckle on the double-paned windows of the sixth apartment we had looked at that afternoon. First had been a loft in Tribeca, then a townhouse in the village that was vetoed simply because it had street access. Two high-rise condos in Midtown, and a classic six on the Upper East Side. Every place had been gorgeous. Stunning. The kind of places where, well, a movie star would live.

And every single one Will had nixed almost immediately, much to the increasing irritation of Benny and the broker, Carol.

"It's the windows," Will said. "We're too exposed here. Come on, Carol, there has to be something better than this."

Benny, Carol, and I all stared out the massive picture windows that provided a panoramic view of Central Park. Several stories below, the trees that carpeted the park rustled noiselessly in the light wind, almost like feathers.

Benny sighed. "Seriously? This again? Who the fuck do you think is going to be looking in here? This is the twentieth floor, my friend, and the only thing you're looking at is green. It's twice what you wanted to pay, but it doesn't get any more private in New York. You know this."

"Private? Then what's that?" Will pointed out the window. "Right there, I can see the twentieth floor of another building. And another. And ten more just like it. Where I'm sure about five different cameras are going to rent windows next week. Don't tell me these fuckers don't have telephoto lenses, Benny."

Benny rolled his eyes. "Come on, man. This is New York. Pull the blinds and get over it."

Will turned to me. "What do you think?"

I shrugged. "I like it."

But I had liked every apartment we'd seen. John Lennon. Madonna. We'd be joining the ranks of some serious star power on this side of town. Walk-in closets. A view to die for. More space than two people would know what to do with. Truth be told, I thought every apartment we'd looked at was way too much. I would have been happy camping out in a studio for a few weeks, or, for the same price, a cheap hotel.

But a hotel wasn't going to be good enough for the great Fitz Baker, and without fail, Will found some kind of problem with every place we'd seen.

Will snorted. "I'm being difficult, aren't I?"

I continued to stare out the window. "I get it. You want to feel safe where you live. You don't even want to be here to begin with, so I don't really blame you for being picky."

Will slipped a hand around my waist and pulled me close. "I want *us* to feel safe where *we* live. And I want to be here with you, Lil. So if you don't like it, that's important."

I blinked up at him. I understood why we needed to stay together. On our way to meet Carol, Benny had asked the driver to pass Calliope's street, which was already horded with cameras. Will was right. I was going to be a target for the press too, and Calliope's walk-up didn't provide anywhere near the security I would need.

But there was still a lot to learn about Will. A whole person's worth of information, actually. There was a part of me that wondered if we weren't diving in a little fast.

So I shrugged again. "It's temporary. I don't really care where we stay. As long as we're safe, whatever you want is fine with me."

Will examined me for a long second, then turned to Carol and Benny, who were both standing by the door, impatiently swiping through their phones. "Guys, could we have a minute in the place alone?"

They both looked up with something resembling relief, or maybe hope.

"Mr. Baker," said Carol. "If this apartment isn't to your liking, we really need to move on quickly before the last building's manager goes home for the night."

"Nah, we don't have time for that," Benny added. "You got dinner with Trish in a few hours. It's this, or we keep looking tomorrow. Choose, Will."

"We'll take the apartment, all right? We just need a minute in it together." Will's tone turned to steel—one I was beginning to recognize. It was the tone he used to cut through the many voices that seemed to surround him here. Voices that wanted things from him. Voices he wanted to silence.

He took my hand and squeezed. I stayed quiet.

Benny sighed irritably, then turned to Carol. "Let's step out and look at the paperwork, Carol."

Carol nodded amiably, seemingly used to the unorthodox requests of high-profile clients. Since she was someone who specialized in showing these kinds of buildings, I wondered how many other famous people she'd met.

The door closed behind them, and Will took my hand and walked me through the rooms again. It was fully furnished—a corner apartment with three full bedrooms, a massive closet, and a huge living space that could probably accommodate a crowd over a hundred. Not that we would *ever* have that many people in here.

The farther in we walked, the more I shrank. The place was huge, and I was so small. What was I even doing here, in this world? Me, with my scuffed Converse and faded t-shirts. I didn't belong here.

"Why did you send them out?" I wondered as I trailed a finger over the crown molding of one window.

"Because I was fucking tired of people," Will said. He pulled me toward him. "And I'm worried about you. You've been too quiet."

He released my hand and leaned back against the wall, then followed as I wandered into a bedroom.

"Would this be—would this be my bedroom or yours?" I wondered. Were we going to live here as roommates? Lovers? We had made up, of course, but I had no idea what this arrangement was going to entail. How do you move in with someone after knowing them—but not *really* knowing them—for a little over a month?

Will's brows rose at the question. "You really think I would ever share an apartment with you and sleep in separate rooms?"

I bit my lip. "Honestly? I don't really know what you want here, Will."

"I swam a mile to get to you at three a.m., Lily pad. What makes you think I would ever find a couple of plaster walls between us acceptable? Why do you think I *really* sent out Benny and Carol?"

I blinked at the window. "I d-don't know. Why did you?"

"Well, for one, I didn't think they needed to be around when I stripped you naked."

I swung around. "Wha-*what*?"

Will smirked, but behind the cocky expression was a bit of empathy. "It's been two weeks. Two weeks since I touched you. Kissed you. Was inside you."

My mouth dropped. "Will…"

"A couple of kisses on Benny's roof aren't enough, beautiful. Come here."

I crossed my legs and leaned back against the windowsill. The city was at my back, the light shining from its rooftops behind me. But the only thing in the world that mattered seemed to be in this room. And here I was…frozen.

Will closed the door. There was the audible click of a lock. He paused.

"I swear to God," he muttered.

"What?"

Will turned back to me. All of the stress, annoyance, and frustration of the afternoon seemed to have concentrated in his deep green eyes—the full extent of which was being fired at me in a very different set of emotions. Need. Desire. Lust.

Each of those fourteen days felt like anchors that Will's heated gaze was cutting free. Other than today, it had been two weeks since I'd felt him touch me. Had his lips on mine. Felt that...moment...where his subtle domination of my body overwhelmed everything else.

Will made me feel big when the world made me small. And here, in this city, I felt smaller than ever.

"Lily," he said, his voice low and serious.

"Y-yes?"

The heat on his face faltered slightly at the sound of my stutter, but only slightly.

"I swear, baby," Will said. "I swear to *God*. If you don't get your ass over here in three fucking seconds, I'm going to spank you until you are black and fucking blue."

My eyes popped open. "Wh-what? You want to *spank* me?"

Will growled. Or maybe he laughed. I couldn't really tell.

"Lil," he said. "Get over here. Now."

The palpable need in his voice set something free, like a spring that had been released. I didn't walk. I didn't run. I *flew* across the room and into his arms, accepting the kiss that was messy, raw, and practically shouted desperation. The two weeks we'd been apârt felt like an eternity, and that Will-shaped space inside me needed to be filled. In every possible way.

The tension between us wasn't fully resolved. Maybe it never would be. After all, he had deceived me for almost the entire time I knew him, and then, of course, I had left him cold. But even as the walls were closing in around us, both of us knew that this—*this*—was the only way that either of us would keep a finger on our freedom.

I hoped. Oh, God, I hoped.

"They're going to come back," I said, heaving for breath as Will's teeth closed around my ear. My core, my center was already pulsing for him. "We should stop, don't you think?"

In response, I was whirled around and shoved against the bedroom door. My shirt and bra were torn off, hips were pulled out, skirt yanked up, panties shoved down.

"Do you really want to stop, Lil?" Will growled. His tongue licked down my earlobe, and when he bit softly, I barely registered the clink of his belt unbuckling before his cock slipped between my legs. "Say the word, and I will."

His hand found the fleshier part of my ass with a loud smack that echoed through the empty space. It was hard, with a sharp sting that made my desire even sharper.

"Say it," repeated Will as he slapped me again. "Yes or no?"

"Mmmm." I was practically wordless, shocked, yet pushing back into his harsh touch, tipped my hips to welcome him. "Y-yesssss."

But he teased, having harnessed his need to keep me waiting.

"Fuck me, you're wet." Will shuddered as he gently thrust between my thighs, keeping his cock trapped between them, the friction creating a slippery preview of what was to come. "Always so ready. You need this as bad as I do, don't you, baby?"

"Y-yes-Oh, *God*!" I whispered, long and loud as he breached my entrance. I did need it, but I still wasn't ready to take him. The sheer size of him simply required more...time.

"Take me, Lil," he said, wrapping an arm around my shoulder as he eased himself in, inch by terrible inch. "God, you're so damn tight."

"I...can't...Will!" I gritted the words through my teeth. He was so big, and it had been so long. He almost—*almost*—hurt, but nothing that came close to how amazing he actually felt, to the exquisite match of our bodies together.

"You can, baby." His low voice rumbled against my neck. "You can, and you will. Because you need to, and I need you to. Take it. Take *me*, Lily. All of me—for all of you."

He sank in that final inch, sheathed completely, and stayed there, perfectly still except for the way I could literally feel him throbbing inside me.

"I could come like this, you know that?" His breath was hot over my neck, and his teeth grazed my nape slightly. "Being in you, feeling you squeeze my dick the way you do. Jesus *Christ*, Lily. Do that again."

Instinctively, I inhaled, pulling up and in with my body, feeling the way he pulsed. I could come this way too. One swipe of his thumb, and I'd be a goner. I was so, *so* ready to let go.

Will's big palms slid up my sides, dipping around my waist, pausing around my rib cage, feeling my curves before he cupped both of my breasts.

"Do you feel that?" he said as he pulled out almost completely, then sank back in to the hilt.

"Mmmm." I was beyond words, my forehead pressed to the wall, urging him shamelessly to shove back in, again and again.

"Say it, Lil. I need to hear you say it."

Out. Back in. His pace was immeasurably slow, centered while his hands kneaded my breasts in time with his movements. He tugged lightly on my nipples. I moaned.

Will paused. I pressed backward into him, urging him on, but he was resolute in his stasis. Then one hand left my breast and threaded into my hair, pulling it tightly so I was yanked against his chest.

"Say it," he ordered.

"S-say what?" My stutter had become so much worse in the past few weeks, but right now, it wasn't out of fear. It was from anticipation. Only Will had the power to undo me this way.

"You know what." He yanked lightly on my hair. The slight pinch made me moan. "Say it, Lily."

So I said the only thing I could think of that hadn't been said. He had murmured the words to me, but I had kept them to myself, letting them sing inside my chest, a vulnerable gift I hadn't quite been ready to give.

But now, the words sang. "I love you."

Will's entire chest relaxed. "Thank fucking God."

In a blur of movement, I was flipped around and picked up, and Will attacked my mouth like he had been starved for days. He took three long steps to the windows, set me atop the deep sill, and plunged back inside me.

"That's right, Lil. Spread out, just like that." Will licked his thumb, then drew it down my torso, between my breasts, grazing my navel, and landing on top of my clit. "Fuck, I could eat you alive, you know that?"

I peered up at him. "Why don't you?"

A sly half grin tugged the corner of his mouth, revealing one dimple that I wanted to lick. "You little vixen. Don't tempt me."

He leaned over and sucked on my lip, giving me a *very* good idea of what it would feel like to have that done lower down. He thrust deeper, and I moaned.

"Sometime soon, when I have more than five damn minutes, I'm going to spend an entire day with my face between your legs." He pushed in again, and the friction of skin on top of skin, rubbing that sensitive spot, caused me to jerk against him. "Breakfast." Thrust. "Lunch." Suck. "Dinner." Shove. "And every snack in between."

He licked his lips—it was all too easy to imagine him licking *me* instead, and the idea was my undoing as he pulled my lower lip between his teeth.

"Will," I hissed. "I'm...oh, *God*, I'm so fucking close!"

"Mr. Baker?"

We both jerked toward the door, where Carol was trying and failing to turn the knob.

"Mr. Baker?" she called again. "Everything all right?"

"Don't stop," Will whispered as he continued to pummel forward.

I arched back into the window, but right as a moan threatened to escape, it was clapped silent by Will's big palm over my mouth.

"We're just talking it over, Carol," he called out, snaking his other arm around my back and yanking me close so we were chest to chest.

"Let go, Lil," he commanded in a whisper only I could hear. The muscles carved into his chest, his abs, his hips, his arms—all of them clenched and rippled with each movement. He dropped his thumb down to my clit and rubbed. "Let go, baby. I'm right here with you. Let me fuckin' feel it."

"Anything I can help with?" I could barely hear Carol's voice as my head tipped back again. The only thing keeping me fully upright was Will's steel arm.

"We're fine, Carol!" he shouted in a choked voice as he pistoned forward. "We'll meet you out front."

As the sound of her heels echoed down the hall, Will gripped my hips and pounded into me with everything he had. I exploded.

"Will!" The name erupted from me, a deep, visceral shout that was quickly swallowed by his kiss. I arched upward as my climax steam-rolled through me, pounding me into the window along with Will's unforgiving movements.

"Fuck, *LILY!*" he shouted in a voice that I swear all of New York could hear.

We grasped at anything and everything—limbs, fingers, hips, hair. Nothing was enough, and yet everything was too much as pleasure roiled through us both. Wave after wave. Sigh after sigh. Until finally, there was nothing left to release.

And then, at last, time and breath slowly put us back together.

"Well," I said, still trying to catch my breath. "That was, um, unexpected."

"That was needed," Will corrected me gently. He cupped my face, urging me to look up at him. "Feel better?"

I nodded. "I do."

His mouth quirked in a funny smile—one he reserved only for me. "So is this it? Is this home, at least for another two weeks?"

I glanced at the windows, which were, ironically, completely uncovered. If Will had issues before about snooping photographers, they were gone now.

"We'll have to draw the blinds next time," he said, with no little resentment as he read my thoughts.

Will slouched over me, skin meeting skin as he slid out. He pressed tender kisses up and down my collarbone, somehow still full of hunger, but a different sort. He needed to be close. We both needed to be close.

"Damn," he muttered. "I wish we could stay here. I want to go to dinner with my mother like I want a hole in my head."

He dropped his forehead onto my shoulder while I threaded a hand into his hair, combing it lightly through my fingers. My stomach dropped too at the mention of tonight. He wanted me to go, but if I was being honest, Tricia Owens-Baker scared the hell out of me.

I wouldn't leave him alone in this, though. Not now. Not ever.

"I love you," I said again, squeezing him with what little comfort I could offer with my small frame.

"Love," Will repeated with no little wonder as he stood up and looked down at me. He pushed a strand of curling hair out of my eyes and smiled ruefully. "What's that, huh? How would I ever know it from anything else?"

"Because you know me," I said.

I cupped his face between my hands, enjoying the feel of his cheekbones under my thumbs. I tipped my head up to kiss him again, and his tongue slipped around mine delicately. Vulnerable.

"Then love is freedom," he whispered between kisses. "Because that's what I feel when I'm with you."

CHAPTER SEVEN

"**A**re you sure you can't come?" I pleaded with Calliope for the fourth time that night.

My friend, soldier that she was, had brought my things herself from her apartment to the new one Will and I were renting, along with a selection of dresses for me to borrow for dinner. We were due at Le Corbeau in thirty minutes—Will didn't want to leave for at least twenty, but Benny had been nagging at us for the last hour, getting visibly more and more stressed every time Will batted his words away. I wasn't so sure being late was the best way to make up with a woman who had literally slapped him across the face that afternoon, but I wasn't much inclined to care about her opinion anyway.

"She can fucking wait," Will kept saying every time Benny or I brought it up.

Benny grumbled and repeated, "Eight o'clock, man. Eight o'clock."

I felt tired. And terrified. And hungry. It had been a crazy day, and there was still more to come. All I wanted to do was crawl into our giant, king-sized bed and keep making up with Will for the rest of the night. But there was no avoiding Tricia Owens-Baker, who had called Benny at least five times in the last hour to make sure Will wasn't skipping out on her again.

Calliope fluffed my hair over my shoulders. She'd come armed with a coconut oil hair mask that my hair desperately needed after taking abuse in the unrelenting Spokane sun and then two more weeks refusing any treatment at all in her apartment.

"I'm sorry, boo," she said. "I can't come. I have to get to another event tonight for one of my clients. You're gonna have to brave the storm on your own."

I scowled into the mirror, and she laughed.

"Stop, you big baby," she said as she looked over the rest of me. "Okay, this is much, *much* better than before. I was about to take you to my girls uptown to shame you into doing something here."

I rolled my eyes, but I couldn't deny that it looked better. Most of the curls and body had returned to my long, dark brown locks, which were piled over my shoulders.

I ran my hands over the sleek silver dress Calliope had loaned me. Between its bustier bodice, tight pencil skirt, and the way the back cut halfway down my spine, the satin basically put every curve I had on display—most of which were a lot tighter after weeks of triathlon training.

"You look gorgeous," Calliope said, wrapping her arms around my waist and setting her chin on my shoulder. "Baby's back, huh?"

I snorted. "I don't know about that."

"For what it's worth, I like him." She stood and walked over to the bureau, where she started putting her supplies in a bag.

I turned. "Who, Will?"

Callie nodded. "I wasn't sure, at first. I hated that he hurt you, obviously, and knowing who he is, his history and everything…yeah, it's all a little alarming. But you seem good together. I don't know. You seem more at peace, I guess, when he's around. Like I haven't seen you in at least four years…maybe ever."

I smiled at my friend, nodding. "I think you're right. I know there are red flags, but we're better together, Cal. I'm sure of it."

She finished packing up her things, and I followed her out of the bedroom and into the living room, where Benny was pacing by the front door and Will was staring out the picture windows grumpily, arms crossed over his chest.

Despite his proclamations that he didn't give a shit what his mother thought of his wardrobe, Will had still gussied up a little for tonight too. He wore the same black, immaculately fitted pants that he had worn on another dinner date—one we were supposed to have the night he found out his father had died—and a pressed charcoal button-down that made his eyes glow against his tan skin and mane of blond waves. He hadn't bothered to tie his hair up—preferring, I suspected, to let it obscure his face. Too bad for him, it made him look that much more edible.

He turned when Calliope and I walked in. Benny stopped in his tracks, and Will's mouth dropped.

"Wow," he said as I walked over to where he stood. "Holy shit, Lil. You look—"

"She looks like a movie star's girlfriend," Calliope said as she walked to the door, slinging her bag of products over her shoulder. "I did good."

But Will shook his head, making his hair swish lightly around his cheeks. "Nah. She looks like a star by herself. Wow." He pulled me close, then ran a hand over my shoulder and down my waist, stopping just short of curving around my backside.

"And...that's my cue. Bye, boo." Calliope waved, ignoring Benny's sly looks.

I waved back. "Bye, girl. Thank you!"

After the door shut, I allowed Will to pull me back toward him so he could look me over more thoroughly.

"This is going to be torture," he said, toying with one strap of the dress, pulling it over my shoulder, then back into place. "I won't be able to think straight with you sitting next to me in this, Lil."

I smiled shyly. "Well, good. Then maybe you'll be too distracted to argue with your mom."

At the mention of Tricia, Will's face collapsed into a frown. He pushed a hand through his hair and sighed. "Ah, well. Here's hoping."

There was a knock on the door panel. We turned to find Benny standing by the exit.

"We ready to go?" he asked. "There's a car at the service entrance."

"Any paps outside?"

Benny shook his head. "No one knows where you are yet. But they're hunting, so I doubt it will take long, especially with Tricia in town."

Will grabbed a pair of sunglasses off a console and tucked them into his shirt pocket. "Better get it over with." He reached out for me and squeezed my arm. "I'm sorry," he said as we followed Benny toward the service elevator.

"For what?" I asked.

Will grimaced. "For whatever is about to happen now."

———

DESPITE WILL'S best intentions to be late, we ended up walking through the kitchen at Le Corbeau, one of the nicest French fusion restaurants in New York, at exactly 8 p.m., and were briskly guided past the open-mouthed kitchen staff by a haughty maître d' to a private room in the back of the restaurant. "Private" was a bit of a misnomer—the room itself was completely visible to the public, with multiple folding glass doors left open, heavy drapery pushed to the sides.

We followed Benny into the room in a slight daze, but Will stopped everyone when he served a nasty glare to the maître d'.

"Did you know I was coming?"

"Y-yes, Mr. Baker," stuttered the host.

"So you do know who I am."

"Will," I murmured, but when I tried to take his hand, I was brushed aside.

"Of course," answered the host again. "I—the others in your party assured us that this would serve your needs exactly, sir."

"Do you think it serves my needs to be stared at like a fucking zoo exhibit?" Will snapped, gesturing toward the restaurant, which had gone relatively quiet with his arrival. His glare remained fixed on the quivering host.

"N-no," said the maître d'. "Of, of course. A terrible oversight on our part." He scurried around the room, closing the glass doors and shutting the curtains over them. "Can I get you anything to drink, sir?"

"Honey, we already ordered a bottle of Macallan 18, your favorite."

Will squinted in the direction of his mother's voice, one that had turned strangely syrupy since we saw her that morning. Then he turned to the maître d'.

"Just a Perrier," he said curtly. "And the same for her. You good with that, Lil?"

I nodded, and the maître d' took Benny's order before fleeing the room and Will's bad temper.

"Well, Mom, I hope you're happy. The place will be crawling with fucking paps by the time we're done." Will straightened his shirt, then pulled out my chair and his. "Let's get this shit show over with."

In the seat next to his, Tricia Owens-Baker smiled sweetly. "Will, there was no need to overreact. This is a nice restaurant. No one here is going to tip anyone off about anything."

Will scowled.

Tricia rolled her eyes. "Good lord, I would have thought you'd grow out of the theatrics during your 'time away.'"

Will remained as stony as ever and squeezed my hand as he sank into his seat. "I learned from the best. It's bred in the bone, isn't it?" Then he looked up at me, all traces of irritation gone. "Babe? You okay? You, um, wanna sit down?"

I didn't answer. I couldn't even move. Not because of the doors or the attention we had. Not because of Will's mother or the other unfamiliar people at the table. I was stuck where I stood because of the one very *familiar* face smirking from across the gleaming wood.

My nightmare, my own personal demon, the man who had tormented my dreams for the last year and spent three before that doing it in real life, pulled his napkin out from beside his plate and fluttered it delicately over his lap before looking directly at me.

"Hello, Flower." He greeted me with a slow, decadent smile. "They said you might be here tonight. So of course, you see, I had to tag along. And it was well worth it, I might say." His black gaze oozed over me. "You look stunning."

I gulped. My chest hurt. It was hard to breathe. "Wha—who—Th-Theo? What—what are you d-doing here?"

The smile widened, showing sharp incisors, like a cat about to bat around its prey. He looked the same as always—gleaming black hair, olive skin with the sheen of good skin care, large, dark eyes that twinkled in the dim restaurant lighting. He was maybe slightly thinner after a two-month stint in a minimum-security prison. It was for sexual assault. "Improper sexual conduct" had been the official verdict.

But we both knew what he had done. Theo del Conte, my ex-boyfriend, lover, abuser, psychotic menace, had raped me. In our home. Two rooms from where his friends were drinking champagne and dancing. Just after he had proposed marriage to me…and I had said no. And if the menace in his smile was any indication, he wasn't anywhere near close to forgiving me for fighting for my justice in return.

Will shoved back in his seat with a loud screech that echoed through the room. "We're going."

"Will—" Tricia cut in.

He whirled. "And *fuck you* very much for springing this shit on us. It's been four years. *Four years.* And the best way you could think of to make peace was to bitch slap me, then corner me with a studio head and his demented son at dinner?"

"Now, Will, wait a second!" Tricia spouted. "What are you talking about, 'demented son'?"

"I think he means me, Trish," Theo put in amiably. He still hadn't stopped staring at me. I wanted to shower.

"*You.*" Will turned to Theo with murder in his eyes. "Motherfucker, I don't know what your game is showing up here. But Maggie isn't alone anymore. She's got me. Read the news, asshole. I'm crazier than you are. I crash boats for the fun of it, and I fuck up strangers like it's nothing. So don't think for a goddamn second that I won't ruin you for looking at my girl the wrong way. *Especially* after what you did to her."

"Well, aren't we gallant." Theo picked up his butter knife and ran the serrated edge lightly over his fingertips, enough that I cringed. "But you can have fun with my sloppy seconds. That pussy is wrecked anyway."

Will lunged forward, only to have his arms neatly captured by Benny.

"Easy, man," Benny muttered. "Let's not get arrested tonight, eh?"

"Say it again," Will dared Theo, a large vein popping out on his forehead. "See if Benny can hold me back this time."

"Will!" shouted Tricia. "What has gotten into you?"

"Chill, man. You gotta chill," Benny said in a low, calm voice like he was taming a wild animal. "This ain't the place, my friend. It ain't. The place."

Outside the curtained doors, the restaurant had gone much quieter. I held onto the top of the chair for dear life, genuinely afraid that I would fall over if I let go.

"That's right, Benny. Calm your client," Theo said.

He turned to the man sitting next to him—an older, suave gentleman in an expensive-looking black suit. He was the kind of man who commanded authority in a room easily without even speaking.

"Right now, he looks more like a beast than a man," Theo continued. "I'm thinking his new contract should include some grooming requirements, don't you think, Dad? No one's going to want to see Fitz Baker on the red carpet looking like *The Walking Dead*."

"Theodore, stop."

The command wiped the smug expression off Theo's face, and he slouched back in his chair to sip on his drink and send me death-glares over the rim of his glass. Will, having relaxed enough that Benny set him free, immediately returned to my side, wrapped a hand around my waist, and guided me toward the exit.

"We're going, Lil," he said. "Walk away."

"Yes, walk away." The deep voice of the well-dressed man, who was apparently Theo's father, brought the room to a halt. "Go ahead. But it will cost you everything you have."

Will stopped. Beside him, I swallowed. Outside, the chatter was audible again—I only wanted out.

"Shit," Will whispered. Then he looked at me with sad, regretful eyes, and turned around.

"Will?" I asked, cowering into his side. "Will, what are we doing?"

Benny now sat at the table, shaking his head. Theo looked incredibly pleased with himself. Tricia glanced between Will and the older man nervously, like she was watching a tennis match. The older man himself folded his hands and waited.

"Fitz*william*!" Tricia hissed, as if no one could see her beckoning her fully grown son with one hand like she was calling a small boy.

The man smiled, and a chill of recognition scampered up my spine. It was a smile I knew. Bright. Slick. Maybe a little demented. Just like the bastard sitting next to him. He reached a hand out, though I was much too far away to grasp it.

"I don't believe we've ever had the pleasure of meeting, Ms. Sharp," he said in a voice that rode the edge of civil and sick. "Though I've heard plenty about you. Maximilian del Conte. You might know me better as Theodore's father, but Mr. Baker knows me as the man who currently owns his last contract. A contract worth millions of dollars. One that he never fulfilled."

"Will."

Benny's voice was low, and it was clear on his face that he had known about this the entire time he was trying to escort us to dinner. He hadn't wanted us to be on time in order to make nice with Tricia. He was doing it so Will wouldn't piss off one of the most powerful men in New York. In the entire entertainment industry. Hell, in the entire world.

Maximilian del Conte. Chairman of Del Conte Entertainment Group. Maker of destinies and crusher of dreams everywhere.

"Shit," Will whispered again. He glanced at Benny. "You knew about this?"

Benny looked between us, his gaze landing on me with a fair amount of regret. "I'm sorry, Maggie," he whispered. "I had to. Max means what he said. Everything is on the line here."

The hand at my back pushed me gently toward the table. My heels were dug so far into the floor, I almost tripped.

I reared. "What?" I looked frantically at Will, whose shoulders were slouched. Desolate. "Why do we have to stay here. Will, we don't need to sit down, do we?" I would have rather been literally anywhere else than at that table. Where the man who had ruined my life would watch me like prey for the rest of the evening.

"Oh, he'll sit down." Max del Conte's sonorous voice again seemed to swallow the silence. "Because if he doesn't, he knows he'll be ruined. He'll sit down, Ms. Sharp, because he knows I own him."

CHAPTER EIGHT

"Y ou look good, Flower."

Theo's eyes slid over me once more in a way that made me squirm. He had always had the ability to make me feel undressed, no matter what I was wearing. "Better than the last time I saw you."

Will gritted his teeth. "And *you* look fucking stupid." He darted a glare at Max del Conte. "He needs to go. Now."

But del Conte only shrugged. "My son is getting ready to assume more leadership positions in the business. He needs more negotiation experience. He'll stay."

"We're not negotiating anything if he's here," Will bit back as he stood back up. "And he has a restraining order that he's already violated once. Does he *want* to go back to prison? The only reason we're staying in town is to make sure justice gets served."

"You may want to rethink that."

I hovered behind my chair, ready to make for the door at a moment's notice, but as del Conte spoke, my skin felt like it turned to glass.

"Sit down," he ordered both of us calmly. He raised an arched brow. "*Fitz.*"

Will's hand around mine squeezed hard enough I thought my fingers might crack. It was one of the only times I'd heard anyone besides photographers, tabloids, and the one fan call Will by his stage name, clearly a shortened version of his full, given name: Fitzwilliam. With one word, del Conte made it indubitably clear exactly what Will was to him: a property. Certainly not a person.

"Will, you need to listen," Tricia put in, though she was quickly silenced by Will's black gaze.

"*You* did this, didn't you?" he hissed. "Some things never change."

She didn't get a chance to answer before del Conte spoke again.

"Five minutes in the same room won't hurt anyone," del Conte continued, caressing the edge of his scotch glass. "And Theo will stay safely on this side of the table from you, Ms. Sharp. After I've said my piece, if you like, both of you can pretend this meeting never happened and continue to make your case in court. Though, as I said before, I wouldn't advise it. Perhaps you'll let me explain why."

Will's jaw flexed as he ground his teeth together. Every muscle in his neck and face seemed to be cast in high relief; even beneath the confines of his shirt, I could see his biceps bunch. He didn't look like a privileged actor sitting down to dinner at a fancy restaurant. He looked like a Viking who wanted to set fire to the whole joint.

"Yo." Benny reached across me to nudge his friend in the shoulder. "I'll take Maggie home if you want. But you need to hear Max out, and I'd prefer to be here with you."

Will darted a nasty glance at him. "I'm sure you do."

Benny shrugged, guilt playing across his face as he glanced at me. "I'm sorry," he whispered to me. "But if you didn't come, he wouldn't have either." Then he looked back at Will. "F, you *need* to listen."

Will opened his mouth to protest, but I shook my head and finally spoke.

"It's fine," I said, finally able to find my voice as I managed to slide into one of the chairs. "I'll stay."

"Lil—"

I looked up, fighting every instinct I had to beg Will to take me out of this room. This restaurant. This city. But something was clearly important enough that Benny was willing to risk his friend's wrath by bringing me here. If Benny was as loyal as Will said he was, that by itself told me we needed to do as he said and hear del Conte out.

"Where you go, I go, right?" My voice sounded small. Pathetic. Even more scared than I felt, which was already genuinely terrified.

The harsh scowl that had been on Will's face since we walked into the room softened slightly. His gaze drifted down to my lips. Then he closed his eyes and blew out a long breath.

"Right," he said as he sat down next to me. He turned to del Conte. "You have five minutes. Starting now."

Again, that terrible, nasty smile appeared. "Good boy. Well, imagine how surprised we all were to read the news two weeks ago." Del Conte took a measured sip of his scotch. "Fitz Baker. One of Beauregard Pictures' most valuable commodities. Back from the dead, wouldn't you know?"

Will ground his teeth. "What do you want, Max?"

"Will, be nice," Tricia started, but quieted quickly when she was once again on the receiving end of her son's foul temper.

"Don't think for a fucking second I don't know you sold me out to these vultures, *Mom*. I'll deal with you later."

My gaze bounced between Will, the del Contes, Tricia, and Benny. The tension in the room was growing exponentially by the second, and by the way Benny was also looking at his friend, we both were coming to the same conclusion: there was no way Will was going to last five minutes.

"Right," Will said, turning back to del Conte. "So. What the fuck do you want?"

Del Conte's eyes turned to steel. He didn't say a word.

Will's eyes narrowed. "I'm out of the game, Max. You know that. I crashed a *boat* to escape this rat race. I'm out."

"Ah, but are you?"

Will's eyes flared, and he opened his mouth like he was about to shout every obscenity in the book at del Conte's smug face when he was interrupted by the entry of a waifish server.

"Hello, everyone," she said as she approached the table looking bored until she caught sight of who was sitting around it. "Oh. Oh! Hel-hello there."

Will rolled his eyes, Benny winked at the waitress, and Tricia snapped her fingers in the air. Several large gold bracelets on her wrist clinked together.

"Can we order sometime this century?" she asked.

The waitress, newly recovered from the shock of seeing Will, straightened toward the rest of the group. "Of course. What can I get for you all tonight? Would you like to hear the specials?"

Del Conte didn't even spare the girl a second glance. Instead, his focus was purely on Will. "You know what I want," he said. "It's not on the menu."

I looked between them, back and forth, without a clue. "Will, what is he talking about?"

"Maybe come back in a few minutes, honey," Benny told the waitress, who, bug-eyed, scurried out of the room, much to Tricia's irritation.

"Ben!" she hissed. "I was hungry!"

Benny shrugged. "You can eat in *five minutes*, Trish. That's all this is gonna take."

"You had a contract, Mr. Baker." Del Conte pulled the attention back to himself. "For three pictures with Beauregard, a studio owned by del Conte Entertainment, you might recall. You only completed two. Now, I'm not a lawyer, son, but I employ some very good, expensive ones. And they all tell me that if you don't fulfill the terms, you're going to be in breach. Which, perhaps you may remember, can get very expensive."

"Fine." Will tipped back in his chair, looking like a kid caught in the principal's office and not an Oscar-nominated actor in a five-star restaurant. "I'll be in breach of contract. What's the penalty?"

"Oh, I don't know." Theo sneered. "How about a hundred mil, asshole?"

Will's chair legs slammed to the ground. "That's *not* what was in the original contract. A breach only cost twenty. Twice my original fee. No more."

"Whoa, whoa, whoa, everyone," Benny said. "Let's not go crazy here."

Tricia grumbled into her glass while my jaw dropped. Will talked about a twenty-million-dollar penalty like it was a few hours of community service, not more money than most people would ever see in their lifetimes.

"That was before you decided to jump ship, my long-haired friend." Del Conte reached across the table and tugged on a loose lock of Will's hair. "This, though. I think my son is right. This is going to need to come off. Can't have my biggest commodity looking like an extra in a Biblical drama."

Will smacked the fingers away with a loud slap that made me flinch. "You can keep your fucking hands to yourself."

Del Conte shook out his hand. And laughed. "Still have that rebellious streak, I see. Well, it was always a money-maker on film. Not so much off, though." His humor turned ice-cold. "Now. It would be better for everyone here if you remembered that I own you. End of discussion."

Will was practically vibrating. "How do you figure, Max?"

The look spreading across the older man's face couldn't be called a smile. Smiles make people happy. They glow. Max del Conte's expression sent chills down my spine. It was nothing short of evil.

"By the time of your 'accident,' your last two films with Beauregard Pictures earned three times their budget, and well over half a billion dollars. Each." He drummed his fingertips on the tabletop. "You owe me one more, which you pulled out of under false pretenses. Fraud, if you will. Beauregard might need to reassess its damages. Emotional, of course. Financial. A lot of people lost their jobs on that final picture because the star wasn't around to do it. Sets were destroyed. Grips, PAs, costume designers, effects people. Everyone lost income. And someone is responsible, don't you think?"

I held my breath. Beside me, Benny studied the table. Will's expression told me that even though he had money, he didn't have *that* much money. Definitely not the kind of money that could take on a beast like Del Conte Entertainment and win.

"All right," he said finally, speaking through his teeth. "So you want me to do one last film?"

"Not just any film," del Conte said. "This one."

A script landed in the middle of the table with a hard slap. Will pulled it in front of us to read the cover.

"*Green Lantern?*" He looked up, disgusted. "Seriously? This is damaged property. No one has been able to make this concept work. You might as well flush three hundred million dollars down the toilet."

"Theo here will be overseeing it. He's got his thumb on the pulse right now. He'll do a good job producing."

I glanced at Theo. He winked. I shuddered.

"I'm not signing on to a franchise, Max," Will said as he flipped through the pages. "And this writing is shit."

"We'll cross the franchise bridge when we get to it," del Conte said as he fondled his scotch glass. He took a long drink and smacked his lips. "Funny thing about superhero movies. They tend to make a lot of money. I'm sure *you* can make it something worth watching. The world is going to clamor for the next Fitz Baker movie. You'll give them a good show."

"Bro." Benny's voice pulled Will's attention. He looked down at the script and back up with raised brows, as if to say, "that's life." To Will's right, Tricia studied her glass, uncharacteristically quiet.

Will looked through a second, smaller stack of papers under the script. "What's this?"

"Your new contract," del Conte replied. "As I said, we require some...addenda to the old one. Consider it a generous penalty for your original breach."

Will flipped through the papers. "Ah. I see. Bit of a finder's fee in here, huh, Mom?"

Tricia examined her French-tipped nails. "It's a standard agent fee that's none of your business. It doesn't come out of your cut, whatever that will be."

Will's brows rose as he thumbed to another page. "Do I look like I'm still fifteen fucking years old to you? It's in *my* contract. And it's not going to be this, I can tell you that." He passed the papers to Benny, who immediately glanced through whatever section they were talking about.

"Oh, hell no!" Benny exclaimed. "That is not what we talked about, Max. This is half what his standard fee was, not to mention there's no back end. You want him to honor a final film, it needs to be fair and square."

Tricia choked on her wine. Benny glanced at her, confused, until he turned back to the contract. "What the..." He glared at Tricia. "You conniving bitch. Did you *really* think you were going to negotiate Will's back end percentage for yourself?"

Tricia shrugged, but wouldn't meet Will's or Benny's eyes. Across the table, Theo chuckled, and del Conte raised a silver brow.

"Tricia was very helpful in locating her son, I must admit," he said. "We agreed she should be compensating for it."

Will's gaze could have turned his mother to salt if she'd actually had the guts to look at him instead of her glass.

Benny shook his head, muttering something under his breath as he paged through the rest of the contract. Then he shoved the contract across the table to del Conte. "It's a no go."

But del Conte didn't even touch the stack of papers. "I think you'll want to reconsider," he said calmly before taking another sip of his scotch.

"And why's that?" Benny demanded. "Will here is the most in-demand name in the world. You said it yourself—he was bankable before he took off. Now he's back, and you want his first film. Maybe his only film. That's gonna cost you, no matter what."

"No, it won't. Because if you fight it, we're happy to leak this." Del Conte looked to Theo, who gleefully pushed a tablet across the table. He licked his teeth all the way around, like a predator getting ready to dive into its kill.

On the screen, what I saw made my entire stomach drop to the floor.

The bar was immediately familiar. The torn vinyl seating. The haze where no one bothered to regulate smokers. The bandstand in the back of the room, and the pool table in the front, where a clearly inebriated woman was currently joking with whoever was holding the camera.

"Come on," cajoled the speaker. "Show us. You said you would. You lost the game, fair and square. Show us them titties."

"Show 'em!" multiple men in the background shouted while the woman grinned lasciviously from beneath blue-shadowed eyelids. She looked around with glazed eyes, back and forth, then giggled and pulled up her top to reveal bare, sagging breasts to the camera.

"Yeah..." cooed the cameraman with a satisfied voice that made me sick. "That's right, honey. Shake 'em."

"Jesus," Will muttered, turning his face away.

"Who is that?" Benny asked.

I gulped, unable to tear my gaze away as the excruciatingly familiar woman beckoned the cameraman to the back of the bar and started to unbutton his jeans as she sank to her knees.

"It's my mother," I said in a voice I barely recognized as my own.

Tricia stared at me with something that could only amount to pure disgust. "*This* is the best you could do, Will? Trailer trash with a mother who can't keep her legs closed?"

I buried my head in my hands as the clear sounds of the camera owner's moans started to fill the room. I felt like I was going to be sick.

"That's enough!" Will reached across the table for del Conte's tablet, but it was swiftly tucked out of reach, the terrible video gone. Will glared. "I don't even want to know how you got that. But you'll delete it right now."

"It wasn't hard. She had no idea who I was in the first place, and unlike her daughter, she wasn't interested in fighting me at all."

My head shot up to find Theo sneering at me.

"You bastard," I whispered.

"No, Flower," he said. "That's you."

I was up and out of my chair like a flash, practically hurling myself across the table with a clang of silverware and dishes. I had never been a violent person, but all of my fears of confronting Theo disappeared at the thought of him subjecting my mother to anything near what he had put me through. He was a monster. A life-ruiner. And all I could think about was getting rid of him in any way possible.

"What the fuck is wrong with you?" I shouted. "What in the hell is wrong with you? Do you enjoy causing people pain, you fucking psycho?"

"Hey, hey, baby." Will pulled me back down to my chair with some difficulty. "Calm, Lil. Calm."

"You'll want to muzzle your dog, there, Baker," Theo said as he picked a piece of lint off his jacket sleeve. "She can be a biter. I should know."

Will looked up like he wanted to jump across the table next, but before he could, Benny cut into the conversation.

"Max," he said as he set a hand on Will's shoulder. "Brass tacks. You knew from the start I was never going to take this, so what do you want?"

"The same thing I've wanted for the last four years," del Conte replied with that same eerie calm he'd exuded the entire time we'd been there. "My money's worth."

Benny sighed as he pulled the contract back. "I have to look things over and get back to you. Some of these terms are embarrassingly bad. If it ever got out, it would ruin my reputation along with Will's. You understand."

"*We're* going to have to look it over," Tricia put in. "Right?"

"What?" Will's scowl beelined back to Max. "What is she talking about?"

"That's messed up, Trish. Even for you," Benny muttered beside him.

"As a matter of course," said del Conte. "We promised to recognize Ms. Owens-Baker as Fitz's representative. We reserve the right to negotiate only as long as she is involved."

I blinked. Could they do that?

"Absolutely not." Will still had his hand on my shoulder. "I don't want her anywhere near this beyond her 'finder's fee' or whatever the fuck you promised. But aside from that, if you want your money, you want my face at the premiere and on the poster, you get my mother and your son the fuck off this project."

"Will, now come on," Trish protested, but Will held his palm toward her while he continued speaking.

"Do your worst, Max. I left this world a long time ago, and that meant the money too. Put out that video and deal with the lawsuit that comes with your son, a convicted sex offender, releasing unlicensed pornography. Bankrupt me if you want. But we both know you won't be getting anywhere near the value of this contract by battling me in court for five years."

I gasped. I understood better that there was no love lost between Will and his mother, but his willingness to sacrifice everything to avoid working with her was jarring.

"It's me or her, me or him," he said to del Conte. "What's it gonna be?"

Del Conte's silvery eyes darted back and forth between Will and

Tricia, not even sparing a glance at his son, but after a moment, he just shrugged. "That's fine. Tricia is off the project and Theo will work remotely. Benny, you'll arrange the final version of the contact."

"Max!" crowed Tricia.

"But there's one other thing." Del Conte ignored both Tricia and Theo's complaints, and this time, he finally turned his black, penetrating stare directly on me. "This one's for you, sweetheart. There's not much we can do about my son's past mistakes with you, but that's what they are: the past. If you'd like this little video of your mother to stay private, I would highly recommend recalling any kind of restraining order you might have against Theo, not to mention any charges filed resulting in a particular hearing coming up."

My mouth dropped, suddenly dry. "What—what?"

"Absolutely *not*," Will put in fiercely. "This son of a bitch has been straight-up harassing her for weeks now. We have documentation, Max."

"It's her decision, not yours," del Conte said. "Theo can do most of his work here, but I can't have my producer unable to work on set if your little friend here chooses to show up." He drained his scotch glass and turned to me. "It's up to you, sweetheart," he said. "But it's all or nothing. Refuse, and there's no movie. Your mother will be masturbatory aid to every fifteen-year-old boy in America while I'll set my lawyers to taking everything your lover has. Or, you can do as I ask and make *all* of our lives a lot easier. You choose."

Before I could answer, Theo held up the tablet and tapped play again, causing the sound of my mother's sloppy moans to fill the room.

"Maggie," Will said beside me. "Don't—"

"Okay," I agreed before he could stop me. "O-okay. I'll do it."

Theo turned off the recording and grinned. Del Conte nodded with satisfaction.

"Good," he said, then looked to Will. "And you'll do the picture, which of course includes a full promotional tour, as well as some other promotional duties to make up for the ones you missed before. I, and everyone else in this room, will sign an NDA when filming wraps, and Theo's phone and all original recordings will be destroyed. If you quit, well…I'll take everything you have in court, *and* this pretty little girl's mother will be trending as the MILF the whole planet wants to fuck." He tipped his head. I wanted to punch him in the face. "Your choice...Fitz."

Beside me, Will recoiled at the second casual use of his stage name. His big shoulders wilted visibly, and Benny rubbed one lightly out of sympathy. I wanted to curl into him and hide away from the shit-eating grin on Theo's face.

"Okay," he said. "Benny and I will go through the contract tonight and have it messengered tomorrow."

Del Conte nodded with approval. Business concluded, the entire table stood up at once, as if none of us ever had any intent to eat once the confrontation was over. Del Conte and Theo immediately turned to the door.

"One more thing."

The men stopped on their way out and turned back to Will. Del Conte appeared mildly irritated at being stalled while Theo looked snide, as usual. Will strode up to him, making it clear just how many inches over Theo's smaller five feet, ten inches he towered. Theo cowered slightly. He had to.

"You might have to be my producer, but let me make one thing clear. You stay the fuck away from Maggie. You don't text her. You don't talk to her. You don't touch her. Like I said before, you fucking look at her wrong one time, and you are going to wish you were dead after what I'll do to you." Will brought a big hand up and hovered it around Theo's neck, almost like he was going to grab him, though no contact was made. "You might have won this battle, but don't think for a second you won the war."

They stared at each other for a long, long time, the din of the restaurant filling the room for a few moments while the two men barely even blinked. But eventually, Theo did, shrinking slightly from Will's fiery gaze. Then he leaned out of Will's reach and ducked to the other side of the table.

"We'll see," Theo said as he followed his father out of the room. To me, he grinned, a cold, nasty smile that chilled me to the core. "See you soon...Flower."

CHAPTER NINE

"That was fucked up, Benny. Really fucked up."

Benny rode the elevator up to Will's—I couldn't yet think of it as our—new apartment, his head hanging low like Charlie Brown. Will *still* hadn't released the white-knuckled grip on my hand that he'd taken as we left the restaurant amid a horde of photographers camped outside both the back and front entrances. I barely noticed, too busy shaking in the corner while I tried to blink away the stars still clouding my vision.

"I'm sorry, man," Benny said for probably the tenth time since leaving the restaurant. It hadn't been easy getting back here without being followed. In the twenty minutes we spent in Le Corbeau, at least forty tweets had announced our presence, tipping off a mass of paparazzi that were waiting for us at the front and back of the building. Will's security team had guided us through the mob to the waiting hired car, but we'd had to switch vehicles twice in underground garages before we lost all the tails. It was completely chaotic, and with every switch Will seemed to grow that much tenser, to the point where I thought that if I touched him, he might snap in half.

"I really didn't know he was going to spring all of that on you," Benny repeated once again. "I didn't know Theo would be there. And I *definitely* didn't know about that recording. You gotta believe me on that." He looked over his shoulder at me. "I'm so sorry, Maggie. Theodore del Conte is scum. Straight up."

I mashed my lips together and pressed my face into Will's shoulder. This was insane. I still didn't know what to think about the fact that there was a recording like that of my mother. That my ex-boyfriend had taken it. That he was now using it in some sick, twisted maneuver to absolve himself of at least some of his crimes.

And, of course, that I had no idea what to do. Is this what it meant to be famous? If so, I was glad I'd never even approached that stratosphere as an artist.

The elevator opened and we filed down the long hallway to the apartment entrance at the end. Will turned after he had unlocked the door. He rubbed a big hand over his face. Dark circles were growing under his eyes—a product of stress and fatigue.

"Just give him what he wants," he said finally to Benny. "Cut out the back end."

Benny did a double take. "Yo, man, *no*, that's gonna be most of your profits—"

"I said cut it," Will snapped. He yanked on his hair, then glared at the curled ends before tossing them over his shoulder. "And cut my fee in half too—no, Ben, do it—in return for a guarantee that both Mom and Theo, that mother*fucker*, stay the fuck away from the project. I'm talking ironclad, man. I'm not working with either of them, and if they come by the set, I want to be able to sue del Conte for every fucking penny he has for emotional distress done to me and Maggie."

Benny opened his mouth a few times like he wanted to argue back, but in the end, he pulled at his loosened tie and stepped back toward the elevator.

"All right, all right," he said lamely. "I'll see what I can do. I know they want you for a first fitting on Friday. Technically, the film is already in production, so Max isn't interested in losing more money than he has to. You cut your fee, I bet he accepts." He looked toward the apartment. "So much for staying in New York, eh?"

I frowned. "What does that mean?"

Benny grimaced and mouthed "sorry" again to Will. "I'll see you tomorrow, bro," he said. "You guys have a good night. Get some rest. You know they'll want you to get your beauty sleep."

Will shut the door behind his friend, then locked all four of the dead-bolts that had been newly installed. When the last one clicked, he laid his palm flat against the wood, hunched over.

"I'm so fucking sorry," he said. When he turned around, his eyes were turquoise rivers of remorse. "This is all my fault."

I frowned. "What? How can you say that?"

Will pulled me roughly to his chest, and I melted into the warm, solid plane of him, listening to the thump of his heart slow against my cheek. The rhythm seemed to calm us both, and eventually, I felt like I could breathe again.

"If anything, this is my fault," I whispered. "I feel like I've ruined your life."

Will held me away slightly so he could look at me directly. "How do you figure, huh? Pretty sure I'm the one who's got half the world looking for me right now. You're just caught in the web."

I sniffed. "It…you…Will, it's because of me that all of this is happening. If you hadn't met me, Lindsay never would have taken that picture. You never would have been found. You wouldn't be harnessed to an industry you hate so much. For me and my disaster of a mother."

The words toppled out before I could think them through—they were instinctual. And true. Tears overflowed *again*. This was my fault. It was all my fault.

Will swayed slowly in time to the song of my cries. "Someone would have figured it out one day, Lil," he murmured into my hair. "Do you really think I would rather be alone still? Stuck in that house, in those woods, living like some crazy troll under the bridge?"

I swiped at my eyes. "Wouldn't you?"

He didn't answer, but continued to rock me back and forth.

"You know, there are rumors that James Dean did the same thing," I said. "Faked his death with the car and escaped to the Canadian forest."

Will chuckled as he laid a cheek on the top of my head. "Well, I don't think I'm going to get away with it again, Lily pad." He framed my face with his hands, tipped it up, and pressed a soft kiss to my lips. "And I wouldn't want to anyway. Things look different—even a shit show like this—when I have someone to face them with me."

We gazed at each other for a long moment, but at the end, something other than love tinged with a bit of sadness, entered Will's expression.

"What is it?" I asked. "What's going on?"

His hands dropped, and Will stepped away guiltily.

"As soon as that contract is signed, I'll have to fly to LA for fittings, a meet and greet with the director, and a few other things. Probably the day after tomorrow. Principal photography is supposed to start next week. If I had to guess, I'm probably stepping in last minute for someone else who dropped out." He shook his head. "Which tells me this film is already a dumpster fire if they lost their lead this late in the game."

My heart sank in my chest. The day after tomorrow. We had been apart for two weeks, and already, this world was tearing us apart again. For the first time I understood why Will had loathed it so much.

And now, this also meant that I was going to be right back where I started. Back in New York alone.

I sighed. Will crossed his arms and worried his lips together as he examined me.

"What are you thinking?" I asked. "What's that face?"

"I'm thinking...don't do it. Don't give in to what del Conte wants."

I looked up. "What? How can I not?"

Will shook his head. "Maggie, your mom's reputation isn't yours to protect. If she doesn't want herself posted online doing shit like that, she shouldn't drink. She shouldn't do the things she does."

My mouth dropped. "Will. You cannot possibly be suggesting that I allow Theo to post that video of my mother sucking—"

"*No*, I'm not," Will cut me off before I could finish.

I was glad for the interruption. The fact of the video was mortifying.

"We'll have the lawyers file, I don't know, a continuance or injunction or whatever they call it," he said. "Delay the hearing, somehow. Benny's already on it. He knows every shark in the city, and I guarantee he wasn't going home to sleep. And besides that, I think it's a bluff. Max cares about the billion dollars he could make on this movie much, much more than he cares about his piece-of-shit son. Let's get a good lawyer. Let them do their job."

But the thought didn't immediately soothe. "Will, I can't afford a shark," I said lamely. "I—I don't even know how I'm going to afford the lawyer I have. Jamie is really nice, and she lets me pay her in installments. But I'm going to need to find a job, do *something* to get her initial retainer in the first place. A shark…I'd have to mortgage the house to do that."

"Maggie, my dad is dead."

There wasn't anything I could really say to that. It was incredibly abrupt, but also, what in the world did it have to do with this conversation?

"My dad's dead," Will repeated. "And I'm not even going to be able to go to his memorial because I have to be on set. So what do you think that means?"

"I—I…"

"It means," he continued, "that the only family I have left in this world is you. Not Benny. Not that fucking vulture I have for a mother. *You*." He swallowed, and the movement caused a small muscle in his jaw to tick. "This isn't a choice. I need to protect my family, Lil. So let me do it, all right?"

He stared at me hard, for a long time, his harsh, immovable gaze refusing to release me until, finally, I gave a tiny nod.

"O-okay," I stuttered lightly.

Will's face softened. "Okay," he said. "Okay." He turned then, picked up the script that Benny had left on the console, and studied it for a moment with disgust.

"I should start practicing lines, you know," he said. He let it drop again. "But fuck 'em. For one more day, fuck them all." He shoved the script lightly across the table. "I'm going to take a shower. Wash this trash can of a city off me. I'll meet you in the bedroom."

With a distant kiss on my shoulder, he strode down the impossibly long hallway, leaving me standing alone by the front door. I hadn't even taken off the strappy black sandals borrowed from Calliope.

I drifted a finger over the plain white pages. Did I feel the animosity coming off the text, or was that my imagination? I stared at it for a long time, trying to understand how something so innocuous-looking could have so much power. You read about the money of a production like this in the news, when film critics or gossip columnists reported on the box office earnings. A movie like this could fetch over a hundred million, sometimes close to two hundred million, in a single weekend. Close to a billion within a few weeks. It was unfathomable.

But was it really worth ruining someone's life? Did they really need Will that badly?

The answer appeared to be yes—or else the del Contes were the type of people who tortured a man for sport. Considering who Theo was, I knew the latter was as likely as anything.

It was then I noticed that there was no sound of running water, which was unusual in an older building like this. I left the script where it was and wandered down the hall, through the master bedroom, and into the bath where I found Will sitting on the edge of the tub, gripping the porcelain while he stared at his stomach, legs, up and down his arms. He had stripped down to his briefs, exposing the long, lean body I had fallen in love with.

"In two days," he said, "everything is going to change. Do you want to know what they're going to do?"

I nodded, though I was uncertain.

"First," he said. "They'll send me to a trainer. And he'll poke at me and pinch me and measure my body fat percentage and all this other bullshit to tell me that I need to put on about twenty more pounds of muscle over the course of filming. But you can't do that in eight weeks, you see. So the next thing they'll do is bring in a nutritionist, maybe even an endocrinologist. They'll start force-feeding me eggs and fish and spinach, and I'll eat probably five pounds of cod and a bag of broccoli every day. But when that doesn't work, the doctor will probably want to shoot me full of testosterone, maybe even HGH. Maybe a combination. Within three weeks, I'll be huge with a temper to match."

I frowned. "Surely you can choose. Do people really do that?"

Will looked up. "You think that doesn't happen? You think all those guys look that way because of natural genetics?"

"I—no! I mean, obviously, they work out really hard and everything, but—"

"Maggie, the last time I did a blockbuster movie, I was seventeen. It was a military film, and those fuckers *still* had me shooting hormones into my ass to square off my jaw so I'd be more of a heartthrob than pimply-faced teenager. They didn't care. None of them did. They care about the buck, about the audience. That's it."

He stood up, and the tensions in his movements made all his muscles flex. Will smirked at his reflection in the mirror and grabbed a handful of his hair.

"Gonna have to come off," he murmured, repeating Max del Conte's snide words. "Well, then. Let's take this shit off ourselves."

I watched in horror as he rummaged through a toiletry bag next to the sink. After locating his razor, he fisted a handful of golden waves and lifted the blade to his hairline.

"Oh my God, *stop*!" I shouted, finally finding my voice.

Will froze, the razor a few scant millimeters from his scalp. "What?"

"Give me that." I plucked the razor away and set it on the counter. "You can't shave off twelve inches of hair, you idiot. To start, it would take forever. If you want to shave your head, you need to buzz it as short as you can before you use a razor." I paused. "But please don't shave your head. I love your hair."

Will's full mouth pressed into a thin line. "Maggie, they're going to cut it anyway. No one is going to want to put a wig on top of all of this. Max already put it in the contract, so I might as well fuck with them. Do it so terribly that they have to get a wig anyway. Nothing in it says I can't cut my own damn hair off first."

My lower lip trembled. I couldn't help it. In my mind, Will was synonymous with his hair. I had grown to love it, loved weaving my fingers through it at the nape of his neck, loved toying with the waves in the early morning, loved staring at the messy knot that perched at the crown of his head with impossible sex appeal.

Even if he did shave his head, it would grow back soon enough. And then his transformation back to that smiling, charismatic movie star would be complete. He wouldn't be my Will anymore.

"Hey," he said, this time more softly. He sat back on the counter and reached out a hand. "Lil. It's still me. Muscle, no muscle. Hair, no hair."

I sniffed. "How do you always know what I'm thinking?"

A smile emerged. My heart thumped, even through my stupid tears.

"Intuition, I guess." Will sighed. "Guess I'll need to get some clippers."

"B-but you're giving them exactly what they want," I argued. "Except you'll look ridiculous. Your scalp is probably whiter than these walls after all those years under that mane."

Will chuckled, but then he shook his head. "Baby, I've been hiding. But I can't do that anymore." He rubbed his face, like he was checking to see if his beard was still there. "If I'm going to play this game, it can't be from the shadows. And it has to be on my own terms."

I sighed and wiped the errant tears off my cheeks. My face felt swollen. I was so, *so* tired of crying, though I had a feeling there were going to be a lot more tears shed in the near future. But a thought occurred to me.

"Hold on," I said. I went back into the bedroom, rummaged around, and returned a few minutes later to Will, whose curiosity turned to surprise when he saw what I was holding.

"You have clippers?"

I shrugged. "I have everything you need to cut hair. It's one of the few transferable skills Mama taught me, and I've already done it once for you, remember? *But*, I'll only do it this time on one condition."

Will leveled his gaze. "Name it."

I stepped close, grabbed a thick handful of his hair, and pulled his face to mine. "You keep their fucking needles away from your ass. Your temper is bad enough as it is."

Will stared at me, but slowly, a wide grin spread across his face. After another few moments, he tipped his head back and laughed, harder than I'd ever heard him.

"God*damn*," he crowed. "You fucking wreck me, you know that, Lil? You are tough as fuck."

I quirked an eyebrow and flipped the clippers on. But even thought my tears, I couldn't help but grin. His laughter lit up the room. It lit up my soul. "Do we have a deal?"

Will grinned. "Fuck yeah, we have a deal."

I nodded. "Good. Now, let's get a chair, sit you down, and do this."

———

Fifteen minutes later, I stood in the middle of the enormous bathroom, staring in horror at the hair lying on the floor, covering the smooth tiles in golden tatters.

"There," Will said hoarsely as he stood up from the dining room chair we'd lugged in. "It's done." He paced in front of the mirror a few times, then came to stop behind me, placed his hands on my hips, and set his chin on my shoulder. "Jesus," he croaked as he stared at himself in the mirror. "Who *are* you?"

It wasn't completely buzzed to the scalp. Though closer to his neck, the dark blond was so short as to be barely visible, I'd convinced Will to let me layer it on the top so his gold waves were still a little evident. Maybe it would even be good enough that they'd keep it on film. The thought cheered—like he'd be taking a piece of me with him on screen.

I reached a hand up to stroke his cheek, and his eyes closed. His stubble scratched my hand, practically the only familiar thing about this face. Gone was the beard now too; now he was all square jaw, chiseled cheeks, full lips, knife-straight nose. His eyes opened, no longer tempered by the beard and long hair. Set into his classical bone structure, the bright green pierced. I couldn't breathe; it was like they shot right through me. There was nowhere for either of us to hide.

"You're beautiful," I whispered as my fingers stroked his skin. I could feel him swallow against my collarbone. But the realization of what he'd been trying to tell me finally sank in. "But you're still Will. You're *my* Will."

His eyes closed again, but this time they didn't wrinkle at the edges. This time there was some serenity there.

"All yours," he murmured, almost so low I couldn't hear him.

His hands slid around my waist, then pulled the zipper down my back. Slowly, he slid one strap of the dress down, then the other, peeling the skintight fabric down my body. I shimmied out of it, then allowed him to remove my bra as well. Finally, his thumbs hooked under the elastic of my underwear, which he slowly drew to the floor, where I kicked them away so that I stood in nothing but my heels. Those, I noticed, he left on.

"You too," I murmured.

Will was already close to naked, but obediently he reached down and removed his briefs. When he returned behind me, slipped his large hands and strong arms around my waist, and pressed my naked back to the bare skin of his front, the warmth of his long body soothing mine from top to bottom. He folded himself around me, inhaling deeply from the curling thickets of my hair, taking handfuls of my flesh—breasts, waist, ass, legs—as if he was trying to memorize every curve I had. As if the touch somehow grounded him.

I understood. I leaned into his hands. I felt the same way.

"Watch us," he rumbled into my ear before setting his teeth lightly over the lobe. Together we stared into the mirror, at our paired image. "It's just us, here, Lil. Remember this when I'm not around."

He drew his hands up my waist to cup my breasts again, then pulled his fingers around my nipples, tugging them lightly. Pressing my palms on the counter, I arched my chest forward into his aching touch.

"Feel it," he ordered, his voice low, ominous. "I know you, Lil. I know this body better than I know my own. It's instinct, baby. Pure and simple."

He tugged again, and a long, low moan escaped my lips as he bit my earlobe again. Will was a master at helping me walk that thin line between pain and pleasure.

"I know you, Lil," he said again. "Like you know me."

He pulled me back to him, so I could feel the hard muscles fit against my back. The solid warmth of his limbs pressed to mine. The long, imposing length of him nestled between my thighs. Pulsing, eager for entry, and yet also content just to be together, skin to skin.

I did know him. Maybe not the large-scale stories. There was so much, after all, that he hadn't told me. So much he had hidden for so long. But I knew Will on a cellular level, deep down, in that place where jobs, even names had no meaning.

His hands continued to memorize every curve, texture, line of my body until I was practically humming with pleasure. They drifted down my back, flattening over the top of my ass.

"One day," he said as his thumb drifted down and toyed briefly with that small, untouched pucker. "I'll know you everywhere. Here too."

I jerked slightly. Even Theo had never gone there with me—his tastes had been decidedly more deviant in some ways, and yet strangely conservative in others. It was a part of me he had never wanted, never taken. And I had never offered.

"For now, I want to be here, though," Will murmured into my ear, even as he pulled my hips toward him. His cock slipped between my thighs. Will shuddered, his breath heavy on my shoulder. "I want to be home."

He entered me with a sudden fullness that made me gasp. I lurched toward the mirror, losing my grip on the counter, but Will's broad hand widened over my chest, keeping me mostly upright as he pushed farther in.

"Stay close," he ordered. "I need you close."

He closed his eyes, holding still for a moment and keeping me in place too. One hand splayed across my sternum; the other kept a solid grip on my hip. I couldn't have moved if I'd wanted, but there was no place else I'd rather be. Love was freedom, Will said, not a prison. How strange, then, that his iron touch, his immovable grasp, was the key to my liberation.

Then he pulled out, almost completely, hauling another gasp from my parched lungs as the friction stole my senses.

"Do you feel that?" he whispered as he left me. "Do you feel that emptiness, baby?"

I nodded, my words choked. The hand at my chest slid up to wrap lightly around the base of my neck.

"You need me, don't you?" Will asked as he rotated his hips, pushing past my entrance yet again, only slightly.

"Mmmmm." I couldn't answer. Speech had abandoned me. My jaw was shaking, my entire body shivering with want. He was torturing me, torturing himself, but why?

It's your reminder, a small voice whispered in the back of my mind. *So you don't forget again. So you don't believe that you can last apart.*

I bit my lip as my tears rose once more. I wouldn't forget it, just as I knew that having him in LA while I went back to Newman Lake would tear my heart out of my chest all over again. It was bad enough when I thought that we were over. It was going to be torture knowing he was miserable, and I couldn't be there to help.

But.

"Soon," Will said as he surged back inside, holding me still, forcing me to take him even deeper. "Soon it will be done. I'll come back to you. And then we get to start our lives together, Lil. Out in the open. No fear. No hiding. Together, we'll be free."

Will's eyes sparked at mine in the mirror, and I could see in them the joy that future offered. There would be no more living in the shadows for Will Baker. Perhaps one joyless film, one last paparazzi cycle was a small price to pay for that kind of freedom.

"And you know it *will* be the rest of our lives, don't you, Lily pad?" His lips dragged up my neck, leaving imprints all over the delicate skin. "You and me, baby. We're not right now. We're forever."

And slowly, slowly, he thrust fully inside, filling me with his cock, his promise, his love, his whole self. Will gave me everything he had with a few small words, a few small movements. And they harnessed me completely.

CHAPTER TEN

"**B**abe. Lil. Come on, beautiful, you need to wake up."

Slowly, I opened my eyes, humming into the warm caress on my shoulder. For a second, I almost thought I was back on the lake, with light streaming through the trees that protected Will's windows. I sighed with contentment, until the glass roof of the MET's atrium gleamed directly in my eye, sharp like the edge of a diamond. I squinted as the light bounced off the gold sconces mounted around the bedroom walls.

I blanched. On a beautiful summer's day, with the benefit of central air and twenty stories up, even the light in this place was sharp.

I sat up, shading my eyes to look at Will. I yawned. "Hey. What time is it?"

He stood from the bed and shoved his hands deep into his pockets. He was fully dressed in blue shorts and a gray t-shirt, despite the fact that both of us had fallen asleep the night before without a scrap of clothing on.

"It's six," he admitted sheepishly. He pushed a hand through his hair, then frowned like he had been expecting its previous weight, not the clipped waves now there. "There's something I need to do before I leave for LA, and I need you there."

"Baker, I hope you're not going to get all Hollywood on me and forget to make requests like a gentleman. I'm not one of your entourage."

It was a joke, but the remark was sharper than I intended. Will slumped as he fell back on the bed.

"Shit," he said. "I'm sorry. I sound like an asshole already."

His despondency erased any irritation I had, and immediately I rustled out of the covers and into his lap.

"I was joking," I said as I leaned my head on his shoulder. "You're kind of always an asshole."

Will chuckled, then wrapped his arms around me and gave a heavy sigh. "You want to get out of the city for a while, Lil? Please?"

I pressed back into him, all fatigue gone. "How soon can we leave?"

———

TWO HOURS LATER, we were navigating my old Passat out of Manhattan, safely protected by its decidedly *un*-movie-star looks and old-school tinted windows. A black SUV containing Will's security detail trailed us as Will drove up the West Side Highway, cut across the Bronx and Queens, and eventually hooked onto I-95 going north along the coast. Clearly he knew this drive well.

I stared out the window, entranced as we left the city and literally crossed into greener pastures, with trees gradually replacing the odd jam of crumbling brick and stone alongside the great metal high-rises of New York that seemed to spear the sky. After we entered Connecticut, occasional glimpses of water held me rapt. Small inlets and harbors decorated with marinas and cattails gleamed through the maples, barberries, birches, and all the other trees that would turn various colors come fall, but for now hugged the turnpike with green.

It reminded me of home, or at least being outside of the city. Even if my reasons for leaving had been the wrong ones, and even if Newman Lake with its sometimes suffocatingly small and narrow-minded community wasn't necessarily the right place for me, I knew now that New York wasn't home either. I needed to be someplace I could swim. Run. Ride. Breathe.

"We're almost there," Will said a little over forty-five minutes later as he took one of the last exits in Stamford. We had driven through downtown, a small urban area, but were back in the suburbs again, on a two-lane road that morphed from strip malls to row houses and eventually to single-family homes on large lawns without even a sidewalk to separate them from the street.

The neighborhood was decidedly mixed-income. Some of the houses were big, newer places that had clearly been built recently or were remodeled colonials. Others, split-level homes or a saltbox here and there, bore the marks of time with peeling paint, chain-link fences, and cars parked outside that were older than I was.

"It's changed a lot," Will said, noting some of the bigger places. "I'm not surprised." He took a right, then a left down another, even smaller street.

"Was this a bad neighborhood or something?" I asked. It was hard to believe as I noted more than one basketball hoop hanging above garages, along with several children's bikes lying on their sides in the front yards. People didn't do that in bad neighborhoods. They kept their things locked up.

Will shook his head.

"Not bad, no. Just always pretty…average." He pulled to a stop on the side of the road, then turned to me with an uncertain, shy expression. "This is where I grew up, Lil. At least…whenever I got the chance."

I peered out the window at the house next to us. It was all very… average, like he said. A two-story split-level. Faded blue paint. Modest, with a two-car garage, a waist-high fence that had probably been white at some point, and a shed on one side that seemed like it needed to have its rusty lock replaced. There were bits of debris on the lawn, forgotten in the summer sun: a set of gardening shears, some old gloves, and a hose that had never been re-coiled.

"I thought you grew up in the city," I said, still taking in the house and the flat, unremarkable piece of grass that included one homely beech tree. "Behind fences and gates and loads of security."

"Mom didn't get an apartment there until I got the role on *Bailey's Life*," Will said. "But even then, I'd come back here on my days off. Dad stayed here."

I turned back to him. "They seem very…different from one another."

"Well, you'll notice that Mom is fairly young," Will said dryly. "She was seventeen when she got pregnant with me."

My eyebrows popped up. Tricia had looked young, but I had assumed that was mostly plastic surgery. Apparently not.

"They met in high school in New Haven. Dad was a fisherman, so he was gone. A lot. Mom was bored and liked to...I don't even know. Go to the mall? She entered me in one of those contests for babies—you know, the ones where they take your picture and enter you to be a spokesbaby for some stupid brand. When I won the whole damn thing, apparently that's when she realized I was her ticket out of New Haven."

I nodded. "So, when did you move here?"

"When I was three, I think. I'm not sure. I don't really remember any other place but this house. I only know that I did a bunch of commercials that earned the down payment."

I frowned. The more I heard about Tricia Owens-Baker, the more I absolutely hated the woman. It was really hard to understand a mother who would use her toddler to mitigate her own boredom and buy herself a house.

"Were they ever actually divorced?" I wondered.

Will shook his head. "No. There was no need. They separated and did their own thing. I think...I think my career actually provided a way for them to live apart without having to face the fact that their marriage was terrible. After a year on *Bailey's Life*, I started getting letters. Threats. Some people even tried to break into the house once. It was pretty clear I couldn't live here anymore, but Dad wouldn't leave his business. He hated the city, and loved the water. So I got to visit on weekends, sometimes. Whenever I had a break longer than a few days. I never wanted to leave."

He stared at the house for a long time, and for a second, I could practically see the ghost of a small, blond-haired boy playing football with his dad in the yard. Pushing a lawnmower. Riding a bike. And just as quickly I saw the arguments, the tears that must have happened when he had to leave his father behind. The begging to stay, only to be told no, time and time again.

It wasn't only Tricia's fault that Will had lived this life, I realized. It was his father's fault too—a father who may have loved his son, but who certainly never fought for him. Not enough, anyway.

Will pulled a set of keys from his pocket. They were worn brass, and had a chipped metal keychain on which I could barely read the words "Stamford Sailing Club" on its glass face.

"I need to go in," Will said, his voice thick. "The house will be gone soon—Mom will sell it, every last bit. So I have to say goodbye before I leave."

I took one of his hands. I felt terrible for not anticipating this on some level. Only a few weeks ago, right before all of the chaos had descended upon us, Will had gotten a terrible letter from Benny, informing him that his father had died of a heart attack. I hadn't forgotten exactly, but Will hadn't said much about it since.

He internalized. Just like me. Which is how I knew the best thing to do wasn't to ask him what he needed in that moment, but to wait for him to tell me. Because eventually, he would. That's why I was here.

Will glanced around the neighborhood, which was practically empty in the mid-morning. There were a few small children running around a yard down the street, but most people here had gone to work, their kids in daycare or summer camps.

"All right," Will said as he pulled a baseball cap low over his face. "Let's go inside."

My hand clasped tightly in his, I followed Will past the creaking front gate and waited patiently while he collected the tools in the yard.

"Fucking waste," he said as he set the tools on the porch. "Dad would have hated that rust."

He unlocked the front door, and we walked into the house. It was dark and smelled like stale coffee and salt water. Dank and gloomy, everything was covered with a fine layer of dust, like no one had been here for weeks.

"What the fuck," Will muttered angrily as he swiped a half-empty coffee cup off the kitchen table. A newspaper was on the corner, open to the Sports section.

He tossed the paper in a bin, then brought the cup to the sink, where he started scrubbing it out immediately, along with a few other bad-smelling dishes.

"No one came," he said. "Can you fucking believe this? *No* one, Lil. His shit has been sitting here since he keeled over."

I gripped the top of one of the kitchen chairs, trying to think of an answer, while Will furiously washed the rest of the dishes. When he was finished, he grabbed a spray bottle and cloth to clean off the tabletop.

"Fuck," he hissed when the nozzle jammed. Maniacally, he clenched the sprayer again and again. "*Fuck!*"

"Let me," I said, taking the bottle from him. I adjusted the stream and sprayed the liquid all over the table. Then I took a rag and began wiping until I realized that Will was now the one watching me.

"What?" I asked as I moved on to the counters.

He took a deep breath, then let it out. "I love you."

I softened. He was so stolid, and yet so broken at the same time.

"I love you too," I said softly. "Let's finish in here, and then we'll move on to the next rooms, okay? Tell me where the vacuum is. We'll take care of everything."

———

THREE HOURS LATER, after having scrubbed, mopped, and vacuumed nearly every surface in the house, Will and I moved to the back porch with the last two drinks in his dad's fridge: a seltzer for me, and Bud Light for Will. There were a few deck chairs that faced the water, and we sat down and cracked open the cans.

"Wow," I said as I looked out.

The lawn, flat and almost lifeless, extended another two hundred feet from the house into cattails and brackish water, out of which a long dock continued the journey into the Long Island Sound, across which you could see the silhouette of Long Island itself. The house, the land— none of it was anything to write home about. But the view was stunning.

Will stared out at the water for a long time. "Yeah," he said. "It is wow." He took a sip of his beer. "If it had been up to me, I would have fought for Dad to be...put to rest...out there. He loved the water."

"Where is he now?"

Will shrugged. "Rotting under some gravestone about an hour from here. Benny said there's even a big monument." He snorted. "Dad would have hated that. He hated any kind of pomp and circumstance."

I nudged his shoulder. "Sounds like someone else I know."

A crooked smile whispered across Will's face, but faded almost instantly. "Yeah. Well."

We sat together for a long time, looking out at the water.

"He would have liked you, you know," Will said after a while longer. "He wanted me to find someone just like you."

"How do you figure?"

Will turned and grinned.

"'Willy,'" he said in a gruff, coarse voice with a thick New England accent slathered on top of it. I knew immediately it was exactly what his father must have sounded like—Will was uncannily good at doing impressions. "'Willy, you listen. When the time comes, and it's comin' sooner'n you think, choose a real woman. A woman who ain't afraid of a little dirt under her nails. That's how you'll know she's someone who's gonna stand by you, through thick and thin.'" He chuckled, took another long swig of beer, then picked up my hand, which currently had *very* dirty fingernails after the morning's labors, and kissed each fingertip reverently. "So I did, Dad. So I did."

He watched me for a moment before turning back to the water.

"Out there, that's where we used to keep the boat." Will looked sadly at the empty dock. "Dad started teaching me to sail when I was maybe four or five. I guess...I guess he never got a new one, though."

I wasn't surprised. I hadn't met Michael Baker, but something told me that the kind of man who would have a heart attack from seeing Will get arrested would be put off sailing after thinking his only son died in a boating accident.

In front of us, the ocean gleamed almost white. Will stared at the expanse, seeing something out there besides the waves. He stared long enough that he forgot to blink, his eyes tearing up in the wind.

"Fuck." The words shuddered, hard, bitter, painful from his throat. "*Fuck.*" Then he turned, pressed his face into my shoulder, and began to shake violently.

As he fell apart, silent and painful sobs wrenching out of him, there was nothing to say, nothing to do but hold him. I did my best, wrapping my arms around his lurching shoulders, and let him keen into me as the waves of emotions I could feel so clearly but knew just the same he couldn't quite name, rolled through us both.

Will didn't need my words. He needed my presence. My strength. My willingness to bear with him the pain that had convinced him at some point in his young life that his parents, his father, would be better off thinking he was dead. Pain that had cost him the last few years of his father's life. Pain that had brought him back here to face a gamut of memories he had shut away for a very long time.

I understood that kind of pain. It was only at this point in my life I was starting to understand the costs of denial. But that was also how I knew, as I rocked him slowly, that I could help Will bear it. That I'd sit here on this lonely porch with the man I loved for hours. Days. The rest of my life. I'd sit here for as long as it took for him to forgive himself and understand that he was no longer alone.

———

AFTER WILL SNOOPED around the house and took a few mementos to keep, he paused one last time at the car, looking over the hood at his childhood home before we left.

"This is it, I guess," he said. "I'll...I'll miss it."

"Why don't you buy it from your mom?" I wondered.

A blond brow rose. The idea had genuinely never occurred to him, though of course, Will could probably afford to purchase the property several times over and not make a dent in his accounts.

"No," he said, turning his back on the house. "It's not my home anymore. It hasn't been for a really long time."

I didn't know what to say. I could only imagine how painful it must have felt to stand on the threshold of your own family's home and feel like it was no longer yours. I had my own issues with returning home, but it was still home. It was still my place, even if it was only in the privacy of that small, simple shack.

My heart ached, and a pang of guilt thrummed in my stomach. I had been gone for almost three weeks now, with hardly a word to Mama.

God knew what she was getting up to without me there, if Theo's video was any indication.

But then there was Will, who was about to return to a life that had almost killed him the last time around. Who, if his visible shaking whenever we encountered a crowd or fans of any sort was an indicator, was going to have to face some serious demons of his own over the next few months. In part because I had brought them to his doorstep. Was it really fair for me to leave him to deal with all of that?

"Come on," he said, slinging an arm around my shoulder. He pushed his sunglasses up his nose and turned us toward the waiting car. "We both need to pack. And you need to go home."

"And what about you?" I asked. "Will you even be able to find an apartment before you have to dive into work? What's going to be your home now?"

Will paused, hand at the top of the door. He looked down at me and grinned—not the cheesy, for-the-cameras grin, but the one I recognized from only a few times before. It was the one he kept for me.

"Lily pad, how many times do I have to tell you? My home is with you."

He leaned down and kissed me, oblivious to the phones held at the ends of outstretched arms across the street. Apparently someone had told their parents who was outside. Then he smiled again, and the world seemed a little brighter.

"Give me a few weeks," he said as he turned back to the car. "And then we can both be home together."

CHAPTER ELEVEN

"Come on, Mama. Time to get up. You have to get to work, and so do I."

It had been two weeks since I left New York, since Will had boarded a private plane, and I'd driven my old Passat across the country for the third time in two months. Two weeks of phone calls back and forth from California to Newman Lake, snapping at each other when the patchy cell service dropped our calls. Two weeks of trying and failing to ignore the incessant news and gossip columns as America adjusted to one of its favorite sons coming back from the dead. And two weeks for me to be completely forgotten from that narrative.

The last part, I was fine with—except when the Botoxed ladies on E! began speculating on who would end up "Fitz Baker's next girl." The only pictures that showed up of him anywhere were the few paparazzi shots people got of him coming in and out of Beauregard studios, but as far as I could tell, no one had figured out where he lived. In all of the photos, he looked grouchy and miserable. Gorgeous, of course, but miserable.

I bunched my hair together and pulled it off my neck for a little fresh air. Late July was already setting records up and down the coast, and a burn ban was in effect for all of Washington. All I wanted was to jump in the water, but instead I needed to go turn down the empty rooms at the Forster Inn, where I'd been hired part-time as a housekeeper until we could start renting out the extra rooms on Mama's property ourselves.

I shook Mama's shoulder. "Mama, come on. You have to do Kerryanne Duff's hair in forty minutes."

Mama groaned. "Heaven above, Maggie Mae, do you *have* to shout like that?" She sat up, clenching her temples, and gave me a black look that matched the eyeliner smudged under her eyes.

I sighed, but turned toward the door. She was up and sober. My work here was done. "I left you coffee on the counter, some ibuprofen, and a yogurt. Don't forget that you have an appointment at one, so no margaritas at lunch, all right?"

"You know, you think you have it all together, Margaret, but you—"

I slammed the bedroom door shut before she could go through her morning ritual of cutting me down a peg. Things between us had been terrible. When I'd come home, instead of welcoming me back with the open arms you'd expect of a good mother, she'd scowled, told me I should be ashamed of myself for leaving in the first place, and finished a fifth of vodka before passing out in front of Anderson Cooper. Lucas and I had tried talking to her about her issues, but it hadn't done anything but add to her resentment. I'd kept the memory of what was on Theo's cell phone to myself, not wanting to damage what little dignity she still had. More likely than not, she didn't even remember it. It was probably better for her sense of self-worth anyway. Especially since she seemed to be continuing to spiral straight downhill.

What a fool I was.

Mama stumbled out of her bedroom, pulling on a tank top before she caught me watching. I turned back to my coffee.

She wrinkled her nose. "I can smell that judgment coming off you like a perfume, Margaret. Kindly douse it with some humility, will you?"

I rolled my eyes and sat down at the counter. "Your breakfast is over here, Mama."

She came to sit next to me, and I tried to ignore the fact that she still smelled of gin. She'd cover it up with coffee and perfume, and by the time she got to the salon, she'd be more interested in gossiping with her clients than being hung over. But right now, it was hard to ignore how sad she was.

She looked me up and down, taking in my outfit. It wasn't anything special—an old pair of black pants, a graphic David Bowie t-shirt that had seen better days, and my Converse. Clothes that were good for cleaning and not much else.

"Did you stay here last night?" Mama wondered.

I shook my head and took another bite of my own yogurt. "No, I was at Will's."

More and more, I had taken to staying at the big house on the other side of the lake instead of my little shack. Will was all for it—he liked seeing me in his home when we were able to video chat, and being there made me feel closer to him anyway. He didn't like the fact that I was cleaning guest rooms instead of taking his money, but he understood why I wanted to do it for myself. We weren't at the point in our relationship where his wealth was mine. Not even close. But sleeping in his house, in a space we had shared…that was a favor I was willing to accept.

The paparazzi had completely disappeared from the lake. No one had discovered which house on it was Will's, and aside from that fact, they all knew he was in LA now. Benny was under strict orders *not* to confirm or deny any rumors concerning me to the press, and after two weeks of no more "Figgie" (as the tabloids had annoyingly christened us) sightings, it seemed that they had officially lost interest in me once the production of *Green Lantern* began.

But staying in Will's house didn't make me miss him any less. If anything, it made it worse. The only bright spot was that it was a particular kind of misery that seemed to be inspirational. I'd written four new songs since coming home and had even recorded a few to send to Calliope, just for kicks. I smiled to myself, remembering our final conversation in New York, when Callie had tried again to convince me to stay.

———

"You don't need to hide from Theo anymore," Calliope said as she stood on the sidewalk, watching me pack the last of my stuff back into the Passat. "He's *not going to do anything—not with his dad putting all this money into the movie."*

Calliope agreed with Will—*that in the end, I shouldn't cave to the del Contes and besmirch my own good name by recanting my statements against Theo. In the end, I'd chosen a compromise—I'd allowed Will to hire a lawyer who would hopefully stop the release of the video and also help me extend the restraining order to include a no-contact clause. But I was also leaving New York instead of staying for the hearing. Callie was right. Will was the real reason I'd stayed anyway.*

My phone buzzed. A picture from Will in some kind of ridiculous costume—a green Spandex suit that fit his body like paint. He was sticking his tongue out while a couple of other people in the photo I didn't recognize were clearly laughing. I smiled and sent a photo back of me in front of the Passat. I didn't smile, though. For someone who hadn't had a cell phone for over four years, he had jumped back into selfie culture like a duck in water. I loved seeing his face every day, but I did wonder if he hated it as much as he claimed.

I put the phone in the back pocket of my jeans and turned to give my friend a hug. "I'm not running, Cal. I just need to take care of some things. This..."

I sighed, looking around me. Calliope lived in a relatively residential part of Manhattan—a tree-lined block close to the West Fourth station, where most of the buildings were brownstones and brick walk-ups. But beyond them, the jagged, sharp tops of skyscrapers at Midtown and the Financial District loomed, like a mouthful of broken teeth, threatening to swallow us whole. I shuddered. New York hadn't felt safe to me for a long time. And now, more than ever, I knew it never really would.

"It's not where I'm supposed to be," I finished.

Calliope pursed her lips and folded her arms. She looked as immaculate and attention-seeking as ever in a bright orange mini dress and hair that she'd teased out into a near-afro. A set of gold bangles clattered on her wrist.

"Well, you don't belong out in the sticks cleaning houses either," she said. "You're too talented."

"Callie—"

"Fine, then. But do me a favor," she interrupted. "Lover boy said you could use his house, right? Take advantage of the recording studio. That's all I'm saying. Don't let your talent go to waste."

She pulled me close for a hug that squeezed my heart and my ribs. "When *you're ready to come out of the shadows again, I'll be here to help you shine, babe. That's a promise."*

———

"You know what that makes you, don't you?" Mama's cracked voice yanked me out of my daydreams.

I pushed my stool back with a screech and got up. "Mama, let's don't start that."

She hadn't forgiven Will for what he did, even if I had. Hadn't forgiven him for being famous, for not telling her, but mostly, I suspected, for not saving her. More than anything, Mama wanted to be saved, preferably by a big, strong man. Never me. Or her friends. And definitely not herself. It had taken me this long, but I was finally coming to see that simple fact.

"His little kept woman," she sneered. "Looks like the apple don't fall far from the tree, don't it, sweetie pie?" She cackled to herself while I washed out my cup.

"You have ten minutes to leave," I reminded her, ignoring her jeers and irritating smile. I grabbed my keys and turned to the sliding glass door. "I'll be home later. It would be good if we could finish cleaning the lower cabin today."

Mama just rolled her eyes, like she was an errant teenager and not my fifty-something mother. But before she could spout another cutting remark, I was gone.

———

Four hours, three bedrooms, two bathrooms, and a very dirty kitchen later, I was beat, driving back home the long way so I could stop at Will's to water a few of the plants I'd brought there over the last few weeks.

At least, I told myself it was the plants, and maybe because I wanted to be away from my mother for a little longer. That was it. Really.

It wasn't because I sometimes wandered into Will's closet to bury my face in the drawer full of t-shirts that smelled exactly like him.

It wasn't because I loved jumping off the dock and swimming out to the lily pads off the end where he'd rescued me.

It wasn't because I liked to sit on his couch, watch the lake ripple down the hill, and pretend that he was there with me, with his characteristic ability to just be. Be quiet.

No. It wasn't any of that.

I unlocked the door to Will's hidden cabin with the key he'd given me the morning he left.

"We already started living together here," he whispered in between kisses that reached my toes. *"We're not going to stop because I'm fifteen hundred miles away for a little while."*

I shut the door behind me for a moment and leaned against it, taking a deep breath of the house that smelled like him, albeit less and less every day. Like pine trees and lake water. Like soap and clean, freshly turned soil. God, I missed him. So, so much.

As if called by my thoughts, my phone buzzed loudly in my pocket. I picked it up and brightened as I saw Will's name flash across the screen.

"I really am convinced you're psychic," I greeted Will as I wandered into the living area and plopped down on the couch. "I was just thinking about you. You got a break today, huh?"

"Sort of." Will's voice was gruff, and I could hear a cacophony of voices shouting in the background. "I said back the fuck off!" he shouted, presumably to the onlookers. There was a scuffle, and then the noise quieted a bit. "Sorry about that. I'm in my car now. Word got out about location shots today and the crowds have been insane."

"Do you, um, want to talk later?"

"Honestly, babe, I can't later. This is pretty much my only free time today. I was actually planning to leave a message."

I said nothing and stared at my lap. He didn't even call to talk? Filming had only just started, and we barely had a minute each day to speak.

"Babe" turned me off too. It's not that he hadn't called me that before, but over the last few weeks, I was less and less frequently Lily, never Maggie, and mostly some version of "babe" or "baby." Will sounded like a caricature of an asshole movie star. I hated it.

"Hold on a second, babe. I'm going to call you back."

Abruptly, the call was cut off. I stared at the black screen, unsure of what to think. I didn't even get a goodbye?

Another ringtone came from the FaceTime app. I answered it immediately to a scowling Will.

"Look at this garbage," he said.

The screen jostled as the camera was turned toward the window, where I could see constant flashes and blurry shapes of uncountable people banging on the car door. Photographers, but also fans. Mostly women. Many of them screaming. One even lifted her shirt. She was definitely not wearing a bra. I cringed.

"Drive, Hakeem. They'll get out of the way," Will ordered from out of the frame, and then he turned the camera back to himself. He gave a grim smile, but there was no dimple. He looked thinner in the face than I remembered, but thicker in the neck and shoulders. His hair had been cut again, with a little more style this time.

"You look tired," I said as the noise of his fans gave way to the hum of the LA freeways.

Will pushed a hand over his face. "I am. The makeup ladies were pissed today. Said I needed to get more sleep."

I tipped my head. "Were you up late last night?"

"Well, we were filming until almost eleven, and then I had to be back on set at six, but my trainer kept me until twelve doing a bunch of crap," he said. "So I got maybe five, six hours, max. Not enough to cure the dark circles."

I stuck out my tongue. That sounded miserable. Will chuckled, then his gaze floated over the screen, like he was taking me in.

"God, you're beautiful," he said, low enough that his driver wouldn't hear him. "No one should look that good after cleaning all morning. What are you up to now?"

I smiled. "I'm at your place. I hope you don't mind."

"For the millionth time, Lil, why would I mind? I gave you a key."

I shrugged, but the pet name warmed me inside. "I don't know. Anyway, yeah. I thought I might go for a swim before I go back to the house and finish the lower cabin. I think we can start renting soon if I hustle tonight."

"A swim, huh?" Will's mouth twisted, and his eyes brightened with a sudden thought. "Does that mean I get to watch you change? Quick, take your top off for me."

I froze. Was he joking? His sly smile made me think he was, but he kept waiting, like he thought I was in the mood to strip down in the middle of his living room. My mind flickered back to the woman who had flashed him literally moments before—is that what he wanted me to do?

"Maggie," Will broke through my thoughts. "I'm joking. I would never ask you to do that." He quirked an eyebrow. "At least not when I can't return the favor."

I exhaled with relief. "Oh. Oh, good."

"I'm sorry, babe. Being here is making me feel…I don't know. Jittery, I guess. I'm being an asshole."

I shrugged. He was, kind of, but saying so wasn't going to help anything. "You're always kind of an asshole," I said.

Will grinned. I told him that all the time now, and it was starting to become a joke.

"How was shooting today?" I asked.

Will sighed. "Shitty. This script is a piece of shit. Some of the dialogue is out-of-this-world terrible."

"Is the director willing to let you change anything?" I didn't even know if it was possible, but I knew how much Will loved writing scripts in his own time. There was no way he didn't have ideas on how to make it better.

"Yeah, Corbyn's great—we go way back, actually, since he directed The Dwelling, you know. He lets me ad lib sometimes when it's really bad. For stuff like this, he's more of a CGI person anyway, so he doesn't really give a shit what comes out of the actors' mouths as long as we look good."

I frowned. That sounded…depressing. "So where are you off to now? Back to the hotel?"

"I wish. I have a call tomorrow at five, so it's going to be an early night, but that means I have to meet up with Adam tonight instead, and then eat about five thousand calories worth of fish before I go to sleep."

I nodded. I'd heard a lot about Adam, the trainer provided by the studio to get Will into superhero-level shape. He seemed nice, at least nice enough to take Will's staunch refusal of any kind of "enhancing" shots to help with his transformation. I didn't really understand why they needed the transformation to begin with anyway. Will's body would make anyone drool.

He made a face. "I would *really* like a big, juicy burger right now. But apparently there are too many simple carbs in a bun. So it's cod and salad tonight. Again. Did I mention how much 'fun' I'm having being an actor?"

I smiled, then pushed a hand over my dirty pants. A burger sounded good, but the lake was calling. I felt grimy and disgusting, and all I wanted to do was get clean and bury myself in Will's arms. Only one of those things was possible at the moment.

"I miss you, Lil."

The note of sorrow in his voice immediately made me regret my earlier resentment. The name plucked a chord inside me and made me thrum. Of course he was sad. This was someone who would literally swim a mile in the dark to be next to me. Neither of us was going to enjoy being apart.

I touched a finger to the screen, wishing I could feel the scratch of his stubble. "I miss you too."

"Call you tomorrow?"

I nodded. "Sounds good."

"It probably won't be until late. The schedule is psychotic."

I shrugged. "It's okay. Call me when you get a break." I hated how needy I sounded asking him that, but I wasn't sure I could do this without hearing from him daily. Things were hard enough as it was.

"Every chance I get." Will smiled, a sad smile, but one that lit up the screen nonetheless. "I love you."

I bit my lip. "I love you too."

———

AFTER COOLING off in the lake, I drove back home and was readying myself for the daily fight to keep Mama in the house when my phone rang again. I pulled it out smugly. He really *did* mean every chance he got, apparently.

But it wasn't Will. Instead, it was a different New York number—my new lawyer's.

"Hello?" I answered.

"Hey, Maggie. How's your day going?" The confident voice of Clay Gronsky echoed through my phone's speakers.

"Good," I replied. "Um…what's up, Clay?"

"Well, I just got out of the hearing. Do you have a second?"

I sat down on the steps. "Oh my God. That's right…that was today."

"I'm surprised you forgot."

"Only temporarily." I tapped my foot on the wood. "Well? What was the, uh, verdict, or whatever you'd call it?"

Again, there was a light chuckle, but it died quickly. "Well, unfortunately, Maggie, I don't have good news. The judge dismissed our petition. In fact, he overturned the whole order."

I was glad I was sitting down, because if I hadn't been, I would have fallen over. "*What?*"

There was another chuckle. Great. My lawyer was a nervous laugher.

"Maggie, did you have dinner with Mr. del Conte and his son?"

"I…what…oh my God. Yes…I mean, I sat down with them. And four other people. For, oh, five minutes or so. But, Clay, I didn't really have a choice. They threatened Will and me, and he said it would be like it never happened."

"But it did happen," Gronsky said. "They're basically using that against you. The argument was that if you agreed to dinner, he must not have been such a threat after all. And the judge bought it. For now."

I held a hand to my chest. It was very hard to breathe. "Oh my God," I gasped again and again. "Oh my *God*."

"Look," Gronsky was saying. "It's not over yet, Maggie. We'll appeal. You have reams of documentation that show Theo del Conte has been harassing you for a year, even from inside prison. One dinner isn't going to change that. In the meantime, if you see him, hear from him, anything, big or small, document it. Write it down. Screenshots. Pictures. Send everything to my office, and I'll have my paralegal add them to the file. We'll beat this."

I listened to him give me more bits of advice on all the things I could keep track of should Theo contact me again, but I could barely hear any of it beyond the roar of my own dread.

"What—what about the video?" I asked once Gronsky had finished.

This time there was no chuckle—only the silence of regret.

"Well, Maggie, I'm afraid the judge wasn't very generous on that count either. Since there was no evidence of the video, not with us or on Mr. del Conte's cell phone, he saw no reason for an injunction."

So. Not only was I unable to keep Theo at arm's length, I also couldn't preserve my mother's dignity. I leaned forward and buried my face in my hands. There was no word for this but one: failure.

CHAPTER TWELVE

I moved through the rest of the day in slow-motion, calling Mama to make sure she made her one o'clock and working on the house before going back to the inn for the afternoon turn-down service. I was pulling a triple-shift today. Linda was holding an event this evening for the local Rotary Club and needed some extra help in the kitchen.

"That's great, hon," Linda said as she looked over the last room I cleaned that afternoon. Linda Forster was the definition of proprietary. It didn't matter that she had known me pretty much my entire life or that I had once been close enough to her family to be like a daughter. I was the first person she'd ever hired outside of the Forsters to work at the inn, so she needed to make sure I was doing it right.

"Empty out the trashes, and I think you're done for the day." She shook her head appreciatively. "What I ever did without you, I'll never know. You're a gem."

She smiled and walked out, leaving me to pack the cleaning materials back into the hall closet and go around to the vacant rooms to double check that all trash had been thrown out. It didn't take long. There were only five rooms on the top floor of the Forster Inn. I cleaned the downstairs in the morning, when most of the guests were asleep. And after other people checked out, I'd return sometime around noon, get the rooms ready for new guests, and turn down the beds. Most days I finished by two at the latest.

In some ways, it felt like I was becoming everything everyone had expected of me. Like the second I picked up a spray bottle, everything they knew about the last eight years of my life—my scholarship, my music, my career—disappeared and I became Ellie Sharp's kid again, doing odd jobs here and there to help pay the bills. The steady to my mother's crazy.

It wasn't a rhythm I ever wanted to keep, but here I was again. And now, with the renewed threat of Theo hanging over me…what the hell else was I going to do?

In the last room, I found a copy of *Us Weekly* stuffed in the bottom drawer of the nightstand. Before I chucked it into the trash bag, a small, grainy photo of a man following a woman down the street in the bottom right corner of the page leapt out with the accompanying headline:

Is Fitz Baker rekindling an old flame?

It was garbage. It wasn't even clear that the photo was him, although those broad shoulders and the cropped blond hair *did* look familiar. But Will told me daily to ignore all of the tabloids, and I knew him well enough to know that he went out of his way to avoid everything they said, not confirm it.

Still…it was as if some masochistic voice in me demanded to know. Demanded to see. *It's LA. There are naked women everywhere, right? Who's to say who he's been talking to off set?*

What did these glossy pages know that I didn't?

I sat down on the bed and flipped through the pictures: celebrities on red carpets and candid photos of them at the beach, the mall, wherever the photographers could find them. "They're just like you!" They all made me feel sick, voyeuristic. Some photos had clearly been staged—they looked too perfect, too coordinated not to. Accessories held exactly right, handbags or sneakers brand new, unused. But in so many others, the subjects were clearly unaware of having their pictures taken or obviously didn't want it. Their body posture was closed, protective. Some of them had small children in tow; others were walking with significant others or friends down the street, shielding their faces.

I snapped the magazine shut. This was wrong. Will had welcomed me into the deepest, most private parts of his life. He deserved privacy as much as anyone else did, and by looking at this crap, I was violating it as much as the photographers.

But…

Is Fitz Baker rekindling an old flame?

The question echoed through my mind as it jumped off the page.

I picked up the magazine again, but before I could open it, there was a loud giggle from down the hall, and by instinct, I shoved the magazine aside and jumped up as Lucas and Lindsay practically toppled into the room, grinning at each other like fools.

"Mom keeps the extra towels in this closet, I think," Lucas was saying while Lindsay continued pawing at his arms and giggling like an anime character until she realized I was there.

"Oh my gosh, Lukey, you're so—oh!"

Lucas turned to me, face red. He usually got to the house to finish the last bits of work on the outer cottages at the same time I left to clean the inn's rooms. Our interactions now were fairly limited, and I was certain that had something to do with the fact that his pseudo-girlfriend—or whatever Lindsay was—was responsible for outing Will to the paparazzi.

Lindsay looked me over with a pointed eyebrow, her slim, tanned hand perched on her waist. They were dressed like they were going out on the Forsters' boat—Lindsay in a string bikini with a pair of tiny shorts, Lucas wearing his swimsuit too. He inhaled, sucking in his stomach a bit. He was still handsome, but the football player's body from high school was definitely a thing of the past.

"Oh, that's *right*," Lindsay said. "I forgot you were the new cleaning lady around here." She snickered. "How's scrubbing toilets treating you? I guess having a famous boyfriend doesn't do much for someone like you, does it?"

"Beats selling out my friends for money," I snapped back. "How was Hawaii, Linds?"

She sniffed. "Fine, thanks. Look, it's not my problem some people can't handle a little attention."

Lucas frowned at her, but didn't say anything. "Everything all right in here, Mags?" he asked me.

I nodded, standing up. "Yeah, just finishing up for the day. You're back early."

He smiled. "We're done at your house. I put in the final light fixtures on the upper cabin. Everything's ready to go."

Twin emotions of relief and fear swept through me. Finally, some good news today. "Really?"

Lucas grinned. "Yup. Airbnb away, Mags. You never know. Maybe having some people around will help keep Ellie busy and out of trouble."

Lindsay snorted. "Not likely."

"Linds—"

"Come on, Lucas, you saw her at Curly's last weekend."

"Lindsay, I said—"

"It's all right." I picked up the trash bag. "I know what she does. And sure, maybe you're right. But we're going to try anyway. Maybe it will help her to have something else to focus on."

"Hey, what's that?" Before I could stop her, Lindsay reached around me and snatched the magazine from the bed, immediately spying the article on Will. "Ooooh," she said as she flipped quickly to the pages. "This must really bum you out."

"I didn't read it," I said, turning to the door. All I wanted was to get out of here.

"Well, it makes sense, of course," she said. "He's back with all of those beautiful women, you know? His fiancée must have been so excited to find out he was alive—she was probably the first person he saw when he went down there."

"Lindsay..." Lucas warned. "Leave it alone."

"Come on, she was just reading the article." Lindsay turned to me with a smirk. "Amelia Craig is so gorgeous, don't you think?"

"Linds."

Lucas's voice was uncharacteristically steely. He grabbed the magazine from her with a glare that made her shrink, then took the garbage bag from me and tossed the magazine inside.

"I'll take this out for you." He gave a small smile. "Let me know if you want help getting furniture for the cottages, Mags. We can use my truck to pick up stuff if you want."

I nodded. "Thanks."

But strangely, it didn't make me feel better. Lucas was kind, but his actions didn't change the fact that Lindsay's words, nasty as they were, could have been true.

———

INSTEAD OF GOING HOME, I ended up driving back to Will's. I didn't like the doubt that was growing in the pit of my stomach. More, it seemed, every day. Our conversations were becoming shorter, more curt, as his days on set grew long, and most of the time when he was off, he was too tired to talk for long.

I opened up the cabin door and was immediately inundated with Will. The scent of fresh water and laundry soap was barely evident, but I could still smell it, especially when I pressed my face into his sheets or wore one of his old, ratty t-shirts to bed.

In the studio, I took a deep breath. Like everywhere else, the room was full of ghosts, but they were friendly. A vision of the first time I'd played in here, when Will had recorded me, had sat with me while I played through my fear, and then afterward, when we'd made love amidst the instruments.

Had that only been a month ago? Had it really only been three since we met?

That night had sparked something else in me: that voice, that song, *something* inside me that called. It had been muted for years, but in the last few months, it had bloomed. And as soon as Will left, a different kind of sadness than the kind that comes from the oppression of abuse— a sadness that simply comes from separation from the one you love— filled me. And inspired.

Over the last few weeks, songs had been flowing out of me like the water outside. I was alone, but that loneliness without Will inspired poetry. *He* inspired poetry, some of the best stuff I'd ever written. Songs about my past, about Theo, about my mother. About us.

I picked up one of the Fenders hanging on the wall and tuned it, leaning close to hear the subtle nuances when I plucked each of the strings. Having perfect pitch meant I never had to use a tuner, never had to listen for the resonance frequency across multiple strings. I could just hear it. It was a gift I often took for granted.

When the guitar was tuned, I set it down on the stand and went into the sound booth to start the recording. As I looked over the massive soundboard, I sighed. Will had enough variations of *Sound Recording for Dummies* lying around that I'd learned to record a few other tracks of me and one of his beautiful guitars. But I yearned for more. In my head, there was a full band to accompany my songs. Complex harmonies with complex instrumental accompaniments. Sometimes even an orchestra. I could maybe lay a few separate tracks of guitar and piano over each other, but I didn't have the vocal range or resources to emulate all of it. The new songs sounded so much fuller than anything I could do on my own.

But that was better than nothing.

I pushed a few buttons and set up the parameters the way I wanted them for this particular piece, then went out to the studio, picked up the guitar, and began to play the song I'd written a few days before.

> *I still see you standing, in a river made of sand,*
> *Where trees don't grow from land, but from the sky.*
> *We grow old so quickly, that we soon forget to breathe,*
> *Our sight reduced to sleep before night.*
>
> *I can't be blamed for going.*
> *Could you be for not knowing? Hey…*
>
> *It was a good dream,*
> *but it was half lies, and that's*
> *All I need asleep from you,*
> *It was a good dream,*
> *And if I'm gonna wake without you…*

Then I…don't need to know the truth…

Walking on the edge
Where the water meets the land
Like we're walking hand in hand to the shore.
These miles seem like inches,
These fathoms become feet
In a place where lovers meet in the dark.

Don't blame me for defending
What you only thought was ending…hey…

It was a good dream,
but it was half lies, and that's
All I need asleep from you,
It was a good dream,
And if I'm gonna wake without you…
Then I…don't need to know the truth…

In the end, I trapped the strings with my fingers and muted the music, frustrated with the sound. I already knew that when I played it back, I wouldn't like it. It was a song that needed more than my fingernails strumming awkwardly on the strings like some kind of faux-Joni Mitchell. It was more than a simple folk melody—this piece was grand, almost symphonic. It was a song I'd written about missing the greatest love of my life. In my mind, I could hear the whirr of cymbals, the hard thrum of a bass line, arpeggios up and down from a piano, even a violin coming in with a slow wail. I could manage some of the tracks, but I wasn't going to be able to learn the violin in a few weeks. I'd never find an orchestra to match the music in my head.

I sighed, frustrated, set the guitar back on its stand, then went into the studio to stop the recording. I removed the memory card to take with me—I'd be able to listen to it and maybe do some editing on my computer later. I had a folder of songs I shared with Calliope, but no one else had heard any of them yet. She was convinced that when I was ready, they'd earn me another showcase.

But showcase for what? So I could go on the road as a folk singer? A rock star? More and more, I was starting to feel like chasing that kind of life wasn't what I wanted anyway. And yet, time and time again, people told me that was the only way to get my music out there. To be heard at all.

After I shut down the studio, my phone vibrated in my back pocket. Outside, the lake was fully abuzz with the sounds of boats, jet skis, country music blaring from loudspeakers. It was peak summer on Newman Lake.

I walked out to the deck where I could watch the water from beneath the shade of the pine trees and smiled when I saw Will's face light up my screen to FaceTime. I swiped right.

"Hey!" I greeted him. "Twice in one day, huh? Lucky me."

He grinned. "I got another break," he said, revealing a bright white smile. "The whole evening, actually. And…I don't know. Things seemed weird when we left off. You seemed, I don't know. Off. God, you're pretty. I miss you."

I sat on one of the big Adirondack chairs with a thump, not even trying to hide my blush. "I miss you too. How'd filming go today?"

He rolled his eyes. "Well, they made the script changes I suggested, so I guess that's good. But I'm so sick of all this CGI crap. You can't trade energy with a tennis ball, you know?"

I nodded, though I didn't know. I could guess, though.

"Did you record anything today?"

I nodded. "Yeah. I just put something else down, actually."

"When are you going to send it to me?"

I bit my lip. I wasn't sure I was ready for that. Calliope was one thing —she had been hearing my music from the start, and I wasn't afraid of her comments, good or bad. But with Will, it was personal. Especially when most of what I was writing these days was about him.

"I don't know," I said. "When it's finished."

"Come on, baby. You gotta give me something. I'm dying down here without you."

I squinted, looking behind him. "Where are you?"

Will turned and looked out at the view. It was fuzzy, but I could make out the shape of a long pier and a Ferris wheel, plus a wide blue sky that never seemed to end. It looked like Santa Monica.

"Well, since I had more than a few hours off, I decided to go to the beach. It's basically the one nice thing about LA. One of the cast members has a house here. It's sort of private, so I figured, why not?"

"Your cast member? Who's that?"

We hadn't really talked much about who he was actually filming with —he'd jumped in so quickly, and I'd avoided any press coverage of him and the movie to be respectful.

"Will! Are you coming, darling? We're about to start the game." A throaty, British, and very female voice sounded behind him. Will started and turned around, but before he could block the screen again, I caught a glimpse of the speaker.

She was tall. Blonde. Tan, and from what I could see, exquisitely pretty. She was also recognizable.

"I'll be there in a second," Will said while my heart turned to glass.

"Will?"

"Huh? What's up, Lil?"

He looked back, his handsome face once more filling the screen. But I was more interested in who was behind it.

I worried my lip between my teeth. "Is that…is that Amelia Craig?"

Will's big green eyes flew open guiltily, and I knew without hearing the answer that it was definitely her.

I pressed my lips together, hating the way that pit in my stomach grew. As if this day could get any worse. "Will…w-why are you with your ex-fiancée?"

At the sound of my stutter, Will's eyes shut tight. I'd never explicitly told him why and how it had developed, but he had obviously figured out enough to know that it emerged when I was stressed. Scared.

His features shuttered. "Well, this is her house."

My chest tightened more. "Your…y-your co-star is your former fiancée? As in, the woman you were planning to marry?"

"Lil, it's not like that—"

"How is it n-not like that?" Dammit, my stutter wouldn't leave. I turned the phone away, not wanting him to see the fear contorting my face.

"Maggie, can you put the phone back, please? I don't want to talk to the wall."

When I did, Will's entire face was crinkled with concern.

"Look, babe, there are a bunch of us here since they are doing stock shots all afternoon. Amy offered to have everyone over, so here we are. You have nothing to worry about."

"Nothing to worry about?" I stood up before I realized it, feeling like an idiot for yelling at a phone. It was so unsatisfying, being this angry with a piece of technology. I wanted to yell at *Will*, touch *his* face, shake *his* arm. Not shout at some blurry facsimile.

"Babe, you have to trust me. Maggie, this isn't going to work if you don't believe me when I tell you the truth."

"But that's the problem, isn't it? You *didn't* tell me the truth. You d-didn't tell me anything. Just like b-before."

I swiped at tears threatening to fall. Behind Will, I could make out the light, lithe form of "Amy" walking on the beach. I covered my face with my hand and looked away.

Will sighed. "I...shit. No, I didn't. Lily, you were already so stressed with everything happening with your mom and the shit with del Conte. Lil, I didn't want to stress you out more. I'm sorry."

I pushed a hand through my hair. "You didn't think I would be stressed when I found out you were working with Amelia Craig?"

Will swallowed.

"Will you—" I hated the question even before I said it. But I had to say it. I *had to*. "Will you have to do any love scenes with her?"

Another visible gulp. "Well, she's the other lead, so…"

My stomach dropped. "I need to go."

"Wait, Lil—"

"I need to go for a run," I said as gently as I could manage, even with the turmoil in my stomach. "And then I have to go back to the inn to help with an event tonight."

"Is Lucas going to be there?"

I sighed, irritated. What right did he have to be annoyed when he was going to be making out with his ex-fiancée all day tomorrow?

"I have to go," I said, more strongly than I felt.

I felt sick from all the nervous energy that bloomed at the idea of Will having a love scene with a woman who wasn't me. Add to that the fact that it was his ex. Someone he, at one point, wanted to marry. Someone who had once been on the cover of *People Magazine*'s Most Beautiful edition. Whom he had neglected to tell me was back in his life on a daily basis.

Yeah. I was about ready to throw up.

"I'll talk to you later," I said and ended the call before Will could respond.

My phone immediately started ringing again. I switched it to silent. All my life, I had lived with shitty excuses for various kinds of disappointment and betrayal. My mother's mistakes flitted through my mind, right alongside the time I'd spent with Theo. I'd thought Will was different, even after the colossal revelation of his secrets. But now I wasn't so sure. And if that was the case, I wasn't sure I could deal with him at all.

————

FOUR HOURS LATER, I was beat. I'd run farther than I intended, ignoring the hot, late July sun to do ten miles to Hauser Lake and back before driving over to the inn to help Linda serve dinner for a group retreat. Mama was gone when I left—out with Barb, her best friend.

There was so much to do. So much to fix. I worked doggedly, running, cleaning, thinking about everyone's future but my own. Maybe this was my future. Let out rooms on the lake. Take care of my mother. Forget about a life beyond these pine trees and hills. Forget about music.

I pulled into the dusty, gravel driveway wanting only my bed and nothing else. Across the lake, Will's house called, but I had the sinking feeling that I didn't belong there. Maybe I never would.

When I rolled to a stop, the dust from the gravel cleared to reveal the hulking shape of a black SUV crowding the easement. I stepped out. The windows were tinted. There were two shapes inside—men the size of linebackers.

But before I could walk closer, something else caught my eye. A shadow crowded the top of the stairs.

The shadow moved. I froze, watching.

Theo.

Was it? No, he wouldn't be that stupid. I hadn't heard anything from him in two weeks. I'd thought that maybe, just *maybe* he'd gotten it through his head that I wasn't worth pursuing. That I wasn't worth the risk. I prayed that was true now that the judge had dismissed my entire protection order.

"C-can I help you?" I asked timidly, wishing my voice sounded stronger. Not as weak as I felt.

Then the shadow stood and turned, revealing the last person I'd expected to see tonight.

His green eyes twinkled under the night sky, hopeful and scared all at once.

"W-Will?" My heart pounded wildly. "What-what are you doing here?"

"What else, Lil?" he asked softly. He pulled his hands out of his pockets and spread them outward, a gesture of pure surrender. "I'm here for you."

CHAPTER THIRTEEN

Will's feet crunched on the gravel as he took a few steps toward me. I stepped back as he did, mirroring his movements. He walked into the light, and we both stopped moving.

He didn't look like himself. I was struck by the difference between now and the last time he'd come to the property, soaked, in nothing but a dirty t-shirt and running gear, a sudden rainstorm cascading down his shoulder-length hair and the beard he trimmed, but never completely shaved off. Now the hair was short, still close to his scalp the way I had done it, but grown out a bit more on the top and styled in that haphazard way that was really hard to do. There were other, smaller differences. His clean-shaven face had grown a slight, perfectly groomed stubble, and his eyebrows had also been groomed, so slightly that anyone else might not have noticed. His body was both leaner and larger at the same time, the muscles tighter underneath a pair of perfectly tailored navy pants and a white button-down shirt, rolled up to his elbows. His hair was blonder. His fingernails were buffed. He was…perfect. Much more so than on any blurry screen.

They were things that erased Will and brought Fitz Baker back from the dead, changes so slight that anyone else might not have noticed. But I did. I knew every tiny line on that face, and every imperfection that had been erased.

He took another step forward, and again, I stepped back. He paused.

"It's all right, Lil. It's just me." I started at the sound of his deep voice. It was almost as if, until he spoke, he'd been a ghost.

I glanced around nervously, wondering if we were being watched. That was what the cameramen did, right? Followed people like him around. Invaded their most personal moments.

"H-how do you know?" I asked.

The reflection of the streetlight lit up his short blond fringe like a halo. But it was more remarkable that his handsome face was so clearly lit. A lens five hundred feet away would have been able to take a recognizable photo of him. He was out in the open for the first time since I'd met him.

"Because I made sure of it," he said. "Two decoys off the set, and I borrowed Corbyn's jet. It's waiting at a private airfield in Liberty Lake, where I wore a wig to get off. No one knew I left. As far as every paparazzi in LA is concerned, I'm asleep in my trailer on set."

I didn't say anything. I didn't even know what to make of that. There was a private airfield in Liberty Lake, the next town over? Will had access to a *jet*? Multiple decoys?

Was I living in a James Bond movie?

"But, Lil?"

I blinked, pulled out of my stupor by that familiar voice, those intense green eyes. Not everything had changed. And yet, the last time I'd seen him here, he'd had the same expression. Frantic. Desperate. Afraid.

Will took another step closer. This time, I didn't move.

"Even if they were here," he said slowly. "Cameras, reporters. Lily, I wouldn't give a shit. I had to come. I had to see you."

We stared at each other for several long seconds, the tension of our last conversation as palpable as before. I opened my mouth to say something, but the light glinting off the chrome hubcaps of the Yukon caught my eye. Maybe there were no cameras, but we still had an audience.

"Security?" I asked, nodding at the car.

Will, as telepathic as ever, followed my gaze and nodded.

"You can't be too careful," he said darkly and walked over to the car. The passenger window rolled down, revealing two of the detail I'd seen in New York.

"We're good, guys," he said. "You can park on the street."

The bodyguards glanced toward me then back at Will like they disagreed, but in the end, nodded and rolled the window back up. We watched as the car moved slowly to the top of the hill, parking just over the ridge.

Will walked back to me. "Better?"

I folded my arms across my chest. "What are you doing here?" I asked again.

Will walked closer, taking careful steps, like he thought I might bolt. He reached out and drifted a finger down my cheek. "I told you, I had to see you."

"Don't you have to film tomorrow?"

He snorted. "Five a.m. call, yeah. But that doesn't matter. So that leaves me…" He checked his watch—a pretty thing, shiny, metal, and new. "About eight hours to convince you to forgive me for being a dick."

I sighed and stepped away again, this time toward the stairs. "Will…"

"Lil, I didn't know. I swear to God, I didn't know Amy was going to be my costar until she showed up on set this week."

I looked away. "Come on…"

"I'm serious! That happens sometimes, all right? Someone drops out, the studio and director have to pinch hit to keep production going. That's how I ended up here, after all. Or maybe—"

"Maybe what?"

Will shoved a hand through his hair, his fingers searching for length that wasn't there anymore. *Good*, I thought, a bit vindictively. But it was nice to know that his new appearance wasn't strange only to me.

"It did occur to me that Max might've done it on purpose," he admitted. "For publicity and buzz. And maybe to get under my skin. It makes sense, right? The paps…they haven't figured out that Amy's there yet, but when they do, it's going to be a shit storm."

It was really, *really* hard not to scowl every time he said her name like that. Not Amelia, the name that everyone else in the world knew. Amy. It was familiar. Intimate. A reminder that once upon a time, Will had looked at her the way he looked at me.

"They know," I said bitterly.

Will looked up. "What?"

I wrapped my arms around my waist. "It was on the cover of a magazine at the inn. Something about you 'rekindling an old flame.' They had pictures of the two of you from, I don't know, somewhere. They know."

"Shit…" Will dropped his hand to his neck and massaged it furiously. "Fuck. God*damn*it. Amy's going to freak."

I turned toward the stairs. I didn't want to see him grappling with this. I had been dealing with it all day, so much worse after I knew who it was in that magazine. Amelia freaking Craig. *Amy.* Every time he said that name, I wanted to hurl a rock at him.

I didn't like the side of myself that I was seeing. I wasn't normally a jealous person. Even with Theo, when I knew he was stepping out, cheating, whatever, I never felt this way. Possessive. Almost animal. It was uncommonly strong, and I didn't know how to deal with it.

"Where do you think you're going?" Will asked, already thundering after me down the stairs.

"I don't want to do this," I said. The wood stairs creaked under my feet, but the repairs to them held strong.

"Don't want to do what?" Will's feet pounded after me, and it only made me jog that much faster.

"This!" I cried, even as he caught my hand and yanked me back around.

The sudden contact between us was electric—the warmth of his hand against my chilled skin, the sudden fact of him after weeks apart. My body caved to him even as my mind continued to fight.

"Please," I said as I struggled to get away. "Please, let me go."

Will ground his teeth hard enough to make a muscle twitch in his jaw. But instead of releasing me, he pulled, hard enough that I had to stumble up two stairs into his arms.

"Never," he said and kissed me.

His lips were insistent, angry, and full of the same desire that vibrated through my bones. This physical connection had always existed on another frequency with us, like a particular sound, a particular music that only we could hear. Our mouths warred, biting, nipping, sucking. But right now it didn't feel like music. It just felt like noise. Chaos.

No! He lied to you! He hid everything from you, and he is still doing it! And that was when my mind won. I yanked my hand out of his clutch and shoved him back up the stairs.

"Lily, *stop it*," Will demanded as he stretched toward me again.

But I danced out of reach. "No, *you* stop it!" I retorted. "You can't show up, manhandle me, force me to feel like it doesn't matter what you did. It's manipulative and completely takes advantage of everything I feel about you, especially when...*fuck*...Will, I am *SO* mad at you right now!"

My words stopped him cold, and the anger and frustration written all over his face scrunched together as his mouth, swollen and full, dropped open.

"I...know," he said.

A solid four breaths passed between us before I could answer.

"You know," I repeated. That was it? That was all he had to say? I was mad, and he...*knew*?

Will took a deep breath. His chest was heaving, like he'd been running at full sprint and stopped on a dime. I was similarly struggling.

"It's been a really long time since I did this," he said. "A relationship. And I'm going to fuck it up. A lot. But, Lil, I need you. I'm dying down there, baby."

At first, I softened. But visions of his increasingly distant video chats and phone calls fluttered through my mind. Especially the one earlier that day.

And the anger was back.

"Oh, you're *dying*?" I asked. "It sure looked like you were having a terrible time partying it up on the beach. Sunshine and sand castles, right?"

Will scowled. "Give me a break—"

"Or *maybe* you didn't want to tell me that either. *Maybe* you're down there having the time of your life, 'rekindling the flame' with your b-beautiful former fiancée."

Will's eyes flared. "That is fucking *ridiculous*, Maggie, and you know it. This is me we're talking about here."

But I kept charging on, all of the resentment I had about not only him, but my entire situation tumbling out of me. "I see the spark in your eye when I talk to you. Even if you are telling the truth about *her*, you're not telling the truth about all of it. I'm up here scrubbing fucking toilets during the day and trying to keep my mother alive at night while you're down there living your dream."

"Lil, seriously—"

"You've got your life back, right?" I rattled on, unable to stop the tears that had been threatening for a while now. "So who cares what I know about it, right? Who cares if I know that you're going to be kissing your 'Amy' tomorrow, or that you're spending time at her house? Who cares if I even know your real name, or anything about your life, right?"

"Maggie—"

"I just wish you would be honest! Because as much as you say you hate it, it seems more like you're having the time of your life."

"No, I'm not!" Will burst out. "And even if I was, it would be fucking terrible!"

"Oh, *really*?" I snapped. "And why is that, pray tell?"

"Because the love of my life is right fucking here, and she's upset, and IT HURTS!" He slammed a palm over his chest—the heel of his hand hit his sternum with an alarming thump. "It fucking hurts, Lil," he went on. "I'm surrounded by people who only want as much money from me as I can make for them, and that includes Amy, someone I was supposed to *marry* at one point."

"Stop!" I cried. "I don't want to hear about that!"

"Listen!" Will cut back. "These people...they're fucking heartless. Lily, I just lost my dad, after four years of pretending I was dead to save his life. And they couldn't delay filming long enough for me to clean out his house. That's what kind of people I'm working with. Do you really think I would choose *them* over you? Over the one person in this entire fucking world who knows me, the real me, underneath this stupid fucking veneer they built?"

He gestured up and down at his new appearance, and my chest

relaxed slightly at the fact that he knew what I saw. That he was as uncomfortable with the little changes as I was.

"Lil, look at me." When I didn't, he exhaled deeply. "Please."

Slowly, I did. His eyes were shadowed here, away from the light, but I could still see his pain.

"Maggie, I'm sorry. I *am* sorry." He shook his head, like he was trying to shake off some invisible weight. "But, baby, I would do so much more than lie to keep you in my life. Lie, cheat, steal, kill. None of it would matter if it meant I kept you."

At first, words wouldn't come out. Was he serious?

"That's ridiculous," I said, stuck in place as he joined me a step lower.

"I never said I was a good man," Will said. "In fact, I think I told you the opposite."

"I'm not your savior, Will," I said, shaking my head.

"No," he agreed. "You're so, so much more."

Our mouths hovered, right at the precipice of a kiss or a bite. Sometimes it was hard to tell the difference, especially with Will. I leaned in. My lips were swollen, dying for another taste. It didn't matter how angry I was—I still wanted him. I knew I always would.

And yet. My heart loathed for me to say it, but I knew I had to. Just as I knew I would have to keep my promise if I was ever going to maintain my self-respect.

"You want to keep me in your life, Will?" I said. "Then you can't do any of those things. You can't cheat. You can't steal. You can't kill. And if you ever, *ever* lie or keep things from me again, I'll be gone. I don't care how much I love you. I don't care how much it hurts. You are not the only one who feels like their guts are being torn out when we're apart. But I can't be with someone I can't trust. I cannot."

Will squeezed his eyes shut, like he was physically feeling the metaphor. I couldn't blame him. I was too. But I absolutely could not be with someone I couldn't trust. "N-never—" I took a deep breath as I regained my voice. At the sound of my stutter, we both winced. "*Never* again."

Will worried his jaw for a moment, then, apparently having made a decision, shot a hand out and captured mine, which he then slapped against his chest.

"Do you feel that?" he demanded.

I tried to pull my hand away, but he wouldn't allow it. "What?" I asked. "*What* am I feeling?"

"My heartbeat, Lil. The one that beats for you."

I scoffed. "Seriously?"

But his eyes held mine, unblinking, and without any trace of a joke. He pressed on my hand hard, forcing me to feel the deep, immediate thump of his heartbeat against my palm.

"If I ever lie or mislead you again, you can shove the knife in yourself," he said solemnly.

I stared at my hand as I felt the solid rhythm.

"You're crazy," I whispered.

"Probably," he agreed. "But I'm also yours."

With the frank admission, something more than the usual possession that Will had said before, something inside me unraveled. Now it was my hand taking a fierce handful of fabric, holding him in place. Daring him to step away.

He remained absolutely still.

"M-mine?" I asked as I moved even closer.

Will exhaled, his sweet, fresh breath harsh and unsteady.

"Every goddamn cell," he confirmed. The muscle in his jaw ticked again, and he stared at my lips. He clearly wanted to kiss me again, but this time was holding back. Not for his sake, but for mine.

I fingered the collar of his shirt.

"Mine," I whispered as I took in his clothes. The ironed Egyptian cotton. The leather shoes that didn't even have one scuff. I wanted to tackle him into the dirty and muddy him up. Like somehow that would make him more recognizable. "*Mine.*"

Our eyes met once more. For a second, the entire world seemed to take a breath. And then it was me...who attacked him. I launched myself at Will, and he caught me, falling easily to sit while he accepted a kiss that was almost violent while giving back as much or more. We tore at each other, tongues dipping, fingers clawing, bodies grinding as we fought each other, ourselves to get closer than we ever could possibly get in reality.

I tackled him into the stairs, my hands ripping at his expensive designer shirt hard enough that the buttons went flying into the pine needles and brush. Will didn't flinch as he slid his own hands up my legs, underneath the hem of my shorts, under the elastic of my panties and gripping my ass so hard I knew there would be fingerprint-shaped bruises marring the skin. My fingers drifted over the hard, contoured edges of his chest, his abs, all of which were now so defined as to look chiseled from stone. Yet another slight change. I loved it…and hated it all at once.

"Mine," I hissed as I bit his shoulder.

"*Mine*," he mirrored with kiss after bruising kiss, so deep and torrid that I knew my lips would be swollen in the morning. We were claiming each other, for anyone to hear. For us to know.

His fingers hooked my underwear and yanked, tearing the thin lace in his hurry to tug them to the side. I had already pulled him out of his pants, could feel him long and heavy, slipping between my thighs, seeking my depths while the hand in my hair gripped even harder.

His other hand lifted, then met my bare ass with a loud crack that echoed through the trees. A lightning bolt of desire shot through me. He did it again, his mouth attached to my neck, and I arched back at the slice of delicious pain. He repeated the action, over and over, hard enough that my skin burned slightly after some countless strokes, and I knew it would be red well after he was finished. And lord, if I didn't want it more than I'd ever wanted anything before.

His cock slipped in, maybe an inch, maybe more. And Will's hand slapped me harder than ever and practically had me soaring right there.

And yet, the sound also made me freeze, knocking me partially back to my senses. What was I doing? Out here, in plain sight, where any one of the neighbors who shared this parking easement with us could pull up at anytime and see me riding a famous movie star like a mechanical bull at the top of my stairs. I was ridiculous. *We* were ridiculous.

"Stop!" I yanked his hand out of my hair painfully, then scurried up as I tugged my shorts back into place, and scampered down a few steps, safely out of his reach.

Will gaped at me, his chest heaving while he flexed his hand. His cock stood straight and long while his eyelids were heavy with desire.

"Don't walk away from me, Lil," he said, the words somehow both a threat and a plea. I could see in his eyes that he meant every word he'd said—he really would die before he let me walk away from him again.

Well. I had no intention of that. But I wasn't willing to sacrifice my dignity or his just to give us what we both wanted in the moment.

"Not here," I said, barely able to find my breath for the two short words. I reached out a hand for him to take. "Follow me."

CHAPTER FOURTEEN

W e practically tumbled down the stairs, fumbling at each other's clothes as we clattered past the house, onto the deck, down the second set of stairs, and toward the dock. We were like a tornado, barely even conscious of where we were going until we were almost falling over the edge.

"Whoa—" Will chuckled as he caught my waist, keeping me from toppling into the lake. The sound held me still. Will so rarely laughed— even now, I didn't think I had ever heard him completely fall apart in joy. Honestly, he'd only really laughed once, and that was when he was so upset, there was nothing else to do.

It reminded me of so many things I had never seen him do—mostly related to being free.

I stepped back. We were both breathing hard, our chests heaving, bodies poised to pounce. Will grinned, his teeth flashing like the stars flickering above. Then he caught my hand, and I watched, a little reluctantly, as that carefree grin disappeared, swallowed by something much more intense.

"Lily."

The word echoed off the water. I swallowed thickly. Will reached up and wiped a bit of sweat that had condensed on his brow. His open shirt fluttered in the breeze, and the smooth contours of his chest and abs flexed slightly in the moonlight—row upon row of tight, corded muscle that had only become that much more refined with the last few weeks of intense training.

I felt ashamed. He might have looked a little different. Smoother. Sleeker. But he was still mine. Still my Will. And suddenly, I couldn't have cared less where we were. We were surrounded by the night, and the lake was quiet. And I needed to feel that connection, that one that spoke to me deep in my bones, before he left again.

"Will," I whispered.

And like sparks caught to a flame, we lunged at each other all over again. And fell into the water with a loud splash.

"Ahhh!" Will cried as he resurfaced.

"Shit!" I wiped water and hair out of my eyes.

We found each other again across the glimmering ripples.

"This way," I said, my voice nearly getting lost as I bobbed beneath the surface.

Will bit his lips as he tread, clearly wanting to grab at me all over again. But instead, he nodded.

He followed me, tickling my feet as I swam around the point to a slightly more secluded area, out of sight from the house. I guided us toward the rock—Moon Rock, my favorite spot on the entire property. I placed my palms on the flat slab and hoisted myself up. Seconds later, we were peeling off our wet shoes and clothes until we lay side by side, stretched out on the still warm granite in nothing but our underwear, looking at the stars. Will's long body glistened. The starlight bounced off the drops of water still clinging to his skin.

"I don't want to go back," he murmured.

I shivered. I didn't want him to go either, but I knew he had to. We both had to bear the next few months so Will could start his life free—or as free as he could ever be.

He took my hand, and for a moment, we listened to our breaths while blinking up at the quiet night sky.

"Lil." Will pulled me to him, uncompromising and strong. Full of the intention I needed. "No more running away now."

And then he kissed me. Not with the fury he had on the stairs or the bumbling need of the dock, but full of a longing that trembled through him from head to toe. His lips were open and insistent, but patient, waiting for me to meet them, kiss for aching kiss. He was afraid, just like I was, that in the short time we had been together, we weren't enough to make it through everything that wanted to tear us apart.

Fame.

Industry.

Ghosts from both our pasts.

Will's arm slid under my neck, tugging me close with the crook of his elbow. The other made fast work of my underwear and his, taking away every barrier until our bodies could press together, naked and wet. He rolled over me, caging me in the night. His knees nudged mine apart, and instinctively, my hips arched toward him, though in my mind, more alarm bells went off.

"Will," I whispered in between kisses that grew increasingly rough. It was becoming harder and harder to think.

"Shhh," he said. "I need this, baby. *We* need this."

The tip of him slipped inside me. Still I was ready for him, ready and *dying*.

"Oh my *God*, Will." I yanked on his hair, forcing him to look at me.

His full mouth fell open, panting slightly.

"Someone might see us!" I said in a loud whisper that could have been heard anywhere.

"They can't see you, Lil. I'm covering you up."

And it was true. Will was so much bigger, so much taller than me, that any onlooker would see my bare legs, and that would be it.

But that was only me.

"They can see you, though," I said. "They can see all of you out here."

Will frowned and shook his head. "Let them see," he growled. "Let them watch if that's what they want."

His mouth closed over mine, and he shoved inside me fully, seating himself with one long, hard thrust. My spine arched toward the glittering sky, pushing my entire body up along with my spirit, and my cries flew upward in some kind of strange, primeval call to the heavens.

"Will!" I screamed, uncaring that half the lake could hear me if they opened their windows to listen.

My body shook around him, but he didn't relent, driving forward, harder, faster, tasting, licking, savoring my mouth, neck, collarbone, breasts, as he thrust, again and again, with a punishing pace that drove every worry, every fear from my poor, helpless mind.

His hands cupped my face, thumbs stroking lightly across my cheeks.

"God," he whispered, eyes full of love as he stroked forward again, and again. "How do you do it?"

I swallowed. "Do what?"

Thrust. Pull. Thrust again.

"Be the air I need and take my breath away all at once."

I swallowed, and then inhaled deeply, like his words robbed my own ability to breathe. My hands slipped around his neck and folded together, pulling him down so his lips hovered over mine.

Will paused, our only movement the slight pulsing of his considerable length. For a moment, we held each other, naked in the moonlight. The whole of the world could look down on us if they liked, but like him, I no longer cared. They could have us as long as we could be together.

His lips touched mine gently, pulling my bottom lip, then the top between his teeth before slipping his tongue around mine as he began to move once more. I opened even more, spreading my legs, my heart, my soul to his merciless drive. It was like the rest of me knew that despite his size and intrusion, Will belonged. That being together, bodies mingled, meant we were home.

"Lil." His breath grew ragged as his hips found a more insistent rhythm. "Do you feel that, baby? Do you feel everything that passes between us?"

I knew. I did. I arched closer, willing him to find the deepest parts of me and plant himself within them. The truth was, all my anger, all my frustration, had only been rooted in the fact that without him, I was incomplete. In such a short time, Will had become essential.

"I'm close," he said, his voice guttural as he pressed his face into my neck. "P-please. Oh *fuck*, Lily, I can't hold it back—"

I grasped his face, held it still and close to mine.

"Then don't," I whispered. "Let it go."

And as I kissed him, he did. A tortured, ruined groan erupted from his throat, and he collapsed over me as every muscle in his beautiful body seized. My legs wrapped around his waist, squeezing him closer, and at the end, as he gave one last push, my body finally joined him. There in the dark, under the stars and the eyes of the whole world, the friction and heat and utter angst of the moment became too much to overcome. So I didn't. I let go too.

———

SLOWLY, once we were able to pick ourselves back up, we stumbled back to my shack, grinning like fools as we hung our sopping clothes up on the clothesline and fell into bed together. It was cool and empty—I hadn't slept there for several days, a fact Will noticed when he saw none of my belongings.

He turned to me, unfazed by his nakedness as he stretched his body and yawned. "You've been staying at my house a lot."

It wasn't a question.

I shrugged as I turned out the light. "Sometimes. You knew that, though."

"I did." He rolled me back to face him. "I like it."

I relaxed and nuzzled into him. "Good."

We lay there together, breathing. I knew I should go to sleep—I had another long day tomorrow at the inn, and I needed to go to the Goodwill to get some furniture for the outer cottages. But my eyes stayed open as I sucked up the last few drops of Will's presence.

Will checked his watch. "I have about three hours, but the plane needs to take off by one if I'm going to get to the set at five."

He was going to have to leave in a few more hours, and I had never wanted him to stay more.

"There isn't a single part of you that's enjoying this at all?" I wondered.

He sighed. And there was a very long pause. My heart sank.

"There is," he admitted. "But it's—it's not the part you think."

I didn't say anything. I wanted him to talk, but I knew it had to come from him.

"The attention, the costumes, the maintenance..." Will drifted off, gesturing up and down his body irritably. "Look at me. I look like a fucking mannequin."

I giggled into his chest. Now that he pointed it out, there *was* a distinct lack of hair there. Will had never been particularly furry, but it was a little odd to see absolutely nothing.

"It's not that bad," I said.

"They waxed my chest, Maggie. I don't even want you to see me on set, when I have ten tons of makeup on. You'd probably mistake me for a Ken Doll."

"A Ken Doll? Really? Even with all that equipment you're packing? I'd at least upgrade you to GI-Joe."

Will snorted, but I could tell it was with pleasure.

"Well, maybe not Ken," he said. "He-Man. Maybe a Power Ranger. That's better."

"Much," I said. "You'll have your own action figure soon anyway, won't you?"

I was joking, but by the way his chest sank, I could tell my words rang true. And not with particularly good news.

"That's what I mean, though," he said. "That shit. It's so fake, Lil. They gotta primp me and style me and make me look...like this. So a bunch of people in China can make shitty toys for rich American kids who will look at me on screen and want to be just like an illusion that doesn't exist. And they'll sell that illusion to a hundred different audiences in a hundred different ways. Fuck..." He rubbed his face. "It's fucking chaos, is what it is. A web of goddamn lies."

We fell silent again until his heart rate calmed. Will brushed his fingertips over my shoulders meditatively, as if the motion soothed him.

"But..." I was still waiting for the part where he said what he liked.

He remained quiet for another minute or so.

"But..." he repeated. "It's...it's hard to explain."

"Try." I pressed his chest. He wasn't getting away with this.

"It's like...okay, so earlier this week, I had this monologue. This script is corny, typical superhero writing, you know? But it's not all bad. And I had to do one of the big scenes, an emotional one, where I tell the girl—"

"Amelia," I put in, ignoring the twinge in my chest at the name.

Will squeezed my shoulder. "Amy. Yeah. Well. Do you really want to hear this?"

I nodded. "I do. Keep going."

Will sighed. "Okay, so, I'm doing the scene. And in the middle of it, finally, I get totally caught up in the words. Not like *I* felt the way the character did, but I felt, I don't know, the real emotion the writers themselves had to invest in the scene to make it work. A great script does that all the way through, but it can still happen with the worst of them. Put you in someone else's mind. Make them feel *exactly* what they feel. And it's...it's addictive. Electric."

I burrowed into his chest. "I get that," I murmured. "It's the same way I feel when I hear a great piece of music."

Will hummed, gently stroking up and down my back. "I wish you could be there. I wish you could see it."

I wondered if Theo would be there. If he would show up now that he wasn't required to stay away from me, Will's contract be damned.

"Lil, what is it?" Will's uncanny ability to read my state of mind appeared yet again.

I sighed and rolled onto my back. "The hearing. It was today."

His response was immediate as he popped up onto his forearm so he could look down at me directly. "Shit, that's right. Dammit, I should have remembered. What happened?"

My face must have shadowed, because immediately, Will frowned. "What? What is it?"

I pulled my sheet tightly up around my chest, refusing to look at him. "It was...everything...e-everything was overturned."

"*What?*"

I rose to get dressed. For some reason, I didn't want to have this conversation naked. "It was the dinner in New York. The one with his dad. The fact that I was willing to sit down with him and didn't leave or call the police or anything. They took it to mean I was no longer scared that he was a credible threat, and the judge overturned the restraining order *and* the injunction."

I finished pulling on a t-shirt and a pair of underwear, then plopped down at the foot of the bed. I'd managed not to think about it all day. Will came to stand in front of me in his birthday suit, completely oblivious to the fact that looking at him like that was more than a little distracting.

But before I could reach out and distract him back, my cell phone lit up on the nightstand with a message.

Thanks for the dinner, Flower. It meant more than you'll ever know.

Slowly, almost imperceptibly, I began to shake.

Will picked up the phone and stared at it for a long time, the blue screen casting a ghostly glow across his face.

"This is from him?" he asked after a few minutes.

I nodded. "Y-yes."

"Has he been texting or calling at any other times?"

I shook my head. "N-not since the triathlon, no."

Will pulled his upper lip between his teeth and closed his eyes, like he was searching for patience with a small child. Then, without speaking, he walked outside and hurled the phone as hard as he could against the boulder outside my front door.

"Hey!" I cried out, jumping to the door.

"I'll buy you a new one," he cut back. "With a new number too."

He pushed by me into the shack, then snatched his underwear off the floor and shoved them back on before he grabbed my empty duffel in the corner and started throwing whatever small belongings he saw into it.

"Will, what are you doing?"

"Packing."

"Why?"

He stopped. "Maggie, you can't possibly think it's safe for you to stay here with that maniac stalking you. You're coming with me to LA."

"What?" I sighed and flopped down on the bed. "Will, it's fine. It was just a text."

He looked at me like I was missing a bunch of brain cells. "Baby, I saw the look on your face when you thought he was in that crowd waiting for you. When you saw him sitting at the table. And don't forget, Lil, I've been in your shoes. It's *never* just a text when it comes to a fucking stalker. Especially one who did what he did."

"Will, I can't leave my mom here again. Look at what happened when I was gone!"

"That's not what I'm suggesting."

"What, then?"

Will stopped, duffel in hand. "Where's Ellie tonight, Lil?"

I swallowed. "You know where she is."

"It's getting worse, isn't it? Every time I ask you that, you say the same thing. Curly's. Some bar. Out with her friends. She's a fifty-something woman who lives like she's twenty-one. What the hell is that?"

I punched lightly into a small throw pillow I held in my lap. "I know that. I *know* that, okay? I know that she's getting worse."

It was the first time I had admitted it out loud. Whenever Lucas gave me knowing looks or other people mentioned seeing my mom at a bar, I would only shrug, act like it was nothing. But with Will, I couldn't keep secrets like that.

"Did you tell her about the video?"

My hands stopped. "Not yet."

"Lily, why?"

Will tipped my chin up so he could look at my face. I pulled it away and stared at the pillow in my lap.

"Maggie, she needs to know. Theo could release that thing at any time. She needs to be prepared. She needs to know what her disease is going to do to her. To you."

I flopped back into my pillow. "So, what are you suggesting? Some kind of intervention?"

Will pressed his lips together. "Call it that if you want. If watching yourself give your daughter's rapist a BJ isn't a wake-up call, I don't know what is, Lil. And if she doesn't want to change after that...I don't know, Maggie. Maybe it's time to let her go."

That was the difference between us. Will had long ago reached a point in his life where he had no problem giving up on the people who truly disappointed him. Which, for him, was many. I was the opposite—I'd only had one. And I wasn't sure I'd ever be able to write off my mother.

But eventually, I nodded. This was the only path I could see forward. For me. Or for her.

Will watched me process his thoughts for a bit, then looked at his watch and tapped the screen. Immediately, a gruff, male voice came through.

"Will. You almost ready?"

"Hey, Gar. Change of plans. I'm staying here tonight. Will you guys stay in the truck, or do you want to set up a camp down here?"

I listened to him jockey for a minute with his bodyguards, who clearly did not want him staying anywhere other than a plane back to LA, but in the end, they came to an agreement, and Will turned to me with a smile.

"Now it's settled," he said. "Tomorrow, we intervene, and then we talk LA." He pulled me back to the bed and into his arms. "Tomorrow, Lil, tomorrow. We figure it out. Together."

CHAPTER FIFTEEN

At seven the next morning, there was a knock on the sliding glass door. I was sitting at the kitchen counter sipping coffee while Will was in the bathroom. Mama had never come home, and the text message from last night was still burning in my memory, though the phone itself was still in splinters outside the shack.

Will might have been furious, but I was only scared. "This isn't over," he said, again and again as he gathered me close and we fell asleep together. But really, that's exactly what I was afraid of.

The knock sounded again, and I got up and pushed back the curtains to reveal Lucas and his mother, Linda, standing behind the glass. I pulled open the door to let them in.

"She's okay," Lucas said. "At least, she was last night when she left Curly's with a friend."

Linda's mouth pressed into a thin line of judgment—clearly "friend" meant one of the male persuasion, and Linda, with her very strict, church-going moral code, definitely disapproved.

She still gave me a kiss on the cheek. "Hi, hon."

"Hey, Linda."

I looked at Lucas, who shrugged. I had only asked him to come today when I'd called on our LAN line—not his mother. As much as I liked

Linda, there was no love lost between her and my mother. Mama was grateful enough for all the times Linda had taken care of her daughter when she couldn't, but she had never appreciated the gossip that often happened afterward, usually in the church basement after services. But aside from that, there was another issue.

"Will's here," I told him as they shuffled into the house.

Lucas turned around, frowning. "I thought you said he went back to Hollywood or whatever to make that movie." His lips curled, like he felt ridiculous for saying it. It did sound far-fetched.

"I did."

Will emerged from the bathroom rolling his cuffs up, but the shirt hanging open, considering all the buttons had been ripped from it. Any other time, I might have been distracted by the muscles on display. His shirt and pants were both wrinkled after a night air-drying on the boulder next to the shack, his short hair was wet and slightly wavy on top after he had attempted to hand-comb it back into place, and a day's worth of stubble had grown out around his jaw. He looked a far sight from the near-perfection of last night. And yet, I was even more attracted to him now, after he looked like he'd been rolling on the floor all night long. His imperfections were perfect to me.

"I'm back for the day," he said as he nodded hello at Linda and Lucas. "No one knows I'm here, and I'd prefer to keep it that way, if you don't mind."

Linda gaped. "I—I won't tell a soul," she promised with star-filled eyes.

Lucas just rolled his. "Whatever," he said. "She'll show up soon. Do you have her things packed?"

I gestured toward the two suitcases I'd stacked by the door. It had been surreal, going through my mother's drawers that morning. How do you pack someone else for rehab?

We had a plan. Confront Mama with what she'd done and give her an ultimatum: come with us to LA, where we could enroll her in Betty Ford and get her the help she needed, or I would leave on my own, and I wouldn't be back until the house was dry.

"Anything less is enabling her," Will had said again and again as he'd helped me fold her clothes this morning. The suitcases were a gesture, of course—more a sign that we were serious than anything else. More than likely, she'd want to redo them, and I'd help her with that too. But anything to convey that this was it.

"You can't let her addiction control your life anymore," Will had said.

And he was right. I couldn't.

There was another knock at the door before it opened and Cathy, the owner of the local store, tiptoed in. I moved into the kitchen to pour her some coffee. Barb, Mama's best friend from down the way, was in charge of making sure she showed up after their bender last night. That was all we were expecting. We could have gotten more, but they were the only ones up this early when I'd made phone calls at 6 a.m. And besides, these were probably all the people who would care about my mother's sobriety anyway.

"Hi, honey," Cathy said as she entered.

She gave me a hug and walked right past to set a tray of cinnamon rolls on the counter. In typical Cathy fashion, she would have only been interested in Will if he had won awards catching bass.

"I brought a little nosh in case anyone is hungry," she said. "Do you have any paper towels?"

Lucas grabbed a roll.

"Damn," Will muttered as he looked on with envy. He rolled his eyes at me as I took a big bite of mine.

"Are you watching your figure or something?" Lucas joked after he swallowed.

I snorted. Will watched intensely as I licked a stray bit of frosting off my bottom lip. There hadn't been anymore time last night or this morning for us to get "reacquainted," and right now, in front of all these people, was definitely not the time.

"Don't start," he muttered as I giggled. "I've got two more months of pretending black coffee is a really big milkshake, and then I'm going to eat my weight in fries. You won't be laughing when you're grabbing my love handles in the middle of the night."

I burst out laughing even harder, much to everyone else's dismay. Really, it was more the idea that Will could ever look anything less than cover-ready that was funny. Will's face reddened, but his eyes twinkled when he looked at me over the rim of his coffee cup.

But the laughter died down quickly when the sounds of footsteps sounded on the stairs outside the house. We quieted, and my stomach, which I hadn't even realized was this clenched, softened slightly as I realized my mom was okay.

I set the cinnamon roll on a paper towel and turned to the group. Everyone wore identical expressions of nervous dread.

"Okay," I said, no longer hungry anymore. "I guess it's time."

Everyone filed into the living room and took awkward seats on the couch and chair surrounding the fireplace—Cathy on the couch, Linda in one of the armchairs with Lucas perched on the arm next to her, and Will in the other while I stood to the side. We didn't have time to get help doing this—no therapist to counsel everyone's words. We were going to speak from the heart.

The sliding glass door opened, and everyone turned to the entrance as Barb, followed by Mama, entered the house.

"For goodness' sake, Barb," Mama was saying blearily. "I would've slept right through Roy's lawn mower, and you know it. I still don't understand why we had to come home this sec—" She stopped cold when she caught sight of everyone perched in the back of the living room.

She looked exactly as I would have expected her to look after a long night out. Her curly brown hair was pulled back into a messy ponytail at the base of her neck, her jeans and rhinestone-decorated blouse rumpled. A smear of blue eyeliner made her look like she had a black eye, and her skin had that yellow, pallid sheen that came when the body was ridding itself of toxins.

"What in the..." Her eyes sharpened on me. "Maggie, what is going on here?"

I stood up, letting Will hold my hand. "Sit down, Mama. We have something to say."

"What?" Her face turned red. "What in heavens can y'all possibly have to say that's so important at seven in the damn morning?"

Linda winced at the mild profanity, and Lucas shook his head.

"Come on, Ellie," Barb said as she guided her into the room. She handed a cinnamon roll and a cup of coffee to Mama, guided her to the armchair we'd left empty, and then took a seat next to Cathy on the couch.

"Margaret." My mother's sharp brown eyes danced between me and Will for a moment before settling solely on me. "What is going on?"

I took a deep breath. Will squeezed my hand.

"Mama, we're here because we all love—"

Mama snorted. "Please. People I hardly know *love* me?"

"Love *and* care about you," I continued. "And we're worried. Mama, I can't keep doing this. I can't keep wondering, night after night, if you're going to come home alive, or with someone, or if you're going to get us both hurt. I—"

"Is that what this is? You're all here to *shame* me?" Mama set her coffee down on the floor and stood right back up. "Well, no to that. I'll say it right now: *no.*"

"Mama, please!" I begged. "Listen. Afterward, you can do what you want. But everyone here took the time out of their mornings because they have things to say. The least you can do is listen to us!"

"Ellie." Will's voice, with its quiet demand, stopped my mother in her tracks. "Please."

She turned slowly, and after a pause, returned to the chair.

"All right, then," she said with a wince—I guessed she had a headache. She look a long sip of her coffee. "Talk."

We glanced around at each other, unsure of where to start.

"Ahem." Lucas cleared his throat. "I'll–um—I'll start."

He ignored everyone's surprised faces and sent a kind look to me before pulling a crinkled receipt out of his pocket.

"Ellie," he said. "I've, um, I've known you a long time."

Mama stared at him. "Well, yes, Lucas, you have."

Lucas laid the receipt down on the coffee table.

"What's this?" Mama asked.

"It's your bar tab. From 2008."

My mouth dropped, and so did my mother's. Lucas shifted on his feet, looking nervously between me and Will.

"When I was sixteen, I fell in love with your daughter, Ellie. Everyone told me I shouldn't get involved because her mom was trouble. But I didn't care. Didn't really understand what that meant, until this night, when Maggie called me from outside Curly's, having to break our date because she'd been called to pick you up."

Mama looked around with shifty eyes. No one seemed surprised by this story but her.

"I knew what you were like, in theory. We'd all seen you have a few too many beers at picnics and things like that. But when I came to the bar to help out, that was when I really learned what it meant for Maggie."

Mama scowled. "I don't know what you're talking about."

"They wouldn't let us go," Lucas replied. "Because you owed the bar a lot of money. They said pay it, or they'd call the cops."

The room was quiet. This time, Mama didn't say anything.

"That was your tab," Lucas continued. "I drained every penny of my savings that summer to pay it off so Maggie wouldn't have to deal with Curly's suing you and contacting social services. Maggie was afraid she'd lose her home. She was afraid she'd lose her mother. I was afraid I'd lose her, so I paid it. But I wish to God I hadn't, because maybe then you would have gotten the help you needed."

He sat back down, and we all stared at the receipt. The number at the bottom stood out: over two thousand dollars in an accrued bar tab over the course of maybe two weeks. Curly's didn't let Mama rack up a tab anymore, and it was because of this.

Mama fingered the receipt for a moment, then sat back in her chair. "I'm sorry for that, Lucas," she said. "I really am. And I'll reimburse you, every penny. I swear it. You've been nothing but a help to me and Maggie here, and I don't want you to feel taken advantage of."

Lucas shrugged, and I shook my head. Obviously that point had passed long ago.

"Just get some help, Ellie," he said. "That's reimbursement enough."

The others continued, offering their stories. Barb talked about how many times she'd had to turn Mama on her side on her couch, how she was afraid to send her home because she worried she'd pass out there and die alone. Cathy told a story about picking up Mama on the side of the road, about when she hit on her husband, and another time when she puked in her car. Mama had no recollection of any of those events. Linda talked about housing me as a teenager at the inn when I didn't feel like it was safe to come home. With every story, my mother's face grew redder, her shame becoming thicker and more palpable.

Finally, everyone had taken their turns, and she turned to me. Her eyes had lost their daze. They were dull and defeated, but when they landed on me, sharpened.

"Well," she said in a voice that had completely lost its previous bravado. "Don't you have a story to tell me too?"

For a second, I wasn't sure I could do this. I wasn't sure I could break my own mother's heart. Beside me, Will took my hand and squeezed. His strength, warm and solid, flowed through me. This was for the best.

"Most of them you know, Mama," I said in a quiet voice. "Because you were there. You were there when I learned, at seven years old, how to turn you on your side so you wouldn't choke on your own vomit. You were there when I had to pretend to my second-grade teacher that the bruise on my cheek wasn't because you pushed me too hard after I spilled your coffee, but because I was clumsy walking down our stairs."

Will's hand squeezed harder as I spoke, but I kept going. There was no stopping now.

"But the biggest problem with all of that wasn't that I was hurt, or disgusted, or even ashamed of you, Mama. It was that I didn't feel safe. I had a mother who taught me that my safety wasn't the most important thing. And I believe that's the reason I was willing to put myself in other relationships where I wasn't safe either. Where I was beaten. Where I was r-raped."

I couldn't help but stumble over the last word, and stared down at my hands after catching the curious glances from the others in the room. Will knew about Theo, of course, as did Mama. But no one else did—not the full extent. I didn't have to look up to know that Linda, Barb, and Cathy had guilt written in triplicate over their kind faces. I didn't even want to know what kind of blend of disgust and anger was on Lucas's. My pain would be gossip fodder for months—but it was worth it if it woke my mother up.

"Margaret."

I looked up, and found my mother crying. For the first time in my life, she looked at me openly.

"I'm sorry those things happened to you, baby," she said as she smeared more of her eyeliner. "I am. And I love you so much. But, Maggie, you cannot blame me for your poor decisions in your life. I've made my share of mistakes, but I am not...that man."

"Mama, I didn't say that—"

"And frankly, it hurts," she continued. The tears were drying now. "It hurts that you would make that connection."

My mouth fell open. She was...was she really mad at me right now?

"Lil." Will sat forward and quietly handed me his phone.

I looked down. There was a still of a video—nothing notable, but the background was familiar. A bar. Curly's.

"What?" I shook my head. "Why do you have that on your phone?"

"It's live," Will said quietly. "Benny texted me earlier. It went live late last night."

"What is that?" Mama asked. "Are we done here?"

I turned to her, full of frustration, even a bit of fury.

"No, we're not *done*, Mama," I said. "I have one more thing for you to see."

I passed the phone to her and pressed play. No one could see the images except Mama, but the familiar sounds of her laughter filled the room.

"That's Theo, Mama," I said quietly. "You might remember him, since that's also you. And until last week, he was trying to hold me and Will hostage with this video. And for a while, we kept it back to save you because you promised to calm down. But now...now it's out there. And I'm not going to be held hostage anymore. If you—if you don't come with us to get some help...then I can't stay. N-none of us can stay any more."

At first, I thought she might agree. She looked up from the phone with tears seeping down her cheeks in dark blue currents. Her nose was red, and she held her head as if in pain. And maybe she was—she was humiliated and astonished, I thought. I hoped.

"Still think there's no connection?" I asked softly, hoping to God she'd say no. That she'd see she needed help. That she'd let me help her get it.

But then she said what, in my heart, I knew it still might come down to.

"Go." Her voice was low, ragged from drink and shame. She tossed the phone back at me as Theo's laughter and her own grotesque noises bounced off the walls. "Get out. All of you. You think you can come in here, humiliate me, and I'll roll over and take it?" She looked up, and her big brown eyes, the same she had given to me, seemed sharp as knives. "And you. Get the hell out of my house. Now."

I stood from my chair, hands reaching out. "Mama, please! Don't you see that you need help? I can't—Mama, I can't be here if you keep going like this—"

"THEN GET OUT!" she shrieked, jumping from her seat and tossing her arms around like a mad woman. The rest of us scattered like seagulls, funneling quickly to the front of the house even as we cried our arguments.

"Come on, Ellie," Lucas tried.

"Eloise, *really*, now—"

"Honestly, Ellie, just listen—"

"No, no, no, no, *NO!*"

As soon as we were all shuttled out the front door, Mama slammed it shut and pulled the blinds. We stood there, the six of us, listening awkwardly as she stomped around the house. There was another slam of a door, and then silence.

From somewhere in the trees, an osprey cried. Will gathered me close and pressed his mouth into my hair.

"I'm sorry," he murmured, again and again. "So fucking sorry."

I said nothing as my tears steadily flowed and my throat closed completely.

"You can't help someone who doesn't want to be helped," Barb said behind me. "Honey, you did all you could do. And now we have to be good on our word. That's what's best for her."

I pulled away, wiping my wet cheeks. Everyone had the same resigned expressions. They knew it was over. Maybe none of them had believed it would work in the first place.

I turned to Will. "Okay," I said softly. "Let's go."

There wasn't anything to bring. All of my things were at his house, and his bodyguards had been sent to retrieve them during the night. We followed Lucas, Linda, Barb, and Cathy up the stairs, all of us moving much more slowly than was necessary. At the top, without a single glance at Will, Lucas tugged me toward him and enveloped me in a massive hug.

"I'm sorry it didn't work, Mags," he said, unwilling to let go just yet. Lucas knew my struggle with my mother better than anyone.

"I know," I said, hugging him back. "I know."

"I'm sorry," he whispered. "So freaking sorry that happened to you."

I didn't have to ask what he was talking about, any more than I needed to wonder if he would ever look at me the same way again.

Lucas released me with watery eyes. "Good luck, Mags."

I exchanged hugs with everyone, and one by one, they left, driving back to their lives with knowing looks on their faces.

"Ready?" Will asked. He wasn't saying anything, but I knew we needed to go soon. He was supposed to be back on set hours ago. Being here, he was risking his professional reputation, not to mention Max del Conte's ire.

I nodded. "Okay."

We got into the car, and I rolled down the back window one last time to look over the property. For better or worse, it would always be my home on some level. This wasn't how I wanted to say goodbye.

"Margaret, wait!"

The car stopped, and I looked through my tears to find Mama at the top of the stairs.

"Wait," I croaked to the drivers. "P-please wait for her."

Finally, she had come to her senses. I knew she would. I knew it wouldn't be for nothing.

But then I saw that she wasn't holding anything. Not a purse. Not a bag. Nothing.

She approached the window and set her hands on the ledge.

"This is really how it's going to be?" she asked as she wiped a tear under one eye. The movement smeared her blue eyeliner even more than it already had been. "You're gonna take off again? Seems that's all you really know how to do anymore."

My heart broke. It tipped off the lonely ledge where it had been perched since I was a girl and broke clean in half.

"I can't—" I shook my head, struggling to get the words out. "I can't let you do this to me anymore, Mama. You—"

"Lily." Will took my hand, beckoning me back.

"You're gonna leave your own kin. Your own *blood* for some stranger you barely know?" She gestured rudely at Will, glaring at him over my shoulder. "If you think a man is going to save you, Maggie Mae, you're even dumber than your mama."

And for a moment, I understood. All my doubts about Will and me bubbled up, and I wondered, as I had days before, whether she was right. Maybe this was where I belonged. Maybe I was no better than her, like everyone had always said.

But then she leaned in, and I could smell the stale alcohol that tinged her breath. I could see how stained her teeth had become, the paper-like quality of her skin, the way her choices had taken a toll on her life, physically and mentally, and now, more than ever, were taking their toll on mine.

I couldn't let her do it.

Maybe I wasn't the bright-eyed eighteen-year-old I'd been when I left the first time. And maybe I wasn't full of the bravado I'd had at twenty, when I promised her once before that I'd never come back unless she was sober. I knew even less now what my life had in store for me.

But I didn't want to be her. I didn't want to be trapped by her. And if I stayed here, that's exactly what would happen.

I wasn't looking for Will to save me. He was helping me save myself.

So I leaned out the window, and for a moment, clasped my hand to her face, my lips to her cheek.

"Good luck with the house, Mama," I said. "When it's dry...I'll come back."

"Margaret!"

But her cries were swallowed as I closed the window.

"Go, guys," Will ordered, and with a rumble of dust, we were on our way.

CHAPTER SIXTEEN

I drove away from Newman Lake and into a new life. A completely new world.

A private plane with butter-soft leather seats.

A luxury SUV at a private airfield near Malibu.

And Will. It seemed like the closer we came to the low, concrete skyline of Los Angeles, the more he closed down again. He hadn't spoken much on the flight, consumed with reviewing lines for the scene he was supposed to be filming that evening. The director had apparently scrambled the schedule to keep up their pace around his absence, but it meant that Will had a new call time later that night.

"It's all on the soundstage," he said when I asked if the time of day mattered. "It might mean paying the crew some overtime, but I doubt the studio cares about that more than going even further past the original schedule."

I nodded. I didn't mind the idea of having a bit of time to myself anyway. I'd been quiet through the fight too, content to watch the clouds for two hours, listen to music, and put the morning's events aside. If I squeezed my eyes hard enough, I wouldn't see my mother's face contorted with hurt. If I turned the music loud enough, I wouldn't hear her voice scratched with anger. Twenty-six years as Ellie Sharp's daughter had made me an expert in the art of denial. And I had one more problem to solve anyway: what the hell I was going to do with myself once we were in LA?

"I'll drop you at the hotel first," Will said as we sped along the 101. We zoomed past Studio City (so said the signs) and eventually got off at an exit in what he said were the Hollywood Hills.

I was too entranced with the new scenery to reply. Though I had spent a bit of time touring up and down the East Coast, I had never been to Los Angeles, or even California.

"Look," Will said, pointing up the hill from Mulholland Drive.

"Holy shit!" I crowed when the Hollywood sign came briefly into view. The pair of security guys in the front seats chuckled.

I turned to Will. "Aren't you glad to be back here? Even a little? LA is pretty iconic."

The sun shone through the window, lighting up Will's face maybe more than he would have wanted. He leaned away, despite the fact that the tinted windows obscured him completely to the few people on the street.

"I..." He rubbed his face. "I like the work all right. I always did, even when I was a kid. I don't think Dad would have let Mom drag me around to all those auditions, put me up for shows if I didn't. It was fun, you know, pretending to be other people. Kind of like playing make-believe when I was little."

I smiled. "Well, I'm glad of that, at least. You're so talented."

Will looked at me with pinked cheeks. "Please tell me you haven't watched any of my films."

I grinned wider and nuzzled into his shoulder. "Only every single one. Twice. I probably watched *The End Zone* about five times, actually. You're a great leading man, especially when you're wearing really tight pants that show off your—"

Will slapped a hand over my mouth and pulled me under his arm, then proceeded to tickle me mercilessly. His bodyguards chuckled while I broke down in hopeless giggles.

"Stop!" I shrieked. "It's not my fault you have dreamy bedroom eyes and abs for days, Mr. Sexiest Man Alive!"

The security team started laughing openly.

"Ain't that the one where you play the has-been quarterback who chases the weather girl?" one of them asked.

"She was a reporter," I corrected him when Will released me only to flop his arm over his face. "And he was *soooo* dreamy. I really liked the part where you swept her into your arms and carried her to the top of the Empire State Building."

"That's right, that's right. I just remember the goatee. You made a chin strap look all right for a white boy," joked the driver. The other giant next to him guffawed.

"Shut up, Hakeem," Will called, but they only laughed harder.

"Seriously, though," I continued. "What was with the kiss at the end? All that lead-up, and then a closed-mouth peck. I know how you kiss, babe. That was like watching two fourth-graders."

"The truth?" Will asked.

I nodded, and up front, Garrett and Hakeem quieted.

Will shrugged. "She had bad breath. She had eaten a bunch of onions before coming on set."

My mouth dropped as the men up front erupted all over again.

"Are you *serious*?" I yelled with a punch to his shoulder. Will was actually red in the face, but grinning, like he was trying to hold back his laugh.

"Yeah, yeah, yeah," Will said. He slouched back into his seat, but the dimple still apparent in his cheek told me he was already more relaxed than he'd been the entire flight. He gave me a dirty look that made me start giggling all over again. "I should French-kiss my co-star just to get back at you for watching that garbage. All the tongue I can muster up."

At that, I stopped laughing, and eventually, so did Garrett and Hakeem. An awkward silence descended.

"Hey," Will said. He sat up and laid a hand on my knee. "Lil, I was joking. Come on, I would never do that."

"But, you will have to kiss her."

It wasn't really a question. Will had already confirmed there would be some kind of love scene with his ex-fiancée, Amelia Craig. And since I'd be watching the film, I'd have to watch that too.

Before he could answer, the SUV pulled to a stop. Hakeem punched a code into a keypad, and in front of us, a large white gate swung open onto a private drive that wound farther up the canyon.

"Lil, you don't need to worry about that," Will said. "I promise. *I'll* eat the bag of onions before that scene. You can feed them to me yourself."

I smirked. "You promise?"

Will grinned. "You bet," he whispered in my ear.

We rode a little longer in awkward silence, until I caught the driver peering at me curiously.

"You guys are Garrett and…" I said, realizing I hadn't been at all introduced to the people who had shadowed Will to Washington and back.

"Hakeem, ma'am," said the driver with a tip of his fingers and pleasant, gleaming eyes through the mirror. "You'll be seeing us around a lot."

"Garrett and Hakeem are the security the studio is paying for while I'm here," Will said. "Sorry, I should have introduced you earlier."

"Yeah, he's rude like that," Garrett said with a grin.

"But you were in New York, too, though," I said. "I recognize both of you." I frowned. "And there was a third guy."

"Benny made sure I got to choose my own security as part of my rider," Will said. "But the studio would only cover two."

"You make it sound like 'Keem and I can't handle your business," Garrett joked. "Because tailing your mopey ass between the studio and your house is so damn hard." He winked at me. "I hope you're gonna give us a little more to do, Ms. Sharp."

Despite Will's groan, I couldn't help but smile. "I'll, um, see what I can do."

The SUV stopped outside a broad white stucco house.

"Come on, Lily pad," Will said. "We're here."

Garrett and Hakeem brought my things in the front door, then came back out as Will took my hand and helped me out of the back seat.

"We'll be in the car," Garrett said knowingly. "But Trish said four o'clock."

Will scowled at the mention of his mother's name.

"I thought she wasn't dealing with this," I said.

Will shook his head. "She's not. But my mother manages to get her fingers into everything. I'll have to call Benny." He turned to Garrett. "Couple of minutes."

He guided me into the house with a hand on the small of my back, and I was ready to interrogate him more about that kiss until I saw exactly what was waiting for me inside.

I stopped short as Will shut the door behind us. "Holy shit."

There was a soft chuckle behind me.

I whirled around. "I thought you said we were going to a hotel."

Will tossed his keys on a marble-topped console with bright blue legs. He looked around sheepishly. "It is a hotel. Sort of. It's a short-term rental."

I looked around, then stopped as I caught the view through the floor-to-ceiling windows at the back of the living room. They looked out onto an impossibly green backyard, full of blooming flowers and weeping vines. "It's nicer than any rental I've ever seen."

In a second, I was wrapped in his arms again, his chin resting on my shoulder while we looked out at the yard together.

"The studio owns it. They offered it to rent, and I said yes. It's private, includes security, and gives us a few thousand square feet where you and I can pretend this litter box of a city doesn't exist." He turned me around so we were facing each other. "Would you like me to ask for some shitty cell block in West Hollywood, Lily pad?" he asked. "Would you be more comfortable some place where the blinds are shut?"

I was taken back to the day spent looking at apartments in New York. They *had* all felt like boxes, even the last one on Central Park. All with windows that would have had to be covered. This one looked out onto a beautifully landscaped yard, beyond which I could see the purple-hued sides of the canyon. The house was surrounded on all other sides by acacia, palms, and brilliantly flowering bougainvillea toppling over a well-hidden wall. Anyone who could take pictures through that would have to be a magician.

I wound my hands around Will's back and tipped up on my toes to kiss him. "It's great. Thank you."

He returned the kiss with something much more promising, but right when I was ready to ask for a tour—specifically to the bedroom—Will stepped back.

"I really wish I could give you a tour, but I do have to get to the studio. The director is about to have a meltdown, and I'm pretty sure that Benny is going to fly out here himself next to make sure Max doesn't sue me for breach of contract." He rolled his eyes, then gave me another quick kiss before pressing a set of keys in my hands. "There's a rental car for you to use in the garage, but make yourself at home. I'll get a break for dinner if you want to come by the set."

I nodded. "I'd like that. I'd love to see where you're working."

Again, there was another eye roll, but this time Will flushed slightly —maybe even with pleasure.

"I'll have one of the guys pick you up around six." He stamped another quick kiss on my lips, and with a regretful look, he left.

I turned to the big house that was suddenly at my disposal. For a moment, I didn't know what to do. I wasn't even sure I could move for fear of screwing something up.

But then I saw the first sign of Will: a worn flannel shirt hanging over the back of a stool in the kitchen. Like a bloodhound drawn to a scent, I beelined for it, picked it up, and buried my nose in the soft fabric. I'd seen Will for less than twenty-four hours, and half that time had been spent plotting an ill-fated intervention for my mother.

The wounds of that failure ached, and I missed Will all over again. The quiet of the last several hours had been necessary, but soon I would be ready to talk. I'd want to process everything that was happening to us. I'd want to figure out where this life was going. Who this man I was with *really* was.

Soon, I reminded myself. He'll be back soon.

And until then, I needed to bide my time and try to be a little more patient.

I walked through the house, exploring the place that Will had been calling home for the last few weeks. House seemed like such an ordinary word; this place was incredible. Much like Will's house at the lake, the living area, dining room, and kitchen all flowed together in one seamless space, spreading outside through retractable walls that opened directly onto a lagoon-like patio. Outside, I found a pool, Jacuzzi, an outdoor kitchen, and alfresco dining area. As I wandered around the house, I quickly realized that the backyard was actually the focus of the entire property, as all of the bedrooms opened onto it with their own retractable walls.

The space, the privacy—I understood why Will needed that part of it. But the rest of the house was so unlike him. It was mostly stark and white, decorated with sudden bright colors, like the midcentury chartreuse couch or the magenta dining table, alongside sleek modern touches like the Lucite chairs or bright brass platform beds. Beautiful, yes. Accessible, no. The Will I knew liked comfort over everything else, and I was afraid to touch most of the things here.

It was in the final bedroom, though, that I finally discovered other signs that Will actually lived in this house—enough that I actually relaxed a bit. There was a computer and a bunch of papers cluttering the desk on one side, a walk-in closet that was empty except for a suitcase that was clearly being lived out of, and a shirt and a pair of pants—previously worn—that had been slung over the bed.

Without thinking, I slipped off my shoes and took a running jump into the bed, scooping up his clothes and squeezing them to my chest as I buried my face in his pillow. I inhaled—there it was, that clean, familiar scent of him. Water. Greenery. Man. Will.

I closed my eyes and continued breathing it in. Though it made me long for the real thing, the scent of him also provided a certain comfort. Outside, the trickle of the pool fountain almost made me believe I was back home, asleep in Will's bed or in the shack while the water lapped on the banks outside my window. And eventually, with that sweet refrain in my ears and Will's clothes in my arms, I drifted off to sleep.

CHAPTER SEVENTEEN

A t six o'clock, after I'd slept for two hours, gone for a dip in the pool, and was thinking about taking the Tesla in the garage out for a spin tomorrow, there was a knock at the door. I found Garrett standing outside, twirling another set of keys in his hand.

"Dinnertime?" he asked.

It took about fifteen minutes to drive to the studio lot, where I handed over my ID with wide eyes to a security guard and was then driven through New York, then the Wild West, and eventually out of a manmade jungle toward a row of giant hangars lined up at the far end of the lot. A cluster of trailers stood together near one of them, while on the other side, several people loitered around what looked like the smashed top of a high-rise building.

"That's the set for next week," Garrett said, pointing at the skyscraper. "They're shooting the finale. Loads of pyrotechnics, from what I hear." He grinned gleefully.

Garrett parked next to the trailers, then escorted me past a hum of people toward a smaller building marked "Stage 6," which looked more like a motel, with two floors of doors facing outward in an L-shape.

"This way," Garrett said as he led me up the stairs. "I think he's in choreography right now. That's down here in 6F."

Most of the doors were closed, and one even had a red light blinking outside that indicated someone was filming, or at least recording, inside. A few other rooms were open, two in which there seemed to be active construction, another containing racks and racks of costumes, another plain room where a few people stood around a table gesturing at what looked like a script. One or two looked up when we passed, but no one paid me much attention.

"In here." Garrett opened the door of 6F and we walked into a sizable room that was almost fully padded on the floor, walls, and even parts of the ceiling. In one corner, most essential equipment was set up for a gym —there for the use of the actors, it looked like, to train when they weren't filming. In another corner, several men were hitting each other against the thick pads while being directed.

"No, no, stop!" called out a little man.

The group fell apart as he walked to the center, where he leaned down to help someone up in the middle: Will.

"Listen, mate, you've got to get that elbow up at the end," said the shorter man in a thick Australian accent. "That's Matt's cue to bounce, and if he can't see it, he keeps going like a bull. That's why he knocks the wind out of you, and if that happens on film, you can't say your lines. And we all know that Corbyn'll have my head if he can't get your sweet voice on camera."

There was a trickle of laughter around the room. Will grinned and shook his head, which was coated with sweat.

"Okay, okay," he said. "I get it, Dom. One more time?"

There was a collective groan around the room.

"Let's break for dinner first," the man called Dom said with a smirk when he realized I was there. He looked around to all of the guys. "Thirty minutes? We gotta have this ready for tomorrow, guys. We're close, but not there yet."

There was a murmur of assent, and then everyone broke off, some jogging out of the room with a curious glance my way. Will traded a few more words with Dom until he looked up and found me. I gave a shy wave. His smile bloomed.

"Lil, come here," he called, waving me over.

"Thanks, Garrett," I said. The big man nodded and took a seat in the corner.

"Lil, this is Dominic, our fight choreographer. He's the one responsible for making sure I don't break my nose. Dom, this is my girl, Maggie."

"Well, if this bastard could figure out how to find his mark, I wouldn't have to work so hard," Dominic said good-naturedly. He shook my hand with a kind smile. "Nice to meet you, love."

I smiled and nodded shyly. "Nice to meet you too. That, um, looked complicated."

Dominic looked back at the set of pads and shrugged. "Come back in two weeks when we do the third fight scene. That one's bound to be a doozy. Poor Fitzy here might chip a tooth."

Will grimaced slightly at the use of his stage name, but Dominic seemed to be joking.

"Lighten up, mate," he said with an elbow to Will's side. "If you can't deal with me saying that, what are you going to do at the junket, eh?"

Will rolled his eyes, but didn't answer.

"All right. I'm going to get some grub. Thirty minutes." Dom strolled off, leaving us together.

Will took my hand and leaned in for a sweaty kiss. It was disturbing how good he smelled, even covered in perspiration.

"Mmmmm," he hummed. "Damn. I *really* wish we could go home and do that a little more."

"Just that?" I joked.

I looked around, but we were alone other than Garrett, who was staring at his phone, so I reached down and squeezed Will's ass. His shorts were clinging to it in a way that was very distracting, and I couldn't help myself. Will groaned and dipped his head for another, much more involved kiss—one that quickly had me as breathless as him.

"Will?"

We broke apart at the sound of a female voice, and Will spun away slightly, though his hand kept mine in a tight clasp. A woman stood in the doorway, her hand braced on the doorframe while she perused the room with a pair of sharp blue eyes that matched her skintight dress. I knew immediately who she was. Tall, willowy, and impossibly blonde and beautiful, Amelia Craig was Will's ex-fiancée and current co-star.

Her gaze traveled over me curiously and perhaps a little cutting. Her perfectly plump lip curled as her eyes met mine.

"Well, hallo there," she said with a bright, plasticine smile over a posh British accent. I didn't know what was worse: the fact that she looked like Malibu Barbie, or that she sounded like the Queen of England. "You must be Maggie. Or shall we call you 'Lily pad'? What an adorable little name. I do hope you didn't get tangled in anything on your way here."

I swallowed, taken aback. Even though to Will, I was Lily or Lil no matter where we were, it felt strange to know that this stranger, whose history with Will went far beyond my own, knew at least some of the details of how we met.

Amelia sauntered into the room, narrow hips swaying from side to side in a pair of skin-tight black pants and a cropped shirt that showed off her enviable waistline. I looked down at my appearance: a pair of torn jeans, a simple black t-shirt, and no makeup. Why I hadn't considered getting a *little* dressed up before visiting a place where actual movie stars spent their days, I didn't know, but I was seriously regretting it.

"Hi," I said, accepting her outstretched hand. Her grip was limp, almost as if she was expecting me to kiss her hand rather than shake it. I let it go quickly. "Nice to meet you."

"You done for the day?" Will asked her.

She nodded, though her deep blue gaze lingered on me for a moment before turning to him with new vigor.

"We finished up the bits in the office. You know, the one where you're saving the world and I'm left to watch next to a computer? You're lucky that set was done ahead of schedule. Corbyn is an absolute beast about time."

"Well, that's one thing that hasn't changed."

The two of them tittered, sharing some inside joke that I clearly didn't understand.

"So, Maggie, how long are you visiting LA?" Amelia asked me.

I shrugged. "I, um, don't really know. I kind of came down last minute."

"Lil's here as long as I am," Will said. He looked down at me hope-fully. "At least, for as long as I can convince her to stay."

"Please illuminate immediately why *anyone* would need convincing to stay with you, darling," Amelia broke in.

This time, it was Will's expression that darkened. I knew what he was thinking of—their nasty breakup, the way it had been splattered all over the papers. The way Amelia had played him to the press for the good of her own career.

The thought gave me about ten more reasons to hate this woman beyond petty jealousy. But the way it clearly bothered Will got to me even more. If it was that far in the past, why did it still get under his skin?

"Well, we're so lucky you stumbled upon Will and got him out of his shell," Amelia said to me. "Honestly, we thought we'd lost him." She gazed at Will almost longingly, and if I wasn't mistaken, there was a sheen of tears in her eyes. "It really did break my heart, thinking you were dead."

Will softened a bit. "Hey, Amy. I'm okay. You know I'm sorry."

Sorry? He was *sorry*? I wondered then how many people Will had been apologizing to while we'd been apart. And how many times he'd had this conversation.

"I've missed you dreadfully, you know," she said quietly.

Will shifted uncomfortably beside me and rubbed the back of his neck. "Yeah. Well. I'm back, I guess."

"And I'm so glad for it." Her voice was breathy, soft. The kind that probably appeared in many, *many* men's fantasies.

Maybe even Will's.

I blinked, trying and failing to shake that image out of my head. If I went down that road, I already knew it would be incredibly hard to dig myself out of it.

We stood there together, the three of us, me feeling uncomfortably like a third wheel. It was very, *very* difficult not to glare at this woman, who, of course, had said nothing but nice things to me for the last few minutes. But I didn't like her. At all.

"Oh, darling, come here," Amelia said. "You're an absolute mess, you know that? Dom's working you much too hard."

She crooked her finger, and after a second, Will stepped toward her, dropping my hand. Amelia tipped up on her toes so they were face to face, their mouths only inches apart. It was all too easy to imagine them closing the gap, his full mouth pressing on hers. They looked very, very good together. Natural.

With her thumb, she wiped a large droplet of sweat from his cheek, and stepped back. "There. All better."

Will gave a tight smile, then turned around to grab a towel off a chair. In the corner, Garrett was watching the entire exchange with veiled curiosity. Amelia looked at me, deliberately stuck her thumb in her mouth and sucked the sweat off of it. My mouth dropped.

"See you around...*Lily pad*," she said with a wink, and sauntered out.

For a few seconds, I stared at the doorway, unsure if what I'd seen had really happened. Had this chick really sucked *sweat* off my boyfriend's forehead? Had he *really* not noticed?

"Hey." Will's calm timbre broke through the fury of questions spinning in my head. "You ready to eat?"

As if in answer, my stomach gave a massive growl. Will chuckled, and took my hand again.

"Come on, Lil," he said. "I might be stuck with steamed vegetables and fish for the next eight weeks, but you can take advantage of the snack table for me."

───────

FIFTEEN MINUTES LATER, we were sitting at a tiny table in his trailer, Will eating not cod, but salmon, me with a plate full of crudité and pizza.

"Not to sound super disappointed or anything, but I expected something nicer," I remarked as I looked around the trailer. "Bigger, maybe."

It was basically like the inside of a roomy RV, with a small kitchenette, a lounge area, and a bed in the back. It was a little claustrophobic, especially for someone who usually prioritized space.

Will looked around and shrugged. "Eh. I never bought my own—this is whatever my mother negotiated as part of the rider in the original contract, and Benny didn't bother to change it. At seventeen, I was just excited to have my own space."

"You didn't have a trailer before that?"

He smirked. "Not one I didn't have to share with my mom or a chaperone." He waggled his eyebrows, and I swallowed a giggle before taking a bite of pizza.

"God," Will said as he watched the cheese meet my mouth. "You're killing me with that, you know?"

I turned the pizza toward him. "Want a bite?"

Will looked pained. "I shouldn't. The call sheet has me shirtless in two weeks."

I quirked an eyebrow. "I'm pretty sure your abs could handle a slice or two."

"That's not what my trainer says. And if they aren't looking good enough by a week from Sunday, I'll be in trouble with the director too. Which means trouble with Max. He's already mad because Theo released the video."

I could sense his distress when he considered Max, and only then did I realize the real pressure he was under. Max had him by the balls, so to speak, which was the main reason Benny had argued not to report Theo for releasing unlicensed pornography. Will had done a very bad thing by shirking his contract, and it was clear that he had to deliver the goods with this movie, or else he'd never get out of it.

I pulled the pizza back. "I shouldn't tease. I'm sorry."

But before I could pull the slice back completely, Will wrapped a hand around my wrist to hold it in place, and took a giant bite with complete and utter glee.

"Ahmmmm, that's good," he moaned as he lay back on the sofa and chewed.

We continued to eat together, but something still bothered me. His call sheet was on the table in front of us—he would be filming into the night to make up for the missed scenes this morning and keep production on track. There was nothing that I could see that involved Amelia, but that didn't keep me from wondering what was next.

"Can I ask you something?" I wondered.

Will took a large bite of salad and looked up, waiting for me to continue.

"Is there—is there going to be a sex scene in this movie?" I asked. "With, um…with her?"

He set his fork down, alarmed. "Jesus, Lil. *No.* I wouldn't do that to you."

"Look, I get it. It's part of the job, so I wouldn't be surprised if—"

Will interrupted me with a hand on my knee. "It is part of the job," he said. "For some. But when I originally signed this deal with Beauregard, I was seventeen, and it was for four films over ten years. I didn't do the last one, which is why I'm stuck on this piece of garbage, but that doesn't mean I don't have rights. And one of those includes a no-nudity clause."

My jaw dropped. "Wait—but—you've done sex scenes before. You—you showed the entire world your ass in *The Playbook.*"

I couldn't lie. As pretty as he had looked in that movie, I wasn't exactly happy about watching my man parade in front of the screen naked and then crawl on top of a ridiculously gorgeous and very naked woman. The scene had faded to black, but not until after a few well-timed thrusts and some tongue-heavy kisses. Sexiest man alive indeed. I was pretty sure that one scene earned him the title.

Will rolled his eyes. "Please don't watch my movies anymore, Lil. That wasn't a Beauregard film either. And anyway, it was just an ass, Lil."

I scowled. "Yeah, but it's *my* ass. And that was *my* dick in the unrated director's cut too."

"No, it's not," he said, "because I was wearing some very sticky tape at the time and humping a pillow that put several inches between us."

I shook my head. "No way."

"Way." Will's eyes gleamed as he took a bite of fish.

"But I could totally see your—"

"Cock sock and CGI, babe."

"And what about her—"

He shook his head, then pulled out his phone, typed in a few words into Google, and then turned a photo of said sex scene to me.

"What's really embarrassing is that my junk gets forty million hits on the internet." He pointed at the picture. "That's not me; that's special effects. You know my dick is bigger than that, anyway."

I smacked him, and Will chuckled, then continued pointing things out.

"Sweat? Water and baby oil. Pubic hair? Nah, that's a merkin on top of a pillow. You can't see her nipples, but they were covered with neon-green pasties and then recreated later. And her mouth? Tasted like cigarettes and Certs." Then he pointed around the screen, outside of the frame, to people and objects we couldn't see. "Director. Continuity. Boom. Camera one and operator. Significant other. Camera two and operator. Script supervisor. Makeup. Wardrobe assistant. First AD. Second AD. Gaffer." He put his phone down. "Want me to keep going?"

I shook my head. "No, I get your point. There's a lot of people around, and most of it is fake."

"Lil, absolutely nothing about this shit is hot. I had to sit there awkwardly, almost naked, pretending to be aroused in front of about fifty other people. The only actors who really get turned on by sex scenes are probably deviants in the first place, and not in a good way."

"Okay, okay, I get it!" I pushed my food away, no longer hungry. "But look at your partner. She's still beautiful. It couldn't have been *all* bad, right?"

I knew what I sounded like: a petty little girl. But I couldn't help it.

"Hey." Will took my hands, and I had to fight not to pull them away. It didn't matter how many times he explained it, I wasn't ever going to like the fact that he was going to kiss his ex on screen.

I mashed my lips together. "I'm sorry."

Will shook his head. "If I could get out of it, I would, Lil. I swear to God, I would."

I sighed. Guilt flooded me—of course he didn't want to do this. The man had faked his own death trying to get away from this industry. And here I was, the person who had brought him right back into it, getting jealous over moments neither of us had any control over.

I placed my hands on his big shoulders and pulled him close.

"I'm sorry," I said. Will closed his eyes as I delivered a slow kiss, full of promise.

"Mmm," he hummed, leaning forward for more.

It was way too easy to forget where I was when he kissed me like that. And much too easy to consider the fact that, other than last night, we had been apart for close to a month at this point. "Will," I whispered as he started twirling his tongue under my jaw. "Will, people are going to—"

"Fuck 'em," he murmured into my lips as he pressed me back into the couch.

"Yeah, but won't they hear—"

"*Fuck* them, Lil." He kissed me again, this one full of lips and tongue and the mild threat of what he would do if I didn't stop worrying.

"Yeah, but—"

"I said, *fuc*—"

"Mr. Baker?" There was a knock at the door, and immediately, I squirmed out from under Will and to the other side of the couch while he sat up and pushed a hand through his hair with a face full of thunder.

"What?" he barked.

The trailer door opened, and the terrified face of a young production assistant popped in. "Oh, um, sorry, sir," he said, his gaze boomeranging between us. "I, um, it's your call to choreography, sir."

Will sat back on his heels and gave me a look that said, clear as day, *next time*, before turning to the PA with a nod. "I'll be right there."

He hopped off the couch and bent over to give me a quick kiss. "No rest for the wicked. I'll be home late. Don't wait up, okay?"

I nodded and scooted back to the food. "I won't," I said and watched him go with regret.

CHAPTER EIGHTEEN

Much, much later that night, after I had ventured to the grocery store, gone for an evening run, picked at my guitar by the pool for a solid hour and a half, and then gone to sleep some time past midnight, I finally felt a long, solid body slide into bed with me.

I had fallen asleep crying as the enormity of the day had finally come crashing down. The things I had done and seen. An intervention. Leaving my mother. Moving to LA. And then, of course, the drama on Will's set.

I didn't move, still half-asleep, lingering at the edge between consciousness and dreams. But a strong arm wound around my waist and pulled me into a wall of warmth, and a pair of lips nestled behind my ear, inhaling deeply.

"Mmmm," I hummed. "That feels good."

But his touch wasn't insistent the way it had been the night before or in New York. For a moment, I was taken back to the lake, to those precious, lazy days before he'd been found out, and the world consisted of us and no one else.

Will drifted a hand down the side of my body, resting a moment on my waist before dragging his fingers back up. He repeated the motion several times, lulling me back into something close to sleep. But not quite.

"Sometimes," he said, his voice coarse, like he'd been speaking for too long, "sometimes I'm still not sure you're real."

I continued to focus on the tickle of his fingernails over my ribs. We lay there together for a long time, until eventually his hand stopped and his breaths started to grow longer. And then, slowly, I turned over to find his eyes wide open, blinking into the dark.

"What is it, Lil?" he asked as his caress moved to my cheek.

I leaned into the touch. "Where...where do you see us? After all of this is over?"

"Where do I see us." He said it like a statement, almost like there was no doubt that he *did* see us—he just hadn't revealed it yet. "You really want to talk about this right now? You don't think you've had enough serious conversations for one day?"

I swallowed, but found that I did. Considering the topsy-turvy nature of my life the past few months, I needed a bit of stability. I needed something resembling a plan, even if it was only for him and me.

"I know...I know we haven't really talked about it, but—"

"Lil—"

"And obviously you're not going to be thinking long term with someone you met a few months ago—"

"*Lil*—"

"So maybe it's dumb, and I shouldn't have asked. Forget I said anything."

Abruptly, I was flipped onto my back, and Will pounced like a panther.

"Stop. Talking," he said as he framed my face with his hands. "For one second." I opened my mouth, but before I could say anything, he pressed a finger to it. "One second, Lil."

Slowly, I nodded and shut my mouth. Maybe I was worrying too much. Maybe I needed to let things unfold naturally.

Then Will leaned down and pressed his lips to mine. The kiss was closed-mouthed. Chaste. Safe.

"For the record," he said quietly, "I see the entire fucking world with you." He grazed his knuckles over my cheek and tucked a strand of my hair around my ear. "When I think about my future, I see you, and no one else."

I inhaled sharply. "Really?"

He nodded. I felt like I could dive into the warm green of his eyes.

"Like…like what?" I asked. I couldn't help it. I had so many visions that danced around in my head, but I wanted to hear his.

He hovered his mouth above mine, then over my cheeks, my eyelids, the rest of my face. "To start," he said. "I'm going to marry you. You're going to be my wife, and I'm going to be your husband, and we are going to belong to each other and no one fucking else."

Oh. I hadn't really been asking about that far in advance, but apparently Will was already heading that direction. Well, fine. I was right there with him. And I liked the sound of *no one else* very much.

"What about…what about a family?" I ventured. "Do you…do you want that too?"

I had never really considered having children before now. This moment, actually. Most of my life had been spent with a parent who didn't really know how to be one, so why would I know how to do any better? On top of that I was a starving artist, planning a career that, even if successful, would have taken me on the road for months at a time, surrounded by all manner of substances, derelicts, and environments that generally weren't good for children. Kids never seemed like they would be in the cards for me.

Until now.

The mouth edging around my jaw stilled. I turned my head, and Will pressed back up, drifting his gaze down to my flat stomach, then back up with an unreadable expression.

"What is it?" I asked. "Do you…do you not want kids?"

He sighed. "It's…complicated, Lil."

I tensed. What did that mean?

"I've thought about it," he continued as he rolled back to lie next to me on his side again. He slipped a hand over my belly and began circling my navel with his thumb. "With you. More than I should probably admit."

A golden warmth expanded in my chest.

"I can see them," he whispered. "Two, maybe three. Their hair is curly like yours, but blond like mine. One has my eyes, and the other two have brown ones, like yours. They are all kind and so damn beautiful, just like their mother. The oldest is a boy, and he's tall and looks like my dad. We'd...maybe we'd name him Michael. We'd raise them near the water, and I could teach them to sail too."

He continued to touch my stomach while I closed my eyes, imagining with him. I could see it so clearly—Will with a small, curly-haired child perched on his shoulders. One running diving off the dock at the lake while I cradled the youngest in my arms. It seemed perfect. So...right.

"But, Lil, how could I bring kids into this chaos? I can barely deal with the bastards who photograph me. I don't even want to think about what will happen when they figure out you're here. How..." He buried his face into my arm, the skin muffling his tortured words. "How could I ever allow someone like that to torment my own child?" When he looked up, his eyes were full of dread. "What kind of parent would I be if I did that?"

In that moment, I knew he wasn't only thinking of this imagined family, but of his own upbringing, at the hands of a father who was at best unnerved by his son's fame and eventually almost indifferent to it, and a mother who nurtured the frenzy despite the fact that her son clearly couldn't deal with it.

"I can't have kids, Lil," he said sadly. "As much as I might want to one day, it wouldn't be right. Because...I'll never escape this life. Not completely. Maybe it's not fair of me to ask you to endure it either. But, like you said, I always was kind of an asshole. And I can't fucking stand the thought of losing you."

I didn't laugh. For the first time, the joke wasn't funny.

"You're not an asshole," I said softly. "And also, for the record, I think you'd be an amazing father."

His eyes closed again and he exhaled, long and low. "Maybe in another life."

His tone was sad, but resolute. Well. Apparently that was it.

"Maybe," I agreed and tried to ignore the heaviness in my chest as the image of those three haloed children disintegrated. "It's not like I bring the greatest gene pool to the table anyway." After all, I came from a family full of addiction, neglect, and absence. It wasn't exactly a winning combination. Maybe this was for the best.

Will's eyes popped open. "Don't do that."

I shrugged. "Do what? It's true."

He shook his head.

When his lips landed on mine, it was a kiss intended for comfort, but the chasteness from before quickly disappeared. It was becoming clear to me that Will and I shared a common protectiveness over each other. Neither of us were willing to hear anyone talk badly about the other— even if it was ourselves.

He rolled on top of me, fitting himself between my legs. I wore only a thin camisole and underwear to bed, and as his tongue continued to probe mine, I quickly felt the evidence of his desire lower down.

"You," he said as he drifted kisses over my neck, "are not allowed to talk about yourself like that. I won't fucking have it."

"Oh no?" My voice was breathy—his tongue was doing things against my collarbone that made it hard to breathe.

One of his hands slipped down my side and yanked his briefs down, followed by my underwear. The silky length of him slipped between my thighs, rubbing against the desire he fed with each light thrust.

"No," he said as he locked a hand around my hip and tipped me to meet him. Our gazes locked, green eyes to brown, as he slowly, gently, pushed inside. He stretched my limits, inch by full inch, until he could go no further. I gasped, arching against him. I wasn't sure I'd ever get used to his size—both because of its undeniable intrusion, but also because of the way his body demanded a response from mine.

"No," he said again as he started to move. This close, his big body rubbed over mine top to bottom, sharp angles meeting soft curves, finding ways to energize that sensitive bundle of nerves between my legs from inside and out.

"Do you hear me?" he asked as he started moving faster. "You are *everything* to me, Maggie. You are amazing, in every way. You're beautiful." Thrust. "Kind." Pull. "Smart." Ache. "Talented. The full fucking package, and then some."

"Will!" I gasped as he rubbed against my clit again. My muscles squeezed, a familiar current starting to run through them.

But he didn't stop, just balanced himself more evenly with his forearms braced on either side of my head so he could kiss me, twist our tongues together, mimicking the union of our bodies lower down. Everywhere else.

"I swear to God, Lil. I'd give you everything I have in the world if it would make you happy," he groaned as he thrust even deeper, finding my limits, and, if his lack of breath indicated anything, his own as well.

I had no words by this point. When we were like this, Will consumed me. Made it impossible to speak, to think, even to feel anything but *him*.

"P-please."

He pushed up on one arm and slipped his other hand between us. His finger found my clit and pinched lightly.

"It's okay, baby," he whispered. "Let go. You're safe."

It was as if he knew exactly what I needed to hear—that curious combination of desire, fear, and safety undid me completely. I came with a loud cry, my fingers clenched in his hair as the currents inside me exploded. My body bucked with his, seizing with each thrust of his hips, flick of his fingers.

"Lily," he murmured as every muscle he had was cast into high relief. "Oh *God*, Lil."

His teeth found my shoulder, and he came in a series of loud grunts, emptying himself into me completely as my legs entwined around his waist, pulling him closer, deeper, as far inside me as he could get.

"Will," I murmured as we both slowly fell. It was the only thing I could think. The only thing I could say.

His face remained pressed into the pillow for a very long time, until slowly, he lifted himself up, though he stayed inside.

"Any man would be lucky to be the father of your children," he said, his forehead damp against mine.

I inhaled, not even bothering to wipe away the tear that trailed from the side of my eye. His admission felt like a loss—another future together we could never have.

But we did have each other. Maybe that was all we would ever really need.

"I love you," he whispered in a low, deep voice, the one that spoke to resonances within me I had never heard until then.

I sighed, letting the calm of night finally wash over me. I should have known better than to try for peace without being in his arms anyway.

CHAPTER NINETEEN

"Come on, Lil, let me see."

A few weeks later, I stood in the middle of Will's walk-in closet, hardly able to recognize myself as I stared at my reflection in the floor-to-ceiling mirror.

"I don't know," I said to Robin, the stylist sent from the studio.

We were getting ready to attend one of five separate premieres over the next year in support of one of Beauregard's movies—a contractual obligation that Benny hadn't been able to get Will out of. Apparently since Will wasn't planning to make any other movies after this, they were going to milk his reappearance into pop culture for everything it was worth. Corbyn wasn't particularly happy with the decision since they were in the middle of filming, but del Conte was adamant. Amelia's new movie, a rom-com that wasn't projected to do well, needed all the promotional boost Will's star power could give it.

The studio, of course, had wanted Will to attend with her. It would be fitting if they were seen together. "Feed the frenzy," in the words of the publicist who had come by Will's trailer the day before to brief us on the event.

Will had given her exactly one second to take it back and then told her to get the hell out of his trailer. A quick phone call to Benny ensured that *I* would be attending every one of those stupid events, or neither of us would be going at all.

"Lil!" Will called from the bedroom. "Come on, baby, you promised I could see."

I sighed and bunched my hair over one shoulder. "Fine. I'm coming out."

I stepped into the gold-heeled Jimmy Choos that Robin insisted went with the dress and walked into the bedroom, where Will was having a suit fitted by an assistant from Tom Ford. It was amazing, really, what the designers were able to do last minute when their stuff was going to be seen on the red carpet.

"Well?" I asked, spreading the blue skirt out from my knees. "What do you think?"

Will looked up, and his handsome face practically turned to ash. "What the fuck is that?"

"Mr. Baker, this is absolutely *en vogue*," Robin said as she came out behind me.

"It's also absolutely fucking see-through," Will retorted, bristling to the point that the assistant, crouched while hemming his pants, had to sit back with a mouth full of pins.

Robin sighed. "This designer is the next Balmain, and we are under orders from the studio that if Ms. Sharp is going to walk the red carpet with you, she needs to pull attention. This dress will do that. It photographs wonderfully, and the satin will positively shine under the lights."

I looked down at the dress. The delicately beaded bustier top with gold over blue satin *was* beautiful and certainly would turn heads, but considering that the knee-length skirt was indeed completely sheer, I wasn't sure it was the kind of attention I wanted. Right now you could completely see my plain black underwear, though Robin had already told me that a dark blue pair came with the dress.

"At least she's got the body for it," remarked Kelly, the seamstress on the ground. She rocked onto her knees and went back to working on Will's hems.

Will's look, also sponsored by the studio and the designers currently hurling their wares at him in hopes he'd get papped anywhere with them on, was relatively simple: an Italian cut, navy blue suit with a crisp, robin's-egg blue shirt underneath that made his tanned skin glow and his eyes look almost turquoise. It was annoying, really, that he got to go the classic route while I had to be a walking attention-seeker.

Will's eyes narrowed at Kelly, who shrank. "Maybe so. But if the studio is that insistent on getting this kind of attention, you might want to remind them about the last time I attended a premiere."

Robin cringed next to me.

"What happened?" I asked.

Will scowled. "I got mobbed. Couldn't even make it out of the car without a super-sized dose of quaaludes, which basically made me the worst interview on the face of the planet. So maybe they should dial back, eh?"

I had no problem with that. I turned to Robin. "Is there anything to try that's maybe a little less…revealing? A little more, I don't know…classic?"

Robin looked me up and down for the millionth time that afternoon. "Kelly, finish picking up Mr. Baker's hemlines, all right? I'm going to make sure Ms. Sharp gets exactly what she needs."

I was spun back into the closet and told to stay still while Robin figured out a new game plan.

"Classic, huh?" she said as she flipped through the clothes on the rack she'd brought with her. "Well, we can't be too plain, you know. You're the arm candy. We want something that pops in photos. So… yellow, no, that's a finicky color, and we don't have time to find the right shade. Red is boring—and I think Ms. Craig is wearing red anyway. Black's out…"

"Why's black out?" I asked.

Robin turned to me with bored eyes, as if I should know the answer. "It doesn't photograph well unless you've got a dramatic cut. Texture, fabric—none of it shows at night with a heavy camera flash. We need color and contrast, and since your skin is a little darker…" She flipped her finger up and down my body, which *had* gotten a bit darker after a month spending half my days by the pool. "Classic? I'm thinking a fantastic summer white."

She yanked out a dress and hung it in front of the others before turning to help me out of the sheer monstrosity.

"I have a feeling about this one," she said. "Just you wait."

———

FOUR HOURS LATER, after Will had gone back to the studio to rehearse a big action scene they were filming later that week, and I had spent most of my afternoon being primped and prodded into oblivion by Robin and her team, I was waiting in the kitchen, standing awkwardly and as still as possible so I wouldn't ruin the "look" that Robin had so assiduously put together. So long as the dress wasn't overly revealing, I trusted her judgment completely, and over the course of four hours, we developed a rapport together I liked a lot. But it was really hard not to ruin it. I desperately wanted a cup of coffee, but was terrified of spilling anything on the sleek white fabric.

Robin was a pro, and after styling half of Hollywood's elite for the last ten years, she had a lot of tips and tricks for me on my first red carpet. I wasn't scared—okay, I was, but not *really*. I'd been on stage plenty of times in the past, and this didn't require anything more than stepping and stopping while Will answered all the questions.

But it was our final chat that put the fear of God in me.

"There," she said as she made the finishing touches on my hair, which had been styled in its natural curls with a bit of added volume, draped over my shoulder in a loose ponytail. "This is going to work. Amateur, my ass."

"What's going to work?" I wondered. "Who's an amateur?" Robin seemed like the picture of professionalism to me.

Robin froze, clearly caught in something she shouldn't have been saying in the first place. I watched as several thoughts clearly flew across her face. And in the end, she settled on candor.

"They're waiting for you to fail," she said as she went back to doing my makeup.

I balked. "What? Who?"

Robin shrugged as Kelly gave her an incredulous look from where she was steaming Will's clothes that would be brought back to the studio.

"What?" she said. "It's the truth."

"Well, yeah," Kelly mumbled, turning back to the clothes. "But that doesn't mean you have to say it."

"Shit," Robin swore when my face must have bloomed red. "Now, don't get all riled up about it. You'll ruin your makeup. That's the nature of this town, you know. Everyone is waiting for someone else to fall on their face so they can use them as a stepladder."

I took deep breaths and tried to remain still as she finished her work. But in the end, my curiosity got the better of me. "Who?"

Robin shrugged. "Oh, no one in particular."

"Robin, come on," Kelly said.

Robin pressed her lips together, then sighed. "All right, fine. You might want to know that the blue dress was suggested by Amelia Craig. I don't know why. I don't know how. But she recommended it to us, and the studio endorsed her decision." She shrugged. "Honestly, it would be a great dress with a bit of lining. We just didn't have time to do that."

I was much too incredulous to think about dress lining. "Why would she do that?"

Over the last several weeks, my relationship with Amelia had been mostly cordial. Conscious of my misgivings about her, Will regularly invited me on set, especially when they had scenes together, but after seeing for myself that Will was nothing but professional with her, and she with him, I had started coming less and less frequently. I didn't want to babysit Will anyway. I wanted to trust him.

Robin shrugged as she pulled out a tube of lip gloss. "Listen. It doesn't really matter. What matters is this." She stepped aside so I could view the total transformation she'd engineered in the giant mirror over the sofa.

"Oh, Robin. It's…"

"Fucking amazing, I know. This is the best way to show those bitches up. They wanted you to arrive looking tacky, but we made you look like a billion dollars instead. You and Mr. Baker are going to look fan-fucking-tastic together, and every reporter there is going to be asking, 'Amelia who?'"

———

As I walked outside to wait for the SUV to arrive that would take Will and me to the screening, I wasn't so sure that was the question I wanted. Shouldn't I have gone for something more sedate? Something a little less attention-seeking, despite what the studio said?

Or maybe I shouldn't have been going at all.

Before I could consider abandoning the night, the familiar Yukon rumbled up the driveway, and through the front window, I could see Garret and Hakeem's faces brighten with surprise.

"Hey!" Garrett shouted as he jumped out. "Somebody cleans up nice."

But before Garrett could open the back door, Will was stepping out, looking, for the first time since I'd ever met him, every inch the movie star he really was. His suit fit immaculately, the blue shirt popping the same color as the sky. His blond hair shone like a mop of gold that matched the gold-trimmed aviators perched over his knife-straight nose and the delectable gold stubble that glimmered over his jaw in the sunshine. He was worlds away from the scruffy, unkempt stranger I'd met on the hillside. I paused, unsure.

And then he took off his sunglasses, and he was my Will again.

"Holy shit," he murmured as he looked me over. "Woman. Jesus. Are you trying to kill me?"

I bit my lip, peering down at the sleek white dress that Robin had picked out. It was about as simple as it got, a dusky silk slip dress that floated over my curves like rain, with whisper-thin straps over my shoulders, and a bias-cut skirt that ended at my knees. I had kept the gold-heeled Jimmy Choos and wore only a thin gold chain around my neck and delicate hoop earrings that Robin had also provided to match a small gold clutch. After hours of primping and polishing, I looked more put together than I ever had in my life. And also felt more terrified.

But when I looked up again to find Will's warm gaze floating over my body, the fear dissipated a little. After all, I wasn't alone in this. And neither was he.

"It's not see-through," I murmured with a shy smile.

He shook his head. "That's not what's going to kill me, Lil. You look incredible."

"You don't look so bad yourself," I said as I walked to the car.

Will took my hand and pulled me close.

"'Taffeta, darling'?" he murmured when I offered my cheek instead of my lips for him to kiss.

I smirked at the familiar Monty Python quote. "I figured you wouldn't want lip gloss on your collar. Robin worked hard on all of this, you know."

For that, my jaw was firmly clasped and turned so that I was looking straight at Will. He stamped a brief, thorough kiss on my lips that took my breath away.

"These lips are mine, Lil," he growled. "Not Robin's. Not any stuck-up designer's. *Mine*."

And as he kissed me again, every inch of polish and sheen fell away to reveal the raw, primal man I had known from the beginning. Apparently dressing up brought out Will's possessive side. Well...I couldn't say I was totally disappointed.

———

WILL WAS quiet as we drove through Los Angeles, and the silence was instead filled by a girl named Gail, another assistant sent from the studio to help us through the process, and likely, to help maneuver Will through awkward situations.

"Gosh, you're pretty," she said again as Garrett turned down Hollywood Boulevard, coming to a stop behind the long queue of cars in line for the arrival. "They really did not tell me you were so pretty."

"Um, thanks," I said. I wasn't sure what to make of her surprise. Instead, I looked out my window toward the growing crowds. "Is the street closed?"

Gail nodded. "Oh, yes. That's pretty standard for a premiere of this size. I mean, it's not an Oscar contender or anything, but the fact that Fitz was coming and he and Amelia are filming together right now is a big deal."

Next to me, Will shuddered at the use of his stage name. I wondered why he kept allowing people to use it if he hated it so much.

"All right. Fitz, Maggie, here's how it will work," Gail said, chipper and oblivious to her client's irritation. "Garrett pulls up the car, and you let Hakeem get out first. The event planner didn't do a very good job of blocking the drop off, so the fans have been a little crazy. There are a few police officers there, but Hakeem will help you through. Once he gives the okay, I'll open your door to let you two out. Come out, wave at the fans, smile. Then step and repeat, and after that I'll escort you to the media outlets that Beauregard is prioritizing for this campaign. Sound good?"

"Do we have leashes too?" Will asked.

Gail blinked. "I'm sorry?"

I chuckled, trying to make light of the comment even though Will's mouth was pressed into a firm scowl. "He's joking. So that's it? Follow you around and we're good?"

Gail grinned. "That's it!"

A roar sounded from down the street, signaling that another big name had arrived. Will hunched down into his seat.

"We're two blocks out," Garrett spoke into his Bluetooth headset.

"Who's that?" I wondered aloud.

Hakeem turned around. "Head of security. Takes a lot of people to put on one of these things. There's usually a lot of dudes like us to make sure the fans don't get out of hand."

He looked forward, where the crowds along the street and sidewalk were getting big enough that several of the police detail had been engaged to make sure everyone kept their distance. We slowed down, stopping and starting behind a few cars as other premiere attendees got out at the roped-off entrance of the red carpet. It was set up to run alongside the theater for a solid block before the actual entrance to the building. The walls of the theater had been painted a bright red, matching the overall color scheme of the film, and several massive movie posters and graphics lined the wall for the celebrities to pose against as they made their way slowly in front of the line of reporters and photographers.

I stared out my window at the scene ahead. The long red carpet was dotted with various people dressed up as much as we were. Some were celebrities I recognized—B- or C-level stars with recognizable faces who likely played supporting roles in the movie at hand or who were there for the exposure. Behind them were the fans—the ones who screamed loudly every time a new celebrity exited their car. Spotlights shot up into the air, crisscrossing here and there while loud music pounded down the boulevard. The whole thing was chaos.

"Looks like it's going to be a good one," Gail said. "Tricia said Amelia brought out the entire cast of her last film too." She looked back at Will. "But they're all waiting for you, you know."

She said it like it was a compliment, but Will just stared fixedly at the floor of the car. You would have thought he was getting ready to jump out of a plane without a parachute rather than meet his adoring fans.

"Will," I said. "Are you okay?"

I reached out tentatively to touch his shoulder and was surprised when he snatched my hand and squeezed it tightly with both hands, forcing me to scoot across the car next to him.

"I fucking hate these things," he said, still studying the floor mats.

"Okay, we're next," Hakeem announced as the car pulled forward and then stopped at the theater entrance. He put on a pair of sunglasses, likely to ward against the constant glare of flash photography. Then, after he got out and scanned the crowd, he turned back to the car and opened our door. Gail hopped out and gestured to me.

"This way!" she said.

I slipped out, grateful that most people still didn't seem to know who I was. The photographers looked away, bored already with me, which gave me a second to process where I was. The crowds. The lights. It felt like this small city block existed in a whole other dimension. This wasn't reality, it was some imaginary space called Hollywood.

I turned back to the car, ready to take Will's hand. I couldn't walk this by myself—we were in it together.

But no one emerged from the car.

I stepped back to the open door and found him still sitting, frozen in place as he stared blankly out toward the wall of cameras.

"Will?" I called, holding out my hand.

My voice was mostly swallowed by the hysteria behind me. I glanced worriedly toward Garrett, who shrugged. There was a long line of cars behind us, all carrying other attendees for the screening. The next driver glared at me.

I got back into the SUV. "Babe. Hon. We have to get out now. We're holding up the line."

I'd read about this in the many, many articles about the "dead" Fitz Baker. That he was terrible with the press. That he was increasingly surly and arrogant the more his fame grew. That he'd suffered from debilitating social anxiety, and in the end had been heavily medicated for it. For the first time, I could see why.

I set a hand on his shoulder, and pressed harder when I found that he was shaking and his breath sounded forced. Will pulled off his sunglasses and closed his eyes.

"We should go," he said. "Max can sue me if he wants. I—they can't see me like this."

I glanced out toward the crowd, all of them peering eagerly toward us to see what the holdup was. There was nothing I'd rather do than shut the door and tell Garrett to keep driving.

But I remembered that nasty look on Max del Conte's face at the idea of ruining Will's future. Like he almost looked forward to that as much as he wanted the money Will's star power could undoubtedly earn. No. I wasn't going to let him get the satisfaction.

"What can I do?" I asked hurriedly, rubbing my hands up Will's arms, face, neck—anything I could possibly think of to mitigate this panic.

My touch seemed to work. Will fixated on my fingers as they encircled his wrists; his breathing regulated a bit when I pressed his face into my neck.

"What helps?" I asked again as I wove my fingers through the hair at the base of his neck.

"You do," he whispered. "Oh, God. You do, Lil."

After another minute or two, long past the time the cars behind us had started honking their horns, Will sat up and straightened his shoulders.

"I'm okay," he said with a long exhale. "I can do this." His shoulders were still shaking slightly and his eyes were wide, but he nodded. "Let's go."

I stepped out of the car, and he followed me

"Lil," he called as the roar from the crowd went up.

I turned around to find him staring right at me, like the crowd and the cameras and the lights and the music didn't exist. "What is it?" I called back, straining my voice to be heard.

Will gulped and reached for my hand. "Don't let go."

CHAPTER TWENTY

"Salmon puff?"

I turned around to find a waiter holding up a tray of hors d'oeuvres with toothpicks. Eagerly, I grabbed one, popped it in my mouth, and snatched another. After the red carpet and sitting through the two-and-a-half-hour movie, I was famished.

Walking past the wall of fans and paparazzi flashes had been the worst part. My vision still hadn't returned a hundred percent, and their screams rang in my ears for hours. Somehow Will had forced himself to smile and wave, following Gail's guidance to step and repeat again and again until she had deemed the photographers had enough shots. I was pretty sure I would come out looking like a deer caught in headlights, but Will had plastered that same smile I recognized from old tabloid photos. The rest of him, however, shivered and shook, showing all the signs of someone trying desperately to ward off a panic attack. My hand was squeezed so hard it lost all feeling until we got inside.

Once we made it past the press, Will relaxed considerably. Most of the reporters asked surprisingly benign questions (Gail told us later they were all instructed *not* to ask about Will's disappearance or his relationship with me). Inside the theater, he remained standoffish whenever other actors approached, though he tended to be nicer to members of the crew or the writers. I, for one, was somewhat starstruck. I had never seen so many famous people in one place, and most of them had been so eager to see Will that they barely noticed me. They were friendly, welcoming back a prodigal son to the industry, and Will smiled, even traded a few jokes here and there. But never, even once, did he let go of my hand.

Will grumbled the entire way to the after-party at a hotel's rooftop lounge a few blocks down from the theater, though I guessed that was partly he was hungry after close to two months of nothing but fish and broccoli, not to mention nothing for dinner that night. It was close to eleven o'clock by the time we got to the lounge.

"Thirty minutes," Gail assured us as she ushered us into the party. "Get your picture taken with a few people—mainly Amelia. I'll let you guys know when you can go." She looked sympathetically at Will as he ducked away to find a bathroom. After watching him stumble down the red carpet for forty-five minutes, Gail had a new understanding of his hatred for the industry. So did I.

"Thanks," I said to the waiter as I took a third bite off the tray. "I needed those."

"You know those are about eighty calories a bite and positively dripping with gluten."

I turned around to find Amelia standing next to me, looking as picture-perfect as ever. We'd seen her briefly at the screening. She had been too busy with her own promotional duties to say more than a quick hello to Will, though I noticed her watching him through half the show from down our row.

She looked me up and down. "Then again, you have the luxury of not watching your weight, don't you?"

I swallowed the salmon puff and dabbed at my mouth. Then I shrugged. "Worth it. Congratulations on the film. It was...entertaining."

That was really the best I could say. It was two and a half hours of watching Amelia play an ingénue pop star—sort of a take on *A Star Is Born*, but with a much happier ending. It might have been fun, if I hadn't already disliked her so much. On top of that, her lip-syncing had been horrendous, and whoever wrote the music for the film had been listening to way too many boy bands.

Amelia took a long drink of what looked and smelled like vodka. "I appreciate that, love. Now, what happened to our man? Did he run off and leave you here?"

I gave a thin smile. *Our* man, huh? I would not let this bitch know how much she and her impossibly perky tits got under my skin. I would not. I would *not*.

"He ran to the restroom, but he needed to make the rounds with some of the producers. Getting some pictures in," I said. "He doesn't want to stay long. I'm sure you know that parties aren't really his thing."

"Parties? Not Will's 'thing'?" Amelia burst into a laugh that sounded more like a cackle. "That's darling, really."

I sipped my water. It was awkward enough being here when a lot of people—most of them female—so clearly didn't want me around. On top of that, being the only one sober made it close to unbearable.

"So, tell me again, how did you two meet?"

I blinked. "I thought he told you that story. I crashed a bike in front of his house, and then got tangled in some lilies in front of his dock."

"Oh, right, right," Amelia said, nodding. "I remember now. How very quaint. And how completely plausible."

I looked up sharply. "What does that mean?"

Amelia's pink lips were pouted and her eyes a little unfocused from the vodka, but none of that could hide her contempt for me.

"Do you really think that anyone believes you just 'happened' to break down outside his house?" She snorted loudly. "Darling, please. That's the oldest trick in the book. You might as well have pretended to be his long-lost childhood friend." Her sharp blue eyes blazed a trail of tiny cuts over me. "He'll get his fill of you. And when he does, he'll come right back to where he belongs." She pointed a manicured finger up and down over me. "You see, Will and I have known each other since we were children. I was fourteen when we met. We grew up in this town together. We were royalty together. At some point in the near future, he'll tire of slumming with peasantry, and when he does, he'll return to his queen. I'll make sure of it."

She giggled to herself, as if the thought of ruining our relationship genuinely amused her. I, for one, was too shocked to reply. Was this chick for real?

"Amelia!" a voice called through the crowd, and immediately, Amelia waved her hand in response.

"Coming!" she called back and then turned to me. "Enjoy the party, darling," she said with a wink. "I know I will."

And before I could summon any kind of reply, she slithered through the crowd, already waving at her next amusement.

"Don't mind her. No one in this town pays attention to a thing she says."

I turned to the friendly voice beside me, still feeling stunned by the exchange. The voice belonged to a short, squat man with a round, friendly face and a head full of bushy gray hair. He pushed a pair of smudged glasses up his nose and grinned at me. His enthusiasm and kindness was so utterly out of place in this room full of splashy, shiny people, I couldn't help but smile back.

"She, you know, has a little...problem." He lifted his pinky finger to his nose, miming the actions of a coke fiend.

I raised an eyebrow. "Really?"

The man chuckled and nodded. "But you didn't hear it from me, of course. And no one will care as long as she's putting out bankable garbage like this every six months."

"You didn't like the film?"

The man shrugged. "What did you think?"

I twisted my mouth around, but decided to be honest. "I thought it had its moments."

"Come on, now, put it out there. You're the target demographic for a movie like this, aren't you? Ms. Craig is trying to grab that coveted eighteen to thirty, and you can't be, what, more than twenty-five?"

"Twenty-six," I murmured, but the man barreled on enthusiastically.

"Well, then, there you have it. So be honest, kid. What are your notes?"

"Well, if you have to know, I thought the music needed a little work," I sputtered, finally giving under pressure.

The man rocked back on his heels. "Is that so? Do tell."

"Well, I mean I'm no expert, but I thought the songs were a little formulaic and mostly unremarkable, especially for a movie like this with some of the biggest stars in the world. You'd think the studio could spring for something better than your average pop crap." The words contained more vitriol than I really intended, or even felt. Apparently I was more bothered by the interaction with Amelia than I thought. "Er, sorry," I said. "That was a little much."

The man only laughed. "No problem, sweetheart. I asked. And can I ask whose opinion is tickling my funny bone at the moment?"

I smiled. I didn't know this man, but I liked him very much. "Maggie," I said. "Maggie Sharp." I held out a hand. "And you are?"

"Rob Reinquist," he said, returning the handshake. "I actually wrote the soundtrack."

My jaw practically hit the floor. "Oh my God, I'm so *sorry*. Shit, I— Jesus, how rude am I? Please, please forgive me. I'm incredibly nervous being here, and maybe even a little jealous of you, and—"

Rob chuckled and patted me on the back. "Hey, hey, relax. I know it's shit, but it's a paycheck. That soundtrack is what happens when the studio asks if I can write music that sounds like the latest Top Forty crap on the radio." He shrugged. "It's formulaic and dull, but it paid for my kids' college tuitions, you know?"

I nodded, taking a sip of water and wishing to God that I had even the slightest taste for vodka. For the first time, I understood why people would try to escape into a vat of alcohol. Mortification.

But Rob's warm smile—and the fact that in his faded pants and slightly stained shirt he was one of the most relatable-looking people here—put me at ease.

"Well, they weren't all bad," I said. "The third number was pretty catchy. I liked the changes between the second verse and the bridge."

Rob looked at me with surprise. "Oh? Do we have another composer in the house tonight?"

I shrugged. "I was out in New York for a while, but I could never get anything off the ground."

"Wait, wait, wait. Are you a composer or a performer? Because they are different beasts, you know."

I blinked. "Well…" I didn't know how to answer that. I knew what he meant. It was a spectrum, of course, but most artists fell on one side of the continuum or the other. People who either lived to perform or lived to write.

I didn't perform anymore. And to be honest, I didn't miss it. At all. It was the music I loved, the music that drove me. I just wanted it out there, no matter what.

"Composer," I said. "Performing was only ever a means to an end. And to be honest, I haven't done it in a very, very long time."

Rob nodded, looking satisfied with the answer.

"Well, hey," he said as he pulled something out of his back pocket. "I've got to go kiss some corporate asses a little bit tonight before I get back to the wife and kids. But if you ever have more solid notes for my stuff, I'd be happy to hear them." He handed me a business card with a wink. "It's good to have at least some friends in this town."

"Oh...thank you..." I took the card and examined it for a moment, stunned by his kindness and openness. I looked up to tell him, but he was already gone.

The party continued in full swing around me, with the drunken laughter and dancing growing louder by the second. I was content to melt back into the wall, study Rob Reinquist's business card, and ponder exactly what I was supposed to do with it.

A few minutes later, Will appeared at my side, looking tired and bedraggled. He'd lost his suit jacket at some point, and his shirt looked like it had been pulled in multiple directions for the last thirty minutes. His hair was sticking up on one side, and part of his shirt was un-tucked.

"God," he said as he wrapped a long arm around my shoulders. "I need a drink."

I looked up sharply. "What?"

He grinned. "I'm joking, Lil. I actually had a couple of shots with some Disney execs, but I'm done now, I promise."

He did sound a little looser. And while I was happy he'd lost that tense, animal-caught-in-a-trap look, I didn't love that it had clearly come from the drinks.

He's not your mother, Maggie. I repeated the phrase in my head several times.

"Relax," Will murmured into my ear. "That's all I'm having. No one's going off the deep end tonight."

"Were you planning to in the future?" The question was sharper than I intended.

Will straightened and looked me straight in the eye. "No."

My shoulders dropped in relief. "Okay."

"Hey, I saw you talking to Rob Reinquist. That guy is such a legend."

I took a long sip of my water and glanced back at the little man, now making his way toward the buffet. "Really?"

Will blinked down at me. "He did the music for *The Dwelling*, and I swear, he completely made that movie. Corbyn loves him. He's won three Oscars for his scores. Didn't you know that?"

I shook my head. "I've never really followed film composers." Maybe I should have. "He gave me his card."

Will grinned and kissed me on the head. "There aren't very many people in this town I'd trust, babe, but Rob is definitely one of them. You should call."

I looked down at the card in my hand. "Maybe I will."

Before I could ponder it some more, the card was plucked out of my hand and tucked into my purse.

"Hey!" I protested, but the playful look on Will's face erased my annoyance.

"Come on, Lily pad, it's a party," he said with a cheeky grin. "Stop brooding, all right? For the first time all night, I don't want to strangle myself. I just want to dance with the prettiest girl in the room."

I rolled my eyes while he tugged on my arm. "Please. There are about a hundred other girls here with flatter abs and tighter asses than me." Amelia's perfectly symmetrical face flashed to mind, and I frowned.

Will yanked me up against him with a growl. "What did I say?" he demanded. "No talking shit about yourself, Lil. You're worth a million of these plastic-looking bitches. Do you understand?"

His hand was steel around my waist, and the rest of the party seemed to fade away. When was the last time Will and I had gotten quality time together that wasn't in his trailer, where we were interrupted every five minutes? For the last few weeks, he'd been pulling sixteen- to eighteen-hour days on set. Sometimes I missed him more than when I was hundreds of miles away.

I popped up onto my tiptoes and touched my nose to his. "Yes, sir," I teased lightly. "Understood."

It was meant as a joke, but as soon as the word "sir" came out of my mouth, Will's face took on a completely different demeanor. One that was pure smolder.

He grabbed my hand roughly and squeezed. "Come with me."

There wasn't any time to respond as I was dragged through the tight crowd, past the people smashed into the VIP section. Will paused at the top of the stairs, looking right and left to see if anyone was watching us. And then he darted into an unmanned coatroom, practically pulling my arm out of its socket in the process.

"Will!" I protested as he led us into the back of the closet.

"Shut up, Lil," he said. He flipped me back against the wall, and then he was pressed against me, all six feet, three inches of him, dressed in Tom Ford's finest with hands, legs, torso, and mouth begging for access.

"What are you doing?" I gasped as his lips found my neck and began to suck.

Will stood up. "What did you expect?" he demanded. "You've been parading around me all damn night with your ass looking grabbable as fuck and your nipples basically staring me in the face."

My mouth dropped, and I looked down at the dress. *What?*

A finger slid under my chin. "I said they were staring at *me*, Lil," Will said with a crooked smile that made my heart thump. He dragged his gaze down, then up with such slow intention that goose bumps broke out all over my body. The smile widened. "Although when you're a little cold, I'm pretty sure *everyone* in the room knows it, baby."

I smacked him on the shoulder with my purse, but he caught my wrist and slammed it high above my head on the wall, effectively trapping me there.

"You're a bit of a caveman, you know that, Baker?" I said, though I made absolutely no move to fight him.

That wicked smile only spread fully, bright and daring in the dark of the closet. His other hand slid up my thigh, seeking skin under the thin silk of my skirt. When he found it, the hand continued up and behind to take a handful of flesh and pulled me taut against his solid and apparently *very* willing body.

"Fuckin' barbaric," he agreed as his fingers sought out my sex. He quirked an eyebrow as he discovered my secret. "Looks like I'm not the only one going back to nature, though, am I?" He closed his eyes as his fingers found pay dirt. "Jesus Christ, Lil, you're completely bare."

I blushed. "Robin, um, said most women don't include underwear when they wear dresses like this. And well, I have, um, dark hair there, so…it needed to go."

One finger dipped inside. "Dresses like what?"

My head fell back against the wall as his thumb pressed on my clit and started to rub.

"Dresses that—oh!—" I arched as another finger joined the first, and the two started to move, slowly fucking me against the wall in time with his thumb.

"Dresses that make me want to fuck you in front of every one of those bastards out there, cameras be damned?"

Will dropped the hand over my head, which fell limp to my side, and then slipped his fingers under the strap of my dress and behind, teasing it over my shoulder while his other hand continued its onslaught lower down. My thighs spread for him as if of their own accord.

"Dresses that make me want to flip you over one of those tables and show the whole fucking world that you're mine?"

As he spoke, his deep voice rumbled over the delicate skin of my neck, over my collarbone, following the strap over my shoulder, and then back up. He kissed me, sucking one lip, then the other into his mouth. Delicately, but with little bite. I moaned against his mouth, and he inhaled sharply.

A third finger joined the other two, and distantly, I sensed the strap of my dress falling down, baring one breast to anyone who might see.

"You make me crazy, you know that, woman?" Will muttered as his hand started to move faster, deeper. My hips began to writhe on it, riding his hand a little faster, a little more furiously. "Goddamn. Look at you."

I couldn't look. I couldn't think. With little else than his touch and a few kisses, Will had rendered me completely speechless. He dipped down and sucked my nipple into his mouth. This time I couldn't silence my moans at all.

So instead of fighting, I followed the rest of my instincts. Arching into his mouth, his touch, I reached down between us, undid his pants, pulled out his cock and squeezed it lightly with both hands.

"Fuuuuuck, Lil," Will moaned against my breast. But he didn't stop what he was doing, and neither did I as I began working my grip up and down his silky length. A pipe was less a cliché and the most apt description in the world.

"Will?"

A high, familiar, *British* voice rang out through the coatroom. Both of us froze. I moved to get away, but Will pressed a hand to my sternum, warning me not to move.

The fingers inside me pulled out. And then pushed back in. And then they did it again while his thumb began to rub over my clit all over again.

"Don't. You. Stop," Will ordered in a harsh whisper as the hand on my chest slid up to fit lightly around my neck, then up farther to cover my mouth. Obediently, my hand continued to move below.

"Will, darling, one of the waiters said they saw you dart in here, you little monkey. Corbyn is asking for you," Amelia called. There was a brief shuffle. "You'd better come."

I buried a laugh into his shirt, and Will pressed his forehead into the wall above my shoulder and grinned.

"I'll be right there," Will called back, his voice creaking with every movement. "I'm just..." Will turned to me with a salacious grin. "Trying to find something."

I tried to smirk, but the flick of his fingers down below wasn't giving me much ability to do anything other than work out his pleasure along with mine. His fingers continued their movements, and my hips gyrated into them, begging for deeper penetration while I helped him along.

His thumb pressed harder, and my mouth opened with a loud cry that Will swallowed with a kiss.

"All right, darling, don't be long."

I writhed against him, coming apart completely as my orgasm overtook me in harsh, unforgiving waves. I spasmed.

"I'm...coming," Will managed to get out as he grabbed his cock, which I'd unfortunately dropped as I'd lost my senses completely. "*Fuck!*" he hissed as he shoved up my skirt.

One, two, three harsh strokes of his fist, and suddenly he was lurching against the wall. I floated down from my euphoria, my hand drifted down to cover his, and we both clutched his pulsing length together as he emptied himself all over my thighs.

And, then, eventually, consciousness returned, along with the cold, hard texture of the brick behind me and the newly suffocating atmosphere of being buried in a pile of coats. Will pushed a hand off the wall, but continued to loom over me.

"Um, can you go get a paper towel or something?" I asked. "I can't go out there like this."

Another slow, wicked smile spread across Will's face. Holding my skirt up with one hand, he reached between my legs with the other and proceeded to smear the remnants of his release down one thigh and up the other. Without moving his gaze from mine, he continued to rub it in until my legs were fully coated with…him. Then, with a smirk, he pulled a white handkerchief out of his pants pocket and proceeded to clean his hand, but left the sticky residue on my skin.

My skirt dropped, but I gawked downward. "I can't believe you just did that."

A finger tipped up my chin, forcing me to look Will in the face. For the first time that night, I saw genuine mirth there. Happiness. I didn't even care where it came from—only that it was directed at me.

"If you're going to wear dresses that bring out my animal side, Lil, then you better be ready for the beast." He kissed me, with a slight bite of my lower lip that had me yearning for more all over again. "Now, let's go schmooze with the studio heads. If I have to watch these assholes ogling my girl for another fifteen minutes, I want to do it knowing she's been claimed."

I rolled my eyes, but didn't argue.

"Animal," I muttered as I followed him out of the coatroom.

Will barked a laugh—a brief, momentary, but one hundred percent *real* laugh, all the way from his belly.

"Only for you," he said and tugged me out with him.

CHAPTER TWENTY-ONE

"Any word from your mom?"

I sighed and sat back in my car—or, I should say, the Tesla that the studio had loaned Will and me while we were in LA. It was a waste, really, since Hakeem and Garrett drove Will everywhere. I was parked outside the lot where Will currently had two more weeks scheduled until principal photography on *Green Lantern* would wrap and we would be free…for six months, anyway.

"No," I told Calliope. "I've been calling, but she's not picking up or returning anything. She finally let her friend Barb come over again, so she's been letting me know how she's doing."

"That's her friend who took part in the intervention?"

"Yeah. So, I guess that's progress."

I plucked at an errant thread on the hem of my skirt. Other than Barb, Mama still hadn't been willing to speak to any of the people who'd showed up that terrible morning. She avoided church like the plague, and so Lucas (via Lindsay, unfortunately) had taken it upon himself to check up on her at Curly's where Mama continued to make a moderate fool of herself several times a week. I had to accept it: I'd failed. And maybe I had to accept too that, as much as it hurt, I couldn't have my mother in my life anymore.

But it did hurt. A lot.

"So, two weeks, huh? What are you guys going to do after that?"

That was the big question. Will wanted to go back to the lake, but I wasn't so sure. What was I supposed to do there? Go back to cleaning rooms at the inn while my mother and I pretended to ignore each other? Leech off my movie star boyfriend while we hid in the woods?

Neither option seemed particularly appealing, and yet…I still didn't have a clue what the alternative was.

"We're still figuring it out," was all I could say.

Will, of course, was dying to go back to the woods. He had big plans to build a massive perimeter around his property and install a permanent security team there until the crazy buzz died down. I wasn't so sure. A cage was still a cage, no matter how big.

We'd attended one more of the five contractually required premieres, plus he'd also done two late night interviews as a way to start building buzz for the upcoming film. Each appearance had been more chaotic than the last, and it had gotten to the point that he regularly had to change SUVs when he drove around to avoid the paparazzi that tended to hover outside the studio lot, hoping to catch a glimpse of him. I began to understand why he had hated this life so much—the poor man barely existed outside of the studio and our rented backyard.

"By the way, that new stuff you sent me is amazing," Calliope said. "Really different from your old work."

I smiled. "You like it?"

While Will had been filming, I spent at least a few hours every day at the house recording something onto my computer. They weren't the best recordings in the world, but it was amazing what you could do with a decent soundboard and mic. I was finally starting to get some of the sounds together that I could hear in my head—at least enough that they made sense.

"Oh, yeah," Calliope said. "They're very…I don't know. Cinematic, maybe. One of them really reminded me of Sigur Ros."

I grinned. "Thanks, girl. I'm glad you like it."

"Have you sent anything to that Rob guy you met?"

Rob Reinquist and I had actually been exchanging emails for a few weeks. I liked him. He sort of reminded me of a corny uncle I never had.

Lately he'd been making noises about having Will and me over to meet his family, but Will had never had a break in filming, and I didn't want to go by myself.

"No," I replied.

"And why not?"

I shrugged. "I don't know. I don't want to seem opportunistic, I guess. Everyone in this town wants something. I kind of think Rob enjoys having a friend to talk shop with who isn't trying to get anything from him."

Calliope scoffed. "Babe, you have to put yourself out there. If you're not going to stand up for your talent, no one will. And you've got too much of it to keep to yourself."

I sighed. "Point taken. But, Cal, I gotta go. Will is supposed to break for lunch soon, and then they are leaving to film some crazy scene in Death Valley for three days, so I won't see him until Friday."

"Got it. Go shtup your man in his trailer so that Kate Moss wannabe can't sink her claws in."

I chuckled. Calliope actually seemed to hate Amelia more than I did. There had been a few more catty moments, but mostly Amelia and I had managed to avoid each other since her premiere. I wondered if she had seen more in the coat closet than we thought.

"Will do, boo." I hung up the phone and got out of the car.

Although Will's schedule definitely wasn't exact, if I did miss his rare moments off, I risked not seeing him for days. This week he'd be gone for a minimum of three, possibly up to a week if things didn't go smoothly. I was spending every spare moment with him in his trailer, since we had next to no time together anywhere else. Everyone was putting in extra hours to make sure things ended on time.

I raced toward the "base camp," where the collection of trailers containing props, costumes, and talent were located along with the second AD's headquarters next to the soundstages for the production.

Most of the production team and even the security guys in the front of the studio were used to my presence by now. I'd been provided with a pass to drive myself on and off the lot, which gave Garrett and Hakeem more time off (to work with other people more in need of their services).

"Hey, Maggie," said Leon, one of the sound guys. "You listening today? They're almost done, I think."

I shrugged and took a seat in one of the extra director's chairs set up around the sound equipment. Leon handed me an extra set of headphones that was hooked up to the equipment and I listened in on the scene currently being filmed on the closed set next to us.

"Guys, I'll be back. I need to take a leak."

I giggled. Will was as blunt as ever—and I doubted that was in the script.

There was an audible sigh over the mic and a rustle on set. I considered getting up to go find Will, but ended up staying put when I heard another familiar voice—this one female and very British.

"Honestly, Corbyn, if you can't elicit some kind of emotion from him in the next take, I'm going to slap him across the face myself," Amelia snapped. "It's like making out with a bloody broom handle."

There was some shuffling, and then the muffled voice of Corbyn, the director, seemingly assuring Amelia that he would fix the problem. I bit my lip. Did I want to be listening to this particular scene?

"Hold on there, hon. Your makeup got smeared during the last take."

Another loud sigh—I was guessing it was Amelia while someone touched up her face.

"Did you see that?" she asked whoever was helping her. "He touches me like I'm a bloody leper. Am I *that* hideous compared to that little urchin he's shacked up with? Must I get a headful of toddler curls like hers to compete?"

The makeup artist laughed, and I reached up self-consciously to pull at one of said curls. My hair had long reverted back to its natural state since arriving in LA. It was so curly these days that I didn't even bother to brush it out anymore. I just gave it its weekly coconut oil mask and let it riot freely. I'd considered another keratin treatment, but Will said he liked it the way it was.

"It used to be *so* much easier," Amelia said. "Once upon a time, a scene like that would have been pure foreplay. Four takes, and he'd have had me over his shoulder and in his trailer with two other women. And by the way, the rumors are *absolutely* true about everything he has going on…down there. More than enough for three of us, if you know what I mean."

My mouth dropped open. There was an audible sigh from the makeup artist.

"'Course, back then he'd be up for a few other types of fun, too. The Fitz Baker I knew would have taken any pill I gave him for the surprise factor alone. Now he's so bloody boring, it's painful."

"He's probably stressed about the movie. Filming is tense, and he's been gone a long time," said the other woman. "The wrap party is just around the corner. I bet you'll be able to get him to loosen up then. Remind him a little of what he's been missing."

There was a shuffle as the boom seemed to move around out of earshot, but afterward, I could hear their voices a bit more faintly as they continued to speak.

"What about his…"

"Darling, please. She's nobody. She's basically a human security blanket. Once Will gets his bearings again, he'll get rid of his wet blankie and come right back to where he belongs." Amelia giggled. "You're going to hold up your end of the bargain, right?"

There was a snicker. I felt like I was going to be sick.

"Yeah," said the other girl. "The old Fitz Baker could never say no to a threesome. Let's see if he's changed as much as everyone's said."

I strained to hear Amelia's response, but the boom moved again. There was more shuffling, and after a minute, I heard Will's voice in the background.

"All right," he said. "Let's get this over with. I've got a hot date I don't want to miss."

I took the headphones off with a smile and handed them back to Leon. With one phrase, I was less interested in hearing the rest of the scene and more concerned with being in Will's trailer when he was finished. I didn't want to miss my "hot date" either.

I hopped off the chair and started toward the other side of the soundstage where his trailer sat by itself. He had requested that it be away from the "base camp" for extra privacy, much to the irritation of the PAs, as I had gathered. I practically skipped down the pavement, rounded a corner, and without looking where I was going, barreled headfirst into another person whose voice was immediately familiar.

"Whoa, there, Flower. Watch your step."

I froze, looking around for any other crew who might be nearby. Of course, there was no one—I was in a part of the lot that was purposefully isolated from the rest. For my misanthropic boyfriend.

I swallowed. I always knew this was a possibility, but over the past several weeks, I'd gotten too comfortable and began to accept the possibility that maybe Theo was done tormenting me. That maybe since I had lost my claims in court, we were done and he was really out of my life. But his presence on set was prohibited by the terms of Will's contract, so what the hell was he doing here now?

I glanced around nervously. If Will knew that Theo was here, I didn't know what he would do. And I didn't know what Theo would do after.

"Flower?"

The word made my skin absolutely crawl. But I didn't want to be bested by this prick. I was in a different place than I was a year ago, even six months ago. I was stronger. I didn't need to live my life in fear of this man anymore.

So, with Herculean effort, I dragged my gaze up to meet his. Theo looked much the same—tanner and a little thicker now that he had been out of jail for a few more months. But otherwise the same lanky frame, the same dark brown eyes, the same curled lip, the same inky black hair. His gaze traveled over me, but when it came back up, it was full of something I have never seen on his face: admiration.

"What—what are you doing here, Theo?" I managed to get out with the stutter that had all but disappeared until now.

Theo smiled. Once upon a time that smile would have made my heart beat faster, but right now it dropped like a stone. "Where's the love, huh?"

I folded my arms across my chest, praying that one of the PAs or *someone* would interrupt us as I stepped backward. "Y-you're not supposed to be around me."

"Ah, ah, ah, *wasn't* supposed to be around you," he corrected me. "The judge overturned that pretty quickly thanks to your little dinner attendance, didn't he? Of course, I'm sure my family's fat contribution to his son's state senate campaign didn't hurt much either." He clicked his tongue like he was chastising a small child. "Oh, Flower. You always were too innocent for your own good."

I opened my mouth to speak. Nothing came out. Was this for real?

"Relax. I'm not here for you, Flower," he said. "I'm here on business. With the studio. Dad wanted me to check in and be here to make sure things wrapped on time."

I balked. "Why do you need to be here for that? They have a million ADs and other people doing the same thing. And y-you're not supposed to be here. It's in Will's contract."

"Well, well, look at you, Miss Hollywood. You really know the lingo now, don't you?"

Again, I didn't reply. I knew by now that arguing with Theo usually only brought out the worst in him. Cowardice combined with aggression was a very dangerous thing.

"Don't you worry," he said, stepping toward me. "Contracts were made to be broken. Dad knows that as well as anyone. Including your boyfriend." He reached out and traced a finger down my jaw lightly, and like a scared rabbit, all I could do was stand there and take it.

"I said don't *fucking* touch me, Amy." The sharp sound of Will's voice echoed from around the corner, and both Theo and I jerked toward the sound.

"Looks like we'll have to get reacquainted later," he said, stepping backward toward base camp. "Later, Flower."

Before I could reply, Theo was jogging in the direction I had come from, away from the six feet, three inches of wrath that he likely knew would be directed at him if he were caught even speaking to me at all.

I turned to find Will rounding the opposite side of the soundstage, tossing the claws of Britain's Top Model herself off his robe-covered shoulder.

I cringed. The robes could only mean one thing—that the scene I'd chosen not to hear was the one and only love scene in the movie. I'd known it was coming; it had been on the call sheet for weeks. It was mild, considering the movie was supposed to be PG-13, but even so, both of them were mostly naked and simulating foreplay in front of an audience of fifty. It wasn't full sex, as Will had said, but it was close enough.

"Darling, really, you never used to be such a drama queen."

"Well, you never used to ignore the word no. The scene was over, Amy. And if I wanted your hands anywhere near my *anything*, I'd come knocking at your door at two a.m. like every other VD-infected prick in this city."

Will thundered toward the trailer, and it was only upon catching sight of me that his expression shifted slightly.

"Thank God you're here," he said as he reached me, taking me with both hands, clasping one around my head, the other around my back.

He smelled of baby oil and the chalky scent of body makeup. Underneath the robe, his body was slick, and his hair had been combed with something greasy. On film he'd undoubtedly look fantastic, but in front of me, it was kind of gross.

"I need a fucking shower," he muttered as Amelia shuffled up behind us. "Hey, are you all right? Lil, you're shaking."

But before I could say anything, we were interrupted again.

"You used to be a lot more bloody fun," Amelia snapped before catching sight of me. Her angry snarl morphed almost immediately into a haughty glare, and she stood behind Will with her hip jutted out with one delicate hand perched on it. She also wore body makeup and a full face of faux-sweat. Their makeup made it look like they had been getting busy for real, not faking it in front of fifty people.

I nuzzled into Will's side and encircled my arms around his waist. It was petty, but I enjoyed the fact that while this bitch was only allowed to touch him in front of a camera, I had free reign—any time I wanted.

"I don't know," I said. "I think he's pretty fun. We have 'fun' all the time. Some people might say we have 'fun' like rabbits, don't you think, babe?"

Will glanced down with a raised brow. He knew exactly what I was doing, and to my surprise, he didn't seem to care. As Amelia watched, he took one of my hands that was holding onto his belt, kissed my knuckles, and then slipped it inside his robe so I could play my hand freely up and down his finely shaped abs and pectoral muscles. If I was going to play this game, he seemed to be saying, he was going to play it with me.

"Hippity fuckin' hop," he said.

I grinned, and he grinned right back.

"You ready for lunch, Lil?" he asked. "Or do you want to have some more 'fun' first?"

Amelia's mouth twisted. "You bloody *bastard*," she spat, then hurried by us in the direction of her own trailer, parked near the others.

Will chuckled, then kissed the top of my head. "Thanks for that. Maybe it'll get her off my damn case for the next two weeks."

I glanced back toward the soundstage with alarm. "Has she been coming onto you a lot?"

Will stiffened, but didn't loosen his hold on me, even though I wanted to take my hand away. His entire body was covered in that combination of oil and makeup.

"It's nothing I can't handle," he replied.

That didn't make me feel better. Not at all.

"God, she's a bitch now," he said as we turned back to his trailer. "She's so much damn worse than she ever was. Power hungry. Manipulative. She's basically a cartoon."

"She wasn't like that before?" It was hard to imagine.

He gave me a crooked smile. "Fame does funny things to people, Lil."

And for a moment, my jealousies disappeared as I realized how often those kinds of changes must have happened in his life. His mother, for instance, who had seen her son first and foremost as a meal ticket. Agents. Managers. How many people in his life had changed or forsaken him for what they thought he could offer? How many people had tricked him, made him believe they cared when really all they wanted was an extra dollar or shout-out from a celebrity?

Theo's appearance could wait another day, I figured. I didn't want to be one of those people who put my own needs on Will's shoulders and made him carry the world on them.

"Guess what?" he said as we entered his trailer.

I shut the door behind me. In the silence, Will's shoulders loosened visibly.

"I have the rest of the afternoon off," he said with a grin. "So before I leave for the desert, I'm taking you out for a surprise."

I sank down into the couch, Amelia and Theo vanished. "Surprise?

For me? What are we doing?" We literally never went anywhere, so the fact that Will wanted to go somewhere besides the walled-in sanctuaries of the rental or his trailer was a complete shock.

He grabbed a towel from one of the shelves.

"First, I need to shower and get all this shit off me," he said. "And then, baby, I'm taking you sailing."

CHAPTER TWENTY-TWO

"Well? What do you think?"

I stood on the edge of a marina in Redondo Beach, pulling my hair into a ponytail over my shoulder while I examined the long, white boat bobbing in front of me.

Hakeem and Garrett lingered a solid fifty feet away, chatting at the marina's entrance and making sure no one disturbed us. After leaving the studio under the cover of another SUV, we'd managed to elude the photographers that always seemed to hover at the entrance. I didn't know where we were going, but I appreciated the way Will's entire body seemed to relax the second the looming buildings of Beauregard dropped out of sight.

"It's...wow." I squatted down to run a hand over the shiny white edge of the boat, then looked up at Will. "Is it yours?"

I didn't know why, but the idea scared me. Was Will the kind of person who would buy a twenty-foot sailboat on a whim? Was he...was he planning to stay in Los Angeles after shooting wrapped in two weeks and hadn't told me?

I still didn't know, did I?

"No, no, no," Will scoffed. "It belongs to Corbyn. He said we could borrow it for the afternoon." He hopped on board and started untying the rope that kept one end of the boat anchored to the dock, then stopped with sudden worry. "You don't get seasick, do you? I figured since you grew up on a lake…"

I shook my head as I stood back up. "No, I don't. But…"

Will began coiling the rope in one corner of the boat. "What, babe?"

"Well, I don't know how to sail. Don't you, um, need some help maneuvering this thing?" I looked doubtfully up and down the boat, which, though very beautiful, also seemed pretty massive.

Will grinned, his smile refracting the bright late summer sunlight. "Lil, you know I basically grew up on one of these things, right?"

"Yeah, but wasn't the last time you were on a boat when you…"

"Crashed one in Maine and faked my own death?" His grin expanded, cheeky. Almost delighted. Out here on the water, Will's face glowed with a boyish light I had never seen before. He started pulling on a few other things.

"Come aboard," he said, holding a hand out to me.

Cautiously, I stepped onto the boat, steadying myself against the light rocking.

"Take a seat over there," Will said, pointing to the bench seats situated around a small table in front of the steering wheel, or whatever it was called.

I did as I was told while he moved around, doing whatever needed to be done to get us going. I watched, enthralled with his obvious competence with all of the equipment that was completely foreign to me.

"How big is it?" I wondered.

"Huh? Oh…she's about eighteen feet, I think."

"She…" I mused to myself when Will lapsed naturally into a sailor's lexicon. I sat back in the seat and continued to watch him. He seemed more at ease going about these little tasks than at any other time I'd seen him.

Then I brightened. "Hey!" I shouted.

Will popped up with alarm. He pulled his sunglasses down, and his green eyes pierced. "What? What's wrong?" He glanced all around the marina. "Is someone here?"

I grinned. "My, *she* sure is yar!" I pronounced, proudly quoting from

Philadelphia Story, which I knew Will owned in his collection back at the lake.

His forehead crinkled adorably for a second or two. But then, as the quote registered, Will tipped his head back and laughed, really and truly, from deep down in his gut, louder and fuller than I'd ever heard him. I grinned back, feeling like I'd won the jackpot.

"Oh, shit," he said as he wiped tears from his eyes. "You're so fucking cute, Lil. You really are." He clambered to me from the front of the boat, clasped my face over the back of the bench seat, and pressed a solid, full kiss to my still smiling lips. "God, I love you," he pronounced as he stood back up. "You don't know shit about sailing, Lily pad, but I love you like crazy."

"Hoist the jib!" I called as he moved back to the front of the boat. "Drop the mainsail! Shiver me timbers! Yo-ho-ho and a bottle of rum!"

Will just laughed even harder with every nonsensical nautical phrase I shouted. I relaxed and watched his perfectly shaped backside as he moved back to the tasks at hand. If this was all we were going to be doing, I was fine with that.

———

It was a good day for sailing, or at least that's what Will said. A decent breeze made the boat fly over the waves, but nothing was so choppy that I ever felt jarred or even the slightest bit scared. For the most part, Will handled everything himself, even when a few big gusts of wind sent the boat off course. Only a few times did he direct me to help—mainly with anchoring—but he was a good teacher and could direct a complete sailing novice like me efficiently and easily.

We dropped anchor somewhere south of LA, in a harbor below steep cliffs covered with succulents and shrubs and topped with a lighthouse. Once we were set, I climbed to the front of the boat, where Will had spread a few large towels. We lay on our backs, watching the clouds rush by while waves lapped at the sides of the boat.

I peered toward the horizon, which was partially blocked by a long, low-lying land mass. "What's that?" I pointed toward the shape.

Will followed my gaze. "Oh, that's Catalina Island. It's pretty, but kind of touristy."

I shielded my eyes to look more closely. "Could we sail there?"

"We could. Not today, but we could. I'd rather go to the upper Channel Islands, though. No hotels or anything, so there aren't as many crowds." He turned to me curiously. "I never asked, but do you like camping, Lil?"

I shrugged. "Sure, it's all right."

Growing up in Eastern Washington, I'd done my fair share of camping around Spokane, Northern Idaho, and Montana, especially when Lucas and I were in high school. The woods were a common way for kids to get out of their parents' supervision and police purview. They were also my escape from my mother's problems (and boyfriends).

Will relaxed back into the towel. "Good," he murmured. "Good."

I sighed, leaning back into his chest while the sun sank a little toward the place where sky met sea.

"Did you always like camping?" I wondered. "When you were younger, I mean?"

Will nodded. "I did, yeah. My dad used to take me sometimes. We would sail, actually. That was originally how I learned, although later on I took lessons too. Dad was a great sailor. One summer we took over a week to sail up the coast of Long Island, all the way out to the east end of it, staying at campgrounds along the way."

I frowned. "Does Long Island have campgrounds? I thought it was all suburbs and ritzy houses."

Will chuckled. "A lot of it is. But there are plenty of places, especially farther out, where you can anchor and camp. Dad had a catamaran, without a cabin or anything, so sometimes we landed right on the beach and slept there. Who knows if we were allowed to? He never cared, actually."

I nuzzled into his chest, enjoying the warmth. Maybe that was why Will always seemed to smell slightly of a spray of water, like fresh rain or a briny wave. The water was where his heart had always been.

"Why didn't you get a boat for the lake?" I wondered. "Most people have speedboats, but I've seen a few little sailboats around."

"I thought about it," he admitted. "But...I don't know, Lil. It always seemed so…exposed. Being out there on the water like that. It's not like the ocean, you know? There's nowhere to run on a lake."

"Well, you managed to hide there successfully for four years," I remarked, only a little bitter.

Will was quiet, sensing my tension. His stomach muscles flexed as he kissed the top of my head. "I'm sorry I never told you," he said quietly, again with that odd ability of his to read my thoughts.

I nosed into his chest. "You're forgiven." And it was true. It was too soon to have forgotten that betrayal, but I meant what I said. I had forgiven him for everything. "There's one thing I still don't understand, though. The logistics of it. How could you have lived there for *years* without anyone seeing you, ever? How did you get food? How did you have the place remodeled like that? What about buying your car or going to the doctor or…"

I continued to gesture with my hand, indicating all of the ways a person had to interact with others at some point. There was no way Will could have avoided them all.

Will squeezed me with the arm around my shoulders, and held up his other hand to count on his fingers as he spoke. "Food: I ordered it. You didn't ask, but I also had a housekeeper who would come twice a month. I'd go camping, and he or she—I never met them—would clean and deliver groceries. Sort of like a property manager, I guess. So that was that." He crossed his ankles, getting more comfortable as he spoke. "The house remodel was harder. I lived in another rental for the better part of six months while Benny acted as a middle man. He really, *really* hated that, but I couldn't risk it. It took me two full years to grow my hair out, you know, and close to one for the beard."

I twisted around to look at him. I'd gotten used to the way he looked now—and he was ridiculously handsome—but I sort of missed the hair and the beard. Though I spent weeks wondering what he looked like under that mask of sorts, I still associated them with the Will I had first met—someone rough, unpolished, beautifully broken. Now, all buffed and perfect for the camera, he often looked almost inaccessible.

Will turned on his side so we were facing each other. His green eyes reflected the blue of the sky and the water, turning them more turquoise than green.

My stomach settled. He was still my Will, no matter what length his hair.

"And the doctor?" I prodded his washboard belly. "Dentist? How did you take care of yourself for all that time?"

"Well, I'll tell you this, Lil." He smiled grimly, revealing teeth that had been whitened since he'd arrived in LA. "I did the best I could, but I still had to have four cavities filled when I got to New York." His smile turned lopsided. "Bad, huh?"

"You don't want to know how much dental work Mama has had." I shook my head. "Was it really that bad before? So bad that you had to flee everything? Everyone? So bad that you couldn't even take care of yourself properly?"

Will sighed again, rolling onto his back. "You want the truth? It didn't really feel like that to me. Not until…well, not until maybe a few months before we met."

"You weren't lonely?"

"No, I was definitely lonely. But no more than when I had millions of people watching my every move. But I…okay, so I guess I thought of it kind of like this. I'd grown up with this incredibly privileged life—a life no normal kid ever comes close to having. I'd never had to do chores. Never had to go to school. Never had a shitty teenager job. I got everything I wanted so long as I memorized a few lines." He folded his long hands over his chest. "And then I was alone. I imagined I was one of those kids out in the bush way back when. I didn't want to be around anyone else because I wanted to see if I could survive without them. Without anyone." He turned again and blinked almost guiltily. "I sound like a jackass, don't I?"

I couldn't help but smile a little. "Maybe a little. I mean, living in a beautiful house on a lake and missing some dentist appointments isn't exactly having to kill your dinner in the woods."

Will snorted. "Yeah, no shit. But in the end, I still found out the same thing. That all I needed was myself."

I closed my eyes. I opened my mouth to say, "all I need is you," but immediately I knew that wasn't true. As much as we wanted to, Will and I couldn't live in a bubble for the rest of our lives. It was a tempting thought—find another lake house, sky-high apartment, bungalow tucked in the hills, and build a fortress around it so no one could bother us again.

But then what? Stay in a cage of our own making? The future in that direction seemed blurry and unclear, probably because there was nowhere to go.

If I looked the other way, though, I saw a mass of possibilities. A house, maybe on the lake or somewhere like it, in a community where we could learn to trust people, be a part of something bigger than ourselves. Raise our children.

The thought made my breath come up short, particularly given the previous conversation we'd had. I had never really thought about having children before that night, but lately I'd found myself imagining those three curly-haired kids all the time.

I had grown up the child of someone who so clearly resented me for existing. What did I know about being a good mother? And yet…when I looked at the man next to me, I knew that I wanted everything with him that was possible. I wanted a home. I wanted a family. I wanted a real future, and not just one that required me to hide away in luxury cages and play shell games with multiple cars.

But…did he? Would he? Ever?

I opened my mouth to ask him, but for some reason, cowered back.

"Where are we?" I asked, gesturing toward the lighthouse atop the cliffs overhead. "This is so private. I didn't realize there were any parts of LA where there were no…"

"People?" Will chuckled, then caught my hand and pulled it over his chest. He had taken his shirt off to enjoy the sunshine, and I luxuriated in the warmth of his skin, not to mention the view it provided.

"Well…yeah."

He smiled. "That's Palos Verdes. Actually, plenty of people live there, on the other side. The cliffs make it harder for spies. I used to know a lot of people who lived in that area, though, because of the relative privacy."

I hated the cynicism in his voice. When I looked closely, I could actually see the edges of a few houses that peeked over, but they weren't as smashed together as other parts of LA.

"Will?" I asked as he drifted a hand lazily over my bare shoulders.

His breaths were starting to grow long. I wondered if he was close to sleep.

"What's that, Lil?"

I swallowed. No, I couldn't let this go. "We need to decide. What we're going to do, I mean. After the shoot."

Underneath my cheek blew a heavy sigh. Will's hand burrowed into my hair, but instead of letting him pull me close, instead I sat up so I could look down at him.

"They're planning to release in May," he said quietly. "Which means starting in April, I'll have to start heavy promotion, and that won't end until close to July, maybe later depending on the international premieres."

The dread in his eyes hurt my heart.

"After that..." He pushed a hand through his hair. "I don't know. Get away. Find someplace they can't bother us anymore. Back to the lake or...or somewhere else."

I watched him for a long time. There wasn't any kind of joy in his suggestion. No hope.

But then another thought occurred to me.

"And so what if they do?" I asked as I rolled over him. "Find us, I mean."

Will blinked as I sat up. One blond brow arched delicately. "You don't know what you're saying, Lil."

I pressed a kiss to his neck, trailing down lightly over his Adam's apple, over the pulse that started to thump a little harder. "What do we have to hide?"

Will didn't reply as I sat back up, and he looked around. We were the only boat in the harbor, and there was no one on the cliffs or down by the sand. For miles, we were the only people in sight. But even if we weren't, I didn't want to live my life on the run, like a pair of criminals.

Slowly, I reached down, took the hem of my t-shirt, and pulled it over my head, maintaining eye contact almost the entire time. Will watched, transfixed, as I reached behind me and unhooked my bra.

His green eyes widened. "Lil..."

"There's no one here, babe."

My hair fell over my shoulders, and a few strands picked up lightly in the wind. When Will looked at me like this, I didn't care where I was. When he looked at me like this, I could do anything.

Will, however, remained frozen except for one particular part of him that had hardened between my legs. Gently, I gyrated my hips over it. Will hissed.

"You're playing with fire, there, Lily pad," he said as his eyes darkened, though his hands had already started to slide up my thighs.

I pulled the straps down my shoulders, one at a time.

I let the garment drop, baring myself completely in the open air. Will didn't even blink, staring at my breasts like he had never seen them before. Slowly, very slowly, he released a long, restrained breath through his nose. The fingers on my thighs tightened.

I leaned down, hovering so that my nipples grazed his chest, making both our breaths come up short.

"Against your shack," I whispered. "Your deck. Moon Rock. The coat closet at the premiere party…I could go on, Baker."

Will licked his lips. "Your point?"

"You have a thing for public places—haven't you noticed." I drifted my mouth over his. "I think you want to live your life in the open. I don't think you want to hide at all."

He sucked in a breath, but didn't move as I continued to play my body over his.

"You want me to stop?" I asked, my voice huskier than normal.

A muscle in Will's jaw ticked. "No," he whispered.

Then he wrapped a big palm around my neck and tugged me down for a kiss. But unlike the ones I had dusted over his neck and shoulder, this one showed no clemency. Will's mouth was insistent. Free.

"More?" he whispered after he finally released me. His fingers were now tangled in the hair above my nape. Our lips hovered again.

I hummed. "Yes. Do you?"

In answer, I was flipped onto my back, then yanked up onto Will's thighs so that we were sitting up, face to face once more. With a solid grip on my legs, Will stood up, walking me over to the cabin entrance despite the rocking of the boat.

"Here comes the caveman," I teased as he wobbled us down the stairs.

"Hush," ordered Will before giving another voracious kiss that silenced my words. Two more seconds, and I was tossed summarily onto a large bed that took up most of the cabin.

"Ahh!" I shrieked as I hit the pillows.

"I said *hush*." His words snapped, but the boyish grin dancing across his features sang a different tune. "And take off your shorts."

I obeyed while Will hurriedly stripped off his own clothes. The second they were off, everything of mine was ripped away and replaced with six feet, three inches of *man* between my thighs. Will buried his face between them like he was starved, sucking, licking, nipping. His tongue found my clit unerringly, and I jerked against him, threading my fingers into his hair to urge him on.

"Oh!" I shouted as two fingers slipped inside me.

But Will didn't quiet me again, with kisses or anything else. Out here, on the open water, we could be as loud as we liked.

"WILL!" His name burst from my chest like a siren while an orgasm seethed through me, shaking me from the tip of my toes to the ends of my hair. My hands gripped his scalp, urging him on, and on until it became too much to bear. "Will..." I whimpered his name again as the last of it coursed through me. An echo.

And at last, he lifted his head, then pressed kisses and licks up my stomach, under my breasts, pausing briefly to suckle each tender nipple, before his cock found me aching for him.

He pushed in slightly, giving me a moment to adjust to his size. My eyes bulged. It didn't matter how many times we did this—he always took some getting used to, a few breaths for my body to mold to his shape all over again.

"Is this what you wanted?" he asked as he pushed in another inch or two. "Up there, teasing me like that?"

I strained slightly against his size. But after a few more seconds, I was able to accommodate him again.

His hand drifted over my body, fingers tickling, tugging my nipples, taking a light grip around my neck, then drifting up to slip a thumb into my mouth.

"Suck," Will ordered as he sank in deeper, eyes closing when he sheathed himself completely in my warm depths.

I hummed around his finger, then sucked obediently as he began to move.

"Mmmmmmm." His hum was an echo of mine, the two of us harmonizing on the same plane of delight, ecstasy. Homecoming.

He pulled his thumb out of my mouth with a light pop, then slid his arm under my back and lifted me, weightlessly, so that I was balanced on his thighs.

"This is all that matters," he whispered as we began to rock together. "Us, Lil. You and me. That's it. That's all."

I knew it wasn't true. I knew that there were others we needed to think about. His relationship with his mother. My relationship with mine. Friends. Family. Jobs. Our lives.

But when we were together, when our bodies met and made such incredible music together, it was easy to block out all the noise that threatened to drown us out.

The delicious pressure between us continued to build, vibrating through me, through him, as we ground into one another, trying to get closer, closer, but never able to get enough.

"Fuck, *Lily*," Will hissed as my teeth found his shoulder. His hand tried to slip between us, but I batted it away. The friction between our bodies was enough.

"It's too much," I moaned as the hand on my hip forced me to take him even deeper.

"It's never enough," he gritted out as he slapped his palm against the wall behind him, his other hand placing an iron grip on my hip to keep me still as he drove into me from below. "You'll take it because it's never enough, Maggie. Do you hear me? It's *never* enough with us."

"*YES!*" I screamed, as a second orgasm tore through me. "Oh God, yes, I hear you!"

Will gave a loud, animal yell as I squeezed around him. "FUCK!" he shouted, his deep voice reverberating off the walls. "Oh, Jesus, *Lily*!"

"Will!"

We fell apart together, diving into each other's bodies like we were diving into the sea—but instead of cold water, we were a refuge of warmth. Will, sweaty and trembling, shook as he finally released all the worries and fears he carried on a daily basis. And I took them all and let them float, lost in a cloud of ecstasy, but also in the knowledge of how much of an anchor this man had become in my life. A life that, before him, had been filled with nothing but questions.

"Do you know?" he asked some time later, as we came down from our mutual highs and the boat slowly rocked us into a hazy dream. "I'm not sure I care."

"Hmm?" Sleepily, I pushed a lock of hair off my forehead, but didn't move. "What about?"

"I don't care where we go. What we do." He nuzzled against my hair, stroking my shoulder lightly as he inhaled. "I don't care where I am so long as I'm with you."

The words were simple, even a bit clichéd. But Will had never been one for flowery statements or poetry. His words were true, clean, and clear, and I knew he meant them.

A cloud lifted as they sank into my soul. The world outside this small room, this small bed, didn't seem so scary. Instead, I could feel it calling to us, expansive and free.

And yet, even as we drifted, I still had this terrible feeling that maybe this afternoon, its idyllic peace, was an illusion. That maybe the freedom I felt wasn't real after all. Maybe we were just in the eye of the storm.

CHAPTER TWENTY-THREE

After a quick catnap, we sailed back to the marina, where Will skillfully berthed (or so he said when he corrected my jargon). But both of us were quiet on the sail back, like we knew that there was something coming. A haze of smoke had settled around LA over the last few days from the end-of-summer wildfires up north. They weren't close, but you always felt the threat.

"So, I was thinking," Will said as he got the boat in order. "I should invite my mom to the wrap party."

I arched a brow in surprise. "Oh?"

In the last two months, Tricia Owens-Baker hadn't been allowed anywhere near production in order to respect the sensitivity of Will as an artist. It was one of the few demands that Beauregard had yielded on— partly, I expected, because of pressure from the director. In the end, getting a good performance from their star, and thus making more money, was more important than Max del Conte's sadistic games. And two months ago, Will had been *so* adamant about keeping her off set. This was definitely an about-face.

Will nodded. "Yeah. I've been thinking about it...I think I need to make peace." He finished tying the rope onto the dock. "We probably won't ever have the greatest relationship, but I can't avoid her forever, right? It's been four years."

I considered while we walked. My mom and I weren't the greatest example of a mother-child relationship. All I knew of Tricia Owens-Baker was that she was the kind of woman who would separate a small boy from his father in order to make money. And that she was the kind of mother who would slap her son across the face after not seeing him for four years. So, no, I definitely wasn't inclined to like Tricia Owens-Baker at all.

But if Will could be magnanimous, then I supposed I could try. For his sake.

"I think that's nice," I said finally. "And I guess I should probably tell you something too."

Will slung a long arm around my neck, tucking me into his side. "What's up, buttercup?"

I didn't laugh. "Um...today...something happened when you were on set, doing your, um, sex scene with Amelia."

The thought erased all the good vibes we'd developed that afternoon. I'd spent the last few hours pretending the incidents with Theo and Amelia hadn't happened. Putting out that fire in the back of my mind. Keeping it far from Will's and my rare moment of peace and solitude.

But just like that, there was smoke on the horizon again.

Will stopped and turned to me. "Maggie, it wasn't a sex scene. Is that what she told you? I swear to God, that little—"

"She didn't tell me anything," I said. "It was...I overheard something on the audio headphones at base camp."

Will frowned. "What did you hear? Because the scene was about two minutes long. We had to be in bed together, but it was thirty seconds of dialogue, a fake kiss, and then I get up and leave. That was it." He sneered. "Can you believe they make us wear full body makeup for that shit?"

I shook my head. I didn't want to think about him in bed with Amelia no matter how briefly. "That's—that's not the point," I said. "Anyway, she was being catty, but it picked up on the mic, and it pissed me off. Talking about how easy it used to be to get you into b-bed or whatever. B-back then."

My lower lip began to quiver before I could stop it. Dammit. I knew that wasn't Will anymore. I knew that wasn't *my* Will, at least. But it didn't make the idea hurt any less.

"Lil. Lily pad."

I looked up, unable to keep my eyes from tearing.

Will cupped my face with both hands. "Baby. You know she's full of shit, right?"

"I...sure. I know. But back then...is it true, the stories about how wild you were?"

Will's shoulders deflated. "Lil, I told you what kind of person I was before. I was empty, looking for the next high that could help me ignore my meaningless fucking life. You...you do a lot of stupid things when you're high out of your mind, babe."

I nodded minutely, but a tear started to fall nonetheless. So it was true, and this was his way of telling me. That the pictures of him stumbling out of nightclubs, about all his wild nights...none of them had been the product of media manipulation.

Would he ever miss that? Was there a part of him that wanted that release again?

Will leaned down and kissed the tear away. "You," he said. "That's all I want, Lil. Just you."

I swallowed and accepted a second kiss he offered. "I know," I said. "But I...I *really* hate it when she talks about you like that. Like, I don't know. You still belong to her. It makes me want to..."

"Want to what?"

A blond brow rose, and a dimple appeared in Will's left cheek. The bastard, he was amused by this.

"It makes me want to kick her bony ass," I said clearly. "And then it makes me want to trap you in your trailer so you don't forget who you *do* belong to."

By the time I was done speaking, I was practically shaking. And when I turned back to Will, he had his arms crossed over his chest, making his forearms and biceps flex distractingly.

"Good," he said.

I gaped. "*Good?*"

He grabbed my chin. "Yeah. Good. Because now you know how I felt every time I had to watch Lucas stare at your ass twenty times a day. And you know how I feel every time I think about what that piece of shit Theo del Conte did to you." He stamped a quick, harsh kiss on my lips. "It's a violent thing, love. It's sharp as a fucking razor and can rip your heart to shreds."

His grip on my chin squeezed a little harder, and for a few seconds, he looked me over the same way you might look at a snake or some other kind of predator. One that you thought might kill you. But in the end, when our eyes met again, his softened, and he released me.

"What I feel for you, baby...sometimes I think it's not natural. Because when you look at me, it's like you see inside, deep down, in the places no one else can reach." He shook his head, like the very idea was impossible. "And you know, if my pain is yours, Lil, then your pain is mine. That's how it works."

He took my hand, running his thumb over my knuckles.

"I know," I said softly. Then, with more conviction: "I *know*."

Will looked at me for a bit longer. "Yeah," he said finally. "I know you do." He exhaled, like some invisible weight had been lifted.

"Will?"

He looked back at me. "Yeah?"

"Theo's here."

Will's eyes became as wide as the sky as he looked frantically around the marina. "*What*?"

I took a step back with my hands raised. "Whoa, calm down. P-please. Not *here* here. I saw him today. At the studio."

He flinched at the sound of my stutter. "Don't tell me to fucking calm down, Maggie! Your rapist showed up at my place of work to harass both of us, and you want me to calm down? Why the fuck didn't you tell me about this?"

"I wanted y-you to take a second to think about it," I said. "You just got done talking about how the idea of him makes you feel v-violent—I didn't want you to risk anything. And I didn't want to ruin what little time together we actually had today!"

"I can't believe you waited this long to tell me." He whipped his phone out and started swiping violently. "Fuck!" he shouted when it was clear he had no service. He snatched my hand and started dragging me back through the marina, around a corner of the dock toward the parking lot where Garrett and Hakeem were still waiting for us in the car.

And somehow, it was like turning that corner brought us immediately back into the real world. Both of our cell phones went off immediately, as we walked back into service raising an alarm of multiple text messages, emails, missed calls, and more. People had been trying to reach us for hours.

"Oh, *shit.*" Will stared at his phone with pure horror.

"What?"

All the anger that had carved up his beautiful face moments before vanished. Now all I saw was regret.

"Oh, Lil," he said as he sank down to a squat. He rocked back until he landed on his ass, then buried his face in his hands.

"Will, what is it?"

"I'm sorry," he said over and over again. He handed me the phone, which had some kind of gallery on it. "So fucking sorry."

He buried his face in his hands, turning back to the ocean while I scrolled dumbfounded, through picture after blurry picture of the two of us only a few hours before. Will lying on his back, long limbs relaxed in bliss. The water on either side of the boat blinking in the light while I took off my shirt, then my bra. Pictures of me kissing him. Of Will kissing me. Of his hands, my hands...*everywhere* until, eventually, he picked me up and we disappeared into the cabin.

It wasn't porn. But it was...close. And it was my body, gyrating atop him like a two-bit dancer at some gentleman's club. Mine and his, so intimately entwined, and completely on display.

I couldn't breathe.

"What—w-what the hell is this?" I stuttered, holding the phone back out. "I d-don't understand. Who took this? Where is that posted?"

My hand shook, but Will managed to take the phone before I dropped it. He clambered back up.

"Some psycho with a telephoto in the trees, I'm guessing," he said as he pulled me into his chest. "Probably sold it to some shitty tabloid sites. Benny says it's on a bunch already."

"In f-four *hours*?" My head hurt trying to process how quickly this was happening. "How—how did they even—where were—" I shook my head, unable to get out a coherent sentence.

"I know, babe, I know." Will shushed into my ear, rocking me lightly. "Come on, let's go home. We *will* find out who did this, Lil. I promise."

Stunned, I let him guide me down the dock while he swiped on his phone. Benny picked up immediately, but I could barely listen while Will shouted.

"The only people who knew we were on that boat were Corbyn, Garrett, and Hakeem. So I want to know who the fuck ratted us out, Benny."

There was a long silence while Benny talked.

"Yeah," Will replied. "She saw it. She's…she's shook up." He listened a few more minutes, then his eyes flashed open. "What? Are you kidding? Benny, how the *fuck* do they even know where we are now?" There was some more talk, and Will swore heavily under his breath. "Fine. No, no, it's fine. I need to get her out of here. Yeah, I'll call you when we're back at the house."

He ended the call and turned to me. "Well, when it rains, it pours, I guess. Things just got a lot worse."

"There is a fucking porn movie of me on the internet, Will! How could things get worse?"

"They could have filmed us inside the cabin too?"

Will was joking, but I only glared at him, not finding the idea at all funny. He wilted, and it was then I realized that familiar weight, which had settled on his broad shoulders ever since he'd left the lake, was back.

"What?" I asked "What made it worse?"

He just pointed down the length of the long dock. I squinted past his shaky fingers.

"Fuck," he said as he scanned the marina parking lot. "Fucking *fuck*."

Will dialed another number, and almost immediately, Hakeem answered.

"Hey, man," he said, his voice sounding clearly through the speaker. "We got a bit of a situation here. About twenty-thirty paps are basically stuck to the gate. You ready to go?"

Will glared down the dock, where we could see Hakeem speaking into the phone while Garrett was doing his best to block off the pack of photographers crowding the entrance. We'd been spotted, and already, flashes were going off.

"What the fuck is going on?" Will snapped. "How did they even know to come here?"

"Man, I don't know." Hakeem's voice was tight. He clearly didn't care for the insinuation on Will's part. "But we need to get you out. Safely. Then we can talk about who the fuck snitched."

I frowned. Hakeem and Garrett wouldn't rat out our location, which meant that it must have gotten out on set somehow. Corbyn had been talking…and someone else had tipped off the paps.

Will shook his head. His entire body was starting to shake. "You didn't think to call some backup?"

"Of course we did," Hakeem snapped. "But it's motherfuckin' rush hour in Los Angeles, and didn't nobody ask you to go European on a boat, did they?"

"So what's the fucking plan?" Will growled. "How the fuck are we supposed to get out of here with that mess?"

I shrank, but he grabbed my hand and pulled me close. His grip was so tight, my bones crunched.

"Don't let go," he whispered, and it was then I realized his gruffness covered his fear. Will wasn't angry at me or anyone else. He was as scared as I was—maybe more.

He continued to listen, holding me close while Hakeem rattled off a set of directions.

"Okay," he said after he ended the call. He shoved his phone in his back pocket and turned to me, sliding his sunglasses back down despite the darkening sky. "Put your shades on, Lil. Otherwise you won't be able to see."

I glanced again toward the photographers, setting off another round of flashes and audible clicks, even from fifty feet away. Then I reached into my purse and did as I was told.

"Garrett and Hakeem are going to do their best to block our way to the car. But it's not going to be like the premiere. There's no blockade or extra security. They are going to shout at us—at you, probably— maybe even grab you, try to get you to look at them. Whatever you do, *don't* let them in, okay? Don't talk. Don't give them anything. Not even a 'no comment.' Hey." Will pulled me back to look at him. "You ready?"

I wished to God I could see his eyes, measure his expression. Was I ready? I didn't know.

"Let's go," I whispered.

I followed him down the dock, and as we approached the entrance where Hakeem and Garrett were forcefully preventing the horde of photographers from crossing through the gate, the flashes went off in a frenzy. They started shouting our names, anything they could think of to get us to look at them.

"Fitz! Where were you and Maggie, Fitz?"

"How does Amelia feel about your new girl?"

"Did you have a nice sail?"

"Whose boat is that?"

"Guys, we just need to get home," Will grumbled as we started to push through the crowd. But there wasn't really a way to get past them completely, since they continued to walk with us, running ahead to snap photos from the front, side, back—whatever angle they could manage. We were squeezed between Hakeem and Garrett, but the two men couldn't protect us completely. Several photographers were in our faces as we tried to get to our car as quickly as we could. Will's arm around me was a vise, and he stared coldly at the ground as he walked fast enough that I had to trot beside him. As the questions and flashes continued, his body began to shake.

"Are the two of you living together?"

"Are you engaged?"

"Maggie, where are you from?"

"Hey!" Will shouted out as we were pushed roughly to one side, then the other, pinballing between them.

"Back off!" Hakeem shouted. He spread his big arms, attempting to make a sort of barrier with his broad body.

But there were too many. And the questions continued as we started to run toward the car.

"Did you have sex on the boat?"

"Oh, honey, don't hide that pretty face."

"Maggie, do you always take your shirt off in public?"

"Maggie, are you a stripper?"

"Did Fitz pay you?"

At the last one, I was jerked backward, out of Will's embrace, hard enough that I fell to the pavement, where I was quickly surrounded by a horde of paparazzi. My sunglasses fell off, and I heard a crunch as they were trampled. Flashes blinded me, and I covered my eyes as I tried to stand.

"Will!" I shouted, though the avalanche of questions obscured my voice. I couldn't see—couldn't tell which direction to go. Where was Will? Where was the security?

"Maggie, are you trying to become an actress?"

"Are you with Fitz for his money?"

"Are you in adult films?"

"Maggie, are you a prostitute?"

One hand, then another grabbed my shoulder, then my shirt, trying to pick me up roughly, but only succeeding at pushing me down more.

"Don't *touch* me!" I shrieked, my arms flailing outward, knuckles scraping on the pavement as I fell back to the ground.

"*GET THE FUCK AWAY FROM HER!*" Will's voice, loud and feral, cut through the crowd as one photographer was yanked back and tossed aside. I heard another loud thwack that sounded like someone's head hitting cement, and another chorus of shouts, among them Hakeem's and Garrett's: "Will, *stop!*"

And then hands—not ones trying to pull or yank on me, but big palms, one my body knew intimately, hands that could slide around my waist with ease, pick me up like I weighed nothing—slipped under my back and my legs and lifted me off the ground. I squeezed my eyes shut as I was enveloped in his scent—light, water, sun, soap. Will.

"Hakeem, open the fucking door!" His voice vibrated against my cheek, but I kept my eyes shut. I didn't want to see the chaos still swirling around us. The shouts, the stares, the reflection of our terror in their long, black lenses.

I was placed roughly in the back of the SUV, and with a fight, Will was able to shut the door behind us, locking us in the back of the truck.

"Oh, *fuck*," I cried softly to myself as the world slowly came back into focus. There were still stars in the periphery of my vision, but soon I could see straight ahead.

"*Go*," Will ordered the second Hakeem clambered into the passenger seat. "I don't care if you run every motherfucking one of those blood-suckers over. Just get us the hell out of here."

I turned away from the window, cowering into Will's shoulder while I tried to ignore the slaps of hands on the glass, the continued flashes through the windows, the shouting and yelling as Garrett backed the car out of the spot, forcing the paparazzi to move with us until finally we were able to turn the car toward the exit and go.

"You've got about five on your tail," Hakeem said as we were turning out of the lot. "And probably ten more getting in their cars." He turned to Garrett. "Do we have shells?"

"Shells?" I asked.

Garrett nodded. "Three."

Beside me, Will shuddered. "A shell game. Remember when we switched cars in New York?"

I nodded, blinking as my vision continued to focus.

He looked at me with dread. "We're going to do that about three times right now, and we have to move fast, okay?"

I frowned. "Won't they—won't they leave us alone when we get to the house?"

"Lily, they don't know where we live, and I'd like to keep it like that, all right?"

There was a grumble in the front of the car, and Will snapped his head forward. "*What?*"

Hakeem shook his head. "Nothing, man. You want to play a shell game, we can do that. But they're going to figure out where you live one way or another. Move a thousand times if you want to, but they always do."

"Just get us home," Will bit out. When my head thumped against his shoulder, he didn't pull me close. Instead, he bent forward and cradled his face in his hands, chanting some unintelligible mantra to himself as we raced up Catalina and then Ripley toward the 405, going much faster than the speed limit.

"Why don't we go to the studio?" I asked. "Couldn't we go there and…"

"Oh, honey, you don't really think it's gonna be that easy anymore, do you?" Hakeem turned back around and smiled at me like he would to a small child. "They know your face *real* well now, sweetheart. Well, to be fair, they know more than that."

"Hakeem!" Will's voice was a bark, though he didn't move from his silent prayer.

Hakeem rolled his eyes, then turned back to me. "For the last two months, they've only been after him. We've done a pretty good job of shielding him. He only gets followed maybe once every other day, but that's only because his life is *boring*. But that little stunt the two of you pulled on the boat? That was *news*. You fed the beast, and now it's gonna want a whole lot more."

"First stop's in five," Garrett called as he pulled onto the freeway. "At least we're not jammed."

The SUV took off like a shot, and it was then I looked over my shoulder to see several other cars weaving around the typical LA traffic behind us. Garrett cut in front of a large semi, earning a middle finger and a loud honk.

"Well, I'd rather be jammed than dead," Hakeem said as he checked his seatbelt. "Let's not get rolled on the freeway, all right?"

"Are you okay?" I asked Will as he remained in his trance. I set a light hand on his back, and he started, popping up with wild eyes.

"No," he said clearly. "No, I'm fucking not."

I watched in shock as he shook off my hand and proceeded to open the center compartment in the armrest and pull out three small bottles of vodka. He unscrewed the top of the first and threw it back like water, the only sign that it was something stronger was the way his eyes watered slightly.

"Will, what are you—" I started, but I was quickly cut off.

"I don't want to hear it," he said before chasing the first shot down with a second. "Right now, I just need to calm the fuck down before my heart explodes like my old man's."

I wanted to take the bottles away from him, but I was too stunned to do or say anything. Will's breath was wheezing, and his face was white.

He shook his head when I reached out again, tossed back the third bottle, and then collapsed backward against the seat. Within minutes, his face took on a rosy glow, nose pink at the tip. It was a look I knew—my mother's face was always unnaturally pink that way.

But before I could say anything else, Garrett was screeching across four lanes of traffic, causing a chorus of car horns to explode as he lost several other cars in pursuit of us.

"How many now?" he asked as he sped off the exit.

"Maybe two," Hakeem replied. "Nice work, man."

Garrett nodded. "Let's see if we can shake the others with only one switcheroo. You two ready?"

"Ready for what?" I asked.

Will looked like he wanted to throw up as Garrett took a sudden turn into a hotel parking garage, wheeling around the spiraled corners with glee until we reached an empty floor containing two other cars.

As soon as we parked, the driver of one of the Town Cars hopped out, and Garrett and Hakeem opened the back doors of the SUV. Will spilled out, a little shaky after drinking all that vodka on an empty stomach.

"Car one, car two," Garrett said, pointing at each of us separately.

"I'm *not* leaving her!" Will spat, his voice a little looser than normal, like his lips were made of rubber.

Garret frowned. "Fine. Be difficult then." He tossed a set of keys to the other driver, who went to take the SUV. "Get in, asshole," he said to Will, who sneered in return before guiding me into the back seat of a shaded Town Car. Hakeem got into the other identical one, and we started the chase again, waiting first for the other man to drive the SUV out of the garage, then Hakeem in the first Town Car, and then us.

Garrett didn't see any other photographers following us directly, but according to both him and Will, that didn't mean they weren't, and so, we repeated the process twice more. Maybe it was a bit extreme, but I could see why it took so long.

I fingered the torn edges of my shirt, pressed my fingertips over the new bruises on my arm, and floated them over the strawberry on my knee. For the first time, I understood something of the deep-seated fear that Will carried of being found. If this was just the tip of what these people were capable of, I didn't want to imagine the kind of terror he faced at the height of his fame.

Eventually, when it was fully dark outside and Will was finally convinced that no one would follow us back to the house in the Hills, he allowed Garrett to drive us home. But when I turned to make sure Will was following me inside, I was shocked to see the car pulling away again.

"Hey!" I shouted, banging on the trunk. "Stop!"

As if the metal heard me, the car jerked to a halt, and the back window opened.

"Where are you going?" I demanded.

Will sighed wearily. The circles under his eyes had deepened, though the shine on his nose hadn't disappeared. "I told you, Maggie. We leave for Palm Desert tonight. I have to be back on set at nine. That's in fifteen minutes."

My mouth hung open. "They can't possibly think you have to go like this. After what just happened to us!"

But Will only stared ahead blankly. His green eyes were dull and dreary, without their usual fierce spark.

"Two weeks," was all he said. "I'd work around the clock if I thought it would get us out of this fucking fishbowl any faster." He reached through the window and took my hand, but didn't pull me in for a kiss. I bit my lip. I could smell the alcohol wafting out of the car—I wondered if he'd taken another few shots when I got out.

"I'll see you in a few days," he said, squeezed my hand, and then let go.

I watched the car drive away while I wrapped my arms around my waist and tried not to cry. Standing in the middle of all of this luxury—I suddenly hated all of it. If its cost was this kind of misery, I'd go back to stripping sheets and emptying the trash any day.

———

A FEW HOURS LATER, right as I was beginning to contemplate trying to sleep, there was a loud knock at the door. I started from where I sat in the living room, picking out another new song on the guitar. It had been my refuge for the evening.

"Maggie, it's me."

I made sure my robe was shut, then opened the door to find Garrett standing there, holding a large bouquet of lilies.

"Apparently my time is better spent delivering flowers than protecting his sorry ass," Garrett said as he handed me the vase.

I accepted it, then set it down on the foyer table and opened the card sticking out of the top. There were only two words in a familiar scrawl: *I'm sorry.*

"Thanks, Garrett," I said as I buried my face in their sweet, soft petals.

Garret tipped an imaginary hat. "Night, Maggie."

I shut the door behind me and carried the flowers into the bedroom. They were the last things I saw as my eyes finally shut—the white and shadows mixed together, their scent lulling me to sleep.

CHAPTER TWENTY-FOUR

"Holy shit! What is *up*, California girl?"

Two weeks later, I grinned as Calliope engulfed me in a massive hug outside of LAX. She looked as outrageous as ever in a bright pink maxi dress, giant hoop earrings extending down to her shoulders, and hair arranged in a massive, intricate pile of braids at the crown of her head. In my humble t-shirt and jean shorts, my hair tied back into a ponytail, I couldn't even begin to compete with my friend's style. She looked much more the part of a movie star's girlfriend than I did.

"Look at you!" She held my arms out wide. "You're *so* tan! How much time have you been spending by the pool, huh?"

"Oh, hush. Not *that* much." I grinned. Maybe I didn't have style, but I had been working out hours every day. There wasn't much else to do besides that and write music when Will was on set, especially with the craziness of the press. So, I'd been doing plenty of both.

"Maggie." Hakeem looked around and twirled a hand in the air, indicating we needed to get inside the car before I was recognized.

"Jeez, paranoid, much?"

I shrugged. He wasn't, actually. In the weeks following the sailboat debacle, I'd been recognized often on the street, followed three times, and had more than a few threats sent by way of the studio. Running by myself—or even in our neighborhood—was a thing of the past.

"It's the way it is right now," I said. "Come on, let's go."

A few moments later, we were on our way to the house. Calliope was in LA to negotiate a new client's record deal with Capitol, but she was staying with us instead of a hotel. "It's on their dime, but I told them I have famous friends," she said. "So you suckers might as well put me up." I was more than excited to see my friend. Until I saw her face, I hadn't realized how lonely LA had been.

"Have you heard from Ellie lately?" she wondered as Hakeem turned down Hollywood Boulevard. This was the part of the drive home that always made me nervous. The boulevard was almost always crawling with tourists and paparazzi, looking for famous people on their way home or somewhere else. Will and I had been spotted a few times, leading to two other fervent car chases all over Los Angeles until we finally lost them.

I pushed my sunglasses up my nose and shook my head. "She still won't answer my calls. Lucas said she was at church again, talking about opening up the outer houses. But he said they still aren't furnished or anything. She spends all her money at Curly's." I shrugged sadly. "It's the same."

I couldn't deny that I was hurt. Here I was, almost two months after giving my mother an ultimatum, without speaking to her, and it didn't seem to matter in the slightest that I was gone.

Calliope rubbed my shoulder. "Hey, she'll come around. It just might take some time."

Slowly, I nodded. "Yeah."

"What about Oscar the Grouch? Has he been any better?"

She was, of course, referring to Will. Two weeks after the sailboat disaster, after Benny, Calliope, and a team of lawyers had been deployed to remove every trace they could find of me and Will from the internet, the hubbub over my unexpected strip show had died down a little. The press attention on Will, however, had not. While Garrett and Hakeem's inventive driving skills continued to keep the paparazzi from figuring out exactly where we lived, they still seemed to hound him no matter where he was: the gym, the studio, and anywhere else he might go. He tried to run once with a team of three other bodyguards and ended up dashing into the canyon and scraping up his leg, much to the irritation of the makeup team.

Unfortunately, his recalcitrance only seemed to make photographers that much more curious. A crowd of at least fifteen of them had basically taken up permanent residence at the studio entrance, and so more than once, Will had chosen to stay there overnight instead of coming home. I had hardly seen him in days. And when I did…it was still like he wasn't there at all.

Calliope grimaced as I recounted all of this and patted my hand. "And…what about the…you know?" She mimed putting back a shot with her hand. "Any more of that happening?"

Hakeem's gaze flickered back to me through the rearview mirror, but he remained quiet.

I shook my head. "Not—not that I know of. But like I said…he hasn't been around as much. The hours at the studio have been so crazy long, I've barely seen him." I didn't want to say that it kept me up at night, wondering if, while I was gone, Will was sitting around his trailer taking shots or doing worse.

"Which means viper lady has been around him instead?"

"Cal…"

She held her hands up, as if in surrender. "Sorry, sorry. I don't mean to suggest."

"Yes, you do. But I can't waste my time being jealous there."

"Maggie, you literally overheard the bitch talking about how she wants to get your man. If it had been me, I would have broken her pretty, plastic nose right there."

In the front, Hakeem chuckled, but assumed a straight face when Calliope turned to him. If I wasn't mistaken, the handsome bodyguard was a little more interested than usual in my friend's comments.

"What am I supposed to do?" I replied. "Track his every move? I trust Will. And he has enough people watching him without me doing it too."

"I'd still like to give Posh Spice a taste of her own medicine," Calliope said with a sympathetic pat. "What about He-Who-Shall-Not-Be-Named? Any more haunting of the set?"

I shook my head. That was the one relief we'd been afforded. As soon as he'd arrived on set after the sailboat debacle, Will had basically thrown holy hell at Corbyn about Theo showing up. Corbyn, feeling guilty that he'd mentioned our use of his sailboat to multiple crew members, instituted a full ban of the studio head's son until Will was done filming. It was a diva approach, but one I appreciated. Finishing the movie on time proved to be more important to the studio than humoring its owner's errant son. Theo hadn't been heard from since.

"Well, at least there's that," Calliope said after I told her everything. "All right, then. So, what's our agenda? Is there going to be press at this party, or can I go in my jeans?"

On top of her business agenda, Calliope's trip coincided with one other event: the wrap party. Principal photography was scheduled to finish today, and in two more days, Corbyn, the director, was hosting a massive party for the cast and crew at his home in Beverly Hills. It would have been a relief, and maybe even something to look forward to if it weren't for a few key things. First, the fact that both Amelia and Tricia were going to be there. Second, that we would all be photographed extensively. And third, that the studio was requiring press as part of Will's promotional duties. Benny was even coming to make sure he cooperated.

I sighed. "*Vanity Fair* is doing an exposé on Will. It's going to be a 'week in the life' feature. Which means I'll be in it too."

Two days ago, the reporter had come to the set and taken candid photos of him and me. Will had sunk into an abysmal mood and hadn't emerged since.

"Well, let's see if we can play that to our advantage, shall we?" Calliope suggested as Hakeem punched the code into the gate and began steering down the long driveway.

"What do you mean?" I asked.

Calliope rolled her eyes. "You guys are such amateurs. You have an excuse, of course, but Will should know this game by now. The trick to getting the press off your back is to give them a little of what they want. Right now they think you're hiding something. You guys run around acting like you're protecting the nuclear codes. Get a stylist. Take a pap stroll or two. Let them see you at the farmer's market or some boring domestic crap like that. Go shopping at Whole Foods and volunteer at a soup kitchen. Sooner or later they won't care anymore and they'll move on to the next drug-laced starlet who's willing to flip their skirts for a few extra headlines. This profile could be a great way to normalize the two of you."

I swallowed. "I don't know. I really don't think Will is going to be open to giving them *more* of himself instead of less."

The car pulled to a stop, and Hakeem hopped out to open Calliope's door with a flourish.

"Think about it," Calliope said. "Now, give me a tour of this palace while you still can."

———

BENNY ARRIVED at the house after Calliope, and we all spent a few hours hanging out around the pool before Will appeared around five, grumpy as usual, but looking relieved. Filming was done, barring any reshoots, and he'd gone to the gym before stopping at the store on the way home. Or, in his case, sending Hakeem inside to get what he wanted.

"Hey!" I called out when he burst into the living room behind us.

But Will just headed straight for the kitchen and started unloading groceries from a paper bag. Benny and Calliope looked at each other and took long sips of their drinks. I, of course, was drinking water, but the two of them had been enjoying cocktails for the last hour. I frowned and padded into the kitchen.

"That bad?" I asked as I slid onto a stool.

Will huffed as he moved around.

"Will," I said. "Hey."

He stopped and turned around. "They're fucking vultures, you know? And it's not just the press. It's everyone in this fucking city. Everyone is an informant, calling in tips for a few extra bucks. I can't even work out without walking outside to a fucking mob."

I cringed. On a scale of one-to-ten, mobs were about an eight.

I put a hand over his. "Well, you only have to stick around for a few more weeks, right?"

He nodded. "Max says I have to attend three more premieres as Oscar season starts, and then I'm done until we start promoting next spring, barring any reshoots." He let out a big breath, like he was expelling the stress of the day. "I can't wait to get the fuck out of here."

Calliope and Benny wandered in from the pool, both a little unsteady after the effects of two mojitos each, courtesy of Benny's mixology skills.

"What's that you have there?" Benny asked, pointing to the paper bag Will dropped in the outdoor kitchen. "Someone's about to binge, I see."

Will looked up gleefully and continued pulling out groceries.

"I had Hakeem run to the store while I was at the gym," he said. "To get me all the stuff I've been banned from eating." One by one, he pointed at the things on the counter. "Salt and vinegar potato chips. Snickers bar. Ice cream. French bread—we're having French toast, bacon, the works for breakfast tomorrow, babe." He continued pulling them out until there was a massive pile of mostly unhealthy food on the outdoor table.

I grinned. "Cheat day?"

"More like a cheat week," Benny pronounced. "Motherfucker wants a dad bod."

Calliope choked on her drink. "Oh good lord, please no."

Will chuckled. "How about a cheat month?" he asked as he leaned over the counter. "You think the paps will be interested in taking pictures of me with a big belly?"

I giggled. Will had the metabolism of a fifteen-year-old. I seriously doubted he could be anything but trim.

"How about you, Lil?" His eyes gleamed, and I grinned, happy to see that spark that had been so absent for the last few weeks. "Would you take me with a beer belly and a double chin?"

I smiled shyly. "I'll take you however you are," I said quietly. And it was the truth.

"Come here."

He tugged me close and nuzzled my hair, then gave me a kiss that lingered a little more than strictly necessary. I sighed. Gratitude. That's what I felt.

"Which makes me the luckiest bastard on the planet," he murmured. "All right, I'm going to put the frozen stuff away. And then we're going to celebrate the end of this shit show."

BECAUSE OF THE PRESS, Robin had been deployed for another round of primping and styling for the party, so Will was only able to put down a bag of chips and a Häagen-Dazs bar before he was forced to get ready like the rest of us. It was for the best. After months of squeaky-clean eating, the rich food made him feel sick.

Much to both Robin's and Benny's irritation, Will had staunchly refused to wear anything fancier than his favorite old Levi's and a concert t-shirt, but begrudgingly allowed Robin to style his hair. I, however, had accepted a little red dress and black strappy heels when Robin informed me that despite Will's stubbornness, most of the people at Corbyn's would actually be dressed for a legitimate party, not a back-yard barbecue. My hair, still in its customary ponytail, had been tousled and teased into a curly mass. Robin had finished the look off with a gold chain and some hoops—relatively similar to the stage looks I had once worn. Unlike at the premiere, I actually felt more like myself. And when I walked into the living room, where Will, Calliope, and Benny were all waiting, Will's reaction was the only one that mattered.

"Holy shit," he muttered as he pushed off the couch. "Woman, you are going to give me a heart attack."

I fingered the short, silk hem. "Too much?" It was definitely brighter than the looks I usually favored, but I couldn't deny that Robin had a great eye for color.

"Absolutely not," Calliope said sharply from the sofa. "You look fantastic, babe."

Will pulled me close and drifted a heated gaze over my entire body. "You look perfect," he pronounced, quiet and fierce. Then a sly half smile emerged. "Maybe we should keep the party here, huh? I could probably make it entertaining for you."

I pushed him lightly on the chest, though I was already blushing. "You're going to get into even more trouble with Max if you do that. We have to go."

He rolled his eyes, but hugged me closer. "All right," he said. "Let's get this garbage over with. And then we are coming back here so we can celebrate the *real* way."

CHAPTER TWENTY-FIVE

Corbyn was sympathetic to Will's anxiety about the press, so instead of having the wrap party thrown at a lounge or club near the studio, he hosted it at his sprawling mansion in Beverly Hills. It wasn't a particularly secret location, and it was clear when we arrived that more than only *Vanity Fair* had been notified of the party's existence.

"Fuck."

Will glared through the tinted windows of our limo at the photographers huddled outside the property gates. Gone was the playful Will who had torn into a bag of chips like a kid on Christmas and copped a feel when no one was looking. He was again primped and polished, his hair a perfectly rumpled mess of golden waves, and the aviators he was currently wearing gave him a rakish look similar to Tom Cruise in *Top Gun*. Robin had allowed him to keep his five-o'clock shadow, but only if he had let her exchange his graphic tee with a button-up Burberry shirt, which he had stubbornly rolled up at the cuffs. I thought he looked absolutely edible, but Will had been pulling irritably at his collar for the last twenty minutes.

"Here we go again," Calliope remarked from her seat across from me. My friend had made no secret of her frustrations with Will's idiosyncrasies. She thought he complained too much, despite the fact that she knew very well about his social anxiety.

She shrank slightly when he turned his glare on her.

"Sorry, sorry," she muttered.

"Hey." I pulled Will's attention back to me with a pat on his knee. "Should we not go? Screw Max. He can deal if the *Vanity Fair* people watch us go to McDonald's or something like that."

Part of me almost wished he'd say yes, even though I'd urged him to come in the first place. Parties were supposed to be fun, but socializing in a room full of drunk people while Amelia and Tricia ran rampant wasn't my idea of a good time. Will and I had gotten so little time together that an evening at home sounded pretty perfect.

Will sighed heavily. "No, you're right. I have to go. It's in the contract. The more we fight the terms, the longer they'll take to fulfill."

"Well, then, is there *any* way we can have a decent time?"

He pulled off his sunglasses, and the anger and fear in his eyes morphed into something closer to shame. He exhaled, long and low. "Got a shot for me?" he joked.

Calliope grunted. I didn't find it particularly funny either.

Will shook his head. "I'm joking, I'm joking. Okay, Lil. Yeah…we can try, okay. And if I start acting like an asshole, tackle me in a closet somewhere, okay?"

One side of his mouth tipped up into a suggestive smile, and immediately, I was taken back to the premiere party where he had done just that to me. I flushed, and Will chuckled.

"Or you can blush like that all night," he whispered in my ear. "That would distract any man from a nuclear bomb."

"Stop," I whispered, turning even brighter red.

"Never," Will said with a broader smirk, and then replaced his sunglasses.

"You guys are nauseating," Calliope pronounced, though her smile said something different.

Will lifted my hand. "Nah, just lucky," he said as he kissed my knuckles.

"All right," Benny said as we pulled to a stop in the roundabout driveway. "Showtime."

———

AFTER DODGING the flurry of flashes and photographers who eagerly snapped away as we walked from the car to the entrance, we managed to get inside safely. We checked our bags with the temporary coat check set up in one of the main floor rooms and wandered to the backyard to join the rest of the party, in full swing around Corbyn's massive pool, set against a panoramic view of Los Angeles.

"Welcome!" Corbyn greeted Will with a slap on the shoulder and a brief kiss to my cheek. "Everything is outside, but feel free to wander the downstairs. The *VF* reporter and photographer are floating around, so try not to get too sloshed until they leave." He winked at me, and I tried to smile back. I could already tell this was the kind of party where I would be uncomfortable within an hour.

Will grabbed my hand and led me to the backyard, where two more people approached that made dread spool in my stomach: Amelia and Tricia, arm in arm, looking thick as thieves.

"Better get it over with early," Will said. "Then we can find a quiet corner somewhere and hibernate for a few hours." He squeezed my hand. "Don't let go."

"Darling!"

Amelia swept in like a tropical fruit-scented breeze and clasped her perfectly manicured fingers on Will's shirt. She looked as stunning as always in a flowing pink dress that clung to her curves like paint. Her blonde hair swished around Will's face as she dropped kisses to each of his cheeks. It smacked me in the face a few times, and I had to brush strands out of my mouth.

"Hey, Amy." Will smiled tightly before pulling me back to his side. "Mom."

Tricia, in a tasteful black dress that showcased her enviable genes, stepped forward, but didn't offer her son any kind of touch. It was almost as if she knew better. "Will. And…" She eyed me carefully.

Will rolled his eyes. "You know Maggie's name, Mom."

For a moment, the resemblance between Tricia Owens-Baker and her son was uncanny. The long, straight nose, the sharp green eyes, the radiant blonde hair. But only for a second before her face twisted into a nasty sneer.

"My goodness. Aren't you a butterfly," she remarked, looking over my dress frankly. "It's a bit different from the outfit you wore on the sailboat."

"*Mom.*"

"I'm surprised," she said, ignoring Will's tone. "I honestly thought this dalliance would have run its course by now."

Will immediately turned away. "This was a mistake. Come on, Lil."

"Come now, darling, it was only a joke," Amelia put in with a hand on his arm. "You can't expect to prance around Corbyn's boat in the nude and not get a bit of ribbing here and there." She winked. "*We* ought to know, hmm?"

Will stared straight ahead without a response. I worked very hard not to slap Amelia's hand away when she tapped him on the shoulder.

"Anyway, there's no need to put your nose out of joint, Willie." She tugged him toward her, but he still didn't let go of my hand.

"It's Will," he said tightly. But when I waited for him to give his mother's nasty comment a harsh rebuke, none came.

"Sorry, sorry. Old habits, of course." Amelia winked at me. "So serious, now. Can't even call you Willie, then? Not ever?"

Will gave her a hard look I didn't quite understand. "You can't do a lot of things anymore, Amy. I thought I made that clear the other night."

Her childlike blue gaze turned icy in a second, then darted quickly between us.

"Did you?" she asked breathily. "Because it rather seemed like something...*else*...thought otherwise."

Will fixed a cold stare that finally made Amelia look away.

"We'll see then," she said and danced around Will, playing a few fingers over his shoulder as she sauntered past us and down the rest of the path.

Tricia watched her go with something like nostalgia. "Why you ever let that girl go is beyond me," she remarked. "She's a darling, and you always looked *so* good together."

"Mom, Maggie is right fucking here."

Tricia shrugged and took a measured sip of her cocktail. "It's only a matter of aesthetic taste, Will. I'm sure Margie here understands what I mean."

"It's Maggie," I corrected her, only to be waved away.

"Because that's really what matters, right?" Will snapped. "How people *look* together?"

Tricia turned back to us, and I found it hard not to look away when, once again, her hard gaze worked incessantly to cut me down. "Some people look wrong from the start," she said. "It's...obvious."

I tried to maintain eye contact. I really did. But Tricia Owens-Baker had the same distinctive talent that her son had of tearing down a person or building them up with a mere look. She was definitely *not* doing the latter with me, and in the end, I looked down at my toes, wishing I'd had time for a nice pedicure before coming here.

"That's it," Will said, turning to leave. "This is bullshit. Maggie, we're going."

"Will, you can't *do* that," his mother said. "You have an obligation to Max, and if you don't—"

Will whirled around with a face full of fire. Even Tricia had to take a step back.

"*Stop*," he ordered emphatically. "You don't have the right to talk to me like that. You haven't had it for a very long time. So stop."

I frowned. "What are you talking about, Will? She's just looking out for you—"

"Please." Will's eyes wavered. "Maggie, let's go."

"Didn't he tell you?" Tricia asked sharply, then darted a look back to Will. "Well, of course he wouldn't, now, would he?" She flipped out a hand. "Will left me. He was eighteen when he chose that idiot savant from Yonkers over his own flesh and blood."

"She means Benny," Will said. "He was the only one who would take me on that young." He looked up at Tricia. "I think you're forgetting why I did that, Mom."

Tricia rolled her eyes. "Please. You can't *still* hold a grudge about that."

"What?" I asked, looking between them.

Amelia snorted. Her blue eyes were a little bigger than usual. I wondered if she had taken something before coming to the party. Or maybe since she got here.

"Sabotaging your own son's college admissions was a good fucking start!"

The chatter around us died down for a moment, but we were in a secluded enough area of the yard that it didn't make that much of a difference.

"Are you forgetting what that did for you?" She wasn't yelling, but she looked like she wanted to. Her eyes flashed exactly like her son's. But unlike him, they lacked the warmth that so easily replaced the anger. "If you had gone to Brown, you would have missed out on several roles of a lifetime! You would have missed out on every one of those nominations. Your entire life!"

"I. Never. Wanted. It." Will's words were brittle.

"You were seventeen years old. You didn't know *what* you wanted. I was doing you a favor until you did!"

"But that's the thing, isn't it, Mom?" Will shoved a hand through his hair. "You never gave me the chance, did you? *That's* why I had to leave you, leave this life, in every sense of the word."

"No, you left me out of some misguided sense of self-righteousness," Tricia retorted. "It was *my* negotiating that put you on the map. *My* hard work that got you every major gig you had before you turned eighteen. You'd be nothing without me. *Nothing.*"

"You don't get it, do you?" Will said in a voice that was quiet, but somehow more intimidating than if he were yelling. "I was nothing *because* of you. I had everything in the world, but my life was completely empty. You stuck me in a fucking gilded cage with no one but coked-up actors and production assistants to keep me company. You took away everything that meant anything to me. My home—"

"*Stop,*" Tricia started.

"My friends—"

"I said *stop it*—"

"My father."

At that, Tricia reared. "You are joking. You can't possibly blame me for Michael's death."

"No, but I do blame you for taking me away from him. For barely giving me any time with him! I'm almost thirty years old. In another life, I could have been working a boat with my dad, bringing my kid to a little league game, worrying about how to pay the mortgage instead of whether or not my latest stalker is going to kill me."

"You mean you could have been *ordinary*."

Will closed his eyes. "I could have been happy."

And there it was. The tradeoff of Will's life, one that had been made for him long before he ever had the knowledge of what choice was made.

But if he's not happy with you, my inner voice asked, what does that say about you together?

Tricia finished the rest of her drink, then slowly set it on the ground next to a palm tree. She smoothed her hands over her skirt and patted her hair before she spoke in an eerily even tone.

"You. Ungrateful. Brat. Literally billions of people would wish to be in your shoes, and it's all because of what *I* built for you. They'd kill to have a mother who's half the manager I am."

"You are not my manager," Will said emphatically. "You are not my publicist. My agent. You are *barely* my mother, and even that's stretching it, all things considered."

He looked her up and down, and Tricia withered slightly. I might have felt bad if by that point I'd had even an inkling that she wanted something beyond financial gains from her own son.

Tricia stared at him for a very long time, and then at me.

"You know what," she said in the end, her voice more immovable than her expression. "You should have stayed dead. If you hated this life so much, you should have gone to the bottom with the rest of that godforsaken boat. Then, at least, everything *I* earned would have come back to its rightful place."

Will caved inward, like he had been hit in the chest. My mouth dropped. How could she say something like that to her son? I watched as Will, despite his height, crumpled slightly while Tricia folded her arms and watched.

Rage, pure and violent, rushed through me like a river. I only had one instinct: protect.

I straightened up and faced Tricia. "You need to go."

She arched a neatly plucked brow, as if she had just realized I was there. "Is that right?"

I took a step toward her. "Yeah, that's right. You might be rich, lady, but you don't want to mess with me. Especially not when it comes to your son."

"Oh, honey. What are you going to do? Start a brawl? Throw a punch?"

Her eyes drifted down my thin body, silently measuring me up. But I was no pushover. Months of training, from the time I'd started the triathlon work and all the weeks since, had given me strength, which was only compounded by Will's presence in my life.

I stepped a little closer. "You want to bring out my inner fighter, Tricia?" I asked softly. "Be my guest. I haven't met her, but I'm pretty sure she would kick your damn ass if I gave her the go-ahead."

Tricia's hard green eyes, so like her son's, held mine for several seconds. This time, I didn't look away. She did, as she took a step back, and then another.

"You know what?" she said softly as she glanced back at Will. "You're not worth it. Neither of you are worth it."

It didn't occur to me until much later to wonder which of us she meant.

"Jesus," Will said once she had gone. "I need a drink."

Without waiting, he turned and started walking toward a drink station at the far end of the pool, towing me along. We moved to the end of the line, and Will smiled and signed a few quick autographs for crew members until he was able to wait alone, staring at the walls behind the servers.

"Willie!" Amelia cried from behind him. Her eyes were even more dilated than before.

Will shuddered, but I watched her curiously. Her comments from before came floating back.

"What was that about?" I asked. "That comment Amelia made. About you and her...the other night?"

Will peered at me like he couldn't believe I was asking about that. I didn't blink.

"It was nothing," he replied, turning back to the bar.

"Will."

He continued to stare ahead.

"Will!"

Finally, he looked down at me. "Look, it wasn't a big deal, so I didn't tell you at the time. But when we were in the middle of doing our final scene, I don't know. Amy got the wrong idea—read too much into it or something—and, well, she tried to kiss me."

My mouth dropped. "She *what*?"

Will shook his head, waving his hands back and forth as if to dispel the words like smoke. "Lil, it didn't mean anything. Obviously, I pushed her away and told her to stop. We finished the scene, everything wrapped, and I came home. To you."

I blinked. "If it didn't mean anything, then why not tell me? Didn't you think I'd find out somehow?"

"I *am* telling you," Will insisted. "That *is* how you're finding out."

I crossed my arms and stared at him. "This is messed up. You know that, don't you? How many people at this party watched what happened, huh? How many are taking bets on how long it takes for the English Princess and America's Heartthrob to get back together? God, your own *mother* is counting the days until I'm out of the way!"

He opened his mouth to argue, but before anything came out, Will's gaze flickered somewhere behind me. I turned around to find Amelia watching us intently, looking more than pleased with herself. She gave a sickening little wave at Will and winked at me.

I whirled back around. "Yeah. She looks like she totally got that message."

"Lil—"

I waved his words away. "I'm going to use the bathroom, all right?" I turned to step away, but was pulled back when Will snatched my hand again.

"Don't do that," he said. "Don't run away from me. Not here."

"Oh, that's rich coming from a man who's barely had a moment for me for the last two weeks. You used to swim across an entire lake at the first sign of any real emotion. You're not exactly an expert at sticking around to deal." I jerked my hand, but he still wouldn't release it. "Let go."

"Not until you let me apologize properly."

I grimaced. "Not here."

"Lil, I'm *sorry*."

I looked down at our joined hands. Around us, I could see the curious onlookers, many waiting for me to leave so they could approach him instead. Will felt their curiosity too, felt pinned by it.

But as much as I wanted to shield him, I was mad too. And I needed a moment to reconstitute myself so I could be the support system he needed. Our reckoning about Amelia would come, but I could see it for what it was: a mistake. The discussion could wait until later.

Summoning all of the forgiveness I felt capable of, I stepped closer to give him a kiss on the cheek, but immediately, he wrapped an arm around my waist to keep me there for a real kiss. One that was insistent and a bit inappropriate for such a crowded setting. A few whistles rose, and when he let go, I was breathless.

"You're mine," he whispered in a low, languid voice. "Say it."

"Yours," I replied immediately. The lazy smile that spread across his face made my insides twist. I grabbed his shirt and pulled him to me. "But you're mine too."

It was a little unsettling how much I meant it. The idea of Amelia touching him, trying to kiss him, made me physically ill. Everyone in the world seemed to feel like they were entitled to a piece of the one person on this planet who was supposed to belong to me.

But…did he feel that way too?

His smile only widened, and Will pulled me in for another open-mouthed, heart-stopping kiss. This time the whistles were much louder.

"Get a room!" someone jeered, followed by a bunch of laughter.

Will let me go, and his body was already more relaxed than before. Come to think of it, so was mine.

"Yours," he repeated in a voice that made my toes curl and my heart thump. "Always. Now go and come right back, promise?"

I was barely able to stand upright, but managed to totter a few steps back. "P-promise."

CHAPTER TWENTY-SIX

I escaped the backyard, looking for the quickest route to the bathroom so I could keep said promise.

Unfortunately, when I found it, there was a line ten-people long.

"Shit," I muttered. I really did have to go.

"Just use the master upstairs."

I swung around to find Tricia holding three drinks. She tipped her head toward the large staircase that wound to the second floor.

"Oh," I said. "I—I thought you'd gone."

She snorted. "Sweetheart, this is a major industry party, and unlike my son, I actually care about my career." She looked me over. "You do need to go to the bathroom, correct?"

"Ah—um, yeah," I ventured. Her response was jarring, considering I'd just threatened to pop her one.

"Upstairs, fourth door on the right," she said with an oddly sweet smile. "I'll try to make nice with our boy while you're gone. Studio's orders."

I looked around nervously. What was going on?

"You're not the first person to threaten me and you won't be the last," Tricia said, nodding again toward the stairs. "Just *go.*"

I peered up to the unlit second floor. Corbyn probably wouldn't care. After all, he and Will were about as tight as a director and actor could get. And…the line was really, really long.

"Okay, thanks," I said.

But Tricia was already gone.

I found the bathroom nested in the giant master bedroom. When I was finished, I lingered a moment on the balcony, looking down on the party below. I spotted Will, with his burnished blond hair, nestled between Benny and Corbyn. He had a drink in his hand, and while that wouldn't ever not make me uncomfortable, he looked reasonably relaxed, actually smiling and chuckling from time to time as Benny told some story. *He's not your mother*, I reminded myself. It was possible for most people, after all, to have a drink or two without flying off the deep end. I was glad to see him relaxed.

I was also glad to see that Amelia and Tricia were both leaving him alone. They were, however, together, chatting amiably on the other size of the yard while sipping the drinks that Tricia had brought out. Absently, I wondered who had gotten the third. A peal of Amelia's high-pitched laughter filtered through the party, and I didn't miss the way she darted another gaze across the yard to Will. He, however, didn't seem to notice.

"Well, hello there, Flower."

As it always did, the voice, with its insidious hum that once upon a time I found attractive, sent a ripple of fear down my spine. My skin immediately prickled all over. Theo. Here.

Why?

I turned around, still praying I'd been hearing things. But no, there was Theo, looking as rakish, handsome, and terrifying as ever. His eyes were glassy and dilated—clearly he was on something, which was made more evident by the way he swaggered unevenly around the room. Ice clinked together in his mostly empty glass, which smelled like whiskey.

"Theo…w-what are you doing here?" I skittered to the side of the balcony, but Theo moved faster, blocking the door back into the bedroom.

"I came to say hello," he murmured. "I saw you standing there, surveying the party like Juliet looking for her Romeo. And I thought to myself, 'well, here I am.' What's the line? 'It is the east, and Juliet is the sun'? That sounds about right, doesn't it?"

I swallowed. "I—I d-don't think so, Theo."

"You know, that's the thing about Romeo and Juliet." He staggered forward again, placing one palm on the wall to balance himself. "Everyone said they couldn't be together. So in the end, they decided it was either love or death." He cocked his head. "Sounds reasonable to me."

Should I scream? Would that help? The music below was pounding. I doubted I would even be heard over the noise. I glanced over my shoulder to the party below, praying that this red dress would shine like a beacon. That Will, with his second sense of what I was feeling, would see me. Would come.

"I wouldn't bother with him," Theo replied. "In another few minutes, your golden boy won't even know his own name."

I blinked. "What-what are you talking about?"

Theo clicked his tongue. "Poor, naive Flower. You were always too trusting. As producer, it's my job to make sure my talent gets what they want. And what your boy wants is pills. Lots and lots of pills."

My hands gripped the iron railing so tightly my knuckles turned white.

"So you see," Theo said as he took a few steps closer, "there's nothing to worry about. There's no one here who's going to save you."

He trailed a finger down my face.

"T-take your hands off me," I ordered, cursing myself for the stutter.

"You were always such a frigid little bitch," he muttered as he cornered me against the guard. Then, like a snake darting out for its prey, his hand shot out and claimed me by the throat. Theo laughed. "That stutter is still cute, though." The hand squeezed tighter. "Annoying as fuck. But cute."

With his violent grip, Theo wrenched me away from the balcony and swept inside, then slammed backward against the bedroom wall, hard enough that the wind was knocked out of me.

"Theo," I wheezed, my heart thumping. "P-please. Just let me go."

My eyes darted toward the bedroom entrance, praying for someone to wander upstairs and find us.

"Do you know I have a record now?" Theo asked conversationally, holding me tightly with one hand while he examined the nails of the other. "Two months in jail were doable. Shitty, but doable. It was basically like living in a country club with bad outfits. I made some decent contacts. But now…" He dropped his hand, and the one around my neck pulled me forward, then slammed me lightly against the wall again. "But now, New York State has me registered as a fucking sex offender, Flower. Because of you. Do you know what that means?"

I didn't answer. I was too terrified.

"It's only level one," he said, like he was talking about a bad drink he got at the bar. "That's 'low risk,' or so says my shit-for-brains lawyer. But the goddamn judge couldn't be bought, you see, and *she* decided to designate me as a violent"—he tapped me on the nose—"sexual"—my chin—"predator"—my chest.

I gulped. His eyes blazed.

"It means," Theo said. "That I'm on a list. That anyone, anywhere, can look up dangerous people in their neighborhood and see my name on it." His eyes flared. "I'm sure you can understand why that's a bit of an inconvenience."

Then, as if it were just occurring to him that I had more than a face to stare at, his gaze slowly raked over my body, taking in the gold chain over my collarbone, down past the short, flared hem of my dress, the long expanse of my legs, and the unusual amount of cleavage. When I'd put the dress on, and especially when I'd seen Will's reaction to it, I'd felt beautiful. Now I wanted to cover up.

"Damn," Theo whispered in a voice that once made me shiver with both desire and fear. Now there was only fear. And revulsion. "Why didn't you wear things like this when we were together, huh?"

He slid a finger down the strap of my dress, past my collarbone, and hovered over the swell of my breast.

"Don't t-*touch* me," I hissed, but the grip around my neck remained strong enough that I could barely get the words out.

The hand continued to travel down, around my breast, lingering over my waist, playing with the hem of my skirt.

"Theo," I whispered. "P-please. Let me g-go."

His dark eyes flickered up. "Or what, Flower? Do you really think anyone would care if I fucked a nobody at a party where everyone else is high or drunk?"

"I'll scream." My voice was tiny, but I knew that in a second, it would blow wide open. *Someone* would hear me over the music. Wouldn't they?

Theo smirked and held me tighter as his other hand traveled up my thigh. He leaned close, his hot breath hovering over my ear.

"Try it," he said. His fingertips brushed the edge of my underwear. "I'll like it better if you do."

Then his fingers, so deceptively smooth and limber dipped under the elastic edge. I opened my mouth, but before the scream erupted, another voice shattered the nasty spell.

"What the *fuck* is going on here?"

"Get *off* me!" I shrieked.

Theo jumped, and immediately, I took the opportunity to bring my knee up as hard as I could, hitting pay dirt between his legs and sending him to the floor, clutching his groin.

"Fuck!" His voice broke with pain. "You fucking *bitch*!"

"That's nothing compared to what I'm going to do to you." In one clean movement, Will lifted Theo by the collar and landed a punch to his nose with a crack.

"Will!" I shouted.

"What the fuck!" Theo's voice was squashed, muted. "You bwoke my dose!"

"I'm about to break a lot more than that, you piece of shit!" Will jumped forward, but was jerked back by the sudden presence of a security guard who grabbed him handily by the arms.

"Theo, what the hell are you doing here?" Corbyn appeared behind the security, looking frantic. "You're supposed to be in New York! Does Max know?"

"Pretty sure *my* company is paying for this little shindig," Theo retorted nastily, even with blood streaming down his face. "It's my right to be here. And besides, it's not my fault if the pretty boy's girl misses the real thing."

"Son of a *bitch*!" Will lunged and was again snapped back by the massive arms of Corbyn's security.

"Listen, man, I don't want to have to hurt you," said the guard. "But this motherfucker needs to get tossed out. You wanna go too? Because I can't take care of him if I gotta hold your crazy ass back."

"It's your father's company, not yours, you entitled little shit," Corbyn snapped at Theo. "And this is my house, so you can get the hell out." He looked around, locating another one of the security guards who had bounded in. "One of you, get this brat off my property. He is *persona non grata* around here."

"Hey, man, easy on the Prada!" Theo's eyes found me as he was yanked out. "You think this is the end? Just *wait*, Flower! You'll get what's coming to you, and don't you fuckin' forget it! OW!" He was smacked in the face by the door as the guard forced him out of the room.

"Okay?" asked the one holding Will once Theo was gone.

Will expelled a long breath, and as his eyes returned to normal, he nodded. "Okay."

The guard released him and followed the others out of the room.

Corbyn darted a gaze between Will and me. "Maggie, you all right?" he asked.

I shuddered, trying to tug my torn dress. I couldn't seem to cover up enough. "I—yeah. I'm ok-kay."

"Should I call the police?" The dread in Corbyn's voice was palpable. This was a Hollywood party. I didn't even want to think about how many illicit activities were probably going on.

Will looked to me. I shook my head a tiny bit. I didn't want to deal with the police any more than they did. After all, what could they do now?

"No," he said tightly. "But we, ah, we need a minute."

Corbyn nodded. "Take your time." And with that, he left, shutting us in the bedroom. Alone.

Will stared, and I tried to maintain eye contact. Tried not to burst into tears, because really, that was the last thing he needed at a party that was no doubt already buzzing with the excitement of the studio head's son getting hauled out.

"How—how did you find me?" I asked finally.

"You'd been gone a long time," he said quietly. "And I—I knew something was off. One of the grips said they saw you go upstairs, so I came to find you."

I swallowed. I thought he would wrap me in his strong arms, shut out the rest of the world in that uncanny way of his. But still he didn't move.

"I'm glad you did," I whispered. A tear finally fell, but before he noticed, I swiped it away.

Will shoved both of his hands through his hair, yearning, it seemed, for its previous length. "I'm so goddamn tired of this," he muttered. "So fucking tired of ripping men's hands off my girlfriend. So tired of chasing people away from what's mine."

And before I could answer, he turned, grabbed the drink that Corbyn had left on the top of the dresser, and tipped the contents down his throat before striding toward the balcony. "Will!" I called as I followed him. "Will!"

He whirled around, a tornado of fury. "*What?*" A cloud of vodka floated off him.

I recoiled. "How—how much have you had to drink?"

He rolled his eyes. "A few. But can you really blame me, Lil? Sometimes that's what I need to deal with all of this bullshit. Dealing with every goddamn stranger in the room wanting a piece of me while my girlfriend is getting off with her ex upstairs."

Several people below us went quiet, though the music obscured most of our conversation.

"You can't actually think he was telling the truth," I said.

"Oh, I definitely think he's a lying sack of shit," Will said. Relief coursed through me, but only until he continued. "But I think you do stupid things when he's around. To the point where I wonder sometimes if you don't want it. Just a little."

My hand slapped over my mouth. "How can you say that? Especially after—"

Will's eyes shone. "After what?"

"After you made out with your ex-fiancée yesterday and shanghaied me in front of her tonight!" My mouth clapped shut. I didn't even know I'd felt that way until the words were out, and now there was no taking them back.

"You could have left immediately when we had that dinner with him and Max. But you didn't, and it cost you the restraining order. He still has your number. I got you a new phone—why haven't you changed it? And now I find myself wondering what the hell you were doing with him on the lot to begin with. Did you *really* 'happen' to run into him? As for right now…"

"D-don't," I whispered. "Don't you even—"

"You come up, alone in a party full of drunks, dressed like that—"

I glanced down at my dress, the one he had complimented so vociferously before the party. "You think my dress caused Theo to try to r-*rape* me for the second fucking time?!" The quaver in my voice was turning violent.

"Well, maybe he wouldn't have done that if you hadn't let Robin dress you up like a two-bit hooker!"

"W-*what*?"

Will squeezed his eyes shut, like the sound of my stutter physically caused him pain. I didn't give a shit. His words were ripping my heart out.

"Honestly, Lil, I don't know what to think right now," Will said. He opened his eyes again, all emotion drained. "I told you before, don't leave me alone."

My mouth dropped. "Are you *serious* right now? I went to the bathroom!"

"*I told you not to leave me alone!*"

Will's eyes widened, and it was then I saw the glaze, the telltale sheen, the slight pinking of the tip of his nose that didn't have anything to do with how upset he was. He hadn't had only a drink or two. The guy was completely sloshed. And, if his slightly dilated pupils were any indication, something more than that too.

"You're drunk," I said, stepping backward.

Will snorted. "Sweetheart, I'm a lot more than that right now."

He stepped toward me, fully imprisoning me against the balcony's edge—exactly where I'd been before. I began to shake.

"It's your fault," he whispered as his hand slipped around my waist. "I don't know how I ended up taking it, but I'm glad I did. It's the only way I know how to bear it without you around."

"You don't mean that," I whispered, trying and failing to blink away my tears. I was a damn mess.

"Maggie?" Calliope's voice sounded like it was filtering through a haze. "Maggie, are you up here?"

Will gulped, his eyes shining as he staggered backward. "I told you that you'd be the death of me. I was right."

Below us, a silence spread across the entire yard. The music had stopped, and hundreds of people, all quiet, all had their mouths open. All looking up. All staring at me.

"Fuck. You," I whispered.

I darted around him, right into Calliope's arms as she stepped onto the balcony. I gripped her forearms, a lifeline in this mess. "Help."

"Come on," Calliope said, looking between Will and me. "Let's get you out of here."

————

"IT'S GOING TO BE OKAY," Calliope said for the fourth time as the Uber driver pulled up to the curb. Thankfully, the driver hadn't seemed to recognize me, but you never could tell. We waited a few minutes for him to drive down the street before walking a few blocks up and walking down the driveway to the hidden villa.

"Is it?" I wondered as I hugged my arms around my waist. "I'm not really sure."

"He loves you," Calliope said.

"He was drunk and high," I bit back. "Regardless of love, I'm not sure what to do about that. And the things he said to me…"

Calliope sighed. "It's going to be okay," she repeated. "I don't know how, but it really is."

My phone chirped in my clutch. I pulled it out—a Google alert about Will.

Old Habits Die Hard—Fitz Baker, Party Boy, is Back!

Underneath the headline was a picture. If the headline shouted, the picture screamed. In it Will sat in the center of one of the outdoor couches around Corbyn's pool, his arms spread across the back while two women sandwiched him. He smirked at the camera with an out-of-focus expression, but it wasn't him that made me feel like someone was shoving a knife into my chest. And it wasn't the girl on the right, one of the makeup girls who was making a peace-sign and holding up her drink to cheer the photographer. It was the other one, the one planting a kiss on his cheek while slipping her hand up the hem of his shirt. It was the sight of her silky blond hair and over-inflated lips that twisted the knife even deeper.

Amelia. Fucking. Craig.

"N-no," I stuttered as I handed the phone to Callie. "It's not."

CHAPTER TWENTY-SEVEN

It took ten minutes of sitting on the couch before I decided I needed to leave the house. Then I darted around, grabbing as many of my things as I could find and stuffing them in my bag. That took thirty.

"I don't know," Calliope said as I took one last look around the villa I had called "home" with Will for the summer. "I still think we should stay."

I wasn't interested in waiting around to see Will stumble in drunk and high and full of more hurtful comments. I didn't want to be a victim anymore. Not to him. Not to anyone.

"Callie, did you or did you not say Capitol was able to put you up anyway?"

She nodded. "Yeah, of course. I made the call while you were packing."

I'd been reliving the events for the last forty minutes. I left the stupid red dress on the bed, feeling more like myself and less like the harlot apparently everyone had seen me as tonight once I was comfortably back in shapeless old jeans and a Blondie t-shirt I'd found at the Goodwill in tenth grade.

I lugged my duffel bag over one shoulder and picked up my guitar with the other, then followed Calliope out to the curb to meet another Uber and put everything in the trunk.

Calliope tried again: "Are you sure you don't want to—"

"No." I got into the passenger seat and folded my arms over my chest. I felt sick to my stomach, but I wasn't willing to listen to my gut on this one. I needed space. Will needed space. In the morning, both of us would see things differently, although I couldn't for the life of me see how we were going to move past any of this. In my heart, I knew this was probably the end.

Calliope slid into the back with me. "Did you at least leave him a note? Maggie, he's going to flip if he gets back and you're not there."

"Why are you defending him?" I snapped. "The man called me a whore in front of hundreds of people, and then a photo was posted of him basically having a threesome with Amelia. What part of *I don't want to fucking see him* don't you understand?"

"*Excuse* me?" Calliope's sharp retort pulled me back to the here and now. She cocked her head, and her braids flipped over her shoulder.

"Shit," I muttered. "Cal, I'm sorry. I'm...no. I didn't leave him a note. I'll come back tomorrow and deal with him. But not now. Not when he's blitzed. Not when I just c-can't..." My words trailed off as tears mounted all over again. Again, I breathed deeply until they receded. I didn't want to let go until I was alone, and that wouldn't be for a good long time.

"Okay," Calliope said. "Let's go."

The hotel wasn't far—only a few minutes' drive. We could see the big disc-shaped Capitol Records building looming a few streets away.

"Are you okay?" Calliope asked after we were standing in front of the hotel. "You look like death."

It wasn't until she asked that I realized I felt legitimately ill. I had thought the ache in my stomach and light nausea was nerves, but when I followed her out of the car, it was clearly something else.

"I'm fin—oh, God!" I made a break for a potted azalea next to the revolving glass doors. The doorman blanched as I emptied my stomach into the soil.

When I was finished, Calliope quirked a finely plucked eyebrow at me. "Um...come with me."

"What? Where are we going? What about our bags? Calliope, I'm sick!"

"Are you really sick? How do you feel now?"

I paused. "Actually, not terrible." Maybe it was just nerves.

"That's what I thought." Calliope handed the doorman a folded bill. "Please take our bags upstairs. Sorry about the plant. We'll be right back."

Before I could argue more, she dragged me down the street. However, it wasn't until she hoofed me down the feminine hygiene aisle of the closest convenience store that I realized what she was after.

"Oh, no," I said when she took a home pregnancy test off the shelf. "No, no, no, no, *no*. Aside from the fact that it's not possible, I cannot deal with this tonight."

"Have you been having sex with your hunky movie star boyfriend?" Calliope smacked herself on the forehead. "What am I saying? You're not insane. Of *course* you've been tapping that. Multiple times a day, I'm guessing. And probably without protection." She patted my arm. "I'm not judging, babycakes. He's hot as sin. I'd probably forget a rubber too."

I crossed my arms around my stomach, which gave another lurch. "I have an IUD. There is no way I'm p-pregnant." The idea sent a chill over my entire body. Two weeks ago, I'd have been happy about it. Scared, but happy. Now all I felt was full-bodied fear.

Callie tapped a fingernail on the box. "IUDs aren't a hundred percent foolproof," she said, then thrust the box into my arms. "Take it. Do it to appease my sad, obsessive mind."

My stomach roiled, and it must have shown on my face.

"We'll pick up some ginger candy too," she said, and patted my shoulder as we turned toward the checkout counter.

THIRTY MINUTES LATER, we were both lying on the bed, staring at the Hollywood sign while we waited for the timer on Calliope's phone to go off. Below it, if I looked hard enough, I thought I could see the exact street lamp next to the entrance to our house. I wondered if Will was home yet. I wondered if he was worried about me. If he wondered where I was too.

In the bathroom were two identical pregnancy tests, set neatly on the counter. Calliope had spent the last two minutes gabbing about her meeting the next day, but I couldn't remember anything she said. My mind raced. What the hell was I going to do if that second pink line showed up?

On the nightstand next to me, my phone beeped for the seventh time that night. I picked it up. Yet another Google alert linking photos from the party. There were more now—pictures of Will dancing, Will with his arms around all number of people, Will lounging on the couch again. And always, always with Amelia somewhere in the frame. In a few of them, I also caught glimpses of Tricia, watching from the margins.

I set the phone back down with a loud clap.

Calliope patted my wrist. "Will knows better than that. Amelia Craig is basic as fuck, and from what Benny says, keeps her legs open just to keep her career afloat."

"Callie, that really doesn't make me feel any better."

She shrugged. "My point is, why would he go for hamburger when he's got steak at home?"

I twisted toward her. "Are you really quoting Paul Newman at me?"

Calliope snorted. "It's a good quote. And it's true."

"I thought he cheated on Joanne Woodward."

"Those are rumors. The hottest man in Hollywood history—and Will gets compared to Paul Newman a *lot*, you know—proclaimed his monogamous love for his wife throughout their very long marriage. I am choosing to believe him, and so should you."

I wished it made me feel better. But the idea of being compared to steak made me even more nauseous.

My phone chirped again with another alert. I turned it off and rolled onto my back.

"This is it, isn't it?" I asked, suddenly having a *really* hard time keeping the tears at bay. If I was pregnant, I doubted I would ever stop crying. "If I leave, I'm going to be miserable because I love him so fucking much. But if I stay, I'm never going to have a normal life, am I?"

Calliope sighed. "Not if you're with him, babe. I don't think that's possible with someone like Will."

My heart fell with the heaviness of two separate realizations. The first, the most obvious: if Will and I stayed together, there was a very real possibility that I'd never be able to go out on my own again without someone following me. Without him being the target of people like Amelia. My safety would always be slightly in jeopardy. Not to mention our kid's, if there even was one.

And that, of course, brought me to the second realization: that life wasn't what I wanted.

For years, I'd chased any measure of success, thinking it had to come in the form of notoriety. Of fame. All I'd wanted was for my music to be heard, and if that meant I was the one to play it, then that's how it was going to be. I'd primped and practiced and done my best to morph myself into the best version of a pop-country star I could be. But it had never been enough. My songs were good, but I'd never be the kind of person who had that natural charisma that made people want to watch them no matter what. I had talent, but I wasn't a star.

And now I knew I didn't want to be. I grabbed my phone again and pulled a business card out of my purse—the creased, worn card of Rob Reinquist, the composer I'd met at Amelia's premiere party. I'd never called him during my time here—only shared a few emails. Now I knew why. I had been scared. Scared that my decisions would chase Will away, with his desire to get out of this town no matter what. Scared that going down that road would also choke the only other career path I'd ever wanted.

All at once, those things didn't matter anymore. And this didn't matter either. And if those sticks in the bathroom said what Calliope thought they would, I wouldn't be calling Rob anytime soon anyway. I didn't know what I'd be doing, but it wouldn't be recording music. With a sigh, I tucked the card away. It was time to let go of pipe dreams. I had a real life to make for myself, and anyone else I might need to care for with that future. And any second now, I was going to find out which direction it would take.

Calliope's phone alarm went off, its twinkling chime waking us both out of our trances.

She sat up. "Judgment Day is here, babe."

I sat up too. "Ha ha. Very funny."

"Do you want to do the honors, or should I?"

I swung my legs off the bed and stood up, wobbling a little when all the blood rushed to my head. "I'll do it."

"All right. I'm here if you need me."

I shuffled into the bathroom and stared at the two sticks. *No*, I thought. *It's not possible.* The nausea was nerves, that was all.

"There's absolutely no way," I informed the sticks, then swiped them off the porcelain. "Do your worst."

And then I held them out, and they did.

Two stripes. One, two. On one stick, then the other. Pink. Small. But very, very present.

I sat heavily on the toilet, holding my forehead as I continued to stare at the stripes.

"Well?"

I looked up.

"Shit," Callie said.

I hung my head. "Oh my God. Oh my *God*, Calliope. What the *fuck* am I going to do?"

"Now, let's calm down for a second. It's not the end of the world."

"Really? Please tell me how this could come at a worse time. My boyfriend is hooking up with a starlet while repressing his social anxiety disorder with drugs and alcohol, my mother is a fall-down drunk whom I'm not even speaking to at the moment, I have no job, no money, no way to support myself, let alone a b-*baby*…" By the time I was done speaking, my words were a garble, buried in tears. I fell forward, face in my hands as I finally, *finally* let out all of the stress of the evening. Amelia, Theo, Will, and now this…everything came crashing down, frustration and sorrow pouring out of me in gut-wracking sobs.

"Shhh, shhh," Calliope crooned as she gathered my rocking form to her. The tenderness only made me cry harder—not because it was unwanted, but because it reminded me so much of the arms I wished desperately were around me.

"It's going to be okay," she said, stroking my hair. "You're not alone, babe. You're not alone."

And I listened as she repeated it over and over, because it was what I needed to hear. But it still hurt, because I had no idea if it was true.

CHAPTER TWENTY-EIGHT

I woke up the next morning with a song dancing in my head. It was a low, mournful melody that rocked me side to side like a boat. It had an oceanic quality, with a full orchestra of strings, timpani drums, even an odaiko, a big bass drum that stood at least ten feet above any man. It wasn't anything like the music I'd written before, and I knew as soon as I woke that I needed to get it down.

Calliope had left early for a SoulCycle class, but by the time she returned, I was sitting on the floor next to the coffee table in front of the tiny hotel couch, scribbling madly on hotel stationery. When she walked in, I jumped, yanked out of the symphonic trance I'd been stuck in for over two hours.

"Well, hello there, Mozart," she greeted me as she dropped her gym bag on her bed. "What do we have here?"

I looked back at the mess of papers, then immediately bent back to them, eager to finish the last few bars I had dancing in my head. It was terrible notation—I'd never been great at it to begin with—but it, combined with the cell phone recordings I'd made by humming the key harmonies, would serve until I could get to a keyboard.

"Denial," I said as I scribbled.

"Maggie," Calliope said again. "Hey, are you okay? Have you..." She glanced around the mess of papers. "Have you eaten anything yet?"

I finished the last two notes with a flourish and looked up triumphantly. But before I could reply, the fact that I'd been up for hours without eating anything caught up to me and my pregnant stomach.

Pregnant. The truth hit like a nausea bomb. Oh. God.

Without answering, I jumped up, sprinted to the bathroom, and proceeded to lose everything I'd ingested in the last twenty-four hours into the toilet. Which admittedly...wasn't much. I'd forced down a few crackers and some coconut water last night before bed, but that was it.

Calliope found me lying on the tiles, my forehead braced over my wrist atop the basin. "The grapevine—and by that, I mean the all-knowing internet—tells me that the best way to ward off morning sickness is to eat when you first wake up." She held out a paper bag that looked like it contained some kind of croissant. "When you're ready."

She left, and a few minutes later, after the nausea had subsided and I had brushed my teeth and washed the sweat off my face, I reentered the room, nibbling on the pastry.

"Thanks," I said, taking a seat on the couch. "I guess I needed this."

"Anytime. Have you heard from...you know?"

My stomach shrank, and I shook my head. "No, he hasn't called."

My voice was small. I'd been too busy working on the music to think about it that much—maybe that's *why* I'd been so busy—but now the fact that it was close to ten in the morning and I hadn't gotten so much as a text from Will hurt. Badly.

"So, what do we have here?" Calliope asked, standing over the table as she drank her coffee. "This looks like quite the magnum opus."

I surveyed the papers. "I don't really know yet. I just needed to write it down. I think I need some time with some keys and a soundboard to really make it work."

"I could probably make that happen."

I looked up. "What?"

Calliope shrugged. "Let me make some calls. But I'm tight with a few of the reps at Capitol. If they have some equipment open today, maybe they'd let you jump on while I'm working."

I gaped. A free sound booth. Free production. At one of the most illustrious recording studios in the country. This never happened.

"Really?" I asked.

She shrugged again as she tossed her towel over her lithe shoulder. "It doesn't hurt to ask, babe."

And that right there was probably the biggest difference between Calliope and me. Whereas asking for what I needed—what I *wanted*—had always been my struggle, Callie was never one to deny herself. Or me.

"Well?" Calliope asked as she sauntered toward the bathroom.

I scrambled up from the couch. "Give me ten minutes."

Calliope laughed. "Girl, please. Rome wasn't built in a day, and I need to shower. We'll call an Uber in an hour."

———

"THANKS, JEFF," Calliope said again to the head of A&R at Capitol Records. She turned to me. "We all good here?"

I checked with the sound technician, an apprentice named Van who was as excited to be getting some time in the sound booth as I was about doing some recording there. He gave me two very enthusiastic thumbs up. I grinned at Calliope and Jeff.

"I think we're good," I said. "Thank you again for letting me do this."

Jeff shrugged. "He needs the practice. The equipment is sitting here until next week." He leered at Calliope, and I had a feeling the gesture was rooted in a little more than simple altruism.

Calliope rolled her eyes. "You've got about two hours," she said. "I'll be back after the meeting."

I nodded. "Sounds good."

They left, and I turned to Van.

"You ready?" he asked.

I walked into the large room that was full of almost every instrument I could possibly want. Sleek. Top of the line. Calling to me.

"Oh, yeah," I whispered as I sat down at the keys. "I've been ready for this my whole life."

"Maggie?" Van's voice was thin through the speakers. "Where do you want to start?"

I pulled out the sheaf of papers I'd brought with me, set them over the top of the piano, and sat down. "I'm, um, I'm going to play some things, okay? Let me get the melody going…and then maybe we can start with the keys, followed by a bass line."

And that was all it took. For the next few hours, Van and I worked, setting down track after track of different instruments, building a sound that was unlike anything I'd ever written before. Using the synths, the guitars, the drums, and a whole host of effects, we were able to recreate the better part of a full orchestra. It wasn't as good as it might have been with a real one, but it gave me a sense of what it would sound like.

It wasn't until they end or the session when finally we came to a section where I wanted some vocals. I stepped up to the microphone, holding an earphone to my ear, and began to sing.

There were no lyrics—just a bunch of layered tones. Keening, they called it in Ireland, maybe in other places too. Sometimes a wail, sometimes a hum, sometimes rounded vowels or even a sigh. I let the sounds flow out of me as pure melody, avoiding the pitfalls of language. There was no logic in this song. Only emotion.

I waited until the final note had dropped, then pulled the earphones down and smiled toward the booth.

Van gave me the thumbs-up, then switched on his intercom. "Holy shit, Maggie. That was…that was incredible. We are going to have something seriously amazing here when we're done."

"Yeah, you are."

The deep voice echoed over the mic, and after that, a face so many knew and loved stepped into the light from the back of the booth.

Van flushed. "Oh, hey. You, um, had a visitor come by to listen. I thought it would be okay."

Will and I stared at each other through the glass.

"Um, yeah," I mumbled. "It's okay."

"Lil, I'm coming in."

Will entered the recording area while Van busied himself with the soundboard. He examined the host of instruments that littered the space and the scattered papers over the top of the keyboard.

"Holy shit," he murmured. "That was…that was yours?"

I nodded. "Um, yeah."

"When did you write that? It's so…Jesus, Lil. It's painfully good. And I mean that in every sense."

My heart thumped, and my stomach flipped. I needed food. Soon. "I wrote it this morning."

Will's eyes darted back to me. "Where? I came home this morning, and you were gone."

"Calliope and I went to a hotel last night. I needed some space." Then I was pulled back to the circumstances at hand. "This morning, huh? So, where were you all night?"

"I—I stayed at Corbyn's. It seemed like the smart thing to do, all things considered."

"Smart because you were too trashed to come home? Or smart because you needed a private spot to get busy with Amelia and that other wench?" The words tasted so much bitterer than they sounded. They made my face twist like I'd sucked on a lemon.

Will blinked, confused. "What are you talking about?"

"I'm…gonna go." Van's thin voice sounded from the booth. "I'll send the track to Calliope when I'm finished."

"Okay. Thanks, Van!" I was cheerier than I felt considering I was busy glaring at the six feet, three inches of frustrated sex symbol in front of me. Emphasis on the word "sex."

I dug out my phone, then swiped angrily to a tabloid site running the article about Will's "wild night."

"I imagine you had a *very* good time after I left," I snarled, thrusting the phone at him.

"What the fuck…" Will scrolled over the photos and the article, then handed it back to me. "Lil, you can't possibly believe this. I told you not to read this kind of shit."

"Why, because the writing's on the wall? You're trashed, that one chick has her hand down your shirt, and Amelia's two seconds from sucking you off."

"Stop it."

"No."

"Lil!"

"Don't call me that!" I shrieked, unable to deal with it anymore. I hurled my phone across the room, and it smacked against the thick, soundproofed walls and fell to the floor. It wasn't quite the same effect as hurling it against a rock, but I didn't care.

"Li—Maggie. Let's calm down a second—"

"Don't tell me to calm down!" I shoved my hands back through my hair, pacing around, unable to keep still. "You—you fucked up here, Will! You said—y-you said you weren't going to fall back into this kind of shit. Not if I was around. Well, I *was* around. I've been around every day, trailing after you like a pathetic lap dog. Dealing with your ex's petty bullshit, the fact that *my* ex has been harassing me! Dealing with the fact that you're never around, that I'm basically alone in that stupid house, day in and day out. That we're both being trailed by photographers and cell phones, and with the fact that your mother thinks I'm no better than a common prostitute. And in the end, none of it mattered. Because *you* pushed me away. *You* called me a whore. *You* still couldn't deal with all of it, and as soon as the opportunity presented itself, you went straight for the bottle and let Amelia get her fucking claws into you all over again while Theo tried. To. *Rape* me!"

"Maggie, that is *not* what happened!" Will's voice bounced around the room. "This is bullshit! Yeah, I was pretty fucked up last night, but I came here to apologize! Do you really think I would cheat on you just because we had a fight?"

"I don't know!"

"You're kidding, right? You're really going to believe one of these fucked-up outlets over *me*?"

"I don't know what to believe right now!" I shouted, unable to keep my hand from sliding around my stomach. "I saw her. With you. In those fucking pictures. And last night, you were blitzed out of your mind! Do you even remember everything that happened? Who the fuck are you? What the fuck happened to *my* Will?!"

"I'm only going to say this one more time. I did not sleep with anyone. Not with Amelia." He held out the phone, and I shied away. I didn't want to see that. "Look at this. *Look* at it, Maggie."

"I don't want to look at that! You don't think I've seen enough of that skank's hands all over you?"

"Fine, then I'll tell you! See that sofa? That's in the middle of Corbyn's backyard. And what you don't see in the photograph are the twenty other people surrounding us. Yeah, I was fucked up last night, Lil. I was, and I apologize for that. But I *didn't do anything with anybody.* You have to believe me. What kind of person do you think I am, anyway?"

"I DON'T REALLY KNOW, DO I?" I screamed, falling backward onto the piano bench from the effort. My heart pounded furiously, and my whole body was shaking. Unconsciously, my hand drifted to my stomach. This couldn't be good for the baby.

The baby.

Everything raced through me. Flowing drinks. Easy pills. Amelia touching him. I was splitting apart.

Will approached, squatting down onto his heels and caging me on the bench.

"Listen to me. There are a shit ton of manipulative people in this business, and Amelia is a pro. She probably fed the outlet this story to begin with in order to build buzz for the movie. That's how it's done, Lil. But one call from Benny, and this gets yanked, okay? That's all we have to do."

"You still don't get it," I said miserably. "It's not the story that bothers me, Will. It's that you were even there at all. It's all the nasty things you said last night." I swiped at the tears that wouldn't stop falling. "It's that in the end...you chose all of that...over me."

"Lil, I said some shitty things, but I did not choose anyone over you."

"You did."

"I didn't!"

"And how would you really know?"

The words fell like bombs between us, and Will took a step back, like he'd been hit. "What?"

I rocked forward. "Will, I have lived my entire life with someone with a substance abuse problem, who only has partial memory recognition half the time because she's too blitzed the other half. You said yourself— you were fucked up last night. So really, how would you know? What did you have? Drinks, and what else? I see you in that photo. I saw you last night. Right there, you look like you couldn't even remember your own name, much less everything that happened."

Will pulled out his phone and swiped to the site again to look at the photo. He studied it again, looking through the rest of the reel. It was obvious on his face that what I said was true—that he didn't actually remember everything that happened.

My heart deflated.

"I didn't take anything," he whispered, but he looked like he didn't even believe it himself. "I didn't..."

"You said you did," I whispered. "Last night, when we—"

He looked up, full of regret. "Please tell me you believe me, Lil. Please. I would *never* do that to you."

I opened my mouth. I didn't know what to believe, but I couldn't take it when he looked at me like that. I clasped a hand over my stomach. *Now,* a small voice said inside me. *Tell him now.*

"Will, it's not only that," I started. "I'm—"

The door to the studio swung open, and Calliope rushed in, phone in hand.

"Maggie?" Her frantic gaze pinballed around the room until she found me. "Oh my God. Maggie. You—you need to call home. You need to call Lucas. Right—right away."

Will practically growled. "We're kind of in the middle of—"

"No." Calliope cut him off, handing me her phone, which was already dialing Lucas's number. I didn't even know she had it. "Here."

Ducking the concerned glances from her and Will, I turned around as Lucas's voice sounded through the speaker.

"Maggie? Mags? Is that you?"

"Y-yeah. Lucas, what is it?" Something in his voice, a peculiar frenzy, made my chest grow cold.

"I—I couldn't reach you. I didn't know who else to call, so I looked up Calliope's number, and—"

"Lucas, what's going on?"

There was a pause. A deep breath. Maybe even the sound of someone crying.

"Mags, you gotta come home," he said with hitched breaths. "You—you need to come back right now."

"What? Why?"

And then the message came, spiraling around me like loose streamers. Disconnected, because how can news like that ever be truly uniform, linear? Instead, the words landed in a cacophony of sharp, staccato notes, shearing through space and time like hand grenades, each one a deadly weapon that somehow cohered into a larger narrative that exploded through me.

Mom.

Sorry.

Ellie.

Driving.

Curly's.

Late.

Drinking.

…

…

Dead.

CHAPTER TWENTY-NINE

"Maggie, we're here, babe."

Calliope tapped my shoulder, almost like she was nervous to do it. It was the same way everyone had been touching me, looking at me, even walking around me for the past ten days.

I let her guide me out of her rental car and into the church parking lot, where people were gathering for my mother's funeral.

Funeral. The concept still hadn't really clicked. It didn't make sense. How could I be here? What was I doing?

We stood outside a pretty typical Presbyterian church—rectangular and white, with a tall spire that reached to the sky, and a gravel parking lot on all sides to accommodate everyone who wanted to say goodbye to Ellie Sharp. The Forsters, God bless them, had walked me through every single step of arranging the funeral. Linda in particular had done almost all of the planning while I had numbly nodded and tried to process what was happening.

Mama was dead. Rolled her car fifty feet off the road into a ditch. The police said that based on the tire tracks, it looked like she had steered into the opposite lane, then over-corrected. She had been going much too fast—at least sixty, given the speed limit on Trent—and the car had flipped.

She was not wearing a seatbelt and was thrown through the windshield.

The coroner estimated she had been killed on impact. Mercifully, he said, though nothing about this seemed like mercy to me. An autopsy revealed that her blood alcohol level was somewhere near .16—almost twice the legal limit.

She had done it to herself, and no one was surprised. Not the police officer, who had showed up to drive her home more than once from Curly's. Not the Forsters, who were sorry, but clearly expected that something like this would happen one of these days. Not Barb, her best friend, who loved her to death, but perhaps knew in the bottom of her heart that Ellie was never going to make it to old age.

Not even me. And I couldn't really forgive myself for that.

Amazingly, Mama had taken out a life insurance policy after I was born. I had looked at it in shock—it was the only evidence that she had ever had more than a few days' prescience when it came to raising me. It wasn't for much, but it was enough to pay for the funeral expenses, finish fixing up the property, and pay the taxes for at least a year. A strange gift that she was only able to give dead, not alive.

I would have given it back in a second if I could have seen her again. However she was.

"Hi, hon." Linda greeted me with a kiss on the cheek as I approached the church.

Calliope and I were late, as I had hemmed and hawed in front of the mirror for more than an hour. How do you dress for your own mother's funeral? In the end, I'd let Callie choose for me—conservative black dress with flower appliqué down the A-line skirt. It swished around my knees. Mama had always liked that cut on me.

"Hey, Mags." Lucas greeted me with a warm, yet uncertain hug, his brown eyes full of sympathy. "You okay?"

I shook my head. This was going to be the hardest part—a million people coming up to me, giving me their condolences. Asking me to express what I couldn't put into words.

I fingered the eulogy folded in my palm. "I'm fine," I said eventually.

Calliope squeezed my shoulder. "Come on. Let's find your seat."

"The guitar?" I wondered. "Where's my—"

"It's by the microphone, hon," Linda said calmly, patting my shoulder. "We brought it this morning."

I looked up toward the altar, where, on the low-lying step of the church I'd attended sporadically as a child and where Mama had tried and failed to fit in most of her life, my Martin had been set on a stand to the right of the closed coffin and the scattered floral arrangements Linda and other people had donated. A blown-up photo of my mom at a local rodeo was propped on the other side of the coffin. She was laughing, holding a cowboy hat on top of her head to keep it from blowing away. It was a good picture of her, but almost felt like a mockery given the day.

"Okay," I murmured, and allowed Calliope to guide me to my seat in the front pew.

"Excuse me, Ms. Sharp?"

I turned to find an unfamiliar man holding a cowboy hat in a rough, weathered hand, extending the other toward me.

"James Edelman," he said as he accepted my weak handshake. "I, ah, was a friend of your mother's. I sure am sorry about your loss."

Great. Another long-lost lover. By the number of men in the crowd, I suspected the place was full of men who had loved and lost Ellie Sharp over the years.

"Nice to meet you," I mumbled. "And thank you for coming. How, um, when did you know my mom?"

"Oh, we knew each other way back," James said. "When I was still playing with my band, back around ninety-one, ninety-two."

I nodded vacantly. Beside me, Calliope stiffened. James stood there awkwardly, showing no sign of moving.

"So," I said. "I'm guessing you and my mom were…"

"Involved, yeah." His shoulders curved sheepishly. "Ellie was…well, I never forgot her, though I messed the whole thing up. She left me after I got a DUI. She was trying to get right back then. I was a slave to the bottle—she was right to do it. I sure am sorry she relapsed."

"Relapsed. Well. Yeah, me too." That was one way of putting it. Dead was another. "Did you manage to…"

"Sober up? Sure did." James pulled a token out of his pants pocket and held it out. "Ten years last month, actually."

"You knew Eloise in nineteen ninety-one, you said?" Calliope nudged my arm, and for the first time, I really looked at the guy.

He wasn't a big man—about average height, with shoulders that slumped a little to the sides with the weight of a harder life than most. He had tight, salt-and-pepper curls that were still mostly black and shorn close to his scalp, and his skin was a dark, rich brown with the sheen of a copper pot. His eyes, a kind, dark brown surrounded by substantial crow's feet, slanted over a long nose and a mouth couched in wrinkles. It wasn't the face of someone who had lived an easy life, but maybe of someone who tried to live a good one.

"Where, um, where did you say you were from?" I asked.

"I didn't—I'm from Spokane. The rez, actually—my mother is Spokane Indian."

"What about your dad?" Calliope's voice was sharp, maybe unnecessarily curious. "What...um, what was he?"

I glanced at her. "Cal." It was inappropriate, asking someone about their race. She knew as much as I did how awkward that felt.

James looked between us uncomfortably. "Oh, him. He was from the Valley. Black guy, disappeared when I was a kid, so we didn't see him much." He folded his lips together—that was clearly all he had to say on the matter.

Calliope's mouth dropped slightly, but because of my hazy state of mind, it took me a few more moments to put together the puzzle she'd already figured out.

Nineteen ninety-one.

Mixed ethnicity.

Musician.

My eyes shot open.

"When did you say you were born again?" James asked. His words slurred together, though I didn't think it was him doing it.

"I didn't," I whispered. "But my birthday is in December."

"December *fourth*," Callie added emphatically.

"Nineteen ninety one," I finished.

James and I stared at each other as a slow realization dawned on both of us.

"I guess we have some talking to do, don't we?" he murmured.

I turned to Calliope. I couldn't do this right now. I really couldn't.

"We'll be around at the reception," she said, stepping in the way only a best friend could.

James rocked back, clearly relieved. It was a lot for both of us, that much was clear. "Certainly," he said. "That sounds…like a plan."

"All right, then." Calliope took hold of my shoulders and guided me toward my seat.

"Was that—did I j-just imagine—"

"'Fraid not, babe," she said as we sat down. "But not now. Put it away. Focus on what you have to do now, and we'll deal with that later."

There I sat, staring at the particleboard walls of the church, the ugly red carpeting, and the red stained-glass window panels while the reverend began the service, calling people to sit while he opened with a prayer.

How was I going to get up there? The same thought had been running through my head for the few weeks it had taken to settle everything: *your fault*. And it was. Nothing I had done had been enough to save her. Not leaving. Not an intervention. I had tried everything, and I had failed. It was my fault that she was dead.

"Babe." Calliope nudged my arm.

I blinked. "Hm?"

"You're up."

I shook slightly. "What?" Then I looked up to the reverend, who was beckoning me to rise. Of course. The eulogy.

I took a deep breath, and eventually I stared out at the congregation of people. They filled the small half-circle of the church seating, so many more than I would have expected. So many more than I even recognized. Who were these people? Were they really here to pay their respects, or were they here for the spectacle of Eloise Sharp's funeral?

I unfolded the short speech I had spent hours poring over and spread it flat on the lectern. Oh, God. Could I really do this?

"Go ahead, Maggie," whispered the reverend kindly.

But I opened my mouth, and nothing came out. I could only stare at the audience. How could I do this? How could I say goodbye to my own mother?

The door in the back of the church opened, and the bright sunlight outside framed the tall, familiar silhouette of a man. My voice stuck in my throat as the last conversation I'd had with Will hurtled through my head.

———

"Lily, please! Maggie! Margaret Mae Sharp, will you stop for one fucking second and talk to me!"

I stopped throwing my things into my bag at the sound of my full, given name—something I'd never actually heard emerge from Will's lips. Calliope stood by the hotel door, waiting for me to finish. There was already a taxi waiting downstairs to take me to LAX—she'd bought a ticket for me while I spoke to Lucas.

When I turned around, Will looked crazed, hair standing on end. More like the odd, surly man I'd met on that mountain months ago, and yet more of a stranger in every way.

"Don't—don't run," he begged, his voice cracking over the words. "Please, Lil. Don't run from me. Stay. We'll talk through this. I only have to be in LA for a few more days, and then I can go up to Spokane with you, help you with everything. Just don't fucking leave right now!"

He was breaking apart in front of me, and I could feel my heart doing the same. But unwittingly, I rested my hand over my still flat belly. I had other things to care for than the broken people in my life, especially since I had failed at that anyway.

My mother was dead. The words still rang through my head, louder than any stupid tabloid. Now I only had one responsibility: to build something better, to be something better for the one thing that was sure to be perfect from the start.

I finished zipping up my duffel bag and slung it over my shoulder.

"I'm not running," I said softly as I stepped toward the door. "I'm going home."

I drove back to Washington on Calliope's dime and proceeded to ignore everything. At first, Will had been frantic, calling, texting, messaging whenever and however he could. He was stuck in LA for promotional duties—parts of his contracts that required him to attend two more premieres, finish the feature with *Vanity Fair*, and do a double interview with Amelia. More pictures from the wrap party leaked, and though it was clear from most that Will wasn't exactly a lively participant in whatever it was that Amelia staged, he wasn't exactly fighting her off either. There were pictures of them sitting cozily on the couch. More from another premiere party they attended. There, he didn't look like he had been drinking—he looked scared in front of the flashing lights. But she was still there. Still with her hand on his knee.

A week passed. Then longer. He was caught up in some reshoots, unable to get away. But he'd be back, said every text, every voice message.

When is the funeral?

WHEN CAN YOU TALK?

PLEASE TALK TO ME, *Maggie.*

SORRY, *so sorry.*

Always sorry.

The phone calls stopped a few days ago. Then texts, then emails.

I replied to none of them.

———

"MAGGIE?" The reverend tapped my shoulder. "Do you need me to read for you?"

I glanced to the back again. Will hadn't moved, and in their focus on me, no one noticed him. He only nodded.

Something deep inside me unclenched.

"Um, no," I mumbled to the reverend. "I can do it."

And then I turned back to the congregation and began to speak.

"I'll, um, keep this short. Mama and I never talked about what kind of funeral she would have wanted, but she didn't like too much fuss. Those of you who knew her know she liked a celebration. She liked a party."

There was a chuckle of acknowledgment, but I couldn't laugh with them. The truth cut. I had to pause, take a deep breath.

"But it can't always be a party, can it, Mama?" I wondered aloud. "Because I can't celebrate your life cut short. I think of all the things you'll never see or experience. You'll never open your bed and breakfast. You'll never get married. You'll never get to retire, or—or meet your grandchildren."

My throat closed slightly as I spoke the last line, and in the back, Will bent his head. In the front row, Calliope winced visibly. She was the only one who knew my secret. It had been easy to pass off the morning sickness and fatigue as grief. It was honestly hard to know what was what.

"Then I remember the things she *did* have," I continued. "The experiences she *did* enjoy. Because above all, that's what my mother lived for—joy. She searched for that her entire life. Maybe not in ways that were the best, but she chose her own path. And for that, I always, always respected and loved her."

There were several nods around the room, and for a second, I wanted to rage at them. These were the same people who talked about her behind her back. *That Ellie*, they'd say before they cast knowing looks at both her and me. Mama's pursuit of joy, men, liquor, and everything else they deemed "un-Christian" had gotten her ostracized from this community for years.

And yet. They were all here. Maybe their reactions to her were only because they were jealous. Maybe it was only because they had wanted to be more like her in some ways that they found it so easy to look down on her.

"Mama wouldn't want me to talk anymore. She didn't love to talk either. But she did love to hear me play. She loved it so much that even when we were going through hard times, she somehow came up with the money for guitar lessons so I could pursue my dream—" My voice cracked again. Just like her, that dream was long gone, wasn't it? "So I could make music. So, Mama. This is for you."

I picked up my guitar and pulled the strap around my back, then stepped to the second microphone next to the lectern so I could play and sing at the same time. With a soft Travis pick, I launched into a version of Mama's favorite Emmylou Harris song, "Boulder to Birmingham," one that was actually written for a friend's death. By the time I was done, several people in the front row were crying. But it wasn't until I flowed seamlessly into a folk rendition of "Amazing Grace" that people really started crying—myself included.

> *Amazing grace, how sweet the sound*
> *That saved a wretch like me…*

My voice broke over "wretch." Because wasn't that what she was— my poor, tortured mother, who lived her life on a knife's edge, hiding from her loneliness, from her past truths? Trying to escape a reputation, and yet still clinging to it because it was the only thing she had left. And in the end, it was what killed her.

> *I once was lost, but now I'm found.*
> *Was blind, but now I see.*

As I sang out my pain and tears, I prayed to God she was found now. I prayed that in death, she had found the peace she'd never managed in life. I hoped that somewhere, above or below, or wherever we went after death, my mother found her absolution, a way to escape her own cycle of fears and doubt. And that through her sacrifice, I could try to break that cycle on my own.

> *Was blind but now I see.*

I managed the last note, choked while I stared out at the congregation, unseeing through my own haze of tears and sorrow. But when I could see through the sheen that covered my vision, it was Will's face I saw, the tears streaming down his cheeks, mirroring my own. Our exchange was intense enough that several people in the room turned around, wanting to see who had caught my fervent gaze. A murmur rose. Some in the back even took out their cell phones to take a picture.

But Will didn't look away. Didn't escape through the back door. Instead, he remained still, hands clasped in front of his belt buckle like a silent gesture of prayer. He watched, letting me know he was there for the last song I would ever sing for my mother.

———

AFTER THE SERVICE WAS FINISHED, I hovered by the front of the church, vacantly allowing people to shake my hand, kiss my cheeks, offer whatever pallid comforts they could. The pall bearers had already brought the coffin to a hearse, and we would follow it to the cemetery, where I would bury my mother.

Calliope stayed at my side the entire time. I hadn't seen Will in a while, but had felt his presence, hiding in the shadows as the crowd dispersed. It wasn't until I had accepted the last wrist-squeeze and awkward embrace, that he reappeared.

"Lil?" he ventured.

I turned around, hating the way my chest froze at the sound of his voice. I wanted to run to him. Wanted to let him pull me into his arms, surround me with his strength.

But how could he support me when he couldn't even support himself?

"It's okay," I said to Calliope. There were things that needed to be said. "This won't take long."

"I'll be waiting in the car," Calliope said and turned to Will. "Be nice. Otherwise you're gonna have to deal with *me*. You got that?"

Will arched a brow, but wisely said nothing as Calliope walked away.

I turned to Will. "Hey."

He shifted slightly from foot to foot, his uncertainty at odds with his magazine-ready looks. He wore a suit—all black, including the shirt and tie that wasn't quite done right. I don't know why, but that was sort of comforting. It meant he had dressed himself somewhere, rather than letting a stylist do it for him. His hair had grown out a little more in the past ten days, the golden waves now brushing the tops of his ears. I knew from recent photos that he had been re-growing his beard, but for today, he had shaved.

"I'd ask how you are, but I have a feeling I know," he said.

He knew? I shook my head. Of course he knew. His own father had passed away only a few months ago. Mentally, I kicked myself.

"I'm sorry," I said quietly. "I can't imagine how hard that was for you, considering what happened with your dad…you didn't need to…"

His finger lifted my chin so I was looking directly at him. "I'd gladly walk through fire for you, and you know it," he said quietly. "So no apologies. Not from you. Not today."

He kept me looking at him for a few more seconds, but when I didn't reply, he released me. I looked away.

"Lil, can we go somewhere for a second? Just to talk?"

I shook my head. "Will, I really can't do this right now. I have to go to the cemetery, and then there's the reception, and then…"

"After the burial. Or the reception. You tell me when, and I'll be there. I don't want drama. But, baby, I…I won't let you do this alone. I know I fucked up, Lil, but the last two weeks with you shutting me out have been fucking killing me."

"They've been *killing* you?"

He swallowed. "Okay, that was a bad choice of words. But, Lily—"

"Please don't call me that right now." I felt like I'd done nothing but cry for weeks now, but today I was allowed as many tears as I wanted. That was what funerals were for. "Will, you should go. I know you don't want to be here. You don't need to do this for me."

"The hell I don't." When I turned toward the door, Will took my arm and pulled me back to face him. His green eyes held me still, mirroring the sorrow and frustration I felt through every cell of my body. "Isn't this what you said?" he demanded. "You said this is what people do for each other, right? That they show up? Well, this is me, Maggie. This is me showing up."

"Well, you don't need to anymore!" I yanked my arm away. "I'm serious, Will, I can't *do* this with you. Not now. Maybe not ever."

Will looked like he'd been stung. "I deserve some answers, Maggie. I've been patient. But you've been ignoring my calls, my texts, my emails every day since you left. We don't have to talk about it all this second, but I need to know when!"

"We don't need to talk," I said.

"And why the fuck not?" His words rang out sharply in the now empty church, his profanity harsh, echoing through what was supposed to be holy ground.

"Because we're *over!*"

The words were heavy, flying out of my mouth and exploding around us like bombs.

Will's entire body practically caved. "You don't mean that. What about your music? What about the promotional tour?"

"I do mean it," I said, swiping at the streams cascading down my face.

Oh God, Mama. Is this how it felt? Is this how it felt when you walked away from your love for me?

"I came to a d-decision." My belly flipped, and not only because of the life inside me. I could do this. "Will, I'm staying here. I'm not going back to LA. My music career is a joke, and you know it. So, I'm going to stay at the house and rent out the other cottages. I'll work at the inn part time, and..." I looked away, toward the fields of overgrown grass waving beyond the church windows. It was fall now. The summer was over. "This is where I need to be."

Will swallowed heavily as he digested the news. "Well...fine. That's fine. If that's what you want to do, sure. We can move back here and rent the places out. I'll still have to leave for the release blitz, but in the meantime, we can up the security around both properties, and—"

"No," I said. "Will, I can't."

"Maggie, come on. You can't give up on us like this. You need us! *I* need us, I—"

"I'm pregnant." I spoke to the fields, to the mountains behind them. To the world that was coming, one I had barely begun to consider.

When I turned back, Will looked like he had been run over by a truck.

"What?" His deep voice, normally so strong, was barely even audible.

I sighed and placed my hand over my stomach. There wasn't even a swelling yet—it maybe looked like I had eaten too much pizza last night, and only when I was naked. But it was there. I felt it with every other change in my body. The mild nausea in the morning. The new weight and tenderness of my breasts. The way my skin seemed to tingle all over.

"You're pregnant?" Will repeated.

I nodded.

He stepped back again. Once, twice, until he hit the edge of a pew and was forced to stop. "I thought you had an IUD."

"It failed."

"But maybe the tests are wrong—"

"They're not."

Will stared at my hand and the muscles in his neck moving thickly as he swallowed several times. "How—how long?"

I chewed on my lower lip. "The doctor says about six weeks."

His gaze bore into my stomach, and reflexively, I covered it with both hands.

"Maggie, we can't do this. *I* can't do this." Will fell into the seat, his green eyes vacant, lost. "Maggie, I can't be a father. Look at me! Look at my fucking *life!*" He whirled back to me. "It's chaos. Everything I do, everyone around me is pure fucking chaos. I can't even protect you, much less a child!"

"I know," I said, thinking of the tabloids. The circus that surrounded him. His inability to deal with it beyond ways that quickly grew out of control.

Will looked up with sudden clarity as he realized what I had been trying to say earlier. That I was choosing this life, one away from Los Angeles, for exactly the reasons he said. It broke him—that much was clear. But not as much as his reaction was breaking me.

Just like I knew it would.

"I have to go," I said, patting his hand while, inside, my heart shattered into a million pieces. "Will, I have to bury my mother."

"Okay," he mumbled as his forehead fell to the top of the pew in front of him. "Oh—okay."

He barely noticed as I turned to leave. I paused for a moment at the door and looked back. Will still sat there, frozen in place, head buried in his hands. Staring down at the floor, like he was trying to determine how it had been ripped out from under him.

CHAPTER THIRTY

The burial passed quickly, or maybe it seemed that way because nothing registered clearly anymore. The world was a haze, a Monet painting, all blotches and swirls rather than clearly defined lines.

I laid Mama to rest under an oak tree at the far end of a cemetery in Post Falls. Barb and I placed late-blooming hydrangeas, her favorite flower, on top of the coffin before she was lowered into the ground. The pastor said a few words. People cried. I wept slow, choked tears as he spoke about her redemption. And then I prayed for her to find the peace in death that she could never manage in life.

By the end, while everyone behind me sniffed back their final tears, mine had finally run dry. I couldn't feel anything at all, scarred by all of the bombs that seemed to keep dropping into my life. The noise was so loud, all I could hear were the echoes of each one.

Will and Amelia. Boom.

My mother. Boom.

My potential father. Boom.

It was too much. Much, much too much. And so, by the time my mother was covered with the first shovelfuls of dirt, I was not only out of tears, I was utterly and totally depleted. And in absolutely no condition to go to the reception that was starting at Mama's—or, I suppose, it was *my*—house, where I'd have to smile and allow people to talk out their grief while I kept mine bottled up inside.

"Where are you going?" Calliope asked as I took off in the opposite direction of the house once we arrived back at the lake. A few guests below were filing down the stairs—had been for a while now to attend the reception that Linda had so carefully prepared.

My heels crunched in the dried pine needles as I turned around. "I need a minute, okay?"

Calliope watched sympathetically, then nodded. "Do you want me to tell him you're here?"

I sighed. I didn't have to ask whom she meant. The black SUV was parked up at the top of the road ahead of the other cars. I should have known Will wasn't going to take my first no for an answer. He was so much more stubborn than that. He'd hovered at the periphery of the burial, and when we had arrived here, the SUV had been empty except for Hakeem in the front seat, playing on his phone.

"No," I said. "I'll—I'll deal with him later. Callie, I can't face all those people. I need a second. I need a breath."

She nodded again and rubbed my shoulder. "Of course. I'll let Linda know you're on the way."

I made my way down the other side of the hill, carefully stepping, and at times slipping, down the trail, past the farthest cabin on the property and all the way to the water. To my favorite spot, Moon Rock—the wide, flat boulder that stuck out onto the lake, where I'd escape my mother's clamor and find some peace.

After leaving my shoes on the bank, I clambered onto the cold slab and sat still, facing the water with my knees pulled into my chest. It was relatively quiet. With September had come the beginning of school, and most of the summer visitors had returned to their cities. The maples and alders mixed in with the pines were starting to change, and the tules scattered around the edges of the water had lost their blooms. Only a few boats were out—mostly fishermen and a few wakeboarders, catching the last few rays of summer. And with them came the last few vestiges of a memory I'd long forgotten.

———

"I'm sorry, Mama." I tossed a stick into the water below the smooth, rounded edge of the rock.

"Maggie Mae."

Her voice was calmer than I'd ever heard it. Since I'd gotten my acceptance to NYU and the scholarship that would make it happen, Mama had moped around the property, sneaking an extra dollop of gin in her soda when she thought I wasn't looking. She complained to inanimate objects that couldn't speak back: the flowers she watered, the grass she cut.

"What does New York have other than filthy streets and filthier people?"

"Why doesn't my daughter love me enough to stay close?"

I turned, ready for another onslaught of her guilt. I was so tired of this fight. She'd never forgive me for leaving, but I'd never forgive myself if I stayed.

She lacked, for once, that omnipresent, slightly manic gleam, the one that came with a strong drink or five and glazed her life with a glee that she had convinced herself replaced true happiness. Without that film, her deep brown eyes clearly conveyed sadness, but also another truth.

"I know sometimes I'm not the mama you wanted," she admitted. *"Certainly not the one you needed. I know I haven't made this decision easy for you."*

I watched the water and the way its ripples drifted outward from the stick.

"But I'm proud of you, Margaret. So very proud."

I looked up. She'd never said it. Not about this, the first accomplishment in my life that really meant something. *"Really?"*

Mama nodded. Her curls bobbed with the moment, joyful in a way her face was not. *"Oh, baby, of course I am. I'm proud of you for everything you are. And I hope..."* She placed a thin, solid hand on my shoulder. It was such a different touch when it was there out of tenderness, rather than the heavy weight of her when I carried her to her room or a harsh smack when she lost her temper. *"In all these years, I hope I've taught you one thing. Maggie Mae, you listen to me. You only got one life to live, baby. And no matter what anyone says, you got to live that life for yourself. You got to live and die for what's right for you. No matter what anyone says. Even if that person is me. Do that, and have no regrets, you hear?"*

The water lapped around us, and for once, Mama didn't look away. Didn't hide her discomfort in a drink or a gale of laughter. Didn't change the subject to *neighborhood gossip or what so-and-so had said at the salon. She waited with uncharacteristic patience as her words sank in.*

"You hear?" she asked after a few more minutes.

Slowly, I nodded. "Yeah, Mama. I hear."

"THEY SAID I might find you here."

I started at a familiar voice that pulled me out of my daydream. Deep. Twisted. Utterly, utterly wrong. At first, I thought he might be a figment of my imagination, another memory springing from beyond. But the scent of his cologne floated over the water, and the hairs on the back of my neck stood up.

I turned around, and there he was, leaning against a tree. His designer jeans and polo shirt were uncharacteristically rumpled. His goatee needed a trim, and the rest of him a good going over. He looked like he hadn't slept in days. And right now, his dark, almost black eyes were trained directly on me.

"Theo," I breathed, edging toward the water. "W-what are you doing here?"

Run, baby. My mother's voice again, speaking from deep within my subconscious. Except I couldn't. Stranded on the rock, there was nowhere to go.

Theo came to stand between the three big boulders couched around the only easy exit off the rock, effectively trapping me against the water. I slid down the slanted plain. Barefoot and cold, I curled into myself, pulling my skirt tighter over my knees.

"I had to pay my condolences," he said, bending over to brace his hands at the top of the slab. "You ran off so quickly last time."

"You mean, after you were kicked out of Corbyn's house?"

Theo's dark eyes sharpened at the mention of the other night. "You didn't really think it was going to be that simple, did you, Flower? You know me." He leaned down so our faces were level. "You know exactly what kind of grudges I can hold. Your boyfriend doesn't. He should, considering there are a few people out there with grudges against him too."

I blinked. "What is that supposed to mean?"

Theo shrugged. "Let's just say I had some help."

It didn't take a rocket scientist to figure out whom he was talking about. There were really only a few other people who would nurse this kind of grudge against Will. Tricia might be a terrible mother, but she was money-hungry, not vindictive.

"Amelia," I breathed. "Tricia?"

Theo nodded. "There we are. Amy was kind enough to let me know where you'd gone. Apparently Mr. Sunshine and she were quite chatty during reshoots. He told her the moment he received the call from your friend." He winked. "They're very close, you know. Almost as close as you and me."

I swallowed as I worried my skirt between my fingers. "You're lying. You shouldn't be here." I looked around, but the lake was empty now—not even a fisherman in sight.

"You really are dense, you know that, Maggie?" Theo's full lips twisted grotesquely. I honestly couldn't remember why I had ever been attracted to them. "All body, but you never had an ounce of brains. Whose idea do you think it was for me to come to the party to begin with? We had it all planned out. I brought the drugs. She dropped them in his drinks. His own mother served them herself. Amy and Tricia got their prize idiot…" He trailed off as his gaze steered down my body and back up. "And I got mine. It was bad luck that your boyfriend turned out to have a better tolerance for Rohypnol than I thought. We underestimated that a bit, but in the end, it didn't matter, did it?"

The revelations took a moment to sink in, but when they did, it was like a veil had been lifted. Rohypnol. Of course. It explained everything—the woozy look in Will's eyes in the photos, the way he didn't move a muscle to stop Amelia, nor to respond to her. My heart plummeted. I believed him, though another part of me wondered if I would ever be free of this kind of targeting. If Will would either.

Theo traced a long finger over a groove in the rock. Once I loved those fingers—loved the way they threaded through my hair, gripped my arms, caressed my body. But even then, his touch was always laced with a threat. Even before he had ever touched me in violence, a part of me must have known that his slender hands contained that potential.

"What is wrong with you?" I asked, hating my voice for warbling the way it did. "Her too. Why can't you let us go?"

"Do you know what I thought the first time I saw you?" he asked. "At your show, remember?"

I remembered. So strange that the two men who would affect my life the most had both seen me on stage that night, so long ago. Even though I hadn't met either of them until much, much later.

"Do you know the first word that went through my mind?"

Wordlessly, I shook my head.

Theo tapped his nose, which was slightly crooked now in the middle. He didn't wear a brace, but there was still a bit of bruising around the bridge. "I'd never seen anything like you. I never liked your music, but it didn't matter because you stunned us all. You were so exquisite. Unfinished, of course. Those terrible clothes, that crazy hair." He pointed at my curls, which flew around me in nearly unmanageable spirals. "But those lips, that body, that beautiful face. I thought, this perfect little diamond in the rough, someone I could remake perfect. Just. For. Me."

I couldn't breathe. Couldn't move. Where was Calliope, Linda, Lucas...*anyone* to help? My cell phone was in the car, and of course, no one would be able to hear me if I yelled from here—all sound was blocked by the giant, bouldered cliff between Moon Rock and the house. Any screams would only echo across the bay to empty houses. The water below the rock masked jagged edges of broken granite—if I jumped in, I risked breaking an ankle, or worse, my head.

Theo stood up straighter. Then he leaned over the rock, close enough that he was less than a foot from me. There was nowhere to go—if I scooted backward, I'd lose my balance and end up toppling into the rocks.

"I thought," he said, as his dark, handsome face contorted with delight, "*Mine.*"

Locked in place, I could hear the ghost of my mother behind me, railing against the men who had loved and hated her all her life. I could feel Will's warm, solid energy emanating from within.

Another memory floated into my conscious thought, this one much more recent.

"You're mine," Will stated in a low, languid voice. "Say it."

"Yours," I replied immediately. The lazy smile that spread across his face made my insides twist. I grabbed his shirt and pulled him to me. "But you're mine too."

"No," I whispered, even as the pain of the memory cut through me. Its pain…and its truth.

Theo's sneer quickly morphed to a snarl. "*What?*"

I cleared my throat. "I s-said *no*. I don't belong to you, Theo. I n-*never* belonged to you. I'm not your flower. I'm not your anything! Your problem is that you could never accept it."

Theo only stood there. It was then I noticed the sheen of something else—drugs, maybe. He had never been one to shy away, and I suspected he was on something now. Which, of course, only made him that much more dangerous.

"Theo, please," I begged, losing any remains of my pride. "Walk away. I won't—I won't call the cops. I won't tell anyone you were here. Please…let me go."

Whether it was my words or pathetic tone, something in Theo moved. Like a rubber band snapping into place, he jerked, and his eyes, black and flashing, zeroed in on me.

"You don't fucking get it, do you?"

Before I could move, he lunged forward and grabbed a nasty handful of my hair, yanking my face six inches from his. The other nabbed both of my wrists behind my back, wrenching my shoulders so that I was both laid across the top of the rock and arched toward him in a painful bind.

"Theo, stop!" I cried, kicking my feet toward the water, but otherwise unable to move.

"You don't get to say no to me!" he hissed. "Are you deaf? You're *mine*, Maggie. You've always been mine. Before. Now. After. Always. And I'm sick and fucking tired of you denying that basic fact."

"You're c-crazy," I said, my voice growing stronger. *Fight it.* My mother's voice was stronger too.

"Shut the fuck up!"

He shook me like a rag doll. I winced, feeling multiple strands of hair pulled out. But I didn't stop talking.

"You've always been crazy," I snapped back, loud enough now that my voice began to echo off the lake. "I don't know why you have this demented belief that I-I belong to you or something, but I don't! I never have. I never ever will!"

His eyes flared. "Is that fucking right?"

He moved like lightning, jumping onto the rock and crouching over me even as he held me still. Theo twisted me around so I sat up against his chest, my face tipped up in an absurd parody of love. He skimmed a finger down my jawline, letting it catch on my skin painfully.

"And you think you belong to *him*?" he wondered.

I tried to jerk away, but the grip on my hair held strong. "You have no idea," I mumbled. *Will*...the name called inside me, full of love and regret. The image of him bent over at the church flashed in front of me. He...oh, God. The things I'd said.

Theo's free arm latched mine behind my back, holding my body still against his. Then his lips followed the line of his nail, pressing cold, rubbery flesh to mine, the scent of his cologne overpowering everything else. Bringing me back to the terrible present.

"Do you remember what I used to do to you, Flower?" His voice was a low purr, like a cat toying with its prey. "Do you remember all those nights, all those days back in New York? The way I'd probe your sweet cunt and make you scream? You loved it. Even when I took you against your will, you secretly loved it."

I jerked again. Perhaps I'd once liked the way Theo touched me, but the longer we were together, the more unforgiving he had become. Even from the beginning, sex had been a way of claiming me, and I had accepted his dominance as intimacy because I was ignorant to the differences between proprietorship and passion. Lines were crossed early on, to the point that it had taken me a very long time to understand how many of our interactions occurred without my consent.

But now I knew better. Now I had experienced the real thing.

"You were a terrible lover," I pronounced. "Everything about it."

"It could have been good if you'd let it." His breath was hot. My stomach lurched.

"You *raped* me," I spat, almost like a reflex. "How the fuck was that *good*?"

"Rape? Oh, Flower, no. That wasn't rape." His teeth closed over the corner of my jaw and bit down. It hurt. "That was games."

"You only ever took what you wanted, and now that when you don't get what you want, it drives you even more batshit crazy. Well, you can't have this. You can't have *me*!"

In response, Theo whipped my hands down and ensnared them between his thighs. I was trapped, while he kept one hand in my hair and the other began tugging my skirt up my thigh.

"Stop." I tried and failed to wriggle away from him, but his thighs were like steel and the hand in my hair yanked again, hard enough that I could feel more hair pulling out.

"No," he said simply while his hand found my underwear and started to pull.

"Theo, stop." My voice was losing its strength. There was no one to hear us. I was completely on my own. "I SAID STOP!"

My body flung into action as I arched against him and twisted with all my might. The movement rolled my ankle in a vicious turn, causing a loud howl to burst from the back of my throat. But at the same moment, it also knocked Theo off-balance.

"Get *off* me!" I shouted, again and again once my arms were free. Lashing out, I kicked and scrambled as he lurched toward me over the slanted surface of the rock.

"Come here!" he shouted.

"NO!"

I kicked again, my injured foot, undercutting his advance. It hurt like hell, but I didn't care. All I knew was that I would not, *could not* allow this man to touch me again. Either I was going in the lake or he was. I glanced out at the water. If I jumped far enough, maybe I could skip the jagged, shallow edges and land where the rocks gave way to the deeper part of the lake. But that was a very big *if*.

"Maggie!"

The sound of Will's voice cut though my panicked thoughts.

"Will!" I screamed. "I'm here!"

His golden head popped through the trees, and the second he saw who was crouched on the rock with me, he doubled his pace down the hillside and came jogging through the trees a moment later, sending pine needles and fallen leaves flying.

"Get the fuck off her!" he yelled as he bounded over the boulders.

Theo made one last frantic grab, and I kicked out, making contact with his legs. "No!" I screamed. "Don't *touch* me!"

Will's fist shot out, a cannon into Theo's face, and knocked him down. His skull slammed against the edge of the rock with a sickening crunch, and then he bounced into the water, face-down. His limbs shook, thrashing on their own. And then...he didn't move.

"Oh my God," I whispered. "Is he..."

Will slid into the water, picked around the rocks, and with Herculean effort, somehow managed to pull Theo out and lay him across the rock beside me. Blood streamed heavily from a nasty cut on his forehead— where he must have hit one of the jagged edges lurking below the surface.

"Will, he's...Will, we have to help him!"

"No the *fuck* we don't!" Will pulled me into him and stared down at the body. His pants were soaked, dripped water all over the rock, while his shirt, damp from lugging the body, soaked into my dress. He looked a little starstruck himself, like he couldn't quite believe this was happening. "He chose this fate, Lil. Let the bastard fucking have it."

For a half second, I actually considered it. All of the moments—the many, *many* times I had felt that my life was in danger because of this man—flashed in through my mind. Part of me wanted to know he was gone.

But no. I couldn't do this, and I couldn't let Will do this. We both carried enough guilt with us, wherever we went. We didn't need this too.

I pushed out of his hold and crouched beside Theo on shaky knees, preparing to administer CPR. I pushed with all my might on his chest, again and again. Nothing.

"Come on," I hummed. "Come on." Again I pushed, then bent down.

"Maggie." Before my lips landed on Theo's, I was pulled back, and Will quickly took my place. Unable to hide his disgust, he took hold of Theo's nose and blew a lungful of air into him. Hands on his chest again, delivering much more powerful thrusts than I could give. More air. More thrusts.

Then Theo lurched.

"Oh, thank God," I breathed as we sat back. Theo coughed and sputtered as water spilled over his chin as his body. We watched as his eyes opened, but didn't focus, only stared blindly at the sky, past the faces looking down at him.

And then they closed, and he didn't move.

"Oh my God," I muttered as I stared down at the cold face of my lover. My attacker. I covered my mouth as I started to shake. "Oh my *God*."

Will pressed his fingers to Theo's throat, but it was clear from his face that there was no pulse.

"We—we have to—"

"No, Lil."

"We have to help him."

"Lil, he's gone."

Will guided me away from the body, pulling me up the face of the rock until I was sitting on the edge, pulled into his chest. I continued to fight him, twisting back around to where Theo's body lay, silent, wet, and cold. But Will's voice was as steely as his arms, and though I struggled, in the end I stopped, and let him keep me still, let him observe the death of the man who had tormented me, stalked me and violated me countless times. He witnessed the end of my enemy so I wouldn't have to.

"Will? Maggie? You guys need to...what the fuck..."

We both twisted at the sound of Calliope's voice. She appeared through the pines, followed closely by Benny.

"Will, I told you, you need to leave her—whoa." Benny stopped short behind Calliope, who was staring at Theo's still form.

Tucked into Will's arms, I began to shake violently.

"This asshole was trying to fucking abduct Maggie," Will bit out. "I punched him, and he slipped on the rocks and fell. We pulled him out, and tried to save him...but it was too late."

Benny's glance darted to Will's scraped knuckles, but he nodded. Will continued to hold me, rocking me from side to side while I tried to breathe.

"Someone needs to call the cops." His voice, strangely calm, vibrated against my cheek while he continued to rock me into him. "We're going to have to give them a statement."

"You sure you want to do that?" The implication was clear. This wasn't the kind of thing that would escape the press or anyone else's scrutiny. It was going to be a battle, he meant. A giant pain in the ass.

But there was no uncertainty in Will's voice. "Yeah," he said. "It's the right thing to do. We're done hiding."

Benny nodded. "Okay. Well, I heard the screaming. We saw the whole thing, didn't we, Ms. Jackson?"

Calliope was still staring at Theo's prone form with something close to bitter satisfaction. "Motherfucker," she muttered. Then she shook her head. "Oh, yeah. We saw it all."

With a nod to Will, the two of them disappeared back around the bend, Benny's cell phone already pressed to his ear. I tried to twist back to look at the body. Was he really dead? Was it my fault?

But Will wouldn't let me move, instead restrained me as trauma turned me into little more than a leaf twisting in a vicious wind.

"Don't," he whispered as his hand cradled my head to his chest. "It's done."

"I-I-c-can't..." I couldn't even get coherent words out as rage and shock rattled through me.

"Shhhhh," Will crooned. I curled into his strong, solid body, and he held me even closer. "I'm here, baby. And I'm never fucking leaving you again."

CHAPTER THIRTY-ONE

I t had been a long time since the residents of Newman Lake had heard a siren anywhere close to the water. Sure, cops showed up from time to time, but usually for domestic disputes. Maybe a boat crash or two. They usually parked silently outside the houses nestled in the trees and allowed people the ability to keep secrets as best they could.

Still, it didn't take long for word to get out that the Newman Lake sheriff had sent an ambulance and three deputies to our house, their red and blue lights blinking through the trees at the top of the hill. It took hours while they collected Theo's body; even longer when Calliope, Benny, Will, and I were all driven to the station in the back of the squad cars to give statements, followed by Hakeem in the SUV. But in the end, everyone was allowed to leave. There were three witnesses who could verify what had happened that night, not to mention the simple fact that I had been stalked here by a man previously convicted of raping me. No one was going to argue that Will shouldn't have defended me, especially not after the police took photos of the bruises and scrapes left all over my body. Theo and I both had remnants of each other's DNA under our fingernails, evidence of the fight. That he had drowned after losing consciousness was just an unfortunate side effect, or so Will said. And the deputies agreed. The pang in my stomach said otherwise.

He was pronounced dead at the scene. His father was notified, and we listened from the other side of the station as Max del Conte screamed through the tinny speakers of the deputy's desk phone. He threatened again and again to charge someone, *anyone* for murder or worse. Privately, Benny said we needed to get a lawyer, and quickly, but no one seemed that alarmed by the threats. Theo del Conte was a known felon who had also broken the terms of his parole by crossing state lines without permission. He had a long history of harassing me, and I had the documentation to prove it. My restraining order might have been over-turned, but in the end, the only person who had killed Theo del Conte was himself.

By the time Hakeem parked at the top of the hill leading down to my house, the sun had already slipped past the trees, and the sky was the dusk color of lavender fields in spring. Benny and Calliope got out quickly.

"We'll go down to the house, make sure everyone is cleared out for the night," Calliope said, and they left.

Will came around to my side of the vehicle. We'd been kept mostly apart while the police had conducted their interviews. And there were a lot of things for us to say.

He opened my door to help me out, but stopped when I placed a hand on his wrist.

"We need to talk," I said softly. I didn't want to do it down at the house, where prying eyes would track our every move.

Will shook his head, concerned only with shuffling me out of the back of the car. "Later," he said. "We need to get you inside. That ankle..." He pointed at my swollen limb, which had been twisted in the scuffle on Moon Rock.

"But, Will—"

His hand floated over my shoulder, around my hip, and paused over my stomach, covering the almost flat expanse with his wide palm. He stared at the spot for a long moment.

"You are not allowed to feel bad about what happened," Will said quietly.

I shook my head. "But—"

"*No*," he said vehemently. "Maggie, he was going to—if I hadn't—he wanted to—" He dropped his head, as if the force of the unfinished statements was too much to handle, then squatted down and laid the side of his face on my belly. "I'm sorry," he whispered. "So fucking sorry I wasn't there earlier. But I won't feel bad for protecting you. The both of you."

Without thinking, I threaded my fingers into his hair, stroking the soft waves while Will's eyes squeezed tightly shut.

"But you did come," I said. "And if you hadn't, I'd be—"

"Don't say it—"

"Dead."

The word hung in the air for a few more seconds, like a gong that had been rung.

Will stood up, and for the first time I noticed a few tiny creases at the sides of his eyes. He looked like he hadn't slept for days.

"I love you so fucking much," he said, his voice ragged and torn. "If anything had happened to you, to..." He gestured toward my stomach. "I swear to God, Maggie, I would have followed you right to the grave."

I blinked, but my body trembled. A breeze shook the trees above us, and a few pine needles flew down, landing on Will's shoulders and my dress.

I brushed them off. "Come on," I said weakly. "Let's go down."

I slid from the car only to find that my ankle was still too bad to walk on.

"Dammit," I muttered as I tried and failed to stand up again.

"Your ankle?" His smile was crooked, and I loved and hated how it tugged at my heart the same way it tugged at his cheek.

Shaking, I nodded my head. "Y-yeah."

Suddenly, I was swept up into Will's very strong, very solid arms. My hands wrapped naturally around his shoulders as he cradled me close.

But I couldn't look at him still. I knew—I *knew*—that he was here in part to make amends, along with the traumas of the evening, but there were still so many things that I wasn't sure how to fix. I didn't want to spend my life hiding. And I didn't want to hide my child either.

"I can walk," I said.

He snorted and carried me toward the path that led to the house.

"Let me help you home," he said quietly. But instead of starting the walk around the property to the house, he stopped before the stairs and sat down on another big rock, keeping me securely in his lap.

"Will—" I started to move, but he just squeezed me to him tighter.

"Please," he said. "Give me a second before I have to face the crowds again." I watched his face, which was etched with frustration.

"Will," I tried again.

It was too far away to see, but I could hear the clamor of people. Even after sitting at the police station, talking about Theo's death for hours, I still had a reception to finish, apparently. A mother to mourn. A house to let. A day that would never end.

But Will only held me tighter, keeping me securely on his lap, and pressed his nose into my hair.

"I didn't do it," he said finally. "I didn't take anything at that party, Lil."

"I know." He had been telling me that for hours, but generally, I'd been too shell-shocked to respond. "But you *were* on something."

He blinked, surprised. "How do you know that?"

I shook my tired head. "Theo actually fessed up to it. He and Amelia apparently were working together. She slipped some Rohypnol in your drink. Amelia and Tricia were supposed to keep you occupied while Theo, um—"

"Son of a *bitch*," Will gritted out. "That fucking snake *roofied* me?"

"Amelia or your mother?"

"Both." He shook his head. "Time to call another lawyer."

I shrugged. "I don't know what that will do without any kind of evidence. Right now it would be my word against theirs. Theo's g-gone." It was still hard to believe. I closed my eyes, and the vision of his body, floating face-down in the water, immediately appeared. I knew it would be a long time before I'd ever be rid of it.

"Yeah, well, there are other ways to blacklist someone in that town," Will said darkly to the trees. "Privilege of being Hollywood's prodigal son."

"No, don't."

I laid a hand on his arm. Despite the fact that I was sitting in his lap, it was the first time I had voluntarily touched him. Will looked at my hand for a moment, his gaze softening before it met mine.

"Why?" he asked. "You can't expect me to do nothing here, Lil."

"Will, you just—" I didn't want to say it. But I had to.

"Killed a man." His voice was tight, but matter-of-fact.

I exhaled. "You punched him. He fell. You were protecting—"

"The love of my life and my child."

I gulped. "Well, y-yes. But this would be different. Don't—don't ruin Amelia's life out of vengeance. Don't attack your own mother. It will eat you up inside. Will, I think you have to learn to forgive."

He looked at me for a long time. "We'll see."

"Will, please."

"Maggie, these people conspired to keep us apart. To ruin you, to ruin what we have. Don't tell me to forgive what's fucking unforgivable."

In the end, I let it go, in part because I understood it. Underneath my shock, there was a small ball of fire that burned when I considered what all had been done to us. If I was asking Will to forgive, I'd need to do that myself. And if I was being honest, I wasn't sure I could.

We sat there for several more minutes. It was clear that neither of us wanted to return to the land of people. There would be more questions, more strangers. The prospect of facing a room full of people hanging around mostly for the gossip potential was disheartening, to say the least.

Particularly considering what still lay between Will and me.

He placed a hand over my stomach. He'd been doing that all afternoon.

"Please," he whispered. "Baby, *please* let me back in."

The uncut pain lacing his voice broke me all over again.

"You…you said you didn't want to be a father," I whimpered into his shoulder. "And then, Will, I was standing in that church, and you blocked me out. *You* wouldn't let *me* in!"

"Maggie, I'm so sorry for that. More than you know. But, baby, you walked away. You *keep* walking away. You left LA knowing that you were pregnant, didn't you?"

I sniffled. He was right, and we both knew it.

"I understand why," he said as his hand came up to stroke my back. "But…fuck, Lil. It hurts. It really, really hurts."

"And what would you have done?" I asked. "Every time things get a little bit crazy, you check out. You run away too, Will. So much more than me. First it was literally running, and then it turned to liquor. Even if Amelia and your mom hadn't slipped you a pill, can you honestly say you hadn't thought about it? I watched you look for the escape, and like you said, it *hurts*." I shook my head, allowing my curls to fall around my face. "Will, I grew up with a parent who wasn't ever really there for me. I was scared, all the time, because the person who was *supposed* to be there no matter what so often wasn't, whether it was because sh-she was literally missing or was so far d-down the bottle she might as well have been gone. I won't do that to my child—I *won't!*"

"And you won't have to!" Swiftly, Will pulled my face to his, cupping my cheek so I was forced to see his wild, anxious eyes.

"Will, I just lost a parent to addiction." My voice choked, and now tears fell freely. "I…I can't deal with losing you too. *We* can't deal with losing you too."

"Lil, you're *never* going to lose me." He pushed my hair away from my face, pressing his lips up and down my cheeks, all around my eyes. Kissing away the tears. "Do you hear me?" he whispered fiercely. "It doesn't matter how many times you try to push me away, Lily pad. You can run all you want, but I'm done with it. The first thing I did when you left LA was find a therapist and sign up for AA."

I hiccuped. "You did?"

Will nodded. "I'm done running, Lil. I won't run to the bottle. Not to pills. And not to the road. And, Lily pad, I will *always* come back for you. You, and one day, this little person in here—I. Belong. To. You." He pulled my face back so he could focus all of his energy on me. So I could see the depth of us in those big green eyes. "All I am. All I'll ever be. All of it belongs to you."

His eyes drifted down, like he wanted to kiss me, but he held still, held *me* still, until I was ready to respond.

One last time, I wondered if I should say no. My soul was torn apart by the people in my life who I'd loved. Theo. My mother. Here stood a man who had torn it up more than most, who had the power to ruin me in every way possible if he so chose. If I stayed and he left me again, I'd never recover. Maybe I wouldn't ever recover now as it was.

But Will's gaze was unwavering, and the currents of love and devotion I saw there matched the intensity of his words. He was mine, he said. And in my heart, I knew I belonged to him as well.

There was never really a choice to leave. Not when it came to him.

"Okay." My voice, my breath, everything shook with the emotion that had been bubbling inside me all day.

"Okay?" The hands on my face softened, and he brushed my cheekbones lightly with his thumbs.

I closed my eyes for a moment, overcome. But when I opened them, he was still there. Still watching. Still waiting.

"Kiss me, Will," I whispered. "Kiss me, and don't stop."

His green eyes popped open, hungry. Maybe even starving.

"Never," he said before his lips crashed into mine.

Kiss wasn't strong enough to describe it. Will kept me on his lap, one hand cupping my face, the other around my waist while he devoured me, tasted me, drank from me like an oasis spring, and he quenched both our thirsty, barren souls.

Because I was equally parched. I grabbed at his hair, pulling him closer, urging his lips to my neck, my chin, my ears, my chest. Our tongues grappled, bodies smashed in a desire to get closer, so much closer than we could ever really achieve. Sob after sob erupted from my throat each time I broke for breath, but Will swallowed them all, taking my pain and burying it with everyone else we'd lost. Replacing it with his love and devotion in every touch of his lips.

"Let's—go—down—" I could barely get out the words as his mouth trailed down my neck. Maybe it was being pregnant, but my skin tingled everywhere—all I wanted to do was feel that healing touch all over. I wanted to shed my clothes like I wanted to shed the past.

"Yessss." Will growled against my neck, then, somewhat reluctantly, pulled away so he could help me stand back up. "Let's go."

But before we could start the rest of the way down, Will's phone buzzed in his pocket. As he read the incoming text, his face whitened.

"What?" I asked, pressing a hand on his chest. "What is it?" How much more could we take?

He swallowed heavily. "It's Benny. I—the press. They're here." Will closed his eyes and took a deep breath. "They're all around your house, apparently." He peered around, and already, I imagined photographers hiding in the brush and trees that covered the hill. A prickle ran down my arms. Will's dread was palpable, especially in the heartbeat that quickened under my palm.

"It's okay," I said, already resigned. "Go. I'll—I'll manage it on my own. Callie's probably already called the police, and they'll clear the property in no time. You can go."

There was still time. He could run back up to the road where Hakeem was still parked, escape the chaos that awaited both of us downstairs. Play another shell game, or even fly back to LA, virtually undetected. Without Will there, the photographers would lose interest quickly, and I'd resume the life I'd planned. Alone.

Ignoring my dread at the thought of Will leaving yet again, I tried to stand up, stumbling slightly on my bad ankle. But before I could take another step, I was swept up once more, with one of Will's strong arms under my knees, the other supporting my back.

"Will—" I protested, but was immediately cut off with a kiss. It started out closed-mouthed, intent, meant mostly to cut off my arguments against his sudden movement. But predictably, it turned into something more, and he and I both poured out the pain, the sorrow, the anger, the confusion of the last few weeks into one kiss. By the time it was over, tears were streaming down my face, and when I pulled back, more than a few trickles fell from his.

He pressed his face against mine with closed eyes. The simple touch, skin to skin, warmed me throughout.

"Walk through fire, remember?" he whispered. "I'm not going to let you face the flames alone, Lil. Never again."

I opened my mouth, ready to tell him it was okay. That he could go. That I could manage it all on my own.

But I couldn't. And so, as he descended the seventy-three stairs to the deck that contained the biggest crowd of people this property had ever seen, I only buried my face in his neck. I took solace in the sweet, fresh scent of him, the solid grip of his hands under my limbs, each one of his steps that were more confident than the last.

We were spotted about halfway down and were immediately swarmed by cameras. Hakeem came jogging from the car—likely alerted by Benny once he realized his friend was entering the fray. The big man jumped ahead and cut a path for us the rest of the way down, pushing away photographers, reporters, neighbors, and anyone else who had appeared on my mother's property.

I shut my eyes as flashes went off, though the questions penetrated nonetheless. Will walked stolidly, his head tucked, but shoulders straight as the onslaught began.

"Fitz!"

'Maggie!"

"Where have you been?"

"Where's Amelia?"

"Is it true she broke you up?"

"Maggie, are you hurt?"

On and on the questions, flashes, pushing and prodding as we made our final descent to the deck, where so many other people stood waiting. Lucas. Linda. Katie. Lindsay. Don. And many others I recognized from the funeral and growing up in a small town.

The paparazzi continued to shout.

"Is your mother really dead?"

"Did you kill Theo del Conte?"

"Maggie, were you and your mother running a brothel?"

"Was Theo del Conte a client?"

"Are you an alcoholic too?"

As we followed Hakeem's hulking form toward the sliding glass entrance, the questions blended with the murmurs of the neighbors.

"Pathetic."

"Look at her—what do you think they're about to do?"

"I bet she's trashed."

"Like mother, like daughter."

It was on the last one that Will stopped right in front of the now open door.

"Goddammit," he muttered, shaking his head.

"Will, don't—" I began, but he had already turned around and was setting me gently on the deck in front of him. I balanced on one foot as he wrapped his arms around my shoulders, caging me against his body. Protecting me.

"Maggie, were you cheating on Fitz with Theo?"

"Did you and Theo have a love child?"

"STOP." Will's voice, with its deep baritone and natural charisma that could take charge of any room he wanted, stilled the crowd immediately. Mouths clamped shut. Heads turned toward the familiar face, the voice that spoke above the rest.

Another round of flashes went off, but Will didn't blink. He didn't even move. Instead of shrinking, he stood taller, rendering himself a beacon in the forest.

"I won't have it," he said, quiet until someone shouted from the back:

"What's that, Fitz?"

"It's *Will*!" Will barked. "My full name is Fitz*william* Michael Baker. I have never in my entire life gone by the name *Fitz* unless it's in the film credits or by people who don't fucking know me."

There was a flurry of flashes, and I noticed more than one cell phone held up in the crowd.

"Will, come on," I murmured, pulling on his sleeve. What did he think he was going to accomplish here?

"No," he said brusquely. "They need to hear this." He turned back to the crowd. "*Everyone* needs to hear this. So you can all *listen the fuck up*."

If it was quiet before, the deck was now completely silent. Quiet enough that I could hear the rustle of the osprey flying through the trees to catch their dinner in the lake. Quiet enough that the wind swishing through the willow branches floated across the crowd. Quiet enough that the lake, lapping peacefully at the water's edge, was louder than my own breath.

"You see this woman?" Will asked as he pulled me back against him. "Every day I have known her, she's been the kind of person who will do more for others than she will for herself. She takes everyone's complaints, everyone's baggage, and bears them like a cross. She gave up a career in music for people she loved, despite the fact that she's one of the most talented people in the world. She is more than anyone else in this life."

I blushed as several eyes flickered to me. But Will didn't stop there.

"This is someone who spent most of her life trying to heal people who didn't want to be healed. Maybe couldn't be healed. She buried one of those people today and lost another and all you can do is stand here and volley idiotic questions that question her character? Well, fuck you. All of you. You should be ashamed of yourselves."

"But, Fitz—I mean, Will—" began one of the reporters in the back, starting off yet another round of flashes.

"But nothing!" Will roared. "I swear to God, if I hear one more person —one more fucking person—treat her with anything less than respect, you're going to have to answer to me. And I am not a particularly nice guy. Especially when it come to people mistreating the one person that makes life worth living when fucking vultures like you suck all the joy out of it. You think I'm moody now? Erratic? A loose cannon? You haven't seen anything compared to what I'll become if I hear even a whisper that this woman is anything less than perfect."

Then Will turned his head slowly, casting a harsh eye across the entire group.

"Lindsay?" he asked with a voice like a drill as he caught the blonde girl standing near the side, trying and failing to hide behind Lucas, who had been watching the proceedings with a somewhat satisfied look.

Lindsay shied, but when Will didn't look away and many others also turned to find her, she bobbed her head.

"Yeah," she said. "Of-of course."

"Ladies?" Will turned again toward the cluster of women near the front. I recognized them from the church—women who had always enjoyed talking about Mama behind her back, and, by extension, me.

"Oh, um, yes, sorry," one of them answered quickly, and the others murmured their agreement.

Will looked around the crowd, picking out faces one by one, reporters, paparazzi, neighbors—anyone he thought had said a disparaging comment or something similar. Each one cowered under the force of his gaze.

"We good?" Will asked the crowd, watching to make sure that everyone nodded.

From up the hill, there was the sound of a siren—again breaking the silence of the strange night. Will turned back to his audience, his lips pulled to one side in a satisfied smirk.

"Good," he said. "So now you can let us mourn in peace. That up there is our backup, and anyone left on this property after the next ten minutes without our permission is going to get arrested for trespassing." He leveled one last glare on the crowd, and several people immediately shuffled toward the stairs. "Now get the hell out."

CHAPTER THIRTY-TWO

I t took several days for people to stop showing up unannounced to the house. They came to bring casseroles and good wishes, but also to get a look at the famous man chopping more wood for the winter down by the dock. To his credit, Will didn't leave. He stayed close, working on the houses, helping me get the property ready for winter.

One man stayed, though, and came a few more times over the next few weeks: James Edelman. Though both of us were fairly certain he was my father, Will insisted on paying for a DNA test to make sure.

"You can't be too careful," he said after we left the doctor's office.

I didn't argue. I now understood all too well the way people came out of the woodwork to target someone like Will, and by extension, me. James was nice. Quiet, and kind of shy. I liked him a lot, and we immediately bonded when I showed him my Martin. He didn't seem to care in the slightest who Will was—honest, he didn't even seem to notice at all. Instead, we had stayed up, singing Johnny Cash songs around the fire together until I was so tired I couldn't keep my eyes open anymore. We wouldn't get the DNA results for a while, but at this point, I wasn't sure I cared.

Fall had fully arrived on Newman Lake, seemingly overnight. The trees lining the south end—the maples, alders, and cottonwoods that stood high over the lily pads and tules, were now a rainbow of reds, oranges, and yellows. Every day, another flock of birds would disappear toward the south, and as soon as the sun set over the mountain, a needle-sharp chill would settle into our bones, the kind that required wool socks and a thick fleece once the sky turned dark.

Eventually, Callie and Benny went back to New York. Will would eventually have to return to LA for reshoots, which he'd managed to delay by a month in order to deal with the fallout of Theo's death. Although they included parts with Amelia—according to Corbyn, their chemistry was absolute crap—Will had renegotiated that any scenes shot with her would be done with a mirror and a stunt double, to be CGI'd together in exchange for not pressing charges against her for drugging him.

Unsurprisingly, she had readily agreed to the terms.

Tricia, however, was another story. She tried more than once to contact her son through Benny, only to be stonewalled again and again. As much as I wanted Will to make peace with his mother, if only for his own sake, I could also see the plain truth. Whether it was because she had been corrupted by a world of money and fame or because she was, to the core, a terrible person, she was absolutely not someone who should be in Will's life. I had never seen any indication that she valued her son as anything more than a commodity. And for that reason alone, I wanted her nowhere near us or our child.

Will felt the same. In fact, he felt so strongly that he wrote a letter to *Vanity Fair* to include with their article on him. The editor was so excited about the coup that she decided to turn it into a double feature: one on the reclusive former star (Will insisted on the word "former"), and the second on mothers of child actors, specifically Tricia Owens-Baker, who had leveraged her success with Will into an agency managing other child actors in Hollywood.

"Everyone should know what she really is," he said as he mailed a copy of his letter to her apartment in New York. It would arrive on the following Monday, the same day the magazine landed on newsstands.

We spent the majority of the next few weeks cleaning out the house and cabins of Mama's things, deciding which pieces I wanted to keep, store, or give away. It was the hardest thing I'd ever done. How do you clean out someone's *life*? How do you do it when it's your own mother?

More than once Will had found me crying over a random photo or an old flannel shirt. And to his credit, he never turned away or tried to help me stop. He pulled me into his chest, clasped my head to his shoulder, and rocked me, whispering nothings until the tears abated and I could keep going.

Eventually, though, the house was cleared out and ready for new tenants. The carpet had been replaced, the bathtub re-caulked, the roof completely re-shingled. I had decided to lease the property to the Forsters as an extension of the inn. Lucas and his family would be good caretakers. I couldn't stay in that house anymore.

Meanwhile, Will and I would head back to LA for the *Green Lantern* reshoots. Once that was finished we had several more months until the promotional tour began. I wouldn't be able to go on the tour—by April of next year, I'd be hugely pregnant and certainly unable to fly around the world from city to city. Will warned me I'd better keep the kid in until he was done—he wasn't missing the birth of our child, no matter what his contract said.

I stood at the edge of the dock, staring out at the lake, and pulled my thick sweater around me and inhaled the cool evening air. I was ready to leave. And this time, it wouldn't be in a rush.

The heavy tread of footsteps on the dock alerted me to Will's presence. A few moments later, I was wrapped in his arms. He smelled of soap and water, like he had just gotten out of the shower.

"So, what do you think?" Will whispered as we surveyed the lake together. "Where do you want to go first after LA? Ireland? Machu Picchu? There's a lot we can do in six months, Lil."

A few days ago when we had come up with a plan to travel between LA and his premiere dates, I was ecstatic. The idea of traveling the world with Will sounded like the best idea ever. He insisted I didn't need to worry about money or anything—it would be our last big hurrah before the baby came. Little no-name. Whoever it was.

But now, the idea made me pull my sweater even tighter around my stomach. Will must have felt me withdraw slightly. The arms around my shoulders tightened, but he waited for me to speak.

"I...what if we don't go?" I wondered quietly.

Will set his chin on my shoulder. "Why not?"

I stared out at the water, wondering at its mirrored surface. In it, I saw every moment in my childhood flash before my eyes, good and bad. I saw my first swim, the first time I ever caught a fish. I saw myself seeking refuge in the waves when my mother was in a particularly bad mood. I saw Lucas, Katie, and other friends, piled in boats and listening to country music. I saw myself sitting on the end of the dock, strumming a guitar with my toes in the water.

And then, of course, I saw Will. Those memories were more recent, but no less meaningful. I saw him climbing out of the water, sun sparkling in the droplets on his body. I saw myself tangled in the lilies, only the second time we met. I saw us falling in, desperate for each other's kiss.

I saw it all. And as I watched, I wanted more.

"I don't want to travel," I said. "I want to find somewhere to stay. Will, our baby needs a home. *I* need a home." I tipped up my head to look at him. "Don't you?"

His quiet was louder than words. Much like the water, it was almost as if I watched our entire emotional history pass through those green eyes, lighting up the gold sparks in the center.

Then, at last, Will stood up straight, releasing me from his embrace. "Come with me," he said, taking my hand. "I want to show you something."

Instead of leading me back up the dock, he gestured toward the boat tied up to one side. A week ago, Will had surprised me when he'd sailed a tiny catamaran with a bright white sail to the house from the boat launch. It had become his nightly ritual, taking her out in the evenings, when the speed boats were done for the night. Sometimes I went, and sometimes I didn't. But he always took me with him: her name was *Lily Pad*, painted right across the stern of one of the pontoons.

We sailed across the lake as night fell and the stars came out, Will perched on the back, manning the rudder and the sails, while I stretched out on the netting between the pontoons. I rested one hand lightly on my belly, which was still only a very slight swelling, but present nonetheless.

The breeze off the lake fluttered my hair around my cheeks, and I closed my eyes, content.

Will tied up the boat at a familiar dock—the one surrounded by lilies, where I had gotten tangled only four months ago. Had it only been that long? The summer felt like it had lasted a lifetime.

"Here, babe," he said as he held out his hand, guiding me onto the wood slats.

I looked around. The dock was different. I was used to it being decrepit and wind-worn, but the wood was newly stained, the sagging ends rebuilt, with shiny new buoys tied to the sides.

I turned back to Will. "What did you do?"

A smile appeared, boyish and bright. Only for me.

"Come on," he said. "There's more."

He led me onto the bank, where the boathouse that used to hold a bunch of CrossFit equipment had been repainted and fit with a new lock. I followed him up the stairs to where his house was tucked into the hillside.

"Will…" I said, taking in all the changes.

"Wait," he said as we walked. "There's more."

And there was. He took me on a tour of the newly refurbished property, which apparently he'd had completely redone while we were in LA during his filming. Gone were the peeling brown exterior and weathered deck—now it was a bright, welcoming white trimmed with a deep green that matched Will's eyes, and the deck was painted to match. The outdoor kitchen had also been completely redone, the counter replaced with granite, and a grill, table and chairs, and lounge furniture taking up the space.

But the biggest change was the extra level that had been built on top of the house. Now it boasted an entirely new third story, with unobstructed views of the water.

"Holy shit," I stammered as I stared up at it. "What did you…what did you *do*?"

"I took a chance," Will said. "And I built us a home."

He tugged on my hand, turning me to face him so he could take my other one. His thumb rubbed over my left ring finger, but he only smiled. My heart picked up a beat.

"Lil, this is for us," he said. "And if you don't like the changes I made, we can tear them down and start over."

I gazed around. "I thought that security was too hard here."

"It was. Which was why I had a fence and cameras installed too. The whole property is fenced in, and there's a gate at the top of the drive-way." There was sadness in his voice, the disappointment that he couldn't ever completely open us up to the world. Our son or daughter wouldn't even know what it was like to run across the street to a friend's house or walk around a neighborhood alone. That wasn't going to be in our future.

But so, so much else was.

"Before Ellie passed..." Will paused, allowing that shadow to move by. "Before that, I thought we'd always come back here, you know? This place, where I met you...when I imagine home, Lil, it's you. Just you."

I turned back to him and cupped his face. "*You* are home to me too," I told him, and was immediately rewarded with a wide smile. I kissed him, pulling him toward me so I could show him with my arms and mouth what words couldn't ever cover.

When we broke apart, Will was out of breath and looked like he desperately wanted to find someplace private.

"All right," I said. "Show me our new house."

With shining eyes, Will unlocked the front door, which was brightly lit by the porch light. The main floor wasn't changed much—still the same comfortable living room, the same large kitchen. But there was one major difference: photographs. Pictures of us over the past few months were everywhere. Some of them I recognized as paparazzi shots, others were from events we had attended, and a few from when we first met. I picked up one from the fireplace mantel.

"This is the photo that Lindsay took," I said, recognizing the two of us curled together, smiling over the flames of the fire near the inn.

Will nodded. "I asked Lucas to get the file. I figured if the press could have it, shouldn't we?"

I replaced the photo, my fingers lingering over the silver frame.

"Yeah," I said. "I think so."

"There's more."

I followed him downstairs, where, again, most of the rooms were still as before, with the exception of his bedroom, which had been emptied completely.

"This is for you," he said, gesturing inside. "An office. A space to do whatever you want. Write music. Be alone. I figured you'd need a place of your own." He quirked an eyebrow. "Sometimes I can be a bit of a handful."

I snorted. "That's one way to put it."

He smacked another warm kiss on my lips and snuck a handful of my ass, causing me to squeak. I nuzzled into him and looked around the room. "Thank you."

He set his chin on top of my head. "It's yours, Lil. Everything else. Come on, I want to show you the upstairs."

"The studio is still here," I said as I followed him back down the hall. I peeked into the room where I had once recorded a song for him, and afterwards, we had recorded ourselves making a different kind of music.

Will wrapped an arm around my shoulders, rubbing his stubbly cheek to mine. "Well, I figured you're going to need it."

I snorted. "Right. For what?"

"Well, after the world hears 'Cavern' in *Green Lantern*, I'm guessing you're going to be in pretty high demand. Corbyn wants to use it in the trailer."

I pushed out from under his arm and turned. "Come again?"

"Cavern" was the name of the song I'd recorded in LA before finding out about Mama. I had felt lost when I'd recorded it, and it certainly wasn't finished. I hadn't even asked about it, just assumed it had been swallowed up in the behemoth of Capitol Records.

Will grinned, and in the middle of his deep green eyes, the gold flecks in the centers sparked. "I hope you don't mind. I got the recording after you left Capitol and passed it on to Corbyn. He didn't know it was you, Lil, only that it was some fresh talent. But the second he heard it, he knew it needed to score the climax. He's been chatting with Calliope all week—she'll probably be calling later tonight with details about the contract."

I slumped down the wall to my heels, suddenly faint. Was I hearing this correctly?

"Next week, when we're filming, Corbyn wants you to work in the studio," he said. "To assist Rob with the orchestra while they record this piece for the final scene of the movie." Will squatted down next to me and placed a hand on my knee. "Lil, what is it? I thought you'd be happy."

I pressed a hand to my chest "Oh, God. Oh…God. I can't breathe."

Will fell all the way to the floor and took my hand in his. "Babe, did I fuck up? Honestly, you can say no, Lil. We can call Corbyn right now and tell him you don't want to have your song in a stupid superhero movie—"

"No!" I broke out. My song. In a movie. It was…it was almost too much. And more than I'd ever hoped for.

Are you a musician or a composer?

Rob's question, asked so long ago, echoed in my mind.

Composer, I'd said. And now it was really true.

"Is this…is it real?" I wondered. "It seems too easy." Even the best things in my life had always come hard.

As if he was reading my thoughts, Will pressed another kiss to my forehead and nuzzled me close. "I think that's why they call it a break, babe," he said. "And it's high time you got yours."

We sat there together in the hall for a moment, digesting the news, the house. The fact that we had a moment just to be together. Nothing to do. Nowhere to go.

Then Will stood and pulled me up beside him. "One more thing."

He led me up the staircase that had been extended to the addition. The new third floor consisted of three large bedrooms, including a master on the far side, with its own large bathtub suite, and a king-size bed that looked out to the water.

"The other rooms are for the kids," Will said as I looked around, taking in the off-white furniture, the wood floors. Everything was comfortable, but luxe.

I turned. "Kids?"

Will smiled and arched a blond brow. "You didn't think we'd stop at one, did you?"

"You're pretty presumptuous, Baker. Who says I want to have any more of your Goldilocks babies? How many extra are we talking here?"

"Not too many. Maybe four or five."

My eyes about bugged out of my head. "Four or *five*?"

"Well, yeah. I figure now that we've gotten started, we should plan on probably one a year until your baby maker breaks down and—"

He couldn't finish, in part because I was busy smacking him on the shoulder, but also because he was too busy laughing. And not just little, subdued chuckles, the way he used in front of a group or when we were out and about. Not just a bark, something that burst out of him before he could clamp it back. These were real, gut-wrenching belly laughs, the kind that came from his toes. The kind he couldn't stop, even if he wanted to.

It was the best sound in the world.

"Oh, Jesus," he wheezed before he broke down all over again. "Holy shit, Lil, your face! I thought your eyes were about to pop out of your head!"

"Well, you looked serious!" I squealed, which only caused him to break down in laughter all over again.

"Oh, Christ, Lil." He slumped against the window, still holding his stomach. "You kill me, baby. You really do."

I threw a pillow at him, which he batted away easily. "You're wicked. You shouldn't mess with a pregnant lady. Don't you know that?"

Will quirked an eyebrow. "Honestly? You want to have one, or you want to have five? I don't really care, Lil. We'll do what's right for us. I just want to start now."

And with that, I was summarily scooped up and tossed onto the bed. Will practically jumped on top of me with another laugh, but his joy quickly turned to something else as my hands wrapped around his neck, and our lips found each other. He pulled off my t-shirt and then his own. A few moments later, we were both naked, skin pressed to warm skin as he caged me against the soft white bedding.

"These," he whispered as his hands found my breasts. "Are getting bigger. Did you know that?"

I arched into his touch, enjoying the tingling of my nipples as his fingers played over them. "More sensitive too. My ass is growing too, if you hadn't noticed."

In response, a hand wormed playfully under my back and began pinching the exact part of my anatomy I'd mentioned.

"Oh, I noticed," Will said in between kisses that left me breathless. "And I'm planning to take full advantage of it for the next seven months."

Both hands slipped under me to do exactly that, and he sat up, rubbing himself over my moist center while he looked me over.

"You know you can't actually get me pregnant now, right?" I said with a smirk as he began to slip inside. "Like, it's already done. We're good for a while."

Will rolled his eyes, then fell back on top of me, hushing my comments with a kiss that wiped away all sarcasm. "Nobody says we can't practice," he murmured.

His mouth drifted reverently over my face, floating over my eyes, my cheeks, my lips. If this was practice, I wondered what he intended for the real thing. He slid inside, finding his place within me. The place that always welcomed him, molded to him.

"I love you," I said opening myself fully.

"I love you," Will whispered, his throat hoarse and full of emotion. His eyes were wide and full of awe. No traces of fear at all.

I smiled.

"I won't tell," I said as I wrapped my hands around his neck. "It will be our little secret."

"That I love you?" Will wondered. "Please. I want to shout it to the whole damn world. There's no need to be discreet."

EPILOGUE

THREE YEARS LATER

Will

"And the award for best original screenplay goes to...Will Baker for *Wind in the Sails*!"

The roar from the audience reaches the sky-high ceilings of the Dolby theater in Los Angeles. The people around us are smiling at me and clapping. A few different cameras have zoomed over the crowd and are pointed at me. But I can barely comprehend what's happening.

"Will?"

I turn when Maggie places her small hand on my arm. Her touch is warm, even through my tuxedo jacket, and when she smiles, my heart practically thumps out of my chest.

She's stunning. Robin, the stylist we usually work with for crap like this, really outdid herself tonight. Not with me—I look the same as ever. If you've worn one black tux, you've worn them all. Maggie cut my hair, like she usually does when she says I'm getting too Yeti-locks for her taste. Right below the ears seems to be her sweet spot, where she gets caught staring at me with her mouth open, just begging for me to slip my tongue in it. Or, you know, something else. Even better if I happen to take my shirt off. Do I do an extra set of sit-ups every day because of the way she looks at my abs? Maybe, maybe not. Okay, yeah. I definitely do. Because three years later, that expression still puts the dirtiest thoughts in my head. Really, you don't want to know.

But somehow, I ended up with a woman who is game for just about anything, including getting busy in the limousine on the way here. She teases me about it, wondering how a guy with a social anxiety disorder gets off on sex in public places. I don't have an answer for that. It's just with her. It's only ever been with her.

But seriously. You try riding next to this woman looking the way she does and keep your hands to yourself. Because when Maggie walked out of the bedroom in our suite, I almost fell over. With her curls piled high and a few soft tendrils loose around her neck, she looked like a Greek goddess, not the girlfriend of a lowly actor/screenwriter. Her light green dress or gown or whatever you want to call it makes her skin glow, is pulled over one shoulder, and flows down the rest of her body. A bunch of designers and jewelers clamored to dress her, and not just because she's my girl. It's her big night as much as mine. And classic Maggie, she couldn't care less about Gucci or Chanel. She went with a local designer and turned down all jewelry except for the pair of diamond earrings and the matching pendant I bought her after she gave birth to our first child, Michaela...

———

I ALMOST MISSED IT.

I was in Tokyo when I got the call, literally about to get out of the car and walk the final red carpet for the Green Lantern press tour. It took me two full hours of meditation and yoga to get ready for that walk, part of the regimen that Dr. Blanchard, my therapist, and I worked out to mitigate anxiety during the campaign. Does it work as well as Valium? No. But it helps. Not as much as having Lil beside me, but it's better than shoving a bunch of pills and drink down my throat to get through it.

Tokyo is the worst of all of them. The crowds are bigger, the craze of the city is contagious. By the end of the junket, I was ready to ask for a straitjacket myself. So when my cell phone rang, and Calliope's frantic voice shouted over the screaming outside the limo, I was more than happy to tell the driver to go straight to the airport.

And I made it just in time. Nine hours to Seattle. Customs, and then another hour to Spokane. Forty-five minutes to the hospital, where I burst into the delivery room right when the doctor was telling Maggie she could push.

"Sir, you need to change—"

"Where is she?" It's a stupid question. There is only one bed in the delivery room, and one person lying on it, her feet in stirrups with a doctor crouched in front of her.

"Just a few more contractions, Maggie, and then I think you can push. Stay with me now, sweetheart."

"Will!" Maggie finds me, her brown eyes frantic, and in another second, I'm at her side, taking her hand and pressing her head into my chest. "You're still in your suit," she whispers, fingering my jacket.

I shuck it immediately, tossing the Armani to the floor, and grab a seat next to her. "Should I put on the Green Lantern costume?"

But the joke is lost as her face screws up in pain as another contraction sweeps through her. A sheen of sweat covers her body, and tiny hairs are plastered on her forehead. She's never looked more beautiful.

"Your hand," she breathes in a voice contorted in her effort. "Oh GODFUCKINGHELLTHATHURTSSS!"

I pivot to the doctor. "Is this normal?"

The doctor just gives me a cheery thumbs-up while she watches whatever is going on down there. "We're almost ready," she calls out.

I turn back to Maggie, whose eyes are now closed. "I'm here, Lil," I say. "I have you." I'd give her any limb she wants. Whatever she needs right now. I just don't want her to make that sound again.

One eye opens, brown and deep. Even in her pain, full of love.

"I knew you'd be here," she whispers. "Don't let go."

I smile. Her words call back to those moments when I'd say the same thing to her. About to do a step-and-repeat, or enter a room full of Hollywood jackals, when I felt the throes of a panic attack snapping at me like wolves. Don't let go, I'd beg, though I was always more scared of losing her than of anything else.

And she never did.

And I never will.

"Okay, Maggie, it's time," the doctor says, popping her head up. "You ready to meet your daughter, guys?"

Maggie grips my hand so hard I swear she's going to crush the bones. Her jaw sets, and she nods. "I'm ready."

I can tell the moment it's about to happen. Something happens to her belly— it moves, clenches with each contraction, but as Maggie starts to push, with grunts, howls, and a bunch of other noises I never knew my girl could even make start pouring out of her. Her face turns purple with the effort, and we're both screaming and moaning together, again and again, until all at once, she deflates and a baby's cry cuts through the thick hospital air.

"Oh God, oh God!" Maggie's crying, over and over again, her eyes glazed and unfocused as she looks around. "Go, Will. Go get her."

But I'm already up and moving to the end of the bed, where the nurses are cleaning our little girl and wrapping her in a loose cloth while the doctor finishes up with Maggie. When women tell you birth is a war zone, believe them. I will respect the hell out of my girl for this for as long as I live.

"Take off your shirt," one of the nurses says, then starts when she actually gets a look at who I am.

"I'm sorry, what?" I've had a lot of inappropriate fans over the years, but this one takes the cake.

Behind me, Maggie laughs. She actually laughs, after all she's been through, after being in labor for almost twenty-four hours, looks like she's been through a major battle, and still hasn't had a chance to see this person she's been growing for the last nine months.

I turn around, hands on my hips. "Seriously, Lily pad?"

She winces a little, but doesn't stop giggling. "No one in here cares about your abs, Baker." She point at the baby. "It's a bonding thing. You're supposed to hold her skin to skin. So strip down and get our daughter so I can meet her, will you?"

My jaw drops, but she's not joking. Vaguely, I remember something about skin on skin and bonding hormones our birth coach mentioned, and then it takes me exactly four seconds to rip off this stupid monkey suit and accept my daughter, who's cooing like a dove, against my bare chest.

She's warm. Tiny, not even as long as my forearm. She has a full head of thick, dark blond hair and skin like a sunset. She's the most beautiful thing I have ever seen in my sad, sorry life.

"Bring her to your wife," says the nurse. "Let's see if she'll latch."

"Oh, we're not married," Maggie says cheerily.

I dart a quick glance at her. "Not yet, anyway."

This has been a point of contention between us for a while now. I asked her nearly every day for two months after we moved back to the lake, but every time, she muttered something about not wanting a shotgun wedding and changed the subject to decorating the baby's bedroom or something equally banal. So I stopped, because you don't want to piss off a pregnant lady. But doesn't mean I ever planned to give up.

Maggie's face reddens again, but I ignore it while I carry the baby to meet her mom. Maggie pulls her hospital gown open, baring her chest the same way I did. With tears flowing openly down her beautiful face, she accepts our daughter into her arms. The baby calms immediately, like she knows this is where she belongs. Where we all belong together.

"Now what?" I find the stool beside them, not sure what I should be doing here.

"Let's see if we can help her latch," says the nurse as she comes to the other side.

We listen only half-way as the nurse gives directions on how to guide the baby to Maggie's breast, help her establish first contact, those first critical bonds. Maggie winces as the baby closes her mouth around her nipple, but after a few moments, it's clear they have both found a rhythm. I just watch in awe. And I know in that moment that this is the best thing I have ever done in my life. This woman. This child. This family. This is all a man could ever need. It's all I could ever want.

Maggie looks up at me, her eyes glossy with pride and joy. "Hey, Daddy," she whispers.

I jerk. And before I realize it, tears are streaming down my cheeks.

"Shi—I mean, shoot," I say, wiping them away.

"It's okay," Maggie says. "Come here."

Keeping the baby in place with one hand, she weaves her other fingers into my hair, which has grown a few more inches in the last six months. I kiss her, feel her warmth, her sigh, her total surrender. That's the thing about Maggie— when she gives of herself, she gives everything she has. I'll never be worthy of it, but I'll never stop trying.

"I love you," I say, low enough that only she can hear me.

She smiles against my lips. "So much."

I look down at our daughter, who's just finished nursing and is drifting off to sleep.

"Michaela?" Maggie asks.

It's a name we've been tossing around since we discovered the sex. The female version of my father's name, Michael.

I nod. "Michaela Grace?"

Maggie's eyes tear up again, and I know it's because she's thinking of her mother.

"Yeah," she whispers. She strokes the tiny head that's cuddled into her breast. "Michaela Grace. Welcome to the world."

———

"WILL." Maggie's voice, sweet and a little husky, pulls me back to the here and now. "Come on, Goldilocks," she teases. "They're waiting for you."

Maggie flashes her bright, brilliant smile and puts her hand back on her belly. She's not showing too much—not under the loose layers of fabric—but in another few weeks, she'll pop out like a basketball, if this is anything like the last one. I smile down at the little man growing inside her. She's five months along with our second, a boy. Not sure how we managed that, and neither are the doctors. After Mickey was born, Maggie went back on birth control as soon as was humanly possible. And, just like the last time, it failed. Looks like I've got some good swimmers down there. Maggie's informed me during her third month of morning sickness that after the birth, she wouldn't be having sex with me until I got snipped. But I don't know, though. I'm sort of holding out for a third. Honestly, I'd keep her pregnant round the clock if I could. That's how damn beautiful she looks.

"Go get your award so we can go back to the hotel, all right?" Her sly grin tells me her libido is calling.

I grin, and then laugh, a big belly laugh that I've only learned to do easily again in the last few years. It's just one more reason to love my Lily pad knocked up—she can't get enough of it. I lay a big kiss on this woman I'm so damn lucky to call my own. It's the kind of kiss I'd never have dreamed of giving out in public before I met her. Then I stand up to collect my prize.

The crowd roars, and without Maggie beside me, it's hard not to freeze up. Hard, but not impossible. I'm still an intensely private person, but things have gotten better with a hell of a lot of therapy and a bunch of coping mechanisms. Meditation. Yoga. Boxing. I do them all.

But the real breakthroughs happened when, after I finished filming the last of the *Green Lantern* and Maggie recorded "Cavern," we moved back to Newman Lake to start our family. We settled in at the new house, into a community that turned out to be way more protective of Maggie— and then of me—than I predicted. Turns out photographers aren't as likely to creep around when your sixty-five-year-old neighbor, Warren, a Vietnam war vet and occasional deer hunter, uses paparazzi for target practice. On top of that, I actually learned to get along with Lucas, since having the Forster family at our back basically meant the entire lake became our extended family. Mickey's got more pretend aunties and uncles than she knows what to do with. Will I be taking the fence down anytime soon? Probably not. But could I? Maybe. And I never thought I'd experience that.

So the last few years gave Maggie and me a bit of peace. Peace to mourn our parents the right way. Peace to learn to be together for the long haul. It wasn't easy—the press tour itself coincided with the last trimester of her pregnancy and had Max del Conte breathing down my neck the entire time, just waiting for a misstep so he could sue my ass for breach of contract. But in the end, he forgot about my role in his son's death when it came out that Theo had sexually assaulted a whole slew of women at Beauregard and del Conte Entertainment. In the end, Max needed me a whole lot more than I ever needed him, to the point where he is *still* throwing money at me, trying to get me to come back for a sequel.

But it ain't gonna happen. Shortly after the *Green Lantern* tour, I announced my retirement from acting. I always felt about acting the way Maggie does about singing live. It's all right, and I'm good at it, but it's never been what I *really* wanted to do, which was come home and be a father to my daughter and a husband to my...well, one day she'll be my wife. My girls give me all the inspiration I could ever need, which is how I ended up writing the screenplay that won tonight's award.

"Wow," I say, speaking directly into the mic. "I mean...wow. Baby, do you see this?"

Lil just gleams from her seat, unconscious of the TV cameras hovering around her. She doesn't react to them anymore the way I do— it's like she only has eyes for me.

I push a hand through my hair, trying to recall the speech I scribbled on hotel stationery last night. Maggie insisted I needed to have something in case I ended up on this stage. I didn't believe I would. No one gives Oscars to first-time screenwriters, especially not when they are washed-up child actors.

"There are about a million people to thank for this," I say, trying and failing to mask the emotion swelling through me. "Um, to all the good people at Warner for buying the script and believing in the project, and especially Corbyn Creighton, Jeffrey Carol, Killian Everett, Sandra Meyers, and everyone else who worked tirelessly to bring this script to life in a way it really deserved—thank you. So much. To Benny Amaya, my brother from another mother, thank you for putting up with all of my B.S. over the years. Your patience is king. To my daughter, Mickey, I love you, bug, but if you're up, tell Grandpa James you need to go back to sleep. But more than everyone else, I have to thank one person in particular. She's the light of my life, the woman who literally brought me back from the dead, the inspiration for this entire story, and without her, I never would have had the guts to write this script, send it in, and get it made."

I pause, finding her face again, feeling our mutual joy. My victories are hers, just like hers are mine. Just like, twenty minutes ago, when she won her own Oscar for best original score, I was on my feet, shouting for her louder than anyone else in the theater. Then I went full Hollywood and swept her up with a kiss that made her stumble on her way to the stage.

So, ignoring the producer, next to the camera man, who is frantically trying to wave me off stage, I grab the mic more purposefully. Because apparently I have a little more Hollywood in me. It's now or never.

"See, we had a couple of bets tonight, you guys, since neither of us thought we'd ever win, but we were both equally sure of each other. If she lost, I said I'd do dishes for a month—and you all know how that ended up. Since my girl is your winner for best original score, she'll be sudsing up for a while."

There's a smatter of laughter around the theater, and Maggie smiles shyly while she cradles her gold statue.

"My bet was a little different, though. I bet her that if *I* lost, she'd have to let me make an honest woman out of her. She agreed, thinking I was joking. Well, Lily pad, joke's on you, baby. Because this was going to happen either way."

A buzz ripples around the theater as I jog off the stage, and multiple cameras move with me as I return to where Maggie is sitting.

My girl. My woman. Light of my goddamn life. Every day I wake up asking myself how the fuck did I ever get so lucky?

I crouch beside her, and slowly, lower one knee to the floor as the auditorium collectively gasps. Lil can't even speak—both of her hands are over her mouth as she watches with moons for eyes.

"This is for you," I said, low enough that only she can hear me.

And then I pull out the box I've been carrying around in my pocket since Mickey was born, watching and waiting for the right time to ask, one last time, the most important question I was ever going to have. It was never a matter of if—just when.

"Lil," I whisper, though by now, there's a boom hanging directly above us so that my voice, no matter how low, is going to be broadcast across the entire room, the entire world. A few years ago, the idea might have sent me running, but right now, I want everyone to hear what I have to say.

"What—what are you doing?" Her voice shakes, but in a good way. In that way that tells me I could probably take her behind the curtains on the stage and have my way with her if I wanted. Her lower lip trembles —that full lower lip I love to suck on like a Jolly Rancher. Jesus Christ. She really has no clue.

Focus, Will. I can hear my dad's voice the back of my mind. *Will, get your mind right. You got a question to ask, son.*

I take a deep breath and hold her eyes with my own. And just for a second, we are the only two people in a room containing several thousand.

"Maggie. Lily pad. Love of my fucking life. You brought me back to life, and you do it every day. There is no one else I want with me on this crazy journey. All I want to do is watch you soar, baby, and fly alongside you. So please. I'm begging you. Will you marry me?" I ask softly.

The entire auditorium is dead silent. Up in the sound booth, the producer is probably going crazy, arguing with the network about whether to go to commercial.

Everyone waits.

And she says...nothing.

For a second, despite the last three years that have been the happiest of both our lives, despite the home we've made together that neither of us ever thought we could have, despite our sunshine-filled daughter and another one on the way—despite all of that, I'm still afraid she'll finally see how unworthy I am of all of it. That she's going to say no.

"Lil," I whisper.

Her big eyes drag up from the ring. "Y-yeah?"

"Lil, you, um, you think you can give me an answer here?" I twist my mouth to the side, that crooked smile I reserve just for her. Her eyes drop —even now, I can tell she wants to kiss me.

"Answer you..." She drifts off, clearly lost in the moment. "Answer you..."

"Yeah. I meant, it's not just me that wants to know what you're thinking?" I tilt my head around the theater, trying to play this cool even though I'm about the explode from the tension. Jesus Christ, she's killing me over here.

But I'd wait forever. I'd keep the world on pins and needles for hours to give her the space she needs.

If she'll just say...

Maggie jerks, as if she's just realized we have an audience. And not just the three thousand or so bodies packed into Dolby, but also the ten million watching us at home.

"Oh my God," she whispers, her brown eyes suddenly wide as the sky. "Oh, Will...oh my *God*, of *course*. Yes! Yesyesyesyes*yes*, of course I'll marry you!"

And that's all it takes. The entire theater erupts into chaos as Maggie jumps out of her chair and into my arms. The force of her small body nearly knocks me off my feet, but I catch her, because that's what I do. We catch each other, Lil and I, no matter what.

"Yeah?" I ask again and again as I slide the ring onto her finger. "Yeah?"

In answer, her lips find mine, and I'm not just a witness to her happiness—I'm fucking immersed in it. Because that's always how it is with Lil. Just looking at her makes me forget where I am. When I taste her, I can't even remember my own name. Will. Fitz. You could call me Donald fucking Duck—it wouldn't matter. Because when she kisses me, I'm hers. And I don't care who sees it.

Whoops and hollers fill the auditorium as everyone cheers for what's probably going to drive gossip columns for the next two weeks. Once upon a time, I'd have closed up, snarled at the cameras. Well, I never would have done this to begin with, and if I had, I would have been torn up with the dread of what's sure to follow—the cameras, a trail of paparazzi while we're still in LA, and a few that might follow us back to the lake until Warren pulls out his gun again. The tabloids publishing way too many pictures of us and trying to find shots of Mickey, and eventually little no-name too.

But tonight, I couldn't care less. For once, I want this news everywhere. I want everyone on the planet to know, see, feel taste one solitary fact: that Maggie Sharp belongs to me. But more importantly, I belong to her.

———

Dying for more Will and Maggie? Go here for another exclusive extended epilogue!

https://bookhip.com/NTRKJP

ALSO BY NICOLE FRENCH

The Spitfire Series

I had a plan.

Finish law school. Start a job. Stay away from men like Brandon Sterling. Cocky, overbearing, and richer than the earth, he thinks the world belongs to him, and that includes me.

Yeah, no. Think again.

It doesn't matter that his blue eyes look straight into my soul, or that his touch melts my icy reserve. It doesn't even matter that past all that swagger, there's a beautiful, damaged man who has so much to offer beyond private planes and jewelry boxes.

But I had a plan: no falling in love.

I just have to convince myself.

Book I is available FREE: www.nicolefrenchromance.com/legallyyours

The Rose Gold Series

Nina Astor gave me one red-hot night and disappeared into the city.

The woman was a phantom, and I was obsessed.

Now she is back in my life, as real as ever.

And completely unattainable.

Because Nina Astor is beyond off-limits.

Daughter of a dynasty.

Cousin of New York's most notorious billionaire.

Married to the scum of the earth—the subject of my next investigation.

As a criminal prosecutor, I'm supposed to be on the right side of the law.

But when it comes to Nina Astor,

I'm a very bad man.

I'll do anything to claim this woman as my own.

And to save her from this monster, I'd sell my soul to the devil himself.

Truth be told…

Maybe I already have.

Start the series here: www.nicolefrenchromance.com/theotherman

The Bad Idea series

Repeat after me: stay away from the hot girl.

The beautiful girl. The f**king ray of sunshine in the middle of your delivery route.

Layla Barros is everything I never knew I wanted. Everything I'll never have.

She's an innocent young student.

I'm a convicted felon.

She's rich girl from a nice family.

I've got nothing but a broken home.

But if I'm an addict, she's my drug. I can't stay away, even though I know I'll ruin her in the end.

She might be the girl of my dreams, but I was always a bad idea.

Book I is available FREE: books2read.com/badidea

ACKNOWLEDGMENTS

First up: Family. Always family. Family, in its various, sometimes fractured forms, is a major theme in all of my work, and that because my beautiful, mixed, devoted, and utterly interesting family is the best one of them all. My husband, who gives me ample time and has never been anything but tirelessly supportive of all my projects. I love you. All three of our kids, who are only just starting to understand who "Nicole French" is and what role she has in their lives. Just today, my youngest said, "I want to be a bookmaker like you." Oh, my heart. I love you, little bear. My aunt, Trish, who thanked me for her cameo before she knew who Tricia Owen-Baker really was. Sorry, by the way. When the characters speak, I listen. The REAL Trish is like a second mom to me—there is no mistaking them for each other. My mom, who always asks about my books, and who gave me the drive and confidence to pursue this dream in the first place. Thank you, all.

Secondly, to my wonderful editorial support team. My amazing alpha readers, Patricia and Danielle, whose arguments about Will and constant cheerleading made this book happen much faster than it would have otherwise. You ladies are the best, both as friends and as readers. This book series is yours. Thank you to Shauna, Erika, and Dee who offered extremely helpful beta notes on the second manuscript. So much gratitude is due to my editor, the eagle-eyed Emily Hainsworth, whose expertise and tongue-in-cheek comments are utterly indispensable. Last (but not least), to Judy Zweifel, who polishes everything into the form you read today. Thank you.

Thirdly, thank you to the author support network that alternately distracts and motivates. To Harloe, Jane, ad Ava, who keep me company, day in and day out. To the wonderful ladies of the DND Book Club and the In the Loop Group, thanks for letting me in the clubs! I am so fortunate to have gained such an incredible group of peers. Other friends whose message and support constantly brighten my days: Maya, Jessica, Laura, Kim, Sierra, and others. I LOVE all your voices in my life.

Most of all, THANK YOU to my other ARC reviewers, reader group members, newsletter subscribers, and basically **EVERY READER** who read this story from beginning to end: Thank you. I would have quit this job long ago without you. Your excitement feeds my stories, and there are so many more on the way. I would not be able to do this at all if it were not for you. All my gratitude, always.